She was risking ever his heart.

As the intruder's footsteps grew more distinct, he calculated they'd soon be discovered and panicked, more for Kaljin than for himself. He'd count himself lucky if he saw another few days of existence. She risked her career, her reputation, and possibly her freedom for this folly.

With two thundering heartbeats to spare, the panel slid open. He gripped Kaljin by the waist and whisked her inside the room.

Dull, amber security lights winked on as the panel closed behind them. Breathing hard, he collapsed against the wall just inside the door. Only when he felt Kaljin's fingers clutching the front of his baggy shirt did he realize he'd swept her into a snug embrace.

She buried her face into the hollow between his shoulder and chest. Her fragrance—a vibrant, vital contrast to the stench of Jarrit's charred flesh—filled the air. With his left arm about her narrow waist, he held her intimately to his body. Somehow, his right hand had come to rest on her delicate nape. The heat of her exquisite satin-smooth skin against his roughed palm sent prickles up his arm and chills down his spine. Fine, springy tendrils of her fiery hair teased his cheek.

As she trembled in the circle of his arms, her sweet vulnerability flooded him with a powerful new urgency to keep her safe. Unlike just minutes before, this time he had no will to flee or fight the instinct.

Briefly, he wondered if her head whirled and her insides clenched with arousal, too. He should push her away.

"Tynan?"

The quiver in her voice reflected his own whipsaw emotions. What did she ask of him? What should he answer?

"We're safe, Kaljin."

But her eyes widened, the dusky pupils overwhelming all but a narrow edge of glimmering irises. Her mouth blossomed with a warm, pulsating color. "Are we?"

"Yes."

But he lied, because he did sense danger. From her. From himself. In that moment, he needed more from her than an intimate embrace. He needed to kiss her—hard and with feeling. He needed to drink from her as a man too long in the desert needs to drink of cool, life-giving water.

This book is dedicated to:

My children—Julia and Brian—who taught me there can be strength in humility and there should be humility in strength.

To my exceptional critique partners Jean Newlin, Laura Renken, and Janet Wiist, with heartfelt thanks.

To the Godmothers of all my books, Jan Hunsicker and Elysa Hendricks, with much affection.

And to my husband, Craig, as always.

Marista

***

Barbara Cary

ImaJinn Books

Marista
Published by ImaJinn Books, a division of ImaJinn

Copyright ©2004 by Barbara Cary
Printed and bound in the United States of America. All rights reserved. No part of this book may be reproduced in any form or by any means (electronic, mechanical, photocopying, recording, or otherwise) without prior written permission of both the copyright holder and the above publisher of this book, except by a reviewer, who may quote brief passages in a review. For information, address: ImaJinn Books, a division of ImaJinn, P.O. Box 545, Canon City, CO 81215-0545, or call toll free 1-877-625-3592.

ISBN: 1-893896-94-3

10 9 8 7 6 5 4 3 2 1

PUBLISHER'S NOTE:
This book is a work of fiction. Names, characters, places and incidents are products of the author's imagination or are used fictitiously. Any resemblance to actual events or locales or persons, living or dead, is entirely coincidental.

Books are available at quantity discounts when used to promote products or services. For information please write to: Marketing Division, ImaJinn Books, P.O. Box 545, Canon City, CO 81215-0545, or call toll free 1-877-625-3592.

Cover design by Rickey Mallory

ImaJinn Books, a division of ImaJinn
P.O. Box 545, Canon City, CO 81215-0545
Toll Free: 1-877-625-3592
http://www.imajinnbooks.com

One

After two standard months of duty at the Terran refugee center on Inara Wadi, Marista could finally tolerate the sight of blood. But the stench of charred flesh that hung heavy in the corridor still forced sourness into her throat.

As she jogged past the human carnage in triage and tried to keep pace with Bram Hyrek's longer strides, she worried her face had turned the same shade of pale gray as her uniform shirt. She had to control the squeamishness. Civilian casualties during planetary civil war were too common. In the next weeks and months she'd likely see and smell far worse.

Out of the corner of her eye, she saw the chief med-tech cast her a sideways glance. "Are you up to this?"

Impatient with her weakness, she cleared the foul taste from her throat and clipped her words. "I'm fine. Just tell me what kind of accident . . ."

"Not accident," Bram cut in. "Incident. The diplomatic kind. That's why I alerted your Office. Where's Bierich?"

Given the uncertain nature of this emergency, Bram's preference for Madame Bierich was understandable. Still, she struggled to control the resentment in her voice. "The chargé is on her way back from the embassy in Timetsuara. However, I'm authorized to deal with the situation. Besides, I speak the Albian dialect, and I'm well versed in the customs of the desert dwellers."

"Don't take this wrong, Marista," Bram replied, "but I think we need more than a linguist or the Deputy Administrator of Humanitarian Services. Unless I miss my guess, we need an honest-to-Creation diplomat. But," he added with a sigh, "I wouldn't have dragged you out of bed in the middle of the night if I thought this could wait. The clansmen probably won't know the difference between you and Bierich anyway."

She raised her brow. "I'll make sure they don't know the difference."

They turned another corner and Bram pulled up short. Hard on his heels, she skidded to a stop in front of Treatment Room Four. An Albian clansman, clutching the butt and barrel of a desert rifle, guarded the door of the self-contained unit. The long, black cylinder of his weapon contrasted sharply with his dingy white burnoose. The man's cobalt eyes glimmered with pure threat.

As she stared in disbelief at the clansman, she forced herself into a tenuous calm despite the jump of her heart. "Bram, what in the name of holy Mother Creation is he doing with a weapon inside the compound?"

The Albian clutched the barrel of his weapon harder. Though she spoke to the med-tech in Terran Standard, she guessed the clansman understood the indignant tone of her voice.

"At least he isn't pointing that thing at us," Bram muttered. "We may have to bend the rules of wartime etiquette on this one. The Albians don't believe our own Terran guard is adequate. They may be right."

When she jerked her gaze back to Bram he held up his hand before she could demand an explanation. "Check out the treatment room, then tell me what you think."

He guided her to the smaller of two viewing windows. Though the glare from an overhead light cast a halo around her field of vision, she clearly saw the gurney filling one entire corner of the room and Zhora Paxton, a nurse, working over it. Easing out of Bram's hold, she shaded her eyes with both hands and inched up on her toes to get a better view.

A man laid face-up on the gurney. A few short, crisp strands of brown-black hair clung to his damp, sun-darkened forehead above heavy brows. The harsh white light set his face in relief and gave his defined cheekbones and square jaw the look of solid cast bronze. His handsome, hard-edged profile lacked any hint of animation except an occasional blink. Neither did the man offer a visible response to Zhora's touch.

Marista let her gaze linger on the striking features a moment longer, then she scanned the man's length. Warmth crept into her face when she realized he was naked except for a swatch of white surgical drape that started at his narrow hips and extended to mid-thigh. The thin material outlined the solid lines of his masculinity.

Aware she'd let her eyes linger too long where they shouldn't, she forced herself to take a more clinical study of the stranger. From the waist up, his broad shoulders and chest made a swarthy contrast to the white linens. The muscles of his left forearm and leg strained against security cuffs affixed to the gurney. His heels overshot the foot of the thin mattress by a good measure.

He was tall. Taller than the rangy clansman standing guard. Taller than most Albians, in fact.

His stoic expression, wide classic features and powerful build resembled the ancient Earth stone-carved renditions of Aztec warrior kings.

She dropped from the balls of her feet back onto her heels. For the first time in two standard months, she worried about her safety as a neutral Terran diplomat stationed on a humanitarian outpost. The clash of culture and politics that pitted the planet's two continent nations of Albia and Krillia against each other had, so far, left this oasis a place of refuge for the nomadic desert dwellers caught in the crossfire.

Now, perhaps, this "incident" breached the neutrality of Terran soil. Anyone could see the man was no simple desert nomad. Injured and restrained he still exuded power and superiority. The clansmen might have reason to be paranoid.

She turned back to Bram. "Who is he? Where did he come from?"

Bram glanced into the treatment room. "The clansmen found him and four others at the wreckage of an air skimmer in the middle of the desert. Most of the crewmembers, except for him, were outfitted in traditional clan robes. The craft, though, wasn't Albian design."

"Are they Krillian?" She suddenly felt a new respect for Albia's sworn enemy. "Do you think there's been an incursion this close to a major city?"

"The clansmen think so," Bram hedged. "Their leader told me that if four of the five survivors hadn't needed critical medical care, he'd have taken them all to the military base at Timetsuara. As a precaution, he posted his own guards throughout the compound."

Apprehension slithered up her back. "These men could be spies."

Bram shrugged. "True, but in the past month, the worst fighting moved south and west by several hundred kilometers. Who knows what they were doing so close to the city."

He paused and shook his head. "Even if they are Krillians they pose no danger to us. One of the survivors died on the way here. Two others suffered severe burns, and one man has massive cranial bleeding. I'd be surprised if any of them lasted the night." He rubbed the furrows in his forehead. "One of the burn cases is a boy no older than sixteen. Damn, Marista, they're fighting this war with children."

For the first time, she saw the strain in Bram's face and laid her hand on his arm. "I know you'll do the best you can. I've seen the practice drills. Your staff is one of the best."

He tried to smile at her words, and then lifted his chin to indicate the man in treatment room four. "At least this one should recover. The clan leader said he put up one hell of a fight at the crash site before they secured him. Except for a gash in his side he's unhurt. Unlike the others he wore a standard flight suit that protected him from the fire. He hasn't said a word, though. Hasn't even groaned in pain."

Aztec warrior kings wouldn't cry out under pain of torture, she mused.

In the next moment, she chided herself for the flight of fancy. She was a member of the Diplomatic Corps, dedicated to finding peace through negotiation, not brute force. She had little patience for men like her father, the General, who made war to solve problems.

"The clan calls him the Silent One," Bram interrupted her thoughts. "I suppose if I were in his place I wouldn't talk much either."

Her skin prickled. "You do think he's Krillian."

Bram glanced at the guard, then back at her. "I can't say for sure. The clothing he wore beneath his flight suit didn't give us a clue to his identity. That's why I called the Chargé's Office. Since this outpost is neutral Terran soil, these men have a right to sanctuary under interplanetary law."

"Which places us diplomatically between hell and a black hole if they are Krillian spies," she finished. "So we have a potential incident."

Bram nodded. "In the end, that man in there may be the only survivor. I'd say that makes him the unlucky one."

When she frowned at the odd comment, Bram cast a furtive glance at the clansman before continuing. "Our desert friends have notified the Albian military in Timetsuara of their find. Lieutenant Sindri should be here with a platoon within the hour, and I have a feeling he's going to insist we release this Silent One into his custody."

"Sindri? Damn!" She exhaled her frustration with the new knowledge she'd have to deal with the arrogant, ambitious officer. In the days after she arrived at the post on Inara Wadi, she had struck up a cordial friendship with the Albian lieutenant. That was before she realized Sindri wielded information, personal or otherwise, like he wielded a deadly weapon—with cold, calculating intent and accuracy.

"I know. Sindri complicates the situation," Bram replied with ironic understatement. "That's why I think our Silent One needs an impartial explanation of his options. The problem is he won't communicate. Whether he doesn't understand us, or he chooses not to talk . . ."

"Is for me to figure out," she concluded, feeling tingles of both anticipation and foreboding. "As Bierich's deputy I'm the closest thing to a diplomat this side of Timetsuara. I'll simply try to conduct a basic interview, so the chargé can form a proper diplomatic response when she returns."

Bram shrugged his agreement and turned his attention to the treatment room. "I told Zhora to give him a relaxant along with a hypo of antibiotics. He should be mildly sedated, but be careful. Remember, the Krillians shot down that Albian civilian transport to start this war. Don't assume they have any more regard for us because we're Terran."

Her heart give a quick double beat. She remembered too well vidscreen images of the charred and melted transport wreckage that washed up on Albia's western equatorial shoreline. The remains of the destroyed civilian transport, Rising Sun, and over a thousand men, women and children didn't fill three fifty-liter drums. Imagining what those people must have suffered in their last moments left her cold with dread. The flames. The asphyxiating smoke. The terror.

Her own worst nightmare come hideously true.

"Are you sure you can handle this, Marista?"

Bram's impatient question cut through her mental lapse. She resisted the urge to grasp the flower pendant that hung from a gold chain inside the vee of her open collar. "Yes, I can handle this."

The little flower talisman gave two mocking jumps with the fitful beat of her pulse.

"Fine," Bram replied, as if he was eager to accept her word. "A second guard is posted just inside the treatment room door. But remember. Watch yourself."

She nodded.

Bram smiled briefly, and then gazed down the corridor. "I should go see if I can do anything for that boy." Already lost in other thoughts, he turned and hurried away from her.

She pivoted toward the window and stared at the stone-like profile of the Silent One. She should have been more afraid. The war had finally caught up with this remote humanitarian outpost. Chance had deposited strangers, possibly Krillian spies, at her doorstep.

But chance also had handed her a real challenge after two long months of bureaucratic data disk jamming, report replication, and disaster drills. With Tessa Bierich absent, she could prove her worth in a crisis. After today, she vowed, even Bierich wouldn't have reason to rate her fieldwork less than excellent.

She finally touched the pendant and gave it a hopeful squeeze. She slid her fingers down to the platinum Terran Diplomatic Corps insignia affixed to the left lapel of her pale gray shirt.

Neither brief ritual helped steady the hammering of her heart as she pressed the door control and took a deep breath.

Zhora glanced up from her duties when Marista strode into the treatment room. "I thought Bram sent for the chargé. What are you doing here?"

Marista flinched inside, but she dredged up a placid smile. "Bierich isn't here right now. I'm in charge."

Zhora turned back to her patient on the gurney. "Well, she'll be sorry she missed this one. We have a certified mystery on our hands."

"Bram told me as much."

Marista moved closer and noted a glimmer of feminine appreciation in Zhora's eyes as the nurse swabbed an antiseptic wash across a deep gash just below the Silent One's rib cage. The sinuous motion of the Zhora's hand seemed in perfect tempo with the steady rise and fall of the man's flat, hard abdomen as he breathed. Though she knew little about medical procedure, she sensed Zhora let her touch linger on the bronze flesh longer than necessary.

A twinge of envy surprised her. Only then she realized how openly she stared at the man's beautiful naked torso.

Embarrassed by the lapse of professionalism, she shook herself mentally and sidled around the foot of the gurney making sure neither her shoes nor the hem of her trousers brushed the scorched and blood-soaked clothing discarded there. Once in position opposite Zhora, she trained her eyes on the nurse. "That flight suit looks as if three men bled into it."

"His wound is deep enough to have caused the bleeding." Zhora glanced down at the wadded flight suit. "By all standards he should be in shock. A gash this deep and wide usually needs minor laser cauterization. Once we strapped him down and he quieted, though, the bleeding stopped. Even more amazing, his blood pressure and heart rate have already dropped to normal."

Zhora smiled more of her feminine appreciation as she set about bandaging the wound. "Of course, you can see he's incredibly fit."

Marista did see, and she suffered a stab of guilt. She had to stay focused on her professional duty.

Zhora glanced up. "I suppose you want to be alone with him."

"Yes, I do."

With a sigh, the nurse sealed the last corner of a synthaflesh bandage over the bronzed skin and stepped back. "He's yours, for the moment. When you finish, send for an orderly to move him into isolation."

"Isolation? Why isn't he being moved to a ward?"

Zhora gave the clansman a glance. "We can lock the isolation room from the outside. The choice is a comfortable bed in there or restraints worse than this. I think our patient would prefer isolation, don't you?"

"But he's injured," Marista said, disgusted.

"Tell that to the clansmen." Zhora stole another glance at the stranger's length. "Besides, he may be injured, but I wouldn't bet that platinum bar of yours he's helpless."

The nurse hurried out of the treatment room. Immediately, the Albian guard positioned himself at the door and lowered the barrel of his weapon a few centimeters.

Marista recoiled at the naked threat of the desert rifle. Even if the wounded man was a suspected spy, he had a right to speak with her in private without fear for his life. She marched over to the sentry and, in desert tradition, nodded with formality to display her authority. "You'll wait outside while I speak with this man."

"No."

She expected his initial stubbornness. Albians boasted about that particular national trait. However, she could match her own will with the Albians any day of the standard year.

Though impatient she smiled warmly. "I know you're concerned for my safety. But this man is injured, restrained, and drugged into submission. He poses no danger to me."

The guard didn't budge. She held her temper and widened her smile. "You've handled your duty well. I'll tell my superiors, and they will be grateful."

The appeal to his Albian sense of duty worked, as she knew it would. He cocked his head as if willing to hear more.

She waved toward the gurney. "But I have my duty as well. I must speak with this man in private, so I can answer to my superiors with as much pride and honor as you."

When the Albian's gaze darted between the gurney and her a half dozen times she knew he was weighing her appeal.

He finally lowered his weapon. "I'll wait outside. Go to your duty."

She nodded formally, the only thanks he'd expect.

When the guard left and shut the door behind him, she let out a relieved breath and hurried over to the gurney. For privacy, she stood at the man's shoulder with her back to the viewing window.

He'd closed his eyes and lay still. She found herself once again struck by his male beauty. Though flame had singed the edges of his dark hair and brows ash white, the perfection of his angular face wanted for nothing, save a trace of animation. She imagined a smile lifting his full, sculpted mouth and deepening the faint lines around his eyes.

Peering at him in repose, she wondered if Bram's medicinal cocktail of antibiotics and relaxants had worked too well. If the Silent One had lapsed into a twilight state, dispensing with the guard had been an exercise in futility.

A glance at the life-sign monitor quashed that worry. She had learned enough about medical instrumentation during her brief time at the outpost to understand he wasn't dozing. His vitals were too strong. In fact, his heart beat fast, and his blood pressure rose a notch while she watched the digital readout.

Hoping he might open his eyes if he more acutely sensed her presence, she leaned forward. He didn't twitch an eyelid, though his chest rose and fell more rapidly. When his arms clenched, she realized he was simply ignoring her.

His response was understandable. Despite the life-sign readings, he was probably disoriented and terrified. She needed to earn a measure of his trust.

Lowering her face, she positioned herself in his direct line of vision. "I'm Marista Kaljin, Deputy Administrator of Humanitarian Services for this Terran outpost," she began, speaking softly and using the Krillian dialect first. "Our chargé, Tessa Bierich, is absent. But I can and will exercise the authority of the diplomatic office in her stead. This is a neutral refugee and humanitarian center. Though you were brought here by Albian nationals, you are under Terran protection. Do you understand?"

He no longer seemed to breathe, though the life-sign monitor indicated his heart rate and blood pressure rose another notch.

Frowning at the disparity between outward appearance and autonomic responses, she repeated herself in Albian just in case everyone's best guess about these strangers was dead wrong. Besides, if the men were infiltrators and had disguised themselves as desert dwellers, surely they were versed in the rudiments of the Albian dialect, as well.

Still no response.

Her patience grew shorter along with her time. "Sir, cooperating with me is in your best interest."

To emphasize her insistence, she spread her hand over his fist. "I can guarantee your safety until . . . Oh!"

In spite of the restraints on his arms, the stranger jerked violently and repulsed her comforting touch. She stumbled back a step. Then she caught her breath, when eyes the color of polished obsidian speared her.

The ancient warrior king had revived. His glower struck at her soul with loathing and menace even as he lay at her mercy.

Instinct warned her to flee. Yet, the stranger's compelling, hate-filled glare held her rooted.

Then, his body shuddered. With a moan and a grimace, he fell back against the pillow.

Forgetting her panic she lurched to his side. "Lie still, or you'll reopen your wound. Do you want me to call back the nurse?"

He shook his head, and his hand flew up as far as the restraints allowed. She glanced at his fan of fingers to make sure she stood well away from his reach when a glint of metal riveted her attention. The tiny gold band encircling his fifth finger winked up at her. The ring looked too small and fragile to be masculine adornment for this intimidating man.

Moreover, the glimpse of the ring settled her suspicions. Albian males considered jewelry effeminate vanity. They didn't even wear simple marriage bands.

She looked back into the stranger's face, still regal and defiant but now beaded with perspiration. As the Silent One struggled with his pain, she struggled with her conscience. Images of the destroyed civilian transport crowded her mind again. By serving the Krillian government in any wartime capacity, this man gave his implied approval of their inhumane conduct.

Yet, as a neutral Terran diplomat, and in the absence of evidence he'd committed any crime, she had a sworn duty to protect and preserve his rights under interplanetary law.

He let out a trembling breath fraught with pain and frustration. Compassion unexpectedly stirred her heart and overrode her instinctive contempt. He might be a Krillian spy, but he was brave and stubborn in the face of peril.

"Please, lie still," she pleaded with him. "Thrashing will only hurt you more."

To calm him, she laid her hand on his shoulder. She didn't expect the charge of energy that raced up her arm at the mere touch of his fevered flesh to her cool fingertips. Neither did she expect the rush of blood to her head.

He flinched and gasped, as if he'd felt the sensation, too. Yet, he quieted under her hand. The hatred in his gaze gave way to bewilderment.

Keenly embarrassed by her own reaction, she simply nodded her satisfaction and attempted a smile. "As a representative of the Terran government, I'll see to your welfare and guarantee you sanctuary."

"I'm sure he feels much better now."

The voice startled her. The sarcasm didn't. She retracted her hand from the stranger and pivoted with as much poise as she could muster.

Mocking blue eyes assessed her up and down. She fought a chill of revulsion, then a flash of disdain as the soldier dipped his head in brief recognition. "How nice to see you again, Marista Kaljin," he greeted without warmth.

She returned his nod with no more respect than he'd shown her. "I wish I could say the same, Lieutenant Sindri."

Two

Sindri's humorless laugh emphasized the long thin line that ran from behind his right ear to the tip of his chin. The scar, a physical badge of highborn rank in the culture of Albian clans, didn't detract from his broad, handsome features.

He wagged his index finger. "A very undiplomatic greeting, Madame Kaljin."

Marista's hackles rose along with her chin. Sindri's swaggering advance gave her the uneasy sense of being stalked by a hungry carnivore. Moreover, four weapons-bearing soldiers, outfitted in sand-colored desert combat fatigues, filed through the door behind the officer.

Unwilling to appear submissive or intimidated, she shrugged as if he and the armed guards were of no consequence. "I'm not at my best in the middle of the night, Lieutenant."

Sindri raised one tawny brow. "Public servants must always be vigilant, regardless of how duty disrupts their lives." He pulled to an abrupt stop. "But I will forgive you."

Biting back a smart retort, she nodded more deeply than his condescension deserved. "How gracious of you."

At her subtle insolence, Sindri's predatory grin slipped a notch. But he stood at ease, lifted his chin, and signaled the guards to disperse. Two men left the room. Two others posted themselves sentry at the door.

She exaggerated her effort to see around Sindri. This time, she didn't hide her sarcasm behind decorum. "I don't suppose you and your men are on routine patrol this evening."

Sindri exhaled as if it pained him. "Official business, Madame. Our desert patriots sent word of their unusual find. Perhaps Madame Bierich's notification of this development reached our base after we deployed."

His insincere deference grated her. Time to establish her authority. "Madame Bierich is absent. I'm in charge, and I have not had time to send any messages. Besides, I didn't want to alert you before I've assessed the situation or determined who these men are."

"Your consideration is flattering," Sindri told her with an oily smile. "Let us say, then, that I'm here to repay your kindness. I extend an offer of my protection to your facility."

Her blood ran cold, but she kept her demeanor calm. "Protection? I haven't yet concluded there is any danger."

Sindri opened his hands in an insincere gesture of conciliation. "Then allow me to help you make that determination, Madame. Considering the location of the crash site, I suspect the air skimmer was a privateer ship from the Borderlands."

She winced before she could catch herself. These strangers might be smugglers, blockade-runners, pirates who profited from war. When her father had been military governor on the colonial planet of Yonar during the Uprisings of 2346, smugglers kept the insurgent forces supplied with arms and food when they might have surrendered. If hostilities had ended even one day sooner, her mother would still be alive.

"I remember you once called such criminals human vultures, Madame Kaljin," Sindri added.

True to his character, Sindri exploited her pain with knowledge she had supplied him. While she collected herself, the lieutenant made a crisp motion with his left hand. One of the guards shouldered his weapon, unsnapped the vest pocket of his fatigues, and removed a portable medical scanner, which he activated while moving toward the gurney.

That snapped her out of the momentary indecision. "Stop!"

The guard ignored her, kicked aside the bloody clothing on the floor, and initiated a body scan of the silent stranger.

Indignant and alarmed, she slid her gaze to meet the pair of obsidian eyes. The stranger glared at her with contempt, as if she was the one violating him.

Didn't he understand she wasn't the enemy? If he had responded to her, he might have avoided this. Angered by his wordless reproach, she spun around to Sindri. "Why are you taking a medical scan?"

Sindri seemed to enjoy her ire. "To help with your assessment of the situation. If this man is physically able, we'll escort him to our base and question him for you."

"No!"

Sindri blinked, as the force of her objection echoed off the walls. "You reject my generous offer, Madame?"

Will power and training leashed her temper, but it didn't moderate the command in her voice. "I not only reject your offer, Lieutenant. I reject your right to be here at all."

Sindri lost his smile altogether. "I beg your pardon?"

"If you truly want forgiveness then leave, Sir," she clarified. "Not only have you trampled this man's rights by subjecting him to unwarranted physical examination, you have breached Terran property without invitation."

Sindri's expression turned as menacing as the enigmatic stranger's had been moments before. "You speak intemperately for a low-level deputy, Madame."

"And you behave intemperately for a mere junior officer."

Crimson stained Sindri's sun-burnished face.

Aware she had let her emotions wreak havoc with her judgment, she decided she had nothing to lose. "This is a neutral, humanitarian outpost, Lieutenant. You have no legal right to march in here and make demands or give orders. If, at a later date, my government deems it necessary to ask for your support, we will do so. Until then, all the men found in the desert, regardless of medical condition, are under my protection."

Sindri narrowed his ice blue eyes. "I caution you to reconsider . . ."

"Lieutenant! You should see this!"

The soldier with the medical scanner startled them both. In her defense of the silent stranger's rights, she had forgotten about what was happening behind her back. She whirled in place and grasped the edge of the gurney with both hands while Sindri assessed the scanner data.

The soldier aimed the instrument at the stranger's right thigh, and then pointed to something on the visual display. While Sindri studied the information, she dared another glance at the hard, dark eyes.

But the silent stranger had turned his face to the opposite wall, even though his tormentors stood on that side. His rebuff bruised her already raw feelings. At the same time, the lack of expression in his profile worried her. She saw nothing of his inner self—no pain, no fury, no resistance. He seemed utterly resigned.

The snap of cloth yanked her attention back to the Albians. Sindri flicked his hand to direct her gaze. The lieutenant had exposed most of the stranger's right hip, leaving only his most private areas covered. Reluctantly she stared at the smooth, muscled juncture of thigh and abdomen.

While her nerves sent out ripples of perverse admiration, her sense of common decency revolted. Seething, she pinned the officer with her glare. "You have no right to humiliate this man and insult me."

"Set your foolish modesty aside, Madame, and take a close look," Sindri cut in. "Then dismiss my offer of protection."

Unwilling to appear weak or, worse, callow she looked again and prayed to Mother Creation the heat gathering in her face didn't flame hellish red. "Just what am I supposed to see?"

"The implant, just below the skin," Sindri coached. "It looks to be a contraceptive device."

She did notice a thin blue line a few centimeters long, and the width of fine conducting wire. "I'd say you're right." She lifted her eyes, squared her shoulders. "Now cover him up."

Sindri thrust out his chin at the command in her voice. But when the scanner-wielding soldier looked to him for permission, he gave a terse nod. "In deference to Madame Kaljin's sensibilities."

When it was done she abandoned all civility. "Explain to me what a simple contraceptive implant proves."

Sindri's expression hardened. "The Krillian Home Guard sterilizes all its dogs before sending them into the field, so when they rape our women they leave behind none of their filthy bastards."

She rolled her eyes. That response seemed marginally preferable to laughing at the officer's bigoted words. "You and I both know better, Sindri. Contraceptive implants are defensive devices, like immunizations. They're standard requirements for a half-dozen other planetary armies."

Her confidence rose as Sindri's face lost color. "If this is your proof he's a Krillian," she continued, "then you must suspect me, as well. All Terrans assigned to a war zone, whether or not they are in a combat role, receive the implants. Brutality has no one racial, ethnic, or planetary identity. It can be found anywhere, even among Albians."

Sindri snapped to, as if she'd struck his face. "That slander could cost you your career."

"Invading neutral territory could do the same for you," she parried. "I'll be discreet. What about you, Lieutenant?"

Sindri opened his mouth.

Tessa Bierich's voice came out. "Can you be discreet in a dignified voice, Kaljin?"

Ah, hell! Marista swore to herself. Not both of them at once!

Hoping for the best but expecting the worst, she looked over her shoulder. Bierich squeezed past the sentry at the door and charged into the room. Bram Hyrek trailed a few steps behind her and cast Marista a fleeting glance of weary resignation.

"Madame Bierich," Sindri greeted as he rounded the gurney and nodded respectfully to the chargé.

Bierich mirrored the gesture, and then gave Marista a suspicious once over before she turned back to the officer. "Hyrek told me the particulars of this situation, Lieutenant. How may I be of assistance?"

Sindri leveled smug blue eyes at Marista for an instant before smiling at Bierich and beginning his petition.

How could she be of assistance to him?

Marista clutched the edge of the gurney to keep from stalking out of the room. Her knuckles brushed warm callused flesh. She realized with a start she had inadvertently touched the silent stranger's restrained hand.

Expecting him to recoil again, she uncurled her hand to let go of the gurney. But the feel of the stranger's skin on hers remained even as she pulled away.

Sindri's verbal list of complaints faded into background noise. Marista lowered her chin and cast a furtive glance at the edge of the gurney. She wasn't mistaken. The stranger's bronzed hand now lay flat with fingers splayed on the white sheet. He stretched his fifth finger, with its curiously feminine ring, to reach her.

The sight of her small, pale knuckles resting tentatively against his large, sun-darkened finger quickened her pulse. When his hand began to tremble with strain, she slid her palm forward so he no longer had to reach. He still didn't retreat.

Summoning courage, she met his mercurial gaze. While there was nothing warm or comforting in his stone-hard eyes, neither was there a sign of his earlier hostility. Exhaustion weighted his eyelids. The stoic effort he made to snag her attention then hold it with the force of his gaze made her ashamed she'd wanted to flee the brewing conflict.

Did he mean to encourage her? Did he finally realize she was his advocate in this battle? Whatever the purpose, his effort renewed her resolve. With a lowering of her lashes she thanked him, let go of the gurney, and jumped back into the fray.

"So you see, Madame Bierich," Sindri wound down, "I offer you my assistance and protection. I urge you to reconsider your deputy's decision."

When the lieutenant emphasized her subordinate status, Marista rose to her own defense. "If you please, Madame Bierich, I've already extended Terran protection to these men, as was within my authority to do so in your absence."

The muscle in Bierich's jaw twitched. Not a good sign. Neither was the calculating set of the chargé's stare. Marista knew she'd based her decision on established, universal humanitarian and legal grounds. However, by confronting Sindri she'd jeopardized local Terran-Albian entente. Bierich obviously didn't appreciate having to smooth ruffled feathers.

Bierich turned her flinty gaze back to Sindri. "Your concern for our safety bodes well for the future of Albian-Terran accords, Lieutenant. However, I am bound to uphold Kaljin's offer of protection to these men. I cannot revoke that protection without a formal due process hearing."

Marista expelled the breath she held.

Sindri started to argue the decision, but Bierich lifted her hand to stop him and flicked a warning glance at Marista. "Whether or not Kaljin exercised good judgment in this case, she does have authority to act in my stead when I'm absent."

The chargé shifted her gaze back to the soldier. "I promise I will take this matter under advisement and order a hearing within the next few days. Meanwhile, if I determine these men are a threat to us or to Albian security, I will extradite them to you."

Sindri clicked his heels. "As you wish, Madame."

Bierich had fashioned a compromise that bought the wounded men time, Marista thought with grudging admiration.

"Meanwhile, Lieutenant," Bierich continued, "I'd be pleased to let you post a guard while we maintain custody of these men."

Sindri flashed his predatory grin.

Marista couldn't believe what she heard. "Madame, we have our own guard . . ."

"Which is limited in scope and size," Bierich interrupted. "Since we don't yet understand the true nature of this situation, we should take precautions."

"Madame, I disagree . . ."

"So noted."

Marista blinked. "You didn't let me finish."

The chargé pinned her with a quelling glare. "You're finished when I say you're finished."

Trembling with rage, Marista kept her expression suitably bland. She'd be damned if she'd let either Sindri or Bierich provoke her to recklessness. After all, she had won the major point of this debate. "Yes, Madame."

Bierich sniffed, and then scanned her head-to-toe. "And next time you act in my stead, Kaljin, at least be certain you're in proper uniform. Button that collar, lose the necklace, and put your hair up, or it comes off."

The petty reprimand took her aback. In reflex, she touched the long, loopy curls at her shoulders, and then glanced down at the gray shirt that should have been buttoned at the throat and hidden by a jacket.

Bram stepped forward. "Marista . . . that is Madame Kaljin . . . was already retired when I called on her tonight."

Bierich turned on him. "This isn't your concern, Hyrek." She faced Marista. "Learn to dress on the run, if you have to, Kaljin. Next time, I'll put you on report."

Incredulous, she gaped at the chargé. Was it possible she'd just witnessed a naked exercise of power at her expense? But why? Because she'd made a proper decision in a crisis and Bierich had been forced to agree with it?

She didn't even bother looking at Sindri. She knew she'd find gloating in the icy-blue eyes. Instead, she waited in resentful silence as Bierich conferred with Bram and sent him on his way before turning back to her.

"Stay here until Hyrek returns to take this wounded man to isolation," Bierich ordered.

Marista lowered her voice to steady it. "Yes, Madame."

Bierich then escorted him and his guard into the hallway.

Marista rubbed the center of her forehead. Tired. She felt so tired. Not just physically, but from the mortifying mental gymnastics Bierich had put her through for reasons she didn't fathom.

"Kaljin?"

The whisper from behind startled her. She spun around toward the gurney, and her gaze connected with the pair of dark eyes. "Yes, what is it?" she asked in the Krillian dialect, since she already assumed he was non-Albian.

The stranger answered with a lazy blink. His eyelids fluttered shut and stayed that way for long seconds before he forced them open again. He tried to form words, but could barely move his lips.

Moved by pity, she leaned over the gurney and brushed back a wisp of black hair that fell across his forehead. The thick, course spikes sifted through her fingers, sending tingles up her arm. "You're exhausted. Don't try to talk. Bram will be coming to take you to the isolation room where you can get some sleep."

He managed a weak nod, and then flicked the tip of tongue over dry lips. "My friends? How many . . . survived? Where are they . . .?"

She strained to understand the slurred Krillian words. And for a cowardly moment, she hoped he'd drift off to sleep. What should she tell him about his comrades—the unvarnished truth, or a mind-soothing lie?

The stoic stranger fought drowsiness. "My friends?"

"This is only a field hospital for refugees," she hedged. "But we have a good medical staff. You and your friends will receive the best of care."

He considered her words, then pressed his lips together and nodded again.

Encouraged, she went on. "In spite of all that bickering, you're safe for the time being."

He squinted. "Why?"

"Because I said so. Even my superior agreed I have that authority."

But he shook his head as if trying to clear it. "No, why . . .?"

"Shhh. Go to sleep now."

His eyes flew open wider. "Wait! Why . . . speak for me?"

She answered without pause. "Because you couldn't, or wouldn't, speak for yourself."

That didn't satisfy him. "If . . . I'm the enemy?"

"I'm Terran," she replied. "I'm not your enemy."

He narrowed his drowsy eyes. "Yes, you are."

Perhaps in his fogged state he didn't understand. "No, I'm not . . ."

"Cold."

Yes, she felt suddenly cold, too, deep in her soul.

Then she noticed gooseflesh rising on his arms. Throughout the entire debate about human rights and diplomatic duty, the wounded stranger lay restrained and nearly naked while bureaucrats and soldiers determined his fate. If Bierich had humiliated her with cutting remarks, imagine how this man must have felt battled over like a trophy.

She hurried to a storage cabinet, retrieved a thermal blanket, and shook it open. When she returned to the gurney, the stranger's eyes were closed.

Carefully, she wrapped him in the blanket and tucked the edges beneath the gurney mattress. Then she leaned forward and, on pure sentimental impulse, pressed her hand to his bronzed cheek and jaw. The stranger's heated skin seared her palm.

He stirred, and labored to move his mouth. "Near . . ."

She smiled sadly at the forced whisper. "Yes, someone's near. And you're wrong, my friend. I'm not the enemy."

Three

Breathe, Tynan, in and out. Slow and easy.

The internal mantra cajoled him until a steady intake of cool, recycled air eased the pitch and roll of his stomach. Feeling stronger, he pushed away from the edge of the bed, and shuffled to the lone window inside the small isolation unit. There he squinted into the Albian morning.

Below him spread the oasis. He knew the place well. Inara Wadi the local clans called it. Far below the desert floor, an artesian spring bubbled to the surface and gave life to lush green vegetation and multi-colored flowers even in this, the dry season.

The weathered, white-stucco building that sheltered him now was once a colonial government site before the founding of the provincial capital city at Timetsuara. From his vantage, he guessed the isolation room was on the second of five levels.

Now he understood why the Albian soldiers appeared so fast at the outpost last night. A military garrison lay not ten kilometers away. The air skimmer must have been further off course before the crash than the pilot reported.

The shimmering heat-haze suddenly made him woozy. A film of perspiration broke out on his forehead. He took a quick, tottering step backward and nearly doubled over. Damn if he hadn't been in less pain two months ago when he'd broken three ribs.

Battling for air he braced his hands on either side of the window casing. He wasn't used to prolonged bouts of physical weakness. Usually, he focused his mind, willed pain into submission, and let his flesh mend.

If Marista Kaljin hadn't disturbed his meditation, he might have been almost healed by now. Every time she touched him last night, his senses and brain short-circuited. He had tried to shut his eyes, shut her out. But even her warm, female scent broke his concentration.

Her image didn't fade from his memory with the dawn of a new day either. In his mind's eye he saw the long, thick strands of gently curled hair that glittered with all the fiery brilliance of a desert sunset. And when she regarded him with her unreserved compassion, her eyes shimmered green as Medan's Ocean.

Sweat trickled across his forehead and slid down his nose. Still unable to let go of the window casing, he shook his head and dislodged the drops, then filled his lungs with air.

What had gotten into him? His mission ended in flaming death. The criminals, Lares and Osten, still walked free. And he lay wounded in the middle of the desert, surrounded by Terran meddlers and swaggering Albian soldiers. Somewhere else on the grounds his friends might be dead or dying.

Yet all he vividly remembered of last night was her face, her voice, her scent.

Perhaps the mental turbulence the little diplomat wrought had triggered the old dream. Dear, sweet Neari had invaded his sleep, after six months of absence. She called to him, surrounded him, and then slipped away before he woke to the blinding sunrise and vivid images of a Terran woman on his mind.

Perhaps this fixation with Marista Kaljin meant only that he needed a quick romp with a woman. Any woman.

Yet, the nurse had touched him, too, and he'd blocked both her and the pain as if they were mere nuisances. Why did the light press of Kaljin's hand skew his pulse and focus?

He had to center himself, and do it fast. Some instinct pegged the unsettling deputy diplomat as his only ally on this so-called "neutral" outpost. Kaljin made it clear last night she disliked and disrespected Sindri. Then she deftly handled the lieutenant's bluff and bluster. Albian officers were not known for their gentle, compromising natures. He knew that better than anyone, and he admired her skill.

He knew, as well, he had to exploit Kaljin's better nature. From the way she passionately defended his rights on idealistic principle, not evidence, he guessed she was relatively inexperienced in the ways of true diplomats. He had to convince her to help him above and beyond what she had already done.

For that reason, and in spite of her disturbing effect on him, he had asked to see her again this morning.

By degrees his breathing slowed and the searing pain subsided. When he finally opened his eyes he noticed the knuckles of both hands were white with the strain of holding himself upright.

He also saw the thin metal wristbands, a reminder the isolation unit doubled as his prison cell. At least the electronic restraints let him move around the room. The med-tech named Hyrek ordered them to replace the mesh and cloth cuffs affixed to the bed, so he could move about the room and regain some strength.

For a Terran, Hyrek seemed to mean well. But the tech didn't understand that his kind gesture mattered little in the long-term. Yes, Sindri did want his prisoner strong and well, but only enough to survive ruthless "interrogation."

He stopped himself before he lapsed into self-pity. He'd always accepted the consequences of his own decisions. On occasion, he'd even pushed his luck. Why did he have regrets or fears now?

A hiss of static startled him. The synthaflesh bandage pulled at his side as he looked over his shoulder.

Kaljin peered at him through the viewing window. The coils of golden-red hair that had lain loose on her shoulders the night before were pulled back and knotted at the crown of her head. Her face, pale in the harsh light, appeared more delicate without curls licking at her chin.

Still, she was as beautiful as when he first saw her through a drug-induced haze. In the span of a half-second, wonder and erotic awareness flooded over him. He struggled to keep his expression flat, while his chest tightened and he labored for air.

Her faint smile faded and the intercom crackled to life. She addressed him in the Krillian dialect. "Hyrek said you asked for me." She gave his length a scan, and then lowered her eyes. "Maybe now is not a good time."

He glanced down at himself. He'd discarded the ridiculous bed shirt and draped it over the back of a chair. The baggy, drawstring leggings Hyrek had given him to wear rode immodestly low on his hips.

For someone of her station and authority, Marista Kaljin didn't mask her private sensibilities well. Her quaint sense of propriety was oddly appealing, and he almost smiled as he retrieved his bed shirt. "No. Come now," he instructed and carefully slipped his arms into the sleeves.

She left the viewing window. A second later, the isolation room door slid open.

In spite of his best intentions, his breath hitched when she stepped through the archway. The gray uniform jacket and trousers molded to her full breasts, narrow waist, and gently rounded hips. She wasn't tall. The guard towered over her. Yet, she carried herself with a dignity and grace that lent her stature.

As he gawked, a bright pink stain sliced across each of her cheeks, and she stared back at him in silence. His attention obviously made her uncomfortable.

Neither did he speak nor move. The green depths of her eyes immobilized him with some strong, but gentle inner force. When her features began to shimmer he forced himself to draw air, unaware until then he hadn't done so for some moments.

"Perhaps you should sit down."

Kaljin's voice was soft, low, and soothing, the kind one used to lull little children and madmen. The notion irritated him. He didn't want her pity or condescension. He wanted . . .

What did he want?

To sit down. He needed to sit down before his knees buckled. Without acknowledging her, he backed against the chair and eased into it.

"You may leave now," she told the guard in the Albian dialect.

The guard leaned forward, muttered into Kaljin's ear, and tried to hand her something.

"Thank you, but no," she replied. Then she directed her gaze and next words at Tynan. "He's so weak he can barely stand. He won't try to harm me. Besides, you'll be right outside the door. I won't need the restraint control."

"He may be stronger than he looks, Madame," the guard insisted. "If you do not take the control, I will stay."

She stared at the small, black box, and then rubbed her palms on the sides of her trousers. "Very well." Reluctantly, she took the box and clipped it to her belt. "Now you may go."

He wondered at the cool command in her voice, when moments before she had reacted to his state of undress with prim embarrassment. This woman seemed to have more facets than a fine cut gem, and he could never quite be sure which face she'd show in response to the situation at hand. As the door slid closed after the guard, he questioned the wisdom of dealing with someone so complex and mutable.

Before his doubts settled, Kaljin strode forward until she stood less than a half-meter away. Hovering above him, she overwhelmed his senses. Her hair glimmered in the diffused, natural light. Her soft brown lashes fanned thick against the translucent skin of her eyelids. She smelled of desert air and new mornings, things feminine, warm, desirable.

Inside him, something gently twisted—something softer and deeper, and more dangerous than simple lust. He'd almost forgotten the stirrings of need. The power of her sensuality and sympathy posed more of a threat than the control hanging from her belt. There was something truly, deeply honest and innocent about her. If that were so, he regretted the need to manipulate and distort such purity of purpose to his advantage.

But he needed her help to carry out his duty. He couldn't let conscience or base desire distract him. Moreover, he had little time to establish himself as a force equal to her. "The guard is right, Kaljin. I'm stronger than I look. I could hurt you before you have a chance to use that control on me."

Wariness clouded her green eyes, but she didn't retreat. Instead, she looked around, found a stool close by, and pulled it forward. When she sat on it, her knees almost touched his.

Leaning slightly forward, she fixed him with a surprisingly hard stare. "You understood what the guard said, didn't you?" She used the Albian dialect, though he had spoken to her in Krillian. Without waiting for an answer, Kaljin pressed ahead. "Last night, when you touched my hand, I thought you understood what happened just from the tone of our voices. But you do know what we said."

To begin earning her trust he decided not to lie. "I speak many dialects," he replied in Albian. "As a diplomat, you must realize it's a useful skill. No doubt you can tell someone to go to perdition so he will look forward to the trip in at least a half-dozen languages."

She raised a narrow eyebrow. "First, I'm not a diplomat. Not yet, anyway. Second, yes, facility with languages is a job requirement for admission to the diplomatic services. For what purposes do you find such skills useful?"

He almost answered. Blunt and brutal interrogation he could withstand. Faced with her gentle, non-intrusive manner, he found himself defenseless. Fortunately, Hyrek hadn't given him another narcotic hypo this morning. Drugged, he'd probably spew out his entire life story to her in thirty seconds.

He nodded in courteous agreement. "For many purposes."

When he didn't elaborate, she narrowed her gaze. "Perhaps I should make myself clear," she told him. "I don't intend to use this restraint control. I can defend myself, but I prefer negotiation to violence. I repeat what I told you last night. I am not your enemy. Moreover, if you believed I was your enemy, you wouldn't have asked me to come here."

Her logic and defiance in the face of his threat astounded him. Didn't the woman have any common sense? Is that the reason she had debated fast and loose with Sindri?

He had to put her in her place. "Perhaps it isn't in my best interest to hurt you. Yet."

She straightened. As much as he wanted to maintain indifference to this Terran woman, he didn't want to alienate her.

When she spread her hands in a conciliatory gesture, however, he realized just how much he'd misinterpreted her reaction. "That is a chance I'm willing to take. By my reasoning, only a fool would harm the one person standing between him and Lieutenant Sindri." Then, she smiled as if they had just been introduced at a social gathering. "You know my name. What shall I call you?"

He hesitated, shaken more by her dazzling smile than her poise. Meanwhile, his mind worked a circular logic. Knowing his name gave her a certain advantage over him beyond her unsettling presence. Still, she didn't seem to notice the agitation she stirred up in him. What she did not understand she could not use. Besides, he had to establish some rapport with her.

"Call me Tynan."

"Just Tynan?"

No first names. Nothing personal, he warned himself.

"For now," he said aloud, and immediately wondered why he had qualified the answer

"What language shall we speak?" she continued in a conversational tone.

Careful, Tynan, an inner voice warned. Don't let her know too much.

"Terran Standard," he answered in her native tongue. "That is, if you don't mind my accent."

She smiled. "You speak Terran well. Though, like the Krillian you spoke last night, neither one is your native dialect, is it?"

Good. She was very good.

Well, so was he. "You may assume what you want. You and the others have already made up your minds about me and my friends."

"It isn't my job to assume anything about you."

"You say that, though you addressed me in Krillian last night and this morning."

"Because of where the clansmen found you," she explained. "Sindri believes you're smugglers from the Borderlands, if not Krillian spies. I reacted on the basis of that information. In addition, though, I noticed you wear a ring, unlike Albian men."

He fisted his left hand, and curled the fifth finger inward until it almost disappeared. Raw sentiment led to that blunder in judgment. The same sentiment roughened his voice. "Thin enough evidence to label a man. Much like the implant Sindri discovered."

"True. My apologies if I have offended you."

When he said nothing for several heartbeats, she tilted her head. "Did you call me here to complain about unfair treatment in our facility? If so, I'll take your statement under advisement. However, if you aren't forthcoming with me, you'll remain under suspicion. I can't change that."

Uncertain her passive demeanor wasn't a ploy to manipulate information from him, he baited her. "How do I know you won't report this conversation to Sindri?"

"You asked specifically for me alone," she replied calmly. "If I believed Sindri had a right to hear our conversation, I would have brought him along. As it is, he doesn't know I'm here. He left at daybreak to investigate the wreck of your air skimmer."

He grunted. "The skimmer's burned to cinders, but he'll find what he wants to find."

The little diplomat's face went white as the desert sand under a midday sun. Terror flickered in her green eyes for a half-second before she blinked it away. "That may be. In any case, I can act as your liaison should you decide to answer Sindri's questions."

Though his curiosity about her sudden pallor chipped some of the edge from his defensiveness, he didn't let down his guard. "I have no use for a liaison."

Color returned to her face. "Then why did you call me here? I thought perhaps you wanted me to contact your family at least . . ."

"I have no family to contact," he cut in with intentional rudeness. "I have only the ones who were with me."

Sadness touched her eyes. "Oh."

Fear constricted his throat. "Are they all dead?"

"No, not all," she answered. "Two of your friends are critical, but stabilized. One has burns over eighty percent of his body. The other has massive head trauma. But one of the men died in transit to the outpost. And the boy . . ." She shook her head. "I'm sorry. The boy died this morning."

He pounded his thigh with a clenched fist. "No!"

"You knew both of the dead well?"

"Well enough," he groaned. "The boy was Jarrit's son."

"We don't know any names. Which is Jarrit?"

His guard had slipped in a moment of anger and grief. Before he could do more damage he clamped his mouth shut.

She eased forward on the stool. "If Jarrit is one of the men left alive, don't you think we should tell him about his son?"

Without asking, she wrapped her hands gently around his wrists, just above the restraint cuffs. Her cool fingers on his heated skin set his body taut, and scattered his thoughts.

Damn the woman! Damn his faltering self-control!

He yanked away and suffered a burning ache in his side.

Kaljin withdrew as if he'd swiped his arm at her. This "touching" nonsense was probably part of her nature that others accepted without objection. His refusal to be petted and lulled stunned her. Good. Maybe she'd keep her distance now.

Still, if he wanted to earn her trust, he needed to compromise something. Besides, her humanitarian instincts might work to his favor. "Yes, Jarrit should be told." He rummaged through memories. "His legs were crushed."

She stiffened. "Yes, I know which one he is now. Our surgeon couldn't save one of his legs. We don't have the facilities and equipment to perform nerve and vascular repair." She swallowed, and then wet her dry lips with the tip of her tongue. "What happened? How did you escape with so little injury?"

She wanted him to be forthcoming. A recount of the crash was a safe enough subject. But he remembered how she'd reacted when he spoke only in passing about the burned-out craft. "Are you sure you want to hear?"

She didn't flinch. "Yes, I do."

He paused, and turned inward where the images, sounds and smells of the fiery crash welled up. "I'm not certain what went wrong," he began. "Everything happened too fast. I think our pilot tried to make an emergency landing. I felt the braking thrusters fire. Instead of a smooth glide we banked sharp right and down, then hit the ground hard."

Kaljin's intense stare blurred in a haze of harsh memories. "Everyone in the cockpit must have died on impact. Most of the men in the main body of the skimmer might have survived if the fuel cells hadn't ruptured and blown."

"How did you survive?"

Her voice cut through the visions of flame and twisted metal. He gave a weak shrug. "The skimmer's main cabin seated only ten, so we tossed dice to see who would sit in the aft storage compartment. I lost and put on a flight suit because that section wasn't heated. Fate and the insulated flight suit saved my life."

He winced in reflex. "When we hit ground, the impact severed the bulkhead at the juncture of the main and aft compartments. My section came to a stop, while the rest of the skimmer traveled a half-kilometer further on the desert floor. By the time I crawled out of the rubble, most of the wreckage ahead was in flames. I ran toward it, but shrapnel from the explosion slashed my side and I couldn't move fast. I didn't have enough time to get everyone out before the ship blew up."

"You pulled five men out of the fire?"

Her hoarse whisper snapped his concentration. He focused on her incredulous stare. "How could I ignore the screams?"

She shuddered, and clasped her hands in her lap. For a moment she appeared ready to flee.

"Kaljin, what's wrong?"

Closing her eyes, she raised her hand. "Nothing."

She lied. If she held herself any more rigid her backbone would snap. Still, she pressed him. "The clansmen found you kilometers from nowhere."

He answered, but watched her carefully. "We were off course."

"Off course?"

"Don't ask more."

"I remind you, this conversation is privileged."

"It is, unless your government finds reason to extradite me to Timetsuara," he pointed out. "In that case, you'll have to repeat our conversations. You can't testify to what you don't know. Ignorance will protect us both."

She regarded him with speculation. "Then I have reason to suspect you and the others are smugglers or spies."

"If we are," he prompted, "would you withdraw your Terran protection?"

"No, of course not," she replied without hesitation. "You have our protection until and unless a due process hearing rules against you."

"Then what you believe doesn't have a bearing on the request I have to make."

"Perhaps not. What is your request?"

He drew himself up as much as his aching wound allowed. "Let me see Jarrit."

Resistance to the idea flicked briefly in her steady gaze. "He isn't often conscious, and he's always under heavy sedation. Neither Madame Bierich nor I have talked with him ourselves yet."

"I have to see Jarrit. It's important."

She eyed him with new suspicion. "Why?"

He realized he seemed too eager, and decided on an appeal to her compassion. "He's my friend. As you said, someone should tell him about his son. I'll do it."

She replied softly, but with skepticism. "I'm not sure I can get permission, even for such a noble cause."

"Don't you have the authority to decide?"

She bristled. "I suppose. That is if I had a mind to cast aside all common sense and put my career on the line to aid and abet a man suspected of criminal activity at best, espionage at worst."

"You make your own assumption about that. I admitted nothing."

"Non-admission isn't denial."

She wasn't as green as he'd guessed. Someday she might make a fine, dissembling diplomat.

Setting aside pride he resorted to supplication. "Consider my request, please. I'll know how to tell Jarrit about his son." He grit his teeth. "Get me in to see him."

"No."

The refusal stunned him. She gave so much without asking, and yet when he did ask . . .

But he hadn't asked. He'd barked an order. Having seen her resistance last night to the chargé's petty tyranny he shouldn't wonder why she refused. This Terran woman had fended off the chargé and Sindri at the same time. She wouldn't be bullied by a total stranger held in check with electronic restraints.

Drawing from limited inner reserves, he steadied his breathing, his heart, his voice. "I have to see Jarrit. The reasons may be more humanitarian than you suspect, or I can fully admit."

He didn't lie. He had to be prepared when Sindri came to collect him.

And Sindri would come to collect him, sooner or later.

"Take me yourself if you want," he pressed.

She stopped him with a slice of her hand. "Nothing in the rule book states you have the privilege to see other patients."

"Then I appeal to your decency and honor."

Her eyes turned hard as emeralds. "Be warned, Tynan. You won't get your way by using flattery."

Her prickly pride intrigued him. "I meant no insult. Neither do I waste my time with flattery. I say what I believe is the truth."

She lapsed into a brooding silence.

He tried one final gambit to convince her. "Why did you defend me last night?"

She looked surprised, and a little irritated. "I have a responsibility to protect your rights."

"The chargé has that responsibility, as well. But I think she would have handed me over to Sindri."

Kaljin twined her fingers into a ball on her lap. "Madame Bierich would have complied with Interplanetary Law."

He crooked his mouth into a humorless smirk. "I admire your loyal defense of a superior. But you don't believe that anymore than I do. That aside, would Madame Bierich be sitting close enough to touch me unless I were tied down to the bed?"

The dark pupils of her eyes nearly blotted out the clear green iris. "I . . . I don't know . . . maybe."

He seized on her momentary confusion, eased forward in his chair, and slowly moved his arm toward her. "Why are you taking this chance with me?"

"Because you . . ." She halted and backtracked. "Because trust has to start somewhere."

"Yes. You don't expect to receive trust unless you give it. Now I place my trust in you. Look at my hand."

"What?"

"Look at my hand," he repeated.

She finally obeyed and let her eyes trail along the thin callused scar that followed the lifeline on his palm. She stifled a cry of surprise. "Is that a clan marking?"

"Yes, it defines my heritage." He paused. "It will condemn me, as well."

She stared, transfixed, at the scar. "You're an Albian national, and a member of an esteemed family."

He withdrew his hand, and then waited until she looked up at him. "That is the reason I speak Krillian poorly and Terran Standard with an accent. That is the reason Sindri will arrest me despite your idealistic protests when he receives the results of last night's data scan. Krillians might be able to claim sanctuary on neutral Terran ground. Albian nationals on the run from their government can't hope for such refuge. Please, Kaljin," he begged in spite of his pride, "let me see my friend, Jarrit, before one or both of us is dead."

Shock. Revulsion. Resentment. They all flickered across her beautiful face before she narrowed her eyes to slits. "Why will Sindri arrest you?"

"Because I'm a danger to the Albian government."

"You are a spy."

"No."

"What are you then?"

"For your own good, I can't tell you more."

She stuck out her chin. "Don't think you can frighten me. I'm no raw intern right out of the academy. No matter what you've done, Sindri can't take you off these premises without benefit of a due process hearing . . ."

"I've seen Albian military justice enforced most of my life," he cut in. "Haven't you heard of the 'Never Born?'"

From her blank stare, he guessed not and pressed the advantage. "Ask Sindri about them. He can and will take me out of here at weapon's point, whether or not you object. I'll be thrown into a prison beneath the streets of Timetsuara, tortured until I break, and executed before you file the first official protest."

Kaljin collected her poise and set her face into a bland expression. For the first time, he couldn't guess what went on behind those green eyes, but her direct gaze made him want to squirm.

She finally replied in a low, tense voice. "You're asking me to risk a great deal. I can sympathize with your request on humanitarian grounds. If, indeed, that is your purpose."

He hardly breathed. "It is."

"And yet," she reasoned aloud, "by permitting it, I might be abetting criminal activity."

"That is a possibility."

He said no more. He'd already said too much. While he didn't enjoy backing her into a corner, or using her sense of fairness and justice against her, he had no choice. He had to see Jarrit and prepare for what lay ahead.

With a sigh she stood and peered down at him as if considering her options.

"Will you tell Sindri who I am?" he prodded her.

"No. I've given you my word this is privileged communication. As a representative of the Terran Diplomatic Corps, my word is my bond."

He rose from the chair. To Kaljin's credit, she didn't give ground though he loomed over her. "I've never trusted diplomats of any world. Too much cunning in words and deeds. I'll accept the word of Marista Kaljin, the woman."

Anger flashed in her eyes, but she replied in a level tone. "You have my personal assurance, too. However," she added with a scowl, "don't mistake my sense of fairness with naiveté. I won't play the fool for my principles."

He stifled a smile of grudging admiration. "I'll consider myself warned. Now, what about my seeing Jarrit?"

From the clench of her delicate jaw line he supposed he'd pressed her too hard, and pressed his luck as well.

"I'll think about it. But I can't make promises." She started to turn.

"Kaljin?"

"What?"

"Don't take too long making your decision." He hesitated. "And thank you. I'm grateful for what you've already done."

With exaggerated deference she nodded. "How kind of you to say so."

The woman could insult as well as appease, he mused as she turned and left the isolation unit.

The door opened and closed behind her. He counted three fast heartbeats until she passed in front of the viewing window. Kaljin held her head aloof, and kept her eyes straight ahead as she disappeared down the corridor.

But she didn't vanish from his thoughts. A survivor's instinct warned him he was more vulnerable placing himself at the mercy of the lovely Terran diplomat than confronting the retribution of the entire Albian military.

Four

The communication server scanned and rejected several programmed locations. Marista twisted in the swivel chair, but she never glanced away from her personal com-terminal screen. Though she'd discarded her jacket and left it on the bed next to her nightgown, a trickle of perspiration slid down her back.

After spending the better part of the morning and early afternoon searching every file in the Terran Embassy databases, she found no evidence that a highborn Albian named "Tynan" existed. It was time to get some expert help.

"Come on, Jace," she railed under her breath. "Where are you these days?"

Lurking somewhere he shouldn't be, she guessed. Jace Ugo, self-educated journalist and general pain in the posterior, seldom covered just "the story." He mucked around until he found the why and wherefore, which made him a most unpopular man. Both the Albian and Krillian governments treated him like contagion.

Despite his faults, and there were many, she dearly loved her oldest friend. Still there were limits to her time and patience. In half an hour she would meet with her twin tormentors, Bierich and Sindri. "Jace, for the love of Creation, this is important!"

The urgency of her own words echoed in the small room. The man named Tynan meant nothing to her personally. He was a high-handed, stubborn Albian, not unlike Sindri.

No, that wasn't true. Tynan was different than Sindri. A deep, personal desperation touched his words and sometimes softened his obsidian eyes to black velvet. The fine grooves on either side of his mouth and at his temples indicated he had, at one time, laughed, and did it often. He only smirked now, but even then a dimple deep enough to hide the tip of her index finger gentled the hard, set lines of his face. The notion of leaving him to the machinations of Madame Bierich and Lieutenant Sindri seemed like a cruel betrayal.

She didn't deny that her physical attraction to Tynan sparked this willingness to invest time and energy on his behalf. Healthy people had healthy libidos, and his powerful virility would arouse any woman's lust. When she saw him standing in the Isolation Room this morning, with his broad shoulders thrown back, his head high and his muscles taut in spite of his injury, a twist of desire actually forced the air from her lungs.

But she knew as well that fighting strong emotions only made them harder to suppress, like swimming against a riptide. She had let the sensations wash over her, certain they would eventually recede and leave her standing on solid ground. For a while, as she conducted her interview with him, the reverse psychology worked.

Then he'd asked about his friends. His grief and outrage were swift and painfully honest. When he recounted how he pulled the survivors from the burning air skimmer, she knew she had waded in too far for self-rescue. Once, two decades ago, she had been at the mercy of runaway flames, scorching heat, and suffocating smoke. She understood what kind of courage Tynan had summoned to brave the inferno for the sake of his friends.

Now, with every rational analytic path polluted by worthless emotionalism, she might have to make her decision whether or not to trust Tynan based on intuition alone.

The servo-voice broke her ruminations. "Terminal connected. Please stand by."

The blue vid-screen jumped, crackled with static, and then focused. She peered into a bright, airy, well lived-in room. Beyond the reclining chairs and low-slung tables strewn with dirty dishes a transparent wall gave her a panoramic view of rolling green hills.

"What the hell is it?"

She grinned at the sound of the scratchy voice. "Good afternoon, Jace. Oh, sorry. It's still morning in Daegal, isn't it?"

"Damn straight it's morning . . . Riss? Is that you?"

The screen became a blur of mahogany flesh. She laughed as Jace pulled his long fingers through the rumpled stubs of salt-and-pepper hair. "Did I get you out of bed?"

Jace settled his long, lean body into a chair and rolled closer to the screen. "Never got that far. Worked through the night."

"I've heard that before."

"No, I did. Big story's breaking. Someone tried to assassinate Prime Minister Lares and Field Marshall Osten."

Her expectations plummeted as she took in the foreboding news about the Albian high officials. "I haven't heard anything about it."

"You will," he assured her.

"Then, I'm sorry to bother you."

"Bother me? You?" He hitched one leg over the other. "Never."

"Good," she answered. "I thought I'd lost my charm after these months in the desert."

"Who said you had any charm to lose? Maybe that's why you don't have a man yet."

Though irritated by the familiar pestering, she offered Jace a flirtatious wink. "I'm waiting for you to grow up."

"Hey, Riss, if I were thirty years younger . . ."

"I've heard that before, too."

"Speaking of old news," he bantered, "heard from the General lately?"

Maintaining her grin, she clenched her hands together on the desk.

"No, we haven't spoken since I left Earth. But I didn't call to discuss Dad or my social life."

"Oh, yeah, sure. What is it?"

She took a breath, leaned closer to the screen. "I need you to find someone for me. A man."

He grunted a laugh. "I thought we weren't talking about your social life."

"Jace, I need your help."

"All right. I give. What man?"

"His name is Tynan. I can transmit a drawing of an Albian clan marking on his right palm. But that's all I have." In a few sentences, she told him about Tynan and the dangers he faced.

"Done," Jace agreed, as if it were no consequence. "You really think Bierich would hand him over to the Albians?"

"She'll hold a due process hearing. But I don't know how vigorously she'll defend his rights."

"Old bitch," he muttered. "She still giving you a bad time?"

"I can handle her," she assured him with a limp smile. "Frankly, Bierich may have the right inclination. Maybe we should let the Albians drag Tynan away in restraints."

"Then why are you going to all this trouble for him?"

Had she been talking to anyone else but Jace, she would have hedged. Instead, she shrugged. "He smells right."

Jace rolled his eyes. "Ah, yes, your old Aunt Mimi's acid test of worthiness. Never could figure out what it had to do with smell, though. Those feelings usually hit me in the gut."

"'Old' Aunt Mimi is ten years younger than you," she kidded. "And neither my nose nor my 'gut' ever failed me before. But this time . . ." She massaged the bridge of her nose. "I don't know. There's so much Tynan refuses to tell me. Before I go sticking my neck out any further, I want to be fairly certain no one can slip a noose around it. That's why I came to you."

"I'll get you answers, Riss."

She grimaced. "I need them fast."

"I'm already on it."

She smiled with genuine fondness. "You're wonderful."

"Isn't that what I keep telling you? Anything else?"

"Yes. What do you know about Albian military prisons?"

He screwed up his face as if someone had pinched him hard. "Don't worry. You've got diplomatic immunity. If you murder Bierich, the Albians can't touch you. Besides, you could claim justifiable homicide."

"Not me," she interrupted with a patient grin.

"Tynan?"

She nodded.

"Don't know much, except people go in and don't come out. On the streets they're called the Never Born.

Tynan had used that same chilling phrase. "Why?"

Jace squirmed in the chair. "Partly because nobody on the outside talks about a person imprisoned under the Albian military. Partly because the people inside the prison wish they were never born."

Her stomach flopped over, and she winced.

"Sorry, Riss. You know I don't mince words. But it kinda makes you wonder who the bad guys are, doesn't it?"

"You can't mean that," she rebuked. "Are you forgetting what the Krillians did to the Rising Sun?"

"Now, don't get your undies in a bunch. But next time we're together, we'll have a little talk about that whole incident."

She frowned. "You're serious, aren't you?"

"Haven't been just warming my ass these past two years. Been out making enemies and raising planet-wide static."

"Jace," she pressed, "what's going on?"

The journalist shook his head and leaned forward as if drawing her into confidence. "Save it for another time, when it's just you, me, and no vid-screen between us."

Sometimes he seemed so paranoid she wanted to laugh. This time, though, his melodramatic pronouncement made her squirm with nagging discomfort. She simply nodded and continued with the business at hand. "I'll look forward to it. One more thing. When you have some information, send it to me via my personal code. No official contact."

His wiry, black brows shot up. "Ho, ho! You wouldn't be doing a bypass around Bierich, would you?"

"I might be. Is the answer relevant to my request?"

Jace grinned and crossed his arms. "Nope. But, damn, I'd swear I was talking to the General himself. Sure as hell, you're the old man's daughter."

"I'm not at all like my father," she blurted out before she could stop herself. Then she drew a calming breath, and cast him what she hoped would look like a comically exaggerated glare. "And unless you want me to come through this vid-screen and wring your scrawny neck, you'll promise never to say that again."

"Hey, watch how you talk to your elders," he joked. "Remember I changed your diapers."

She failed to suppress a reluctant grin. "And I'll dance on your grave. The way you look right now, that'll be sooner than later."

He scrubbed his face hard with one hand. "The way I feel this morning I'd lay odds you're right. But don't worry. I'll get on this project before I hit the sack."

She gentled her smile. "I don't know how I can thank you."

"I do. Call your old man to say hi."

She sighed loud enough for Jace to hear. "I have a meeting with

Bierich in five minutes. Have to go."

"Okay. Bye, Riss. Kick Bierich's ass."

The vid-screen went blue. She switched off her terminal, sank back in her chair, and rubbed her burning eyes.

Poor, dear Jace. He'd never understand that she'd rather confront Tessa Bierich sixteen times every day than call her father just to say "hi."

***

Bierich sat at her desk with her hands folded in front of her as Sindri reported his initial findings. Though sunshine streamed into the airy office through an overhead skylight, a downward draft of recycled air chilled Marista to her fingertips.

Yet, despite her physical discomfort, she felt a surge of relief. So far, the Albian officer revealed nothing about the skimmer crash she hadn't already heard from Tynan.

Sindri read from a display screen in the palm of his hand. "The air skimmer's navigation logs were severely damaged, but seem to suggest the crew was indeed on a heading for the Borderlands."

He glanced up and smiled faintly at the chargé. "Rest assured, Madame, the Albian government prosecutes smugglers with as much prejudice as it does spies."

In light of her recent conversation with Jace about Albian prisons, Marista shivered at the threat. "You found hard evidence of smuggling activity, Lieutenant?"

Sindri clasped his hands behind his back. "My investigation is not complete. Requests for data from our central government files have been given secondary priority due to a rather more important situation that has occurred in Fremandri Province."

Was that "situation" the assassination attempt about which Jace spoke? she wondered. If so, diversion of intelligence resources to the other side of the planet might buy Tynan and his friends even more precious time.

Bierich frowned. "How unfortunate."

Sindri cocked a brow. "Unfortunate, too, that Madame Kaljin adheres to strict confidentiality regarding her conversations with the detainee in isolation. But, we may learn more once we have the results of the body scan we took of the one man and compare it to our population data file."

Marista checked her temper at Sindri's refusal to address her directly. She didn't check her tongue. "I'm afraid, Lieutenant, you will not be able to submit that scan as evidence in a due process hearing. You conducted the procedure without the man's permission and outside your legal jurisdiction."

"I'll decide the admissibility of evidence, Kaljin."

Bierich's interruption didn't anger her as much as it startled her. The chargé glared. Her eyes reminded Marista of the clansmen's desert rifles—cold, steely, threatening.

The unspoken warning only stiffened Marista's resolve. "But, Madame, the scan violated the man's rights."

"Kaljin, Albian law does not hold the individual's rights inviolate when there is overwhelming evidence of wrong-doing."

"However, Madame, there is no overwhelming evidence of wrong-doing, and this is not Albian territory. This is a Terran facility."

"I must balance our neutrality against the good of our entente with the Albian government," Bierich answered. "The Lieutenant is not asking our cooperation in the prosecution of these men. He's merely asking we release them into Albian custody so the authorities can finish the investigation."

"Finish it how?" Marista demanded.

Bierich's jaw twitched. "That is not our concern."

"I think it is very much our concern."

"I didn't ask for your opinion, Kaljin."

Her glare clashed with Bierich's, but Marista refused to be intimidated. "For the record, I have a right to give my opinion and lodge a protest."

"For the record," Bierich mocked her, "you've exercised that right, and your protest is noted." She turned her attention to the soldier. "Now, Lieutenant, in two days I will convene a formal due process hearing at which time I will determine the matter of extradition. Our chief medical technician assures me the ambulatory man will be strong enough by then to attend the proceedings on behalf of all three survivors. I trust you will have sufficient time to finish your investigation and prepare your arguments."

Seething, Marista watched as Sindri bowed his head and tried to hide a triumphant smile. "More than enough time, Madame. On behalf of the Albian government, I thank you. Now, I'll take my leave."

"Lieutenant, wait," Marista called before Sindri finished a smart pivot toward the door.

"Yes, Madame Kaljin?"

As much as she despised the sight of him, she locked her eyes into his. "Tell me, who are the 'Never Born?'"

Sindri blinked twice before masking his surprise. "I'm sure I don't know."

He lied. That intuition strengthened her resolve. "I'm sure you do, Lieutenant."

"Kaljin, that's enough!" Bierich snarled, and then flattened her tone. "Lieutenant, we'll keep you no longer."

Sindri nodded again and left.

Before the door slid completely closed, Marista stalked to the desk. "How can you consider turning those men over to that self-important martinet? Why did we bother trying to save their lives, when they'll die inside an Albian prison anyway?"

Bierich dismissed her with a backhanded wave. "I have no direct knowledge that will happen."

"'Direct knowledge?'" Marista echoed, her voice rising. "You and I both know that's diplomatic language for 'don't ask, don't tell.'"

Bierich fisted her hands at her sides. "You're insubordinate!"

"I'll be sure to mention that in the letter of protest I send to our embassy in Timetsuara."

The chargé squared her wide shoulders. "Do you think the ambassador will pay you the least bit of attention? Don't flatter yourself, Kaljin. You don't make Terran foreign policy. You just carry it out. Under my direction."

"That 'direction' is flawed."

Bierich's face went slack. "Why? Because I try to keep your brash conduct from landing us in the middle of a diplomatic crisis? Your gall is astounding. Sindri is ready to call for your dismissal himself. Your reference to rumors about the 'Never Born' was as offensive to him as an insult to his clan's integrity."

"Unlike Sindri, the only weapons I have are my words and actions," Marista pointed out. "And I've taken an oath to use them when the need arises."

"I took the same oath, Kaljin. But experience has taught me to use my words judiciously. You're a reckless and foolish idealist, one who takes herself far too seriously, considering who you are and why you're even here."

The derision in Bierich's voice gave her pause. "What are you talking about?"

Bierich lifted a brow, shook her head. "You really don't know, do you? Tell me, why do you suppose you received this field assignment?"

The question sounded more like an accusation. "I graduated in the top ten percent of my class at the academy. I speak the offshoot dialects of Terran Standard fluently. And I asked specifically for humanitarian services," Marista recounted.

Bierich chortled. "Not even close. I didn't need you. I can pick and choose help any time I want from the embassy in Timetsuara. And even if I needed a deputy, the rule of thumb is that only trained and seasoned representatives are posted in hostile zones. Yet, you swaggered in here two months ago with an appointment that, in effect, makes you my second-in-command."

She leaned forward, clasped her hands on the desk. "Kaljin, I was forty before I had my first administrative posting, and then it was on Malvi, the yawn of the planetary confederation. You aren't yet thirty and you've been thrown into a position of authority that would give veterans nightmares. Someone wants you to rise far and fast. Someone who is well-connected to the powers that be—General Anthony Henson."

Fury set Marista trembling. "My father has nothing to do with my success. I've come this far on my own merits!"

Bierich's steel-blue eyes turned hard as agate. "Are you so sure?"

Sudden doubt assailed her. In truth, the career-launching assignment on Serraine had been as much of a surprise as it had been a rich reward for years of hard work, dedication, and discipline. Yet she had set aside her amazement and immersed herself in the job. Never once did she imagine her father might have whispered in someone's ear.

No, he couldn't have. He wouldn't have!

"Yes, I'm sure," she answered.

Bierich spread her hands and smirked. "Well, fine then. I hope you and your inflated ego will be happy. As for me, I need someone at my side who'll support my decisions, not challenge me every step of the way. Neither am I afraid of some retired general who has nothing better to do than meddle in his daughter's life. I'm requesting that you be reassigned to Earth."

"No!" Desperation edged Marista's voice. "This fieldwork is an important step in my career!"

"You came too far, too fast. You're not ready."

"I've done everything and more that my job requires."

"Compromise is the essence of that job, Kaljin."

"I can't compromise away human life. How can you?"

Bierich's face blanched. "The evidence indicates that those men are, at the very least, smugglers, and at the worst Krillian agents. My conscience is clear."

"What conscience?"

Even as it left her mouth Marista knew the reproach went beyond all reason. Yet, she didn't regret it and stood taller when Bierich came slowly out of her seat and fisted her hands at her sides.

"Careful, young woman," the chargé warned her in a low, menacing tone. "There are places in this galaxy you can languish where even your father won't be able to save you."

The warning left Marista cold with fury but not with fear. "I've never asked for my father's help, and I won't now. But that doesn't mean I'll go quietly. Everyone from the ambassador in Timetsuara to the Inspector General on Earth will know my side of this."

Bierich's glare narrowed. "If you want to stay in the Corps and make a name for yourself, I'd advise against that."

The couched warning set her on guard. "Are you threatening my career?"

"No, you are."

Bierich was right. Whatever her principled intentions might have been, Marista had forgotten the first rule of bureaucratic survival—don't burn any bridges. She'd let her passions overrule reason. She had been insubordinate and had given Bierich just cause to fault her.

Now fate rested in her own hands. The manner in which she accepted reprimand and dismissal, vindictive as it might be, determined the course of her career. Bierich simply stood ready to facilitate her ruin.

Tears stung her eyes, but she held them back. Life had taught her weeping and supplication wasted time and energy. Tears hadn't saved her mother's life. Begging hadn't kept her father near when she needed him most.

Dredging up strength from a deep well inside her soul, she extinguished her inflamed emotions. With deliberate dignity, she straightened her shoulders and held the chargé's gaze. "Very well, Madame, I'll see to my regular duties until the reassignment comes through. If that meets with your approval."

The passivity seemed to deflate the worst of Bierich's ballooning anger. The chargé stared at her for long, uncomfortable seconds before she eased back into the chair behind the desk. "This sudden willingness of yours to comply will not change my mind."

Drawing a shaky breath, Marista nodded once. "I'm aware of that. Am I free to continue my duties?"

Though she still seemed wary, Bierich agreed with a dip of head. "Of course."

A resolution formed in Marista's heart as she spoke. "Then you'll want me to debrief the man in Isolation as a matter of record for the due process hearing?"

Bierich's expression shifted from surprise to contentment. "Yes, good idea. See what you can get from him. If he refuses to cooperate, at least our log will show we made an attempt to help him."

Before we send him to his death, she silently finished for the chargé. Out loud, she agreed. "Yes, Madame. Is there anything else?"

"No. You're dismissed."

With a crispness that would have put Sindri to shame, Marista wheeled in place and left the office. She hadn't spent the formative years of her childhood on military outposts at her father's side for nothing, after all.

Once in the hallway, she ran back to her private quarters. Bolting into her room, she slammed the door behind her, lunged for the com-terminal, and keyed Jace Ugo's number.

She wasn't about to let Sindri run roughshod over Terran neutrality, even if Bierich was inclined to let him for the sake of entente. But more than pride and principle lay at stake here. A man's life, perhaps three lives, hung in the balance. She couldn't bow to intimidation and still live with her conscience.

Her career be damned.

The screen blipped and clarified. Jace squinted at her. "When you said fast, you meant fast. Don't have anything yet, Riss."

"That's not why I called. Jace, I need another favor . . ."

Five

The Terran guards came for Tynan soon after the evening meal. They gave him tan trousers, an overlarge light green shirt, and a pair of ankle-boots. In sign language they ordered him to dress.

He didn't ask questions for fear his accent would give him away. It was bad enough Kaljin knew of his heritage, and that the knowledge gave her an advantage.

Yet, she did promise her protection. In her ocean-colored eyes he'd glimpsed the honesty of someone who never promised anything she wouldn't deliver, and the tenderness of a woman who truly cared.

After he finished dressing in silence, the guards bound his wrists with mechanical shackles over the electronic restraints, and walked him into an elevator.

To his bewilderment, the Terrans escorted him to an underground interrogation room. Every official Albian-built facility had at least one such place, he knew, though this particular setting seemed less intimidating than most. The softer overhead lights and padded chairs were certainly Terran additions.

Though the soldiers removed his metal shackles before they sealed him in, his imagination ran amok. As minutes passed, he paced the length of the room until the heel seam of his left boot chafed at the ankle, and his injured side ached. Finally he retreated to the back wall, pressed his spine into it, and crossed his arms.

Judging from the number of strides it took him to pace from the left dun-colored wall to the right, he determined the room measured longer and wider than his isolation unit. The two cushioned chairs were pushed beneath a long table. Both front and rear entrances were sealed with security-coded locks.

The wall he faced was transparent from the ceiling to a meter from the floor and was probably weapons-proof. Beyond the viewing window lay a smaller anteroom. Mounted into the ventilation fixtures, he guessed, were audio and video recording devices.

Only one of the guards who escorted him down in the freight elevator remained at his post in the anteroom near the main corridor's entrance. Though alert and serious, the young soldier regarded him with none of the fierce intensity Sindri's men had. Even the guard's pale blue uniform seemed less threatening than the Albian combat-fitted desert fatigues.

He had little time to concentrate his thoughts before the corridor entrance to the anteroom slid open. He stood straight and held his breath for what seemed an eternity. When Marista Kaljin walked in, he nearly broke into a relieved smile.

Her expression, however, remained as neutral as her Terran citizenship, until she turned to the guard and graced him with a brilliant smile.

His gut twisted with a sudden, fierce desire to rush to the window and steal her attention. He took a faltering step before reason yanked him back in line. The short-lived spasm of raw emotion disturbed him more than the uncertainty of his situation.

She chatted briefly with the young man. The soldier appeared uncomfortable with something she said, but nodded, pulled to respectful attention, and left. She then closed the entrance to the corridor behind him.

When she finally came to the window and switched on the audio-speaker her smile was as stilted as her voice. "I see our staff found you some suitable clothing."

He stalked to the window. "The shirt doesn't fit and the boots hurt my feet."

"Sorry," she apologized without feeling. "I didn't give Hyrek much warning. He must have grabbed whatever was handy."

Self-consciously, he shoved the already rolled sleeves of the shirt past his elbows and tucked some of the bulky sides further into the waist of the trousers. "I could use a belt."

Amusement crinkled the corners of her eyes. "Hyrek probably thought you might try to hang yourself with it."

"There are more efficient methods of suicide."

Her grin faded. "Of course. But you practically flew at the window when I came in, which means you still have some will to live."

Will to live had little to do with it, the dour voice of reality stated inside his head. Out loud he demanded, "What am I doing here?"

Her eyes widened a moment, but she remained calm. "Madame Bierich scheduled a due process hearing for the day after tomorrow to determine the matter of your extradition to Timetsuara. She instructed me to obtain a recorded statement from you to use in your defense."

The possibility that Kaljin abandoned her principled protection of him and his friends and was now in league with Sindri and the chargé wrenched his gut. "I have nothing to say, Madame."

He started to turn away.

"I know."

He swung back around. If her admission surprised him, the sound of the interrogation room door sliding open fed his confusion and doubled his wariness.

Kaljin disappeared from the window. Seconds later she stepped into the interrogation room. The door remained open behind her, and she rested her hand on the electronic restraint control attached to her belt. "We have a little less than an hour, Tynan. Do you still want to see your friend?"

Hope propelled him forward. As if responding to an awkward dance, she moved backward until her heel touched the threshold.

He halted and spread his hands to soothe her. "Yes. Did you receive permission to take me to him?"

"No," she admitted. "As I said, I'm officially here to record your statement."

He didn't try to hide his disbelief. "Are you saying the statement, and the guards marching me down here, are a ruse?"

She nodded. "I'll tell Bierich you refused to cooperate, which is the truth, so I didn't bother recording any of our conversation. We'll now make different use of this time. I told the guard I had to take your statement in private. He won't try to come in unless I flash a green light over the hallway door."

Suspicious, he shook his head. "Why? You said yourself there's nothing in the rule book about giving me access to my friends."

"Not the official rule book," she replied. "But this is the decent thing to do. Jarrit hasn't responded to any of us. We don't know if he can't understand or won't talk, as you did at first. But he should know about his son. Maybe you can get through to him."

When he continued to stare incredulously, she released an impatient sigh. "Look, Tynan, I'll be brutally honest. This is a gesture of compassion, nothing more. I'm running out of time and options to keep you and your friends out of Sindri's custody. I can't even help myself anymore."

"What do you mean, you can't help yourself?"

"I mean I'll be leaving Inara Wadi on the next transport back to Earth. You might say, I'm being extradited, too. Bierich's transferring me because I refuse to march in lockstep with her."

Kaljin had been exiled for defending his rights. She might be gone before Sindri hauled him away. The sudden jolt of loss and emptiness stunned him.

For her part, she seemed to accept her fate with better grace, continuing to speak with her usual quiet confidence. "We can't use the elevators without risking detection, so we'll have to climb five flights of stairs to the fourth floor above ground. Are you up to it?"

Her question tweaked his pride. "Do I look unfit?"

She scanned his length, then hit the door control and let the open panel behind her close. "No. Come on, then. We don't have much time."

She headed for the rear door. The unspoken assumption he would simply follow amazed him. So did her seeming disregard for the danger he still might pose. Or did she think he was some sort of passive dolt? The implied insult angered him, but no more than her lack of common sense.

He snagged her arm as she passed less than half a meter from him. "Are you sure this is about ideals and compassion, Little Diplomat? Or is this your way of spiting Bierich, even if she never finds out?"

Though her jaw twitched when he snidely called her "diplomat" she didn't correct him this time. "Why does it matter? You're getting what you want."

She yanked her arm to be free of him, but he tightened his grip. "Make no mistake, Kaljin, I want to see Jarrit. But I won't be a pawn in a reckless game of retaliation."

"A cautious smuggler with principles?" she mused.

"I'm only considering the odds of success."

She gave another futile tug to free herself. "Do you think I want to get caught? Bierich has already banished me from field service. I won't allow her to drum me out of the Corps altogether for aiding and abetting a criminal. I've planned everything well. You may be half-suicidal. I'm not."

He yanked her closer until her arm lay rigid on his chest. "My trusting you isn't the problem. Has it crossed your mind I might kill you and escape?"

She peered at him as if he spoke a dialect she didn't understand. "I doubt you'd give me fair warning first. Besides, I have the restraint controls . . ."

Before all the words left her mouth, he grabbed her free wrist and spun her to face him. Ignoring her warm, womanly scent, he baited her. "So much for reaching those controls. Now scream. The room is probably soundproof. The guard won't hear you."

Her eyes flew open. "You can't leave this room without my palm identification. The scanner recognizes only living tissue."

"That's the easy part, Little Diplomat."

He dragged her to the rear door. Finally goaded, she struggled until he pinned her to the wall with his powerful legs. Without much exertion, he forced her arm upward until her hand rested near the scan plate. "Done."

Breathing hard, she stared at the hand, then at him. "I have to key in my security code."

"Do you think I couldn't 'coax' the numbers from you?"

At that, she wrenched futilely from side to side. But she wasn't the only victim of the physical intimacy he forced on her. Heat pooled where her slender body clashed with his. Tendrils of desire curled inside his belly, spread outward, and scattered his concentration. If he didn't break with her soon, his effort to mock her trusting nature would mock his own self-control.

Suddenly, Kaljin stilled beneath him, and she rebuked him with her glare. "All right, fine. I won't force you to hurt me just for a series of numbers. But you'll never get off this wadi without tripping at least twenty other alarms. Taking a risk like that is suicidal."

Angry that she wouldn't admit he was right, and disgusted with body's treacherous response to her nearness, he grit his teeth. "Maybe suicide is better than letting you Terrans turn me over to Sindri."

She stared at him a moment longer, then slumped against the wall. "You may be a smuggler or even a spy. At this point, it doesn't matter which. But I do know you hold life dearer than you admit. No one who rescues five others from a fire would give up his own life so wantonly. Why are you wasting our time and your energy trying to convince me otherwise?"

If she believed giving up would calm him, she'd used the wrong psychology. She was a non-violent little fool who trusted too damn easily. Instead of slackening his hold, he gripped her wrists harder. "Someday, Kaljin, that Terran naiveté will get you hurt. Or maybe killed."

Her ocean green eyes narrowed to slits. "Why should it matter to you?"

The demand for truth repelled him with the force of an impulse from the restraint control. He released her arms, and took two hasty steps backward.

Putting distance between himself and the beautiful Terran didn't calm his racing pulse or stop the rush of adrenaline to his trembling limbs. Once again her physical presence singed him. Worse, he hungered for more.

She dropped her arms to her sides and peered up at him with silent confusion, and her question echoed in his mind. Why should it matter to you?

When he stood mute, unwilling and unable to answer the question in her eyes, she gave the hem of her rumpled jacket a straightening tug. "Shall we go or stay?"

He had to see Jarrit. If nothing else, his friend deserved to learn of his son's death. Moreover, he had to seek final guidance from the mission leader. "Go."

She cast him a wary glare, placed her palm on the scanning plate, and entered her security code.

He followed into the corridor, making sure he stayed at least two strides behind her.

***

Marista feared her wobbly legs wouldn't carry her past the second flight of stairs, much less propel her up three more. Tynan's brutish lesson on the hazards of trusting unwisely didn't frighten her as he intended. Nevertheless, the incident left her shaken and dazed.

The grip of his hands on her arms had sent ripples of excitement, not shafts of panic, through her. The lengthwise crush of his body filled her with the heat of arousal, not the chill of terror. She clung to her anger in order to cling to her wits and counter the awakening of desires she hadn't felt in a very long time.

No, she wasn't afraid of the man. He "smelled right," as her Aunt Mimi termed that mysterious chemistry between people, the human sixth sense.

Until last night, when she had her first looked at Tynan, she'd never really experienced such intense gut instinct about anything or anyone. Then and there, she knew she had to help him with all means at her disposal. Just as certainly, she knew he wouldn't hurt her.

What she hadn't anticipated was the effect of his overwhelming physical magnetism.

For the second time that day, unfamiliar and disquieting doubts assailed her. Was she using compassion as an excuse to rationalize some less worthy motive? Was simple lust the reason she ran this wild gambit to take him to his friend? Did she risk her career because he made her hormones flow hot and wild?

"Bierich's right, you know."

Tynan's comment, coming after two flights of silence, startled her into missing a step. She grabbed the handrail and swung around. "Right about what?"

When he pulled up next to her she noted he didn't even breathe hard, while she strained to catch air. "Bierich needs a loyal aide, not someone who debates every decision."

Feeling somehow betrayed by this man she was helping, she resumed the climb with an angry energy. "And I deserve a fair hearing from my superior. If I wanted nothing more than to obey blindly, I'd have joined the military."

"Do you know so much about the military?"

"Only a decade's worth of involuntary enlistment. My father was a general in the Terran Security Forces. He dragged my mother, my sister and me all over Creation as if we were his own, personal platoon. He expected no complaints."

"I see. But I suppose you did complain?"

"No," she admitted, staring straight ahead to avoid his searching eyes. "I followed my mother's example. She never complained about anything. Not in front of me."

"Maybe she didn't mind."

The comment gave her pause as they reached the third floor. "Maybe."

"Did you ever ask her?"

The empty pain of loneliness expanded inside her chest as it always did when she thought of her mother. Before answering she swallowed hard, twice. "I never had a chance. When my father was the military governor of Yonar an insurgent group invaded the Terran compound. They blew up headquarters and the fire spread to adjoining dependent housing. My mother got me out of our home, but she went back inside for my sister."

She slowed her progression up the stairs as the emptiness inside grew hideously large. "I never saw my mother or sister again."

"I'm sorry."

The genuine sympathy in his voice startled her. But she didn't want pity from anyone, particularly him, so she resumed a crisper pace up the stairs. "It happened a long time ago. I was ten. My father made me leave Yonar before the funerals. Back on Earth I watched vidscreen reports about the attack. My father told the journalists there had been 'collateral civilian casualties.'"

Long simmering anger filled the empty void in her chest. "He sounded so cold and unfeeling." She drew air into her aching lungs. "I lived with my aunt from then on. My father and I rarely saw each other, and we never talked about what happened on Yonar."

"Maybe he felt responsible and couldn't bring himself to talk about it."

She barely heard his quiet words over the clatter of their boots on the steps. But as she took a long, furtive look at Tynan's handsome profile she gleaned little from his impassive expression. "I'm sure that was part of it. And I know he grieved. But I needed him to grieve with me."

Tynan faced her then, his dark eyes curious and gentle and sad. Suddenly she realized he held secrets in his heart, too—secrets that might put her ancient grievances to shame. Yet he didn't voice them. His stoicism made her feel petty.

No longer able to meet his gaze, she faced forward as they turned the bend of the fourth flight. "Needless to say, I don't have a great deal of confidence or trust in the military mind-set."

Tynan said nothing more until they had ascended several more steps. "Is that why you chose to enter the Diplomatic Corps, because it seemed the opposite of your father's profession?"

"It would seem so, wouldn't it?" She sighed. "Maybe because of what happened on Yonar I believe warfare is nothing but failed diplomacy. Negotiated settlement is always preferable to a violent solution."

"In my experience actions speak truer than words."

"Violent 'action' left my family either dead or alienated," she retorted. "Like my father, I want to make a difference. But I'll be a peacemaker, not a warrior."

"Everyone, even warriors, have noble intentions in the beginning. Reality eventually kills the nobility."

"I won't let that happen."

"You won't be able to help it. Especially if you think the Diplomatic Corps is a place where you can express yourself without consequence."

The mocking tone in his voice made her bristle. "I understand discipline and attention to duty. I can follow orders, too. But I won't do so at the expense of my conscience."

"Then you might as well turn in your platinum bar now. Conscience only hinders diplomats."

"I told you I'm not yet a . . ." She waved off her own objection. "Never mind. How do you know so much about diplomats?"

"I've known my share."

"How?"

"What difference does it make?"

She knew he wouldn't answer, even if she prodded. "I'm different," she said, defending herself.

"Yes. For now."

The clipped agreement sounded less complimentary than cautionary. After experiencing the less noble aspects of Corps bureaucracy over the past two days, she was afraid he might be right, and she didn't look at him as they mounted the final steps. "It seems neither you nor I will find common ground over this."

He drew in air, but didn't reply.

Irrational annoyance with him propelled her ahead. She sprinted the last three steps and waited at the door that opened onto the fourth floor. By the time Tynan caught up to her she had retrieved a data disk three times the size of her fingernail from her trouser pocket.

Holding the disk between her thumb and index finger, she explained the plan. "Your friend is down that hallway in a special life support pod. The floor should be clear of most personnel at this time of night, so we should be able to get inside his room easily.

"But," she warned, "a video camera monitors the life pod. The medical telemetry is relayed to the nurse's station at the end of the floor. This disk will create a feedback loop so the cameras won't record us when we're close to the pod. The telemetry won't show we're stimulating Jarrit in any way."

She closed her fingers around the disk. "The problem is I can't rerun any more than five minutes of the data before someone notices the glitch and comes to check. Understand? Five minutes is all you have."

He nodded. "You thought this out well. You're a natural at subterfuge. Maybe you'll be a good diplomat after all."

His snide comment ratcheted her annoyance. For an instant, she felt the urge to leave him standing at the door and run back down the five flights of stairs.

But a niggling voice inside her head warned that this man needed—and deserved—her help.

She laid her hand on the identity plate, entered her security code, and opened the door.

Six

Lurking in the shadowy stairwell, Tynan peeked through a sliver of open door, and allowed himself a half-smile. Kaljin walked alone down the corridor and scouted the inside of the critical care unit where Jarrit lay. He had to admire her ingenuity and poise. She had a liberal measure of initiative, as well.

He was wrong to accuse her of recklessness. If this visit to Jarrit was indeed her way of striking out at Madame Bierich, she planned the retaliation with a cool, keen intent of keeping the risk of discovery low. He had a notion Marista Kaljin approached most everything with that calculated reason—after she relied on gut instinct and adherence to principle.

There had been a time when he'd approached decisions in a like manner. Then stark reality had flung him off-center, made him doubt all those intuitions she still trusted. He feared the same disillusionment lay ahead for her.

But the near certainty that harsh reality would grind her rock solid idealism to dust wasn't his concern. She was nothing to him save a means to see Jarrit. She was passing through his life, not settling into it. He had no reason to care about her future when he wasn't likely to see much more of his own.

Yet, when she turned and fixed her trusting, eager gaze on him, he knew he lied to himself. He did care what happened to her, perhaps because she cared what happened to him. In her naïveté she didn't realize the chargé might have saved her soul with the transfer back to dull, peaceful, duplicitous Earth.

She waved him forward. Rolling his steps to soften the noise of his footfalls, he hurried to her side and peered into the critical care unit. The dim, overhead room lights cast everything in long, deep shadows, including the life pod against the back wall. Even squinting he discerned little except the outline of Jarrit's motionless body inside the clear, oblong bubble. The touch of cool fingers on his bare forearm startled him.

Kaljin retracted her hand and held up the data disk. "Remember, Tynan, from the second I insert this you have five minutes. After that, the cameras start real-time recording."

He nodded.

As if she might be reconsidering, she trapped her full lower lip between her teeth. The pose she struck just then was innocently and sweetly sensual. Erotic imaginings slipped through his mind. He jerked his gaze back around to the life pod, afraid that she would glimpse in his eyes the substance of those rogue thoughts. Surely then she'd be tempted to slap her palm to the restraint control clipped to her belt and send him to the floor in spasms of bone-breaking pain.

He deserved it. He had no right to let his mind wander in that direction about her now—or ever.

She released her lower lip. "Ready?"

Expelling his breath, he nodded again.

She inserted the disk into the control and pressed the door release. The panel opened. "Go."

He followed her into the room and squinted until his eyes adjusted to the murkiness. The air felt markedly warmer than it had in the corridor, and hung heavy with a sickeningly sweet odor. He took shallow breaths to lessen the smell, but it grew stronger as he approached Jarrit.

The intricate configuration of the life pod emerged from the gloom. Three tubes snaked from the bubble-like transparent shell. Two were intravenous lines, probably attached to bags of liquid that fed and medicated Jarrit. A third line carried away his wastes. A portable respirator stood nearby, but its readout panel was dark and its attachments were coiled in storage. At least his friend still breathed on his own.

When he finally lowered his gaze to the inside of the pod that fact didn't comfort him long. Jarrit lay naked in a bath of pale green gelatinous solution that gently washed over his charred arms and torso. Over three-quarters his body was nothing but a mass of raw, seeping wounds. The sweet odor emanated from the pod itself. Tynan guessed it was the grisly fusion of seared flesh and the medicating wash. A traction device elevated the bandage-encased stump of Jarrit's left leg. A similar appliance lifted and immobilized his head.

He drew in short, shallow gulps of air to keep his stomach from turning over.

"Hurry!"

At the whispered croak, he glanced over his shoulder. Kaljin stood three paces behind him. She was too pale and looked ready to flee.

Her mother and sister had died in flames, he remembered. No wonder she had momentarily recoiled when he told her about the skimmer crash in the desert. No wonder she recoiled now at the sight of this tortured man. Yet, she summoned the will to stay at his side. She was either more stubborn, or more courageous, than he imagined.

"Tynan, hurry, please."

Responding as much to Kaljin's pallor as to the urgency of her words, he swung back around to the pod and leaned forward. "Jarrit?"

His harsh whisper was barely louder than the soft whine of life support machines. Gripping the safety rail, he waited. The odor of the circulating fluids filled his nose and clogged his throat. The man didn't respond.

"Jarrit?"

"He may not be aware enough to hear you."

He held up his hand for silence. "Jarrit, it's Tynan. Answer."

Jarrit's eyelids fluttered.

"That might be an autonomic reflex," Kaljin muttered.

He ignored her. "Jarrit, can you understand what I'm saying?"

The man's eyelids fluttered again, this time with conscious purpose? Tynan dared hope so as Jarrit lifted his lids with agonizing effort and tried to turn his head to the side.

"No, don't move," Tynan whispered. "I'll come closer."

Jarrit ceased the effort. He swallowed once; then again. "Who? Who . . ."

"It's Tynan. Can you hear me?"

Jarrit squinted. "Can't see . . . blur . . . Tynan? Yes . . . has to be . . . you were aft . . ."

Suddenly, Jarrit sucked back and went rigid.

From behind, Kaljin grabbed his arm. When he turned to her, she pointed at the life scan monitoring board. "His heart rate and blood pressure spiked. He can't take this. He's too weak."

Shrugging her off, he fixed his attention back on the man in the pod.

"Who . . . who . . . with you?" Panic edged Jarrit's voice.

"Her name is Marista Kaljin."

Jarrit's gaze widened. "Albian?"

"Terran. A hunting party of Albian clansmen found our wreckage and brought us to a neutral field hospital outside Timetsuara."

"Trust her?"

"Yes, I trust her," he answered, surprised by his own immediate certainty. "She brought me here to see you at personal and professional risk."

"She knows?"

Aware Kaljin heard every word he paused. "Some. Enough. Not all."

"Interrogation?"

"No, not yet. The Terrans are protecting us at present."

"Tynan, his heart rate."

He disregarded the breathy warning as Jarrit tried to form more words.

Jarrit worked dry lips. "Others?"

He gripped the pod rail harder. "Bohara has severe head injuries, but he's still alive. I had only minor injuries. The rest . . ." He paused, swallowed. "Marcus and the rest are dead."

Jarrit gasped. "My son? Dead?"

"Yes. I'm sorry."

Jarrit struggled for air, yet spoke with command. "I'm dead, too. You're alone now. No interrogation. Telemetry sent, but ship locator beam inoperative. Up to you . . . follow procedure. Understood?"

Follow procedure. In the past months there were many close calls during the sorties over the desert. But not once had Jarrit seen fit to utter those desperate words: Follow procedure.

Hardly hearing himself above the roar of blood in his ears, he answered, "Yes, I understand."

Jarrit exhaled, and his eyes fluttered shut. Tynan glanced at the life scan monitor to reassure himself the man still clung to life.

"I'm not sure he was strong enough to withstand this."

Drawing a breath to steady himself, he spun around to face Kaljin. "He had to know about Marcus and the others. Moreover, our mission was under his command. He has the right to give the final orders."

She blinked. "Mission? Final orders?"

Aware he'd let slip too much, he snatched her arm to stifle the questions and escorted her to the door. "Our five minutes should be about up. We better leave."

She couldn't argue. He let her loose to open the door, then hovered over her shoulder as she removed the data disk and rebooted the monitoring system. Kaljin's hand shook so hard she fumbled the disk. Only his quick reflexes kept it from bouncing off the console and on to the floor.

When he offered the disk back to her, she only stared at it. Her poise finally had worn too thin.

Less worried than moved to sympathy, he cupped her hand in his and laid the disk in her palm. When she looked at him in surprise, he forced a wan smile. "Knowing what I do about your mother and sister, I realize seeing Jarrit in that condition wasn't easy."

His attempt at kindness brought the snap of anger to her eyes, and she twisted away from him. "Is that so?"

The snide edge to her voice cut at his pride. "Yes, that's so. I understand. More than you realize."

She jammed the disk into her pocket and opened her mouth to reply. But she stopped herself just as fast and stiffened to attention.

"What is it?" he coaxed.

She put her finger to her mouth, demanding silence. He listened and, by degrees, heard it, too—a shuffle of feet in the corridor perpendicular to where they stood. When he took a bearing on the noise his gut clenched. They'd never make it back to the stairway entrance before the intruders turned the corner.

Pivoting, he scanned the length of the corridor and pointed to a door panel less than ten paces across the way. "Where does that lead?"

"It looks like a storage unit."

"Can you access the security lock with your code?"

"I . . . I don't know."

He grabbed her right arm and dragged her after him to the door. "Let's find out before someone finds us."

This time, when he lifted her hand as he'd done in the interrogation room, he made sure her palm fit precisely over the identity plate. After an eternal moment, the plate glowed green. The digital readout asked politely for a personal security code.

Kaljin shook off his grip to enter a series of six numbers. The screen flashed a line of red letters: "Access Denied."

"That can't be," she groaned. "Not if the plate went green with my palm print."

"Try again. Maybe you keyed wrong."

She did so, choosing the numbers more carefully.

As the intruder's footsteps grew more distinct he knew they'd soon be discovered, and he panicked more for Kaljin than for himself. He'd count himself lucky if he saw another few days of existence. She risked her career, her reputation, and possibly her freedom for this folly.

With two thundering heartbeats to spare, the panel slid open. He gripped Kaljin by the waist and whisked her inside the room.

Dull, amber security lights winked on as the panel closed behind them. Breathing hard, he collapsed against the wall just inside the door. Only when he felt Kaljin's fingers clutching the front of his baggy shirt did he realize he'd swept her into a snug embrace.

She buried her face into the hollow between his shoulder and chest. Her fragrance—a vibrant, vital contrast to the stench of Jarrit's charred flesh—filled the air. With his left arm about her narrow waist, he held her intimately to his body. Somehow, his right hand had come to rest on her delicate nape. The heat of her exquisite satin-smooth skin against his roughed palm sent prickles up his arm, and chills down his spine. Fine, springy tendrils of her fiery hair teased his cheek.

As she trembled in the circle of his arms, her sweet vulnerability flooded him with a powerful new urgency to keep her safe. Unlike just minutes before, this time he had no will to flee or fight the instinct.

Briefly he wondered if her head whirled and her insides clenched with arousal, too. He should push her away.

He banished the thought as soon as it formed.

She loosened her grip on his shirt and leaned back just enough to look up at him. In the amber light, her eyes shimmered iridescent green-gold. Emotions flickered in her gaze, but changed before he could pin them down. He clearly recognized relief and bemusement.

What else did he see? Fear?

Yes, fear. He saw it in her eyes, and sensed it at the same moment in himself.

But fear of what? That they might be found? Discovery wasn't likely, concealed as they were inside the storage room.

"Tynan?"

The quiver in her voice reflected his own whipsaw emotions. What did she ask of him? What should he answer?

"We're safe, Kaljin."

But her eyes widened, the dusky pupils overwhelming all but a narrow edge of glimmering irises. Her mouth blossomed with a warm, pulsating color. "Are we?"

"Yes."

But he lied, because he did sense danger. From her. From himself. In that moment, he needed more from her than an intimate embrace. He needed to kiss her—hard and with feeling. He needed to drink from her as a man too long in the desert needs to drink of cool, life-giving water.

No longer attending the whining voice of reason, he slid his hand from her nape to her jaw and traced the soft roundness of her chin before testing the full curve of her bottom lip with hesitant fingertips.

Yes, he wanted to kiss her. He would kiss her. And she would allow it, even welcome it. He felt her need, as any man senses when a woman is about to surrender to desire. When she let her eyelids flutter shut and lifted her face toward him, he smiled with satisfaction and gave in to the inevitable.

Her lips were already warm with anticipation and soft as a night breeze. They quivered beneath the flick of his tongue, but opened when he pressed his suit. He drank deeply to quench his long denied thirst.

But he soon realized this one, brief taste of the beautiful Terran would never be enough. As he claimed her lips, she claimed his soul, meeting the force of his desperate kisses with a powerful need of her own. With fingertip caresses on his face and feather-light combing through the bristled strands of his hair, she gifted him with a tenderness he never anticipated. It flowed from her, through him. It left his knees weak, his pulse erratic.

Too late he realized she offered him more than one long, cool drink of pleasure before he died. Instead, she flooded him with a torrent of honest passion. Now he could never leave her without regrets.

Why did she do this to him? Why had he let it happen?

Furious with her and with himself, he pushed away from the wall, and then shoved her backward. Deprived of her body heat, he shivered. Kaljin gasped and put her hand to her throat.

Guilt and regret sharpened his voice. "Don't look at me with those sad, sympathetic eyes," he warned. "This is not what I want from you."

The fingers lying at her throat curled into a fist. For a second, he thought she might strike out at him. Good. He could defend himself against physical blows.

But she held her ground. "Just what do what from me?"

He smirked with a false bravado. "Wasn't it plain enough, Little Diplomat? I could be dead in two days. One last time I want a willing woman spread out beneath me."

The crude proposition nearly choked him. But how else could he disguise the true depth of his reaction to her?

She stared at him with hurt in her wide eyes. To halt her stinging, silent accusations, he grasped her forearms and dragged her close until his face almost touched hers again. "Maybe you want bragging rights about a romp with the mysterious condemned stranger? Would you share the details with your friends on a cold, lonely night, Little Diplomat?"

When her stare went blank with bewilderment, he gave her a shake. "What about it? I'll be happy to oblige. If you're not too keen about comfort, I can take you on the floor, or up against the wall."

She tore from his hold. But before she put her back to him and her hands to her face, he glimpsed anguish, not the anger or revulsion he expected.

He swallowed the lump of remorse in his throat, but the sour aftertaste thickened the words he forced out. "Make up your mind. It's now or never. Do you submit to the last wish of a walking dead man? Or do you get us out of here?"

Her back went rigid, and she whirled in place. Even before she spoke, her unflinching gaze warned him he'd underestimated her again. "I'm no simpering fool, Tynan. I've been kissed before. I've made love, too, in places that would make the floor feel like a soft bed."

Sudden fury at the knowledge she'd taken pleasure with another man, maybe several men, tightened his throat. Yet he waved a dismissive hand at her.

She took a tottering step forward and swatted his hand aside with her own. "I know the difference between raw desire and honest need. Maybe what happened between us wasn't all sweetness and purity, but it wasn't simple lust. And if you didn't feel anything more, then what happens to you the day after tomorrow doesn't matter. Inside you're already dead."

He could take no more of the harangue. "Maybe I am!"

Again he lied. Inside he felt anything but dead. The sizzle of electricity sparked by her kisses still heated his skin. Jealousy of her past lovers clawed at his insides.

He had no right to those feelings. Not one of them. Yet, she dragged them out of the darkest recesses of his being into the light of day. He was better off soul-dead. He should hate her for reviving him.

But it wasn't hate he felt as he glared at her in the dull, amber light. He dared not define the emotion seething inside him. Giving it a name meant giving it power over him. He'd already surrendered enough of himself to this Terran female. "Stop trying to save me, Kaljin. I don't want it. I don't need it . . ."

"I don't believe it!"

Any other woman, and most men he knew, would cower or sulk in the wake of the last few minutes. Marista Kaljin only lifted her head higher, as if the pose gave her some sort of moral authority. The woman wouldn't give up!

Frustrated to the point of weariness, he balled his hands. "What would you have me do? Start something I can't finish? I've never done that, and I won't now. I have no future. Nor does anyone who takes my part."

She blew out a hard breath of disgust. "Mother Creation, you don't deserve my help."

He snorted. "We finally agree on something . . ."

Her fierce scowl cut off his words. "You don't deserve my help, but damn it all, Tynan, you're going to get it whether you want it or not. I don't start something, either, unless I intend to finish it."

Before he could argue, she pushed past him and used the manual controls to open the door panel just enough to peek into the corridor. After a moment, she motioned him to follow her.

In less than thirty seconds they reached the stairway entrance and headed down the five flights. Nothing but the echo of their footsteps disturbed the silence between them.

She raced ahead. When he caught up with her at the interrogation room a full minute later, she didn't look back at him before placing her palm on the identity plate and entering her code. Once inside the room, she waited until he seated himself at the table, and then went for the outer door.

"Kaljin?"

She whirled around. Her face was scarlet, and her mouth was set in an imperious frown. For one, dreadful moment he feared he'd never see her smile again.

Shaking off the self-pity, he nodded in the formal Albian way. "Thank you for taking me to see Jarrit."

Apparently surprised, she blinked, but then imitated his polite gesture. "It was my duty." Then she quickly exited.

He didn't watch her leave the anteroom. Instead, he set his elbows on the table and buried his face into his palms until the Terran guards came for him.

Seven

Tynan sat in profile near his window in the isolation unit. With his shoulders relaxed, head dipped forward, and eyes closed, Marista guessed he'd dozed off in the afternoon sunshine.

He wore serenity like a flight suit three sizes too small—temporary and ill-fitted, unable to conceal his energy. From the moment she set eyes on him, she was drawn to his inner vitality. Then she drank deeply of it last night in the storage room.

Even in repose he exuded the same potent male sexuality he'd unleashed on her. He blamed his actions on lust. She knew better. Her year of joy and agony with Daniel, the one man she might have eventually married, had taught her to trust her instincts and intuitions.

Yet not even bold, intense Daniel had kissed her with such furious, desperate need like Tynan had. His assault on her senses had unloosed secret inhibitions and undermined her self-control. In the gray, sleepless hours before dawn that morning, she'd confessed to herself that if he had acted further on his impulses, she'd have set aside professional ethics and common sense and surrendered to him.

Without a qualm.

She should have been ashamed. But as she stared at Tynan through the plastiglass barrier, her insides quivered with arousal and anticipation.

Assailed by second thoughts, she backed away from the window. The message she carried could wait. Perhaps she could even delegate the task to some lower level aide. Yes, that way she could avoid him until the hearing.

As she started to turn away, she noticed his hands resting palm-side up on his thighs. He wasn't dozing in the sun, she realized, but was posed in deep meditation.

How odd. Albians in general preferred action over reflection. Tynan didn't seem the type, Albian or not, who would put much stock in transcendental exercises. Still, if he was mentally preparing for tomorrow, she didn't want to disturb him.

His eyes snapped open, and he blinked twice before twisting toward the viewing window. He looked irritated, though she'd done nothing to disturb him.

Bracing herself, she activated the audio speakers. "I don't want to interrupt your meditation. I'll come back."

As if clearing a fog from his brain he shook his head. Then he braced his hands on the arms of the chair and hoisted himself to his feet. "You're here. Come in now."

Though the invitation lacked enthusiasm, he was right. She might as well deliver her message and be about the rest of her day's business.

She left the window and accepted the restraint controls from the

Albian guard at the door. A moment later, she crossed the threshold into the isolation unit.

Before she had the chance to apologize further, he scowled. "What do you know about meditation?"

From the sharp edge in his voice, she guessed he hadn't yet achieved mental serenity. "I know the neo-ascetic cults on Malvi resurrected the exercises from the dust bins of history over a century ago. The practice supposedly centers thought and emotion."

He lifted his chin. "Meditation exercises aren't widely used or recognized. Your academic training must have been thorough."

"As is my practical experience," she rejoined with a hint of her own irritation. "By the time I was ten, my sister and I had called three different planets, not including Earth, our home. My parents immersed us in every local culture and history."

Her memories stirred an insight. "I recall that sometimes meditation helps the body repair itself. Is that how your wounds healed so quickly?"

He regarded her with wariness. "Yes, but I wasn't hurt badly in the first place."

"Even so, few people besides the cultists on Malvi practice that sort of deep trance meditation. The Albian society in particular scoffs at such mysticism."

"Not all Albians fall into your neat cultural stereotypes, Madame Diplomat. Sindri and I are nothing alike, even though . . ." He stopped his lecture, winced, and then folded his arms. "Why are you here? If you want an apology for what happened last night, then you have it. I made a mistake."

The perfunctory contrition hurt worse than an outright insult. Anger heated her skin, but she kept her words cool. "The 'mistake' was a mutual one. I want no apology, especially one so dishonest."

He merely shrugged. "As you wish. Why did you come?"

She struggled to maintain a level tone. "I was sent, by Madame Bierich."

"Is that so?"

She countered his ennui with exaggerated formality. "Yes, it is so. You may not want me to serve as a liaison, but Tessa Bierich ordered me to do otherwise. Isn't that the sort of loyalty and obedience you admire?"

He smirked. "So you've decided to follow directions to the letter during these last few days on Serraine."

Suspecting that he was bent on goading her, she refused to take the bait. Besides, she couldn't in all good conscience deliver the message to him laced with petty, personal anger.

"I'll make this quick," she said softly. "During the night Jarrit lapsed into a coma, and our physician had to put him on a respirator."

He said nothing. Neither did he flinch a muscle.

She resisted the urge to frown her confusion at his impassiveness.

"Then, early this morning," she continued, "Hyrek pronounced the man named Bohara brain dead and disconnected his life-support. I'm sorry. You're friend is gone."

Slowly, he folded his arms across his chest. "Is that all?"

The apathy galled her. "Is that all? Mother Creation, one more of your friends is dead, and another may soon join him. If meditation 'centers' a person into an emotional coma, I'll avoid it for the rest of my life."

She spun toward the door.

"Kaljin, wait."

She paused but didn't remove her hand from the door release. Behind her, she heard the soft roll of his footsteps. When his clean, male scent surrounded her, she knew he stood not more than a half-meter distant.

"What would you have me say?" His voice dropped to a gruff whisper. "Bohara's gone. And Jarrit's no longer in any pain, at least. By tomorrow at this time I may envy their good fortune. If you want me to grieve, let me do it in my own way."

He slowly retreated, and she now understood he held himself in tenuous control with a stubborn nobility that would have impressed even the warrior-kings of ancient times. Yet, because of last night's folly, she judged him with a bruised heart, instead of trying to understand him with trained reason.

She looked over her shoulder, but she couldn't look him in the eye. "Of course, you're right. I've been unfair and unkind. I'm sorry about your loss. I'll leave you now to your meditation."

"You might benefit from meditative training."

He no longer sounded tense or gruff, but genuinely cordial. Without thinking, she turned toward him. "I beg your pardon?"

Tynan resumed his chair and motioned to the stool she used on her first visit to the isolation unit. Eyeing it, then him, with wariness, she hesitated. What did he want from her? Companionship? Forgiveness for his rude behavior? Both? Nothing?

"Meditation would focus your streak of impulsiveness, Kaljin." He obviously wanted to continue the conversation.

Trying not to be offended by his observation, she ambled to the seat across from him and slid onto it. "I like the way I am. I'd rather not have all the spirit tamed out of me."

"Meditation doesn't rob one of spirit. It helps focus and direct that spirit."

"I'm focused and directed enough."

"Yes, you're directed right back to Earth." Before she could retort, he added, "Is Bierich sending you home so soon?"

The change of subject puzzled her. "What?"

He gave her length a once-over. "I wondered if Bierich moved up your orders to return to Earth. You're not wearing regulation grays today."

His casual, but thorough scan of her body sent a rush of warmth through her. In nervous reflex, she laid her hand on the small, white metal-worked flower that hung from a gold chain around her neck, and rolled it between her fingers. "Today is my scheduled holiday. I'm taking the next transport into Timetsuara to meet a friend." She brushed the leg of her golden-yellow jumpsuit. "These are my civilian clothes. The necklace I wear always, but beneath my uniform."

Tynan cocked his head, as if amused. "You touch it reverently. Is your necklace a talisman?"

She immediately dropped her hand from her throat. "It isn't a charm in the usual sense. The necklace is precious and magical only because my mother gave it to me. The flower is my namesake."

"You were named after a marista flower?"

"No." She smiled cautiously. "The scientific name is 'maris stella'. It means 'Star of the Sea.'"

Tynan leaned forward as if to encourage her. But why did he now engage her in light conversation when minutes before he almost verbally threw her out the door?

She clasped her hands in her lap. "My mother was a marine exo-biologist before she married my father. On a scientific expedition under the Great Salt Sea of Galleron, she and another expedition member discovered a little white flower. For some reason, the petals attract and hold sea minerals. If the flower is brought to the surface and dried, it glistens like a star. That's why it's called a 'maris stella'."

She found herself smiling at the memory. "The flower was always one of my mother's favorites. When I was born, she created my name from the two words of the name."

"Marista," he repeated with unusually gentle respect. "Is that what you are, a Terran sea star? Do you enjoy the water?"

Her memories now bittersweet, she shook her head. "Not like my mother did. We moved so much with my father, she didn't have the time or the opportunity to pursue her work often. But she always made sure we had aquariums full of non-terrestrial underwater life forms. A few times, when we were home on Earth, she took my sister and me sailing in a skiff. I was never much of a deckhand. I'd rather skim the clouds than waves."

Though Tynan looked at her, she sensed his thoughts drifted in time and space. "A little sea flower that prefers the sky." He took a shallow breath. "I've always enjoyed the water, and with it the wind and open space and fresh air. Drifting on the waves, feeling the roll and pitch of the currents is better than meditation. On Medan's Ocean we had a bi-sail."

His reverie jogged her memory of Serraine's global geography. "Medan's Ocean borders western Albia, doesn't it?"

He drew up inside the chair, as if catching himself before falling off. "Yes."

Her pulse thrummed a little faster. "Did you live in Nadiv Province?"

"Once. I no longer have a home there."

His tone and unblinking stare hinted he wanted the subject closed. But in his rush to do so, he let slip another tidbit of information.

She seized the opportunity. "If Nadiv was your home, surely you've been to Antor, the provincial capital."

Tynan pushed out of his chair and paced to the window. She'd hit a nerve. Now wasn't the time to give up, so she swiveled on the stool to look at him. "I've been told Antor is a lovely city, rich in culture and tradition. And the university there is the finest on Serraine."

He continued to stare out at the wadi landscape. "Don't bother accessing official records. I didn't attend the university."

His warning didn't deter her. "You did attend some other institution of higher learning though, didn't you? You have the swagger and appearance of a pirate, but the intellect and speech of a well-educated man."

Tynan glanced over at her and scowled. "For someone with so delicate a flower name, you act more like a kae-a-tek with its prey."

She bristled. "I'm not sure I appreciate being likened to a horned desert lizard."

"You have the tenacity of an entire den of them."

"Tenacity has allowed me to accomplish my goals."

"As well as showing your father you could make a life separate and wholly different from his?"

She answered him with seething silence.

"Well, you've accomplished your goal, Little Diplomat," he said with a weary sigh. "You've become a fine emissary for interplanetary peace and human rights. I'm glad my friends and I have had a small part to play in your achievement. If we've made a measurable contribution to your field work then maybe, in some perverted cosmic sense, our losses have meaning."

Furious with his cruel sarcasm, she wanted to bolt off the stool and head for the door. She might have, too, had he not stalked back to her and stared down until she looked up into his hard gaze.

"Trust me, Kaljin," he rasped out in a near whisper, "a war zone is no place to heal personal pain."

Then she understood. "You know that firsthand, don't you?"

He went rigid. "Don't try to get inside my head."

She smiled serenely. "You just let me in."

A sound, like the growl of a wounded animal, left his throat. As a pinch of salt dissolves in a freshwater sea, her anger gentled into tender pity. His heart ached with some terrible pain of its own, perhaps the pain she'd glimpsed in his eyes last night as they climbed the stairway to see Jarrit.

But a proud man stood before her. She dared not allow him to glimpse her pity. She set her expression with cool professionalism and rose from the stool. "Motivations, either yours or mine, are not at question. I'm just asking you to be honest with me. However, I'm not sure you can be honest even with yourself."

He pinned her with his dark, uncompromising eyes. "I've never lied to you."

"But you've withheld from me."

"To know more about me would put you at risk."

"Perhaps you should let me be the judge of that. At least tell me about the 'mission' you and Jarrit conducted."

"No."

The fierce determination in his glare matched the tone of his refusal. Further debate was futile. "Very well," she conceded, "the choice is yours. I'll have to make do with the information I have. Tomorrow at the hearing I'll speak on your behalf . . ."

"I don't want your representation."

The declaration stunned her. "You don't want . . . Tynan, you need an advocate!"

"I have the right to refuse advocacy, don't I?"

She sputtered a string of nonsense syllables until she formed a suitable response. "Yes, but . . ."

"I don't want you to speak on my behalf. I'll make that clear in a statement before the hearing. Better still, don't come at all." He grabbed her wrist and dragged her toward the door. After depositing her at the threshold he backed up three paces. "Go home to your Earth, Kaljin. Do good deeds for someone who cares. But in the future, don't be so quick to honor a man under your protection with 'special' favors. You might lose your dignity along with your precious idealism."

Blood rushed to her already stinging cheeks. She should have faced his mock with calm professionalism. But he'd directed the insult at her personally.

Moisture collected behind her eyes, but she refused to vent the tears. No swaggering smuggler would make her cry for shame or regret. Still, fury and hurt made her reckless. "Fine. You can burn in hell. Or worse, rot in an Albian prison."

His malicious smile stung worse than a hard slap. "Ideals wear thin when pride is at stake, don't they? Maybe you and Bierich aren't so different after all."

That was the most hurtful insult yet. "And you wear cruelty as if it were a badge of honor. What makes you any better than Lieutenant Sindri?"

Even as the words left her mouth, she regretted them. In a fit of raw emotion, she'd bludgeoned his ego because he'd bludgeoned hers. The flattening of his smug, superior smile gave her no satisfaction. "I'm sorry, Tynan. I didn't mean . . ."

He turned his back to her and paced to the window. "Your ignorance would be a joke if it weren't so pathetic. Spare me your apologies. I despise you and your kind. I will for the rest of my life, and then some."

"Why?" she demanded. "Why do you despise diplomats? Why do you despise me even though I've proven I want only to help you?"

He refused to turn and face her. "Diplomats, especially Terrans, nurture and prolong this war."

Stunned by the indictment, she took a moment to find her voice. "I don't understand."

He growled a laugh. "You don't want to understand."

She fisted her hands. "My patience is wearing thin. Explain what you mean."

He spun around so fast it made her dizzy. "The time for talking is long past. I no longer have faith in 'meaningful dialogue.' I have faith only in raw force."

She met his fiery gaze head on. "Of course. You are Albian, after all."

"Yes, and I act," he agreed fiercely. "Now I dismiss you. Get out of here and leave me alone."

The cold invective swept over her like a blast of polar wind, freezing her in place. Once before a man had rejected her comfort and companionship with words that would haunt her beyond this life. *I want you to go,* her father had said. *It's for your own good, Rissy. You'll be safe with Aunt Mimi on Earth. You can't help me here, so I want you to leave.*

That rejection had left her floundering and helpless and sad for more years than she could count. But she was no longer a child at the mercy of a higher authority. "No."

"What?"

She stared at Tynan without flinching. "I said no."

He ground his teeth. "You don't have a choice."

"Oh, yes, I do," she argued. "This time, I do have a choice. I'll be at your side during the hearing tomorrow morning."

"Then I'll state for the record that you do not speak on my behalf."

"My presence itself will make a statement."

"Don't try to save me. You'll only condemn yourself."

"That's my concern, isn't it?"

Tynan clenched his fists. "What do you want? A thank you?"

"I never expected gratitude for doing my job. But neither did I expect disdain. I'm sorry if you believe my willingness to defend you is a character flaw, but I will not stand down."

"Dammit, Kaljin, I never said anything about a character flaw."

She waved her hand. "Your opinion matters little to me."

But his opinion did matter. Beneath the bluff and swagger Tynan was a noble soul. He'd risked his life to save his friends from fiery death. His grief over the boy, Marcus, was genuine.

So yes, the opinion of a good man, this Warrior King incarnate, did matter. She craved his respect, and he withheld it. She wanted to stand with him against Sindri, but like her father, he wanted to cast her aside. She wished to see just one hint of gentle sentiment for her in his dark eyes. Instead his obsidian sharp glare slashed her feelings to bloody shreds.

She set her gaze on the door controls before her eyes betrayed her, but she had less success hiding the rasp in her voice. "Try to get a good night's sleep. I'll ask Hyrek to find you some better fitting clothes so you'll at least make a good visual impression."

He said nothing.

She cleared her throat. "Until tomorrow, then?"

He didn't reply. The Silent One had fallen silent once again.

She slammed her palm to the door release, lurched into the corridor, and tore the restraint control from her belt. The Albian guard juggled the black box when she threw it at him, but she didn't take time to mumble an apology.

As her footsteps echoed off the tile floor, she focused her thoughts on the afternoon ahead. She'd deal with the ache inside her later.

Right now, she had people to see, and a job to finish.

Eight

Tynan labored through a pre-dawn meditation. By the time four Terran guards appeared mid-morning, he had prepared himself to face Sindri and his fate at the due process hearing. However, instead of escorting him to the sham deliberations, the guards took him once again to the subterranean interrogation room.

Leaning against the back wall, he crossed his arms over his chest and struggled to maintain a centered calm. At any moment he expected the viewing room door to slide open and Marista Kaljin to appear. He dreaded that moment. Why wouldn't she leave him alone? He wanted her to stay away.

That dishonesty made his gut twist.

He did want her here, now, close enough to touch and smell. In what might well be the last few hours of his life, he obsessed over a woman who drove him to distraction by merely entering the room. He wanted what he couldn't have. How ironic. How pathetic.

Analyzing the dilemma didn't solve it, any more than meditation excised Kaljin's face from his mind. He knew when she finally walked through the door his heart would thunder, his body would heat, and his control would slip until he spewed his frustration in a fit of anger toward the object of his desire.

He despised his own weakness. He resented Kaljin for sparking it to life.

Where was she?

When the outer room door slid open he lurched forward. "Kaljin, I told you . . ."

He pulled up halfway to the viewing window as a gaunt, lanky man sauntered across the threshold. Though the transparent barrier separated them, and the stranger's weathered face and wiry graying hair made him appear at least double Tynan's own age, he assumed a defense-ready stance and assessed the man.

Garbed in the loose white trousers and tunic of a desert city-dweller, the stranger might have been an Albian merchant or craftsman. There was nothing particularly notable about his long, leathery face, except crystalline blue eyes that seemed an electric contrast to the man's dark skin.

Those eyes snapped with intelligence and curiosity, and narrowed in amusement. The man tilted his head and the corner of his mouth at the same time. "So, you're the one who has Riss chasing her tail."

The man spoke Terran Standard. Tynan recognized most of the grumbled words. He just didn't understand their meaning. "Riss? Tail?"

The stranger threw his head back and laughed. Sure the joke was at his expense, Tynan fisted his hands. "Who are you? What are you talking about?"

With long, lazy strides, the stranger moved to the viewing window and plopped into a chair in front of the command console. "The name's Jace Ugo," he answered as he extended his legs and cupped the back of his head with both hands. "I'm a freelance journalist and general pain in the ass. Riss is the woman you call Kaljin. And if you haven't noticed her tail, boy, you were hurt worse than she said."

Heat rushed to Tynan's face. "I don't know every turn of phrase in your Terran dialect, just as I don't know Kaljin by the name you use for her."

Ugo grinned, flashing perfect, white teeth. "It's a pet name I call her. Have for years."

The blood that pooled in Tynan's cheeks drained away, leaving behind a nasty whine in his ears. "Are you the one who is her lover?"

Ugo squinted those preternatural blue eyes. "Got a good reason to ask that?"

Further chagrinned by his open, undue interest in Kaljin's personal life, Tynan only glared.

Ugo squinted harder. "You know what curiosity did to the cat?"

"No."

Ugo snorted a laugh and dropped his hands to grip the arms of the chair. "You're no fun, boy. No fun at all."

Fun would be feeling his fist connect with the end of Ugo's wedge-like nose, Tynan decided.

Ugo slid forward in the chair. "Fair's fair. Riss and I are old friends. Very old friends. I was there when she was born. Got to hold her before her daddy, the General, held her, though he doesn't know it to this day.

"Yeah, Riss and I go way back," Ugo said with a sigh. "Watched her become a fine woman. Got her mama's looks, her daddy's pride, and a sweet way all of her own. Deadly mix. Hard to resist. Can't deny her a thing. That's why I'm here." Ugo lifted one shaggy brow. "She wants me to help you, boy, though Creation only knows why."

Tynan had enough of this annoying Terran and his aggravating ridicule. He crossed his arms and looked down his nose at the seated man. "You're on a fool's errand. I don't want Kaljin's help. I want her to leave me alone."

Ugo threw up his hands. "She can't do that. Not who she is. That pretty package of hers hides a core of pure titanium. She's got a hell of a will behind that sweet smile. Don't ever doubt it."

Tynan didn't doubt it. "You're like a kae-a-tek with its prey," he remembered saying to her. According to Ugo, the comparison wasn't far wrong. "We agree on something."

The journalist cast him a crooked smile. Amazingly, Tynan felt the tension ease from his shoulders, and he propped his hip on the conference table behind him. "Tell me, Ugo, why do you want to help a total stranger?"

All traces of humor left Ugo's grizzled features. "You're important to Riss, so you're important to me. She's not one to beg favors on a whim."

Add another admirable quality to Marista Kaljin's long list of damn fine traits, Tynan grumped to himself. "She's a hopeless idealist, and it cost her this field assignment," he felt the need to point out.

"Oh, you mean her little problem with Bierich?"

"Little problem? Chances are she'll be shipped off this outpost before I am."

Ugo grinned, a wholly threatening expression that made Tynan thankful for the transparent barrier between them. "Once my story breaks, Bierich will be gone and Riss will be promoted out of this hellhole."

At the hint of mercenary intent on Kaljin's part, disappointment settled over Tynan like a shroud. "So, she called you in to help save her career?"

Ugo's wry expression flattened into stone-cold menace. "Riss has one thing on her agenda—keeping you out of an Albian military prison. She's asked nothing for herself. Told you she had pride. Wouldn't take my help, if I were too stupid to offer it." His chin went up. "One thing I'm not, boy, is stupid. You take my meaning?"

Though relieved to learn of Kaljin's selfless intentions, Tynan eyed the man with renewed wariness. "You have your own plan to help her, then?"

"Damn straight." Ugo settled back into his chair with a smug grin. "There's no reason I can't save her while she's trying to save you."

The man's pomposity propelled Tynan off the edge of the table. "Just how do you plan to accomplish that?"

Like a bird displaying plumage, Ugo puffed out his narrow chest. "I write stories. Some big. Some small. Every one important. People read. People listen. People complain. But someone always reacts. When I write about you and your friends, and this travesty of justice in the disguise of interplanetary entente, you'll be a heroic victim of bureaucratic intrigue. Riss will have a promotion."

"Before anyone reads your story," Tynan argued, "I'll be dead and Kaljin will be on the express flight back to Earth. You can't work miracles."

"I've managed one or two in my day."

Tynan ground his teeth until his jaw hurt. "Then consider this. You can't save someone who doesn't want to be saved. Neither you nor Kaljin understand that."

Slowly, Ugo lifted his lean body out of the chair. "Riss really doesn't want to lose her career, and I'll bet you really don't want to lose your life. Seems like both you and she have too damn much pride to realize that right now. Some poor bastard has to keep the pair of you from destroying yourselves with mutual self-sacrifice."

"I suppose you're that 'poor bastard?'"

Ugo made loopy circles around his head with his scrawny arms. "Don't see anyone else who wants the job."

Half-amused, half-disgusted, Tynan swiped the air with his hand, a gesture of grand dismissal. "You're daft."

"Sure am. Worked hard to get that way. Now, how about you show me yours, if I show you mine?"

The man was incomprehensible. "What?"

Ugo frowned and rubbed his pointed chin. "Okay, I'll go first. Worked my ass off trying to find out who the hell you are. Got every one of my sources chained to com-terminals. Now, I've managed to slap together profiles with half as much information as Riss gave me about you. But you're a puzzle, boy. An honest-to-Creation, skull-numbing puzzle. None of the pieces I have snap together."

A ripple of tension spread outward from the pit of Tynan's stomach and made his limbs twitch. If Jace Ugo thought he'd be any more forthcoming than he'd been with Kaljin . . .

"Like that scar on your palm, boy."

Tynan wasn't sure he heard right. "Kaljin told you about the scar?"

"Drew me a diagram."

"I gave her that information in confidence."

Ugo arched one brow until it disappeared into the folds of his forehead. "Yeah. So? She's trying to help you."

The journalist's dismissal of Kaljin's betrayal brought him to the edge of control. He gave the table a shove and spun a quarter turn to face the nondescript tan wall.

The display of temper didn't seem to faze Ugo. "She's a sucker for the underdog, but she's no fool. You come in here, flash a clan scar in her face but don't explain it, and you expect she won't look for answers? How would you have her protect herself?"

Once again Ugo prattled on, using words he didn't comprehend, yet he did understand the logic. Still, the excuse did little to soothe his fury with Kaljin's breach of confidence. He focused on a dent in the wall, a place where the color wash had been chipped away.

"Couldn't match the scar to a name until I accessed the Terran colonial archives," Ugo blathered on. "Then I hit pay dirt. Askanati was the name, a minor but wealthy clan that laid claim to property along the coast of Medan's Ocean in Nadiv Province. Loosen any memories?"

Too many memories that washed over Tynan like storm driven waves over a derelict bi-sail. He tried to go inside himself, to his centering point. He tried to blank out Ugo's voice and words. He failed.

"The Askanati's have an interesting and distinguished history," Ugo pushed on. "Especially one clan unit. The patriarch of that clan, a man named Dav, died five years ago. The wife, Jamilia, became matriarch and still lives in Nadiv. An older son began his own clan unit. A daughter married into a prominent clan in Prokopios Province."

The waves crashed around Tynan, pounded him, suffocated him. His lungs strained for air . . .

"But there was another son, the youngest kid," he heard Ugo say somewhere in the far distance. "Name was Quint. A rebel, that one. Joined the military instead of following the usual path of highborn Albians. Graduated from the Security Forces Academy ten years ago. Must have been a good soldier. He made captain by age thirty. Assigned to 'Special Sections.' On Earth we call it Intelligence Operations."

Tynan shut his eyes, let the waves drown him. The memories would come now whether or not he struggled against them.

"Quint might have made a fine career officer." Ugo paused. "But official records claim he died during training maneuvers not long after the war started two years ago."

Tynan held his composure together by frayed threads of will. The strain lowered his voice to rasp. "I have no sympathy for dead Albian soldiers."

Ugo snorted. "Figures. Albian soldiers don't have much sympathy for you. Still, it's too bad about Quint. He had a fine future in the making. Could have become a distinguished clan leader in his own right someday."

"Too bad," Tynan murmured.

"Boy?"

Bristling at the persistent condescension, Tynan cast the journalist a disgusted sideways glance.

Ugo stepped flush to the window. His ice-hard stare sent chills down Tynan's spine. "You fuck with Riss, and you fuck with me. And that's dangerous shit. You understand?"

At the end of his self-control, Tynan rushed at the window. "What would you do, little man? Turn this research over to Sindri? That would make Riss happy, wouldn't it?"

The corner of Ugo's mouth lifted into a nasty grin. "What I'd do is move heaven and earth to get you out of this over-baked pest hole. Then I'd turn you over to the General. Between him and me, you'd wish Sindri had thrown you in with the Never Born."

Tynan clenched his teeth in frustration. "You're delusional."

"And you're Quint, son of the Askanati Clan."

Tynan's heart gave a breath-stealing double beat as the charge rang in his ears.

"Deny it," Ugo goaded.

"My name is Tynan . . ."

"There is no such Albian name—first, last, or middle," Ugo cut in. "Never has been. It's not Krillian either. But I know where it is from. I've made it my business to know the name along with a thousand others. It was listed on the passenger manifest of the transport, Rising Sun."

Each word slashed like a dagger at Tynan's heart. Trembling with a rush of adrenaline he put his back to the viewing window.

But the rudeness didn't stop Ugo. He went on in a persistent monotone as if reading from a script. "The name Tynan belonged to a Malvian woman who died on that flight. Her family included scholars, poets and mystics. You sure as hell aren't one of those."

Rigid with pain and fury, Tynan breathed hard a half-dozen times before he trusted the steadiness of his voice. "Leave. Now."

"Why? Why did you let Quint of the Askanati Clan die and steal the name of a dead Malvian national?"

Tynan spun in place. "I'll call the guard!"

"Is it because you know the truth about what really happened to the Rising Sun?"

The grated question stunned Tynan into silence. From the satisfied glimmer in Ugo's keen blue eyes, he supposed that's just what the journalist had in mind. "What truth?" he finally croaked.

Ugo's shoulders sagged, as if his body could no longer support its defensive stance. "The truth about what really took the transport down. Not the excuses or the flaming rhetoric. Not the formal assignment of blame by the Interplanetary Council of Inquiry. We both know the official report isn't worth the cyberplane it's recorded on." Ugo cocked his head. "Don't we, boy?"

"How do you know that?" Tynan challenged, unwilling to concede anything. Yet.

Ugo chuckled with sour humor. "You have enough self-righteous ego for three men. Do you think you're the only Albian with a conscience?"

Sudden nausea threatened to bring up the little breakfast Tynan had managed to swallow that morning. In a handful of minutes this strange man, this journalist, this self-appointed guardian of Marista Kaljin and crusader of truth, dredged up the pain and self-loathing months of meditative discipline had finally suppressed. Tynan wasn't sure he could face, much less bury it, all over again.

Yet, if Ugo did know the truth about the transport . . .

"I suppose you don't know anything about that failed attempt to assassinate the Prime Minister and Field Marshall either," Ugo prodded.

In reflex, Tynan bolted to attention. Damn, he'd let Ugo take him off guard again.

"I know all about it, boy. Told you I had global contacts. Nasty business, but understandable if a man had reason to hold a grudge against the architects of this war. Where exactly did the clansmen find you and your friends? Out in the middle of nowhere? Funny place for smugglers who would keep to mountain air space if they wanted to hide."

Ugo smirked. "But maybe not so funny if someone on board knew the desert well and could hide in plain sight, as we say on Earth." He tiled his grizzled head. "A former Albian officer of Special Sections would know all the really good places to hide in the desert, wouldn't he?"

Tynan maintained silence in front of his inquisitor.

Ugo pounced on the concession. "We're on the same side, boy. I'm not your enemy."

Kaljin had told him the same thing. He wanted to believe someone. Anyone. Still . . .

"You said yourself Albians of good conscience have already come forward about what really happened to the Rising Sun," Tynan argued. "No one but the Krillians listened. Terrans especially want to deny the truth."

"Terrans like me?" Ugo snapped.

"You want a story. You're as suspect for mercenary reasons as the Krillians."

"And Riss?" Ugo pointed out. "What does she want? Her career is already half-wrecked. At least it's derailed. Tell me, what do you think she wants?"

Tynan didn't want to think about what Marista Kaljin really wanted from him. He saw the frightening truth too clearly in her sea green eyes. He covered his cowardice with gruff bravado. "What have you told her?"

"Nothing. I wanted to rattle your cage first."

Tynan let go an impatient sigh. "I'm not sure exactly what you just said, but I think I've been outmaneuvered."

Ugo grinned, wide and cocky. "You understand me fine. Now spill your guts."

Tynan glared at he journalist, annoyed that he might be starting to follow Jace Ugo's strange way with words.

***

The retracted conference room window shades allowed a glorious view of the lush oasis outside. Though the climate-controlled temperature and midmorning sunshine gave the room an airy, springtime ambiance, Marista felt as if the walls were closing in on her.

In less than half an hour, she would represent a man who wanted no representation, and make her arguments before an adjudicator who had exiled her back to Earth. Worse, Jace hadn't returned from the interrogation room after nearly fifty, nerve-racking minutes. What was taking him so long?

Evil butterflies swarmed in her stomach. Perhaps she should have notified Bierich that she had issued Jace Ugo press credentials. Then, of course, Bierich might have overruled her plan to publicize this so-called "due process" hearing. One way or the other she risked the chargé's wrath. Another line or two of official reprimand would be of little consequence. Would it?

The butterflies in her stomach morphed into vultures and stirred up roils of nausea with their powerful wings. She should have eaten more than a few bites of a grain biscuit for breakfast. But she'd barely managed to swallow that with a full cup of sweet palm leaf tea.

There would be time later to tend to her hunger. Time and more time. Her flight off-world didn't leave until evening. She'd already packed her personal belongings. She would finish her last official report after the hearing.

A deep, sad regret nipped at the edges of her heart, but she willed it away. She could brood later, too. In the meantime, she had a duty to perform to the best of her ability.

She skimmed her cold fingertips over the smooth platinum bar on her lapel. The single chevron symbolized her identity and her dreams. Now, both her identity and her dreams were in jeopardy.

Before she could sink deeper into self-pity, the conference room door slid open and Jace rushed to her side. "Riss," he panted, "we have to talk."

He grabbed her hand and held her fingers tightly as he pinned her with an almost desperate stare. "Listen, we're in way over our heads. You have to convince Bierich to postpone the hearing. You can't let the Albians haul Tynan away."

She frowned. "That's been my goal from the start. But the only reason I've stalled Bierich this long is because Sindri's waiting for results of his own investigation. We're talking bureaucracy, Jace. Two bureaucracies—Terran and Albian. No force in Creation outside of a supernova is going to stop them."

Jace gripped her hand so hard she flinched. "Well, you have to try. Tynan has to remain under Terran protection until I can pull some strings. I think he's the key to ending this stupid war."

Intuition struck her like a lightning bolt. "Dammit, Jace, what did Tynan tell you that he didn't tell me?"

Nine

Jace hesitated, a sure sign of guilt. "Riss, I know things you don't. I got to him in ways you can't."

Marista tore her hand from the journalist's grip. "I'll bet," she snapped, unable to hide the hurt she felt. "Out with it. I want straight answers."

"So do I, Kaljin!"

She pivoted at Madame Bierich's command. The chargé stood in the doorway. Lieutenant Sindri led his cadre of four armed guards a deferential step behind.

Though the chargé directed her words at Marista, she leveled her glare at Jace as she stalked across the room. "What's going on here? Who is this man?"

Marista opened her mouth to reply.

Jace edged in front of her and grinned at the chargé while he flashed his official press credentials. "Ugo's the name. Terran by birth. Journalist by conviction. Here to report on our judicial process in action and verify official transcripts of this proceeding."

Sindri pushed forward. "Madame Bierich, I object."

Bierich ignored the soldier and fixed Marista with a wrathful glare. "Kaljin, on whose authority did Mr. Ugo receive press credentials?"

The chargé's anger didn't frighten her. At this point, she had precious little left to lose. "I issued the credentials on my own authority. Jace Ugo is a respected journalist who has covered the Serrainian conflict since its beginning."

Bierich narrowed her flinty glare. "You invited him here to embarrass me, didn't you?"

Jace tucked his chin, gave a snort. "Now, Madame Chargé, what would be embarrassing about a routine due process hearing?"

Bierich's face went scarlet. "I want you to leave, Mr. Ugo."

Jace clucked his tongue. "Don't think you want to kick me out. Not when Madame Kaljin officially invited me in. I'd feel duty bound to mention it in my next dispatch. Freedom of the press, the public's right to know, and all."

Marista tried to snag Jace's attention and warn him with her eyes to shut up and let her handle the situation.

But the journalist focused on the chargé. "People back home might wonder just how well the Diplomatic Corps represents traditional democratic principles on Serraine. Your boss—I know Dimitri, by the way—might even have a doubt or two."

As quickly as Bierich flushed red, she paled. "Are you threatening me?"

Jace spread his hands wide in mock submission. "I'm a journalist. I report the truth. How could a statement of fact threaten someone conducting a fair hearing?"

Sindri lurched forward. "This is unacceptable!"

Jace cocked a bushy brow. "This is Terran soil, Lieutenant. Madame doesn't have a choice." He shifted his gaze to Bierich. "Does Madame?"

The chargé clenched and unclenched her jaw a half dozen times before she gave a curt shake of her head.

Sindri blinked his astonishment. "But, Madame!"

Bierich cast him a sharp glance. "I suggest you take your place, Lieutenant. We'll finish this proceeding as quickly as possible."

Sindri fumed in silence, but nodded with forced courtesy. Ignoring Marista, he marched toward his designated chair at the conference table.

Bierich directed the cold fury of her glare and whispered to Marista, "You had no right to bypass me. Your actions constitute gross insubordination."

"I never superseded my authority." Marista's voice held steadier than her pulse. "I felt it necessary to invite Mr. Ugo without your knowledge. You would have tried to bar him."

"With good reason."

"I disagree."

The chargé took two steps forward until her shoulder nearly touched Marista's. "You're finished, Kaljin!"

Jace leaned in from the other side. "Don't bet your pension, Madame."

Bierich huffed her disdain and stalked away to take her chair.

Despite Jace's insinuations to the contrary, Bierich's warning rang true. Marista had just dealt the deathblow to what was left of her already wounded career. All for a man who placed his ultimate trust in someone else.

"The old bitch is bluffing, Riss," Jace whispered. "Bierich can't blackball you without casting doubt on her own motives. Besides, I won't let her get away with it."

She snapped open her eyes and forced her voice to remain low and calm. "Stay out of my business with Bierich. I ran the risk. Now I'll accept the consequences. But since you hold all the right cards where Tynan is concerned, just do what I asked. Help him stay out of an Albian prison. Understand?"

Jace flinched at her angry words. "Riss, this isn't a competition between the two of us."

"Yes, it is," she interrupted, unable to subdue her bitterness. "You won. I lost. Tynan prefers your counsel. He's your problem now. Don't screw it up."

Jace's slack-jawed astonishment pricked her conscience. She'd taken out her resentment and disappointment with Tynan on her oldest and dearest friend. Yet, she wasn't ready to apologize.

Later. Once again, later . . .

Tense murmuring wafted through the room. She peeled her attention from Jace just as Tynan stepped across the threshold.

Taller than any one of the six Terran soldiers who surrounded him, he appeared more like an ancient god with a host of mortal guards than a prisoner still bound with electronic restraint cuffs. The strong morning light cast his face in smooth, handsome relief. With his head held high, his shoulders thrown back, and his hands loose and steady at his sides he exuded an air of complete control.

Though she should have been immune to his male beauty, her face warmed, and cloying regret tightened her throat.

Then Tynan let his gaze linger on Ailsa Griff, a pretty media-tech who stood by to record the proceedings. Marista's heated blood turned to ice. What in the name of Holy Mother Creation was happening to her? This adolescent reaction to his natural curiosity about Ailsa had no bearing on her own professional concern for the man's fate. After today she'd never see him again. He'd be nothing more than an entry on an official report.

Yet, the moment he turned his gaze to her, she realized how thoroughly she deceived herself. Despite his belligerent refusal to trust her or accept her help, his plight had become personal.

As he and his escort neared, Tynan shifted his gaze between her and Jace twice before settling it on Marista. Then, amazingly, he nodded in a greeting Albians usually reserved for their social equals.

Easy for him to be gracious now. He'd held his silence and gotten his way in spite of her reasoned arguments. At the bitter end, he'd chosen Jace's help over hers. This final rejection hurt worst of all.

Unable to look at him without wincing, she tore her eyes from Tynan's face. She felt him pass on his way to the conference table and focused again on Jace. "I mean it. Don't screw this up."

Jace caught her arm before she turned away. "Tynan still needs you."

She wiggled out of his grasp. "He has you."

Jace shook his head. "Not good enough. I have no official standing here."

"Jace, please . . ."

He grinned in his cockeyed way and gave her a quick nod. "You'll understand. Trust me."

Torn, she glanced at Sindri, who looked down his nose at a data recorder. Though the Albian lieutenant maintained an outward reserve, his bearing and demeanor spoke of a smug confidence. With a deep sigh, she gave Jace a warning glare. "All right, I'll trust you. This better be good."

Jace's grin blossomed into a smile. "Atta, girl!"

Ashamed of her base emotions, she turned away from the encouragement. Tynan had already taken his seat at the table across from

Sindri and perpendicular to the dais where Bierich presided. A Terran guard holding the electronic restraint controls positioned himself several discreet paces behind Tynan's chair.

As she rounded the conference table and headed for her seat, she met Tynan's stare. With his eyes narrowed and his mouth in a straight line, he seemed to question her. She pulled out her chair and sat down, neither saying nor doing a thing to allay his concerns.

Spiteful, yes. But that was the least ignoble emotion raking her insides just then.

"Lieutenant Sindri," Bierich addressed the Albian, "are you prepared to begin?"

Sindri stood. "I beg Madame's indulgence, if I could have a moment or two. I'm just now receiving an update from our central com-terminal in Timetsuara."

Marista groaned and shuffled the papers of a hard copy report in front of her. "Wonderful. What now?"

"Is something wrong?"

She glanced up at Tynan's whisper to find him leaning closer. So close, in fact, she felt the warmth of his breath against her cheek.

"I don't know," she whispered back, then returned to her papers and feigned more interest in them than in the well-defined curves of Tynan's mouth. "Sindri doesn't share his secrets with me." She paused. "He isn't the only one."

"Something is wrong."

She refused to look at him. "Actually Jace tells me things might just work out right for you."

"No, something is wrong with you. I felt your anger when I came into the room."

Better to ignore him than brush him off with a lie. Or worse, she decided, answer with the truth. "I understand you had a meaningful talk with Jace."

Tynan hesitated, but answered. "Yes, we talked. He's hard to understand but easy to like."

"Interesting," she muttered. "I love the man and sometimes even I don't like him very much. You must have found it easy to trust him, as well."

"You're angry because I talked with him?" he guessed, his voice tight. "Why? You arranged the interview. What did you expect?"

She cast him a sideways glare. "I expected that over the past days you would have been as forthcoming with me as you were with Jace after less than an hour."

"I was forthcoming with you," he retorted, keeping his voice low with effort. "And what did you do? You told Ugo about my scar. You betrayed our confidence."

"I tried to help you."

"As I tried to help you."

She faced him squarely. "How? By blocking me every step of the way?"

"I told you, there are things you shouldn't know. For your own good."

"Let me be the judge of what is or is not good for me," she lashed back, barely maintaining a whisper. "I don't need or want either you or Jace running my life."

"No, you don't need us. You can throw away your career by yourself."

No longer wishing to suffer the cold honesty in his hard, dark eyes she turned away from him. She had enough guilt and regret without adding his opinions of her incompetence.

"Kaljin?"

She heard his cajoling whisper of her name past the buzz in her ears.

"Kaljin, that was cruel of me. I know how you must feel right now. But know that I do appreciate what you've done for me. I'm . . . I'm sorry."

She felt sorry, too, that she had lost the final shred of her dignity.

"Will you forgive me?"

Ancient warrior kings seldom, if ever, begged forgiveness. When she moved her gaze back to his face she saw that Tynan no longer appeared the embodiment of male perfection and nobility. His dark gaze had mellowed, and his brow wore a deep furrow. His wide, expressive mouth had thinned to a tense line.

He was only a man after all. When he'd kissed her, she'd tasted the needy tenderness of his soul beneath the instinctive responses of his flesh. Given half a chance, she'd have given her body over to this man who refused her on every other level. He didn't even want her compassion. They were both fools.

Her anger seeped away. Resigned sadness softened her voice to a murmur. "I only want to help you."

"I can't let you."

The final decree. Time grew short. Further debate would only prolong the pain.

She would not send him out of her life with acrimony unresolved between them. "Very well, I accept your apology. All is settled between us."

The crack of Bierich's gavel signaled the beginning of the end.

***

Sindri's voice filtered to his brain. Tynan listened to none of the words. He stared at the graceful lines of Kaljin's profile. Did she mean to insult him? Or was she really so unaware?

Nothing was settled between them. Didn't she understand that?

How could he expect her to understand? He'd told her little about himself. He'd made a damn good show of rejecting everything about her. The consequences of his strategy registered in the dullness of her eyes, and the weighty sadness around the soft edges of her mouth.

But, in fairness, she should have heeded his warning. He didn't want her help. He didn't want to let her into his life.

Yet, she slipped in like an airy sprite of desert folklore, touching his frozen heart and soul with the magic warmth of her charity. She gave without taking, upended his notions of diplomatic deviousness and the Terrans' corruption. Then she ignited an ember of need he thought cold and dead.

I never wanted it! he railed silently as she gazed straight ahead, unaware. I never wanted you to settle in that empty, aching place. I never wanted to feel this obligation toward another woman! No, Marista Kaljin, I never wanted it!

Neither had she sought it out, he admitted as Sindri droned on. Still, he knew she felt as bound to him as he was to her. Only she'd touched her feelings long before he'd admitted his own. That much she'd tried to tell him in the storage room.

Too much had happened that should never have happened. Now they both suffered the consequences.

Kaljin lifted her head a notch, as if she'd keyed into his ruminations. A flame-red tendril of hair slipped from the hairpins at her crown and kissed her cheek. Absently, she tucked the loose strand behind her ear. His fingers, clenched together in a single fist on the tabletop, strained with the urge to help her with the task.

But she was unaware of his rogue impulses, and narrowed the steady gaze she had kept fixed on Sindri. The lieutenant finally must have said something important.

He smothered the embers of desire in his gut and focused on the proceedings that would determine his fate.

"Madame Bierich, your deputy has not been generous with her research and findings, though it's documented she's spent a great deal of time with the detainee," Sindri complained. "We don't know this man's name, or the name he assumes. Since our data information systems are engaged in more pressing matters at the moment, I regret to inform you our investigation is not complete."

Kaljin smiled without the generosity Tynan admired. "Did I hear you correctly, Lieutenant? Even your illegal bio-scan matched nothing in your databases?"

At the cold contempt in Kaljin's voice, Sindri glared at her with ill-concealed animosity.

Bierich rapped her gavel twice. "Kaljin, you'll refrain from editorial comment."

Kaljin stood. "Madame, Lieutenant Sindri did take an illegal bio-scan, according to my understanding of basic human rights."

Bierich leaned forward in her chair. "We are not here to discuss the legality of the sampling . . ."

"No, we are not," Kaljin interrupted, startling her superior into vapid silence. "We're here to determine if the Albian government has a valid claim on this man and his one surviving companion, despite the fact that I granted them protection under the neutrality clause of Interplanetary Law. After learning the results of Lieutenant Sindri's inconclusive, if not incompetent investigation, I move we adjourn these proceedings."

"Madame, this is ridiculous!"

Kaljin ignored Sindri's sputtering. "Further, I request a continuance of this hearing until Lieutenant Sindri finds evidence these men deserve extradition under Terran-Albian accords."

Fascinated and amazed by Kaljin's spirited, logical statement of her demands, Tynan almost forgot she did so in his defense—a defense he didn't want. He smiled with a strange sense of personal satisfaction.

Sindri ruined his pleasure. "Madame Bierich, the fact we cannot find this man's identity in our databases should cause alarm not relief, and gives you reason enough to commend him to our detention facilities for further interrogation."

Kaljin stuck out her chin. "He's on Terran soil," she reminded Sindri, dragging out the words as she might in the presence of a dunce.

The clan scar snaking along Sindri's jaw line stood pallid against the furious red of his skin. "His ship crashed in the Albian desert. I claim sovereignty over his person."

"He's not a piece of property," Kaljin retorted. "He has basic civil rights. Madame Bierich, the very language of Lieutenant Sindri's statement should convince you of his ultimate intentions . . ."

"Enough! Both of you!"

Bierich's command brought immediate silence to the room. Sindri nodded his curt deference. Kaljin, however, stood unbowed.

A core of titanium in a pretty package. That's what Ugo had said of Marista Kaljin. A strong will behind a sweet smile. Ugo was dead right about this woman he'd pet-named "Riss."

Tynan moved to the edge of his chair. Every fiber of his being urged him to stand up in a show of solidarity with this strong, beautiful woman. He restrained the impulse only in deference to Kaljin's professional authority. Besides, she was doing just fine without anyone's help.

After a moment Bierich collected her composure and turned to Sindri. "Lieutenant, will you take your seat for a moment while I deal with Madame Kaljin's argument?"

Though he obliged without question, Sindri scowled.

Bierich focused on Kaljin. "You want a continuance of this hearing?"

"Yes, Madame."

"Yet, this man and his companions came into our custody under suspicious circumstances, to say the least."

Kaljin shook her head. "That has no bearing . . ."

"Do you or do you not agree?" the chargé demanded.

Unable to do otherwise, Kaljin nodded. "Yes, Madame."

"Then would you have me further risk the security of this outpost, not to mention spend time and resources, in an effort to keep this man under de facto house arrest while the Lieutenant continues his investigation?"

"Madame," Kaljin replied, "this is not a question of our security or use of our resources."

Bierich groaned. "Yes, I know. The issue is human rights. Well, do you have anything to say on this man's behalf? Something that might give me good cause to grant your request?"

For the first time, Kaljin faltered. She opened her mouth, closed it, and then wet her lips. "He . . . No, Madame."

Bierich looked surprised. "He didn't record a statement?"

"No, Madame. He refused."

"You've had three days worth of access to him, yet you have no solid information to offer this hearing?"

Tynan's palms began to sweat. He'd given Kaljin nothing with which to defend him. Now she looked like a fool.

"No, Madame," Kaljin answered coolly in spite of the embarrassment.

"He wishes to make no statement on his own behalf?" the chargé needled.

Kaljin shook her head. "No . . ."

"Yes, I do!"

Tynan bolted from his chair. Beside him Kaljin gasped and took a step backward. Around him, the room echoed with the menacing click of desert rifles cocked in response to his sudden movement.

All too aware the Terran guard stood behind him ready to use the restraint controls, he held up both hands in non-threatening passivity.

Sindri, too, launched off his chair, and set his hand on his sidearm. "So, the Silent One does have a voice."

"A voice you don't want raised," he replied in the unaccented cadences of the Albian dialect.

Tynan had no time to enjoy the officer's slack-jawed confusion. Fingernails drove deep into his arm. When he glanced down, Kaljin's taut knuckles stood out bloodless against the dark blue of his shirtsleeve.

"What's going on?" Her whisper trembled. "Sit down and let me handle this."

He peered into her disbelieving eyes. Her fear for him was as real and intense as the bite of her grip. Poor little Terran. His heart ached for the disillusionment she would suffer for the sake of her misplaced idealism.

But his heart ached, too, with the emptiness he already felt knowing she'd soon be gone from his life.

He peeled Kaljin's hand from his arm. "I know what I'm doing. Trust me."

She shook her head. "No, please."

Unable and unwilling to answer the dozens of questions in her eyes, he turned toward Bierich. "Madame Chargé," he announced in Terran Standard, "I am part of the reason the Albian data systems cannot process the Lieutenant's requests. I was a member of the commando unit that attacked Albian Field Headquarters five days ago."

Sindri went florid. "You were part of the assassination attempt?"

He cast the soldier a disparaging sideways glance. "Not an assassination attempt. A retrieval of Prime Minister Lares and Field Marshall Osten to face charges of war crimes against the people of both Krillia and Albia."

Sound and fury erupted. Sindri demanded answers. The Albian guards scattered and took defensive positions, two near the door and two behind their lieutenant. Bierich ordered Kaljin to explain, but Tynan heard only a choked reply amidst the swirl of raucous confusion.

Finally, Bierich slammed her gavel on its stand with such force he expected the handle to snap. "Silence! I demand silence! Now!"

By degrees the chaos subsided enough that Bierich returned her attention to Kaljin. "Explain."

Kaljin drew a shaky breath. "Madame, I . . ."

"She knows nothing of this," he came to her defense.

Bierich squinted her disbelief. "Kaljin, is this true?"

She nodded once and caught her breath. "Yes, Madame, but . . ."

"Like you, she suspected me of common criminal smuggling," he pressed before Kaljin did herself accidental harm. "In fact, I am one of only two survivors of a failed mission. I held my silence to protect myself . . ." He avoided Kaljin's sea green eyes and amended, "Myself and others. But the situation has changed. I realize now, for the sake of my cause, I should reveal myself and the reason I participated in the strike against Lares and Osten."

He looked down at the woman who'd defended him blindly and would pay too much for doing so. "I'm sorry," he told her in a voice for all to hear.

Then he faced Sindri. "You didn't find me in your databases because I no longer exist. My family and my society buried me, deep and for good. I know things I shouldn't know, and I took those secrets to my official grave."

He pulled himself into rigid attention. "My given name is Quint. I am third born to Dav and Jamilia of the Askanati Clan. Nadiv Province is my home. Until my death over a year ago I was a Captain in the Albian Security Forces."

"What?"

He resisted the impulse to turn toward Kaljin's strangled cry of disbelief.

Sindri pounded the table with his fist. "Traitor! Deserter! Worse than a smuggler!"

"A refugee of conscience," he retorted. "My conscience now demands I speak out. Madame Bierich, I request political asylum. I have information . . ."

A brilliant light halted him in mid-sentence. He barely had time to throw up his arms to shield his face before a concussion wave snatched his legs out from under him.

The explosion shattered the air, reverberated through his head, and stunned his reflexes. His ears rang. His eyes stung from some acrid stench. Though he landed hard on the floor, the blast only knocked the wind from him. He curled into a protective ball as chunks of mortar and wood and shards of splintered glass glanced off his body.

When his insides stopped quivering, he coughed, rolled to his side, sat up.

Amid the smoke and debris and the screams of panic his mind raced with only two thoughts:

The locator implant worked.

Marista was no longer at his side!

Ten

Marista choked and struggled for breath. But the air was filled with noxious fumes, and she choked again.

At least she knew she was alive. Prone, dazed, and possibly broken, but alive.

So were others alive. A dull buzz blunted her hearing, but she heard discordant human commotion. Frantic voices called out names. Boot heels crunched glass. A woman shrieked. A man shouted an answer. When she recognized Jace's scratchy but vital voice, she set her hand to the floor and pushed up to go find him.

Something cold and sharp raked her right palm and her elbow buckled. She groaned before her shoulder thumped against the floor.

The physical pain ripped through the gauzy veil of her mind's numbness. Stark, paralyzing fear rushed in behind. Lying still to gather her strength, she felt her heart slam against her ribs and listened to the floor rumble beneath her ear.

Had an earthquake shaken the wadi? But then what was the blinding flash? One moment she had been gripping Tynan's arm . . .

Tynan! Mother Creation, he might be buried alive or bleeding to death!

She ratcheted herself up on one shaky elbow and opened her eyes a slit. The thick haze forced out tears that blurred her vision. She made out the legs of a toppled chair to the right. Directly in front of her stood the conference table, its fractured surface bowed under ceiling debris. Beyond that were only stiff, slow moving shadows backlit with desert sunshine.

"Tynan?" she croaked. Heat from the desert poured in through the shattered window and robbed her lungs of air. She tried to sit up. "Tynan, answer me! Ah!"

A vice grip around her ribs forced the rest of the air from her lungs. The room spun. Her arms and legs went flying as the powerful clamp yanked her off the floor, and dragged her a short distance. An instant later, she did a belly flop back onto the dust-coated tile.

She coughed, and then gasped when a heavy weight slammed lengthwise over her body.

For a panicked moment, she thought the ceiling had collapsed on top of her. But the weight pinning her was sleek and warm, not sharp and cold. The familiar masculine scent filled her with relief.

"Tynan! You're not dead! Thank Creation . . ."

"Kaljin, are you hurt?"

"No . . . not hurt, but . . ."

"Then lie still and shut up!"

As if she could do otherwise. Every nerve in her body vibrated, every muscle was clenched taut. Her ribs seemed jammed into her lungs, and her spine felt ready to snap. Tynan seemed intent on succeeding where the cave-in failed. He slowly crushed the life out of her.

Desperate for air, she lifted her trembling hand to catch his attention. "Let me up!"

Faster than an attacking viper Tynan struck out, snatched her hand inside his, and tucked both their arms securely beneath her.

"Tynan . . ." she tried to warn him as her air supply dwindled.

"Lie still!"

"What . . . what just happened?"

"For once just do as I say!" he commanded and held her fast.

"Tynan . . . please . . . let . . . me . . . up . . ."

He ignored her plea. She wiggled her foot.

Tynan countered by digging his knee further into the back of her leg. "Stay still, and maybe you won't get hurt!"

The growled warning startled her into obedience. She lay beneath him, feeling his labored breaths stream across her face. His heart beat like a war drum against her backbone. His cheek burned hot against hers. He was shielding her from some kind of danger, she realized, though his weighty protection just might kill her anyway.

Seconds passed. Painful, agonizing seconds. Purple spots danced in front of her eyes. The chaotic noise dulled to a background hum. Her eyelids fluttered shut. A sweet, peaceful lethargy stole over her. Oxygen deprivation, some rational part of her knew.

Yet, she felt no fear, not with Tynan so close. He protected her from . . . what?

It didn't matter. What did matter was that he was protecting her with his own body. So heroic. So noble. So . . .

Wild screams and staccato explosions jerked her back to sharp awareness. From floor level she watched furniture upended and the guards still standing propelled backward into the rubble. Wordless, guttural screams of agony rent the air.

Tynan curled further into her. The shift of his body allowed her to gasp in air. But she gagged on the odor of fresh blood and the weapons' after burn that came with the oxygen. A heartbeat later, the conference table they laid under overturned and crashed behind them. The toe of a jackboot stirred up masonry dust, then skidded to a halt centimeters from the tip of her nose.

The scuffed and dusty boot didn't belong to the Terran guards. Neither was the owner one of the impeccably uniformed soldiers of Sindri's command. When the barrel end of an assault weapon jabbed her shoulder, she knew the room had been stormed by strangers. Some gut instinct warned her that death loomed.

A round of weapon's fire burst over her head, and Tynan's body fell away.

Her scream sounded more like a raw sob in the back of her throat. They'd killed Tynan in cold blood, and she'd be next . . .

Hands gripped her shoulders and rolled her over. Strong fingers then clasped her chin and gave her head a shake. With her last ounce of strength, she answered the tormenting with a weak swipe of her hand.

Past the buzzing in her ears she heard a hoarse laugh and words in heavily accented Albian. "She'll live."

"No thanks to you, Gaer."

Tynan? Was that his voice?

Another laugh, more like a snort, came at her. "You're welcome. Captain."

The formal address conveyed insolence, not respect. Still woozy, she squinted. Her vision waved and wobbled, but it finally focused on a set of amber eyes and a vicious, thin-lipped scowl.

When she turned her face away from the man, strong fingers, Tynan's fingers, brought her back around.

"Kaljin, stay with me."

Tynan leaned over her, mercifully blocking the sight of the terrifying stranger. She sucked in a full breath of air, the first in too many minutes, and managed a whimper.

"I think you squashed her, Captain."

"Shut up, Gaer. She's lucky you didn't kill her. Kill us all, for that matter. You were supposed to get us out of here alive. What was that explosion all about?"

"Sosan packed too much igniter gel," the man named Gaer quipped. "He'll know better next time."

Tynan grumbled something in Albian, phrases she couldn't translate to standard Terran.

Gaer took exception to the words. "You be thankful Colonel Varden bothered to send a rescue mission, Captain. I'd just as soon let you rot in your precious desert."

"Then I'm glad you're just the errand boy."

"I command here, Albian. Don't forget that while I hold the weapon."

She had heard enough of the argument and batted Tynan's fingers away from her chin.

He snapped his attention back to her. "I landed on you hard. Did I hurt you?"

Before she could answer, he slid his hands across her ribs, down her hips, and over her thighs. Startled by the unsolicited intimacy of his probes, she raised her knees, shook him off, and scrambled to sit up.

Gaer let out a bawdy guffaw.

Tynan shot the man a murderous glare, but redirected his concern to her. "Good. Nothing's broken. Can you stand?"

Though her vision no longer wavered, the sudden shift of position made her nauseous. Worse, she trembled from head to foot. "I'm not sure."

"Try."

Without waiting for her consent, Tynan grabbed her left arm, draped it around his neck, and anchored his right hand at her waist. Suddenly, she was airborne and upright.

Almost immediately her knees wobbled. She tried to lock them, failed, and gasped a warning as she crumbled back toward the tile floor. But she didn't hit ground. To banish the dizziness and the wretched stench of destruction, she shook her head. As her senses cleared, she realized Tynan supported her weight. Her cheek rested against his wide chest, and his arms held her tight.

He wouldn't let her fall. Though he didn't trust her with his secrets, she trusted him to keep her safe.

With her ear pressed to his heart, she heard him rumble a command. "Turn that chair upright."

"Of course, Captain," Gaer grumbled, again with insolence. But he obeyed, lifted a chair out of the rubble, and set it down with a crash.

Tynan dragged her to the seat, lowered her gently into it, and then bent down on one knee in front of her. Cupping her chin with his hand, he softened his voice. "Sit a while and you'll feel better."

She tried to focus on his face—any one of the three that floated in a circle would have been sufficient. "My head is spinning."

"From the explosion," Tynan explained. "My ears are ringing."

She swallowed the bitter taste of the weapon's after burn. "What explosion? What happened?"

"A botched rescue."

"Personnel and data retrieval," Gaer countered Tynan's disgusted reply. "Where are the controls to those cuffs?"

Tynan turned a quarter circle, but didn't let go of her. "Over there. The guard has them."

When Gaer moved away, she watched him and immediately wished she hadn't. The scruffy raider squatted next to a lifeless form. The young Terran guard lay amid crumbled mortar and splintered wood. The remains of his body were little more than a bloody heap.

The sight of carnage sent her reeling again. She moaned and clutched at Tynan's arms as awareness slid away.

He gave her a shake. "Fight it, Kaljin."

The words echoed through her head. She wanted to fight. Didn't he understand that? She blinked hard and willed her spine rigid.

By then, Gaer returned with the restraint controls. "At least the new locator implants worked as you claimed they would, Albian. Give me your wrist."

Tynan's hand left her face, and her skin chilled. "What are locator implants?" she muttered.

Tynan fixed his gaze on his wrist as Gaer relieved him of one cuff. "The device you thought was a contraceptive. It's experimental Albian technology. One of the secrets I took with me when I died."

She swayed but didn't topple when Tynan set her free.

Gaer unlocked Tynan's second restraint cuff and tossed the control aside. "Fitting that you were the field test subject, Albian."

"Field test?" she echoed.

"I wasn't sure the technology would work at such a distance," Tynan explained. "Neither was I sure the device hadn't been damaged in the crash."

Gaer's surly chuckle raised the hair on the back of her neck. "Why such a puzzled face, pretty lady? Did Tynan lead you to believe he was neutered instead of wired? Did you trust this Albian deserter with your honor?"

Tynan shot to his feet. His fist cracked into Gaer's jaw before she saw the swing of his arm. The raider staggered backward two paces before catching himself.

Before she had time to wonder at the violent but chivalrous defense of her virtue, Gaer leveled his weapon at Tynan's chest. "Fine Albian! I'd just as soon claim you as a casualty of the rescue!"

Ignoring the buzz in her ears and the pitch of her stomach, she lunged in front of Tynan and threw her arms wide. Her smaller body covered little of his, but it shielded enough to make a clean blast from Gaer's weapon impossible.

Tynan gripped her shoulders from behind and shouted a profanity.

Somehow she found the strength to dig in her heels and extend her palm toward Gaer. "Stop this! I don't understand half of what's happening here, but you're supposed to be saving his life! There's been enough killing!"

Gaer cocked his head and lowered the rifle a few centimeters.

From behind, Tynan grabbed her upper arms, pulled her up until her heels left the floor, and set her aside with a thud. "You fool!"

Gaer snorted, but banked his weapon to the left. "You're right, Captain. She's a fool to save your worthless life. Or at least your right arm. I'd have been satisfied separating it from your body."

Amazingly, Tynan glared at her, not the raider who'd almost maimed him in a fit of anger. "What were you thinking?"

She refused to flinch at the reproach and wrenched from his hold though it sent her a tottering step backward. "I didn't think I wanted to see you dead at my feet!"

"Instead you almost got yourself killed!" Tynan fired back.

Gaer jammed the barrel of his weapon between them. "Shut up, both of you! The shuttle's waiting and we can't hold the outpost forever. Where are the others?"

Tynan set his hard glare on the raider and shoved the rifle aside. "All dead, except for Jarrit. He's in the medical wing."

"Take me there."

Tynan shook his head. "I can't. The guards brought me in from a subterranean level. I'm not sure of our location in the complex."

Gaer snatched her arm, and dragged her to him before either she or Tynan could react. "You know where Jarrit is. Take me to him."

She struggled to twist free. Gaer only tightened his hold until her fingers pulsed with backed up blood.

Tynan stumbled forward over rubble. "Leave her alone."

"I'm in command!" the raider reminded Tynan before he gave her a bone-rattling shake. "She'll take me to Jarrit."

Gaer didn't wait for a reply but turned toward the doorway with her in tow. Though she dragged her heels, Gaer yanked her arm with such force that she gave up, preferring the man's repulsive touch to a broken wrist.

Trying to avoid mangled bodies and choking down her revulsion, she heard Tynan plow through the debris behind them. "Gaer, let her go."

The raider ignored his plea. She had to use her own wits to deal with this evil man. "Jarrit's in a life support pod," she told Gaer. "He can't be disconnected. He'll die."

"She's telling the truth," Tynan agreed as he caught up with them at the door.

Gaer halted in the door's arch and glared at Tynan. "You and I both know what has to be done, don't we, Albian?"

Tynan's jaw twitched. "Jarrit's going to die anyway."

The raider tilted the barrel of his weapon toward Tynan's face. "I do my job so others don't have to come and clean up my mess. If you have no stomach for it, run off to the escape shuttle now."

She winced, not at the bite of Gaer's hold, but at the foreboding of the man's words. "Tynan, what does he mean? What has to be done? Jarrit cannot be moved!"

He seemed not to hear her. "All right, Gaer. Kaljin will take us to Jarrit so you can judge for yourself," he finally conceded, his voice so low she barely heard it.

Horrified, she gave a futile tug at her captor's hold. "No!"

Tynan jerked around toward her. "He'll take you by force anyway. Just go and be done with it."

Gaer swung her around and shoved her over the threshold. Whirling blindly, she hit her foot on a slab of ceiling tile, and lost her balance. The raider wrenched her upward, nearly tearing her shoulder from its socket.

The burning pain forced a cry from her. Tynan barked another curse at the raider. At the same moment, she heard Jace's indignant screech.

"You son-of-bitch! Get your hands off her!"

Righting herself she homed in on her friend. He was under guard with the rest of the blast survivors. Plastered against the wall and facing three raiders who looked no less like killers than did Gaer, the journalist managed to appear both endearing and enraged.

"Riss, you okay? You hurt?"

She wanted to reassure him, but she couldn't get so much as a wan smile past her fear and pain. "I'm not hurt badly. Are you?"

Jace shook his head, and then glanced over at the others. Bierich sat slumped against the wall with her right arm crimped at an unnatural angle. She faded in and out of consciousness.

Next to the chargé, Sindri applied a tourniquet to a gaping wound in his own leg. His face was ashen and bloody from deep lacerations. Yet he gritted his teeth and cast Gaer and Tynan a murderous scowl as he lashed out, "You're both dead men!"

"Not today," Gaer snarled and glanced at Tynan. "Get everyone up and take them to the main portico. You do know where that is, don't you?"

Tynan let his gaze dart between Gaer and her. "Yes, but I'm coming with you first."

Gaer's crooked mouth split into a chilling grin. "No need." He gave her arm a jerk. "'Riss' and I will get along just fine, won't we?"

Tynan drew himself up. "I will not let you go without me!"

Though her heart beat so hard she feared it would burst, she shouted into Tynan's reckless fury. "I'll go alone with him!"

Tynan gaped at her. "What? No!"

But she knew separating these two men was the only way to defuse the explosive hostility between them. "I'll be all right," she insisted, however much she feared and despised her captor. "Go and do as he says."

Tynan didn't give in. "You don't understand . . ."

"Go, Tynan," Gaer taunted in a falsetto voice. "Listen to the pretty lady."

She had never seen Tynan so conflicted. He held himself back from Gaer, but just barely.

As much as she wanted him to stay at her side, she resorted to pleading. "Please, Tynan, go."

Before he voiced another objection, Gaer shouted at the guard closest to him, "Give the Captain your sidearm."

The guard complied. Tynan accepted the weapon as if Gaer ordered him to commit self-destruction with it. After letting the sidearm lay in his flaccid palm a few seconds, he snapped his fingers over the wide handle and assumed a commanding stance.

"Take care of it, Gaer. Fast," Tynan growled while the guards assisted Bierich and Sindri to their feet.

"Do not give me orders, Albian," the raider warned and started to turn.

Tynan grabbed Gaer's arm and yanked him to a dead stop. "Listen hard. If you hurt Kaljin in any way—*any way*—you'll answer to me."

The threat should have filled her with new fear for her safety. Instead, the fierce intensity of Tynan's vow, and the seething protectiveness in his obsidian eyes, swelled her heart with tender gratitude. Mother Creation, he did care what happened to her.

"Riss?" Jace called to her as one of the raiders prodded him with a weapon.

"Don't worry," she called back to him, and then glanced up at Tynan. "I'll see you in the portico."

Uncertainty shadowed his expression, but he said nothing and turned away to follow the queue down the hallway. She watched him retreat until Gaer yanked on her arm.

"You'll be reunited soon enough. Get going." Gaer shoved her ahead of him.

Free of the raider's grip and glad of it, she obeyed as she had promised.

***

Marista stumbled out of the elevator ahead of Gaer's weapon. As she had hoped, the raider wasn't so belligerent once he didn't have Tynan to harangue. He grunted only a word or two after they left the wrecked conference room. Now that she had rendered her service to him, perhaps he'd set her free.

Rounding the corner into the last hallway, she spotted two more raiders already stationed outside Jarrit's unit. One of the men came forward and met them halfway.

"We can't get in," the raider said, talking as they approached the window. "One of the techs locked himself inside with Jarrit. We don't have time to cut through the shielded window."

Gaer pulled her to a stop at the edge of the viewing plate and jammed his weapon into her backbone. "Get us into that room."

With her heart skipping every other beat, she shook her head. "I can't if the door is locked from the inside."

Gaer sank his meaty fingers into the thick roll of hair at her nape. She gave a yelp of pain and surprise, but when she felt the press of Gaer's weapon to her temple and heard him cock the trigger she sucked it all back in her throat.

The cold metal cut into her skin. She squeezed her eyes shut as panic blanked her mind. Suddenly, she didn't doubt he'd kill her for her ignorance.

Gaer steered her forward then pulled her to a halt so hard her neck cracked. "Open your eyes!"

She did and saw Hyrek inside the unit. He grimaced at the sight of her dilemma. Then, his figure blurred. A heartbeat later, the door opened with an ironic, apathetic yawn.

Still grasping her hair, Gaer rammed her inside the unit. Once beyond the doorway, he handed her off to one of the other raiders. Then he trained his weapon on Hyrek. "Shut off the life support."

Hyrek stared at him in stunned disbelief. "No! He'll die!"

She could have told Hyrek to spare his appeals to Gaer's sense of decency. She knew the raider had none.

As if to prove her right, Gaer jammed his weapon into Hyrek's chest. "Shut it off!"

Even as Hyrek stared at the weapon, he shook his head. "This man isn't brain dead. I won't be a party to murder."

For one, unguarded second, Gaer seemed confused by the principled refusal and let his gaze stray to the pod. Hyrek took advantage of that second by grabbing the end of the weapon and pushing it up and away from his chest.

But Hyrek's self-defense skills were no match for Gaer's strength and reflexes. The raider bent the tech backward and had Hyrek on his knees in less time than Marista could draw a breath and warn her friend. In one fluid motion, Gaer lifted the end of his weapon and smacked Hyrek's jaw. The tech sank to the floor, unconscious.

Gaer spun around and aimed his weapon at her. "You shut it off!"

She shrank away from him, but the guard at her back thrust her toward the pod. She stumbled forward and regained her balance just before crashing into the plastic bubble.

Trembling violently, she drew her arms over her breasts. "Gaer, you don't have to do this. Tynan didn't lie. Jarrit won't live much longer anyway."

"A few hours might be too long," Gaer shot back. "Albian interrogators can wring information from a stone, woman. Now do it. Turn off the life support."

She stared down at the weapon, black and ugly and pointed at her heart. She sucked in ragged breaths of air, holding back hysteria by mere threads of will. "I can't."

Gaer's jaw quivered. "You will, or . . ."

Her control slipped one too many notches. "I can't turn it off! Even if I wanted to, I don't know how!"

Gaer narrowed his eyes with what seemed to be honest puzzlement.

"I don't know what to do!" she shouted, as if saying it louder would make him comprehend. "There's a sequence of steps that has to be followed. If I shut down the oxygen units wrong I'll blow us all halfway across the desert!"

"You lie!"

"No, I'm not!"

Within a span of three seconds he considered her honesty. Then, his face smoothed, and he appeared almost rational.

A sigh of relief stuck in her chest when Gaer shouldered his weapon and withdrew a guttered combat knife from a sheath at his waist. With his free hand, he tore away the protective bubble from the life pod and expertly drew the blade across Jarrit's throat. One by one the lights on the life monitor winked out until the entire board went dark.

A scream ripped from her chest and echoed off the walls.

Eleven

As the minutes ticked by Tynan's nerves strung tighter. Where was Gaer? The Krillian commander was reckless and ruthless. But even Gaer had to realize the quicker they made an escape from Albian air space the better their chances of survival.

He slid his index finger along the trigger of his weapon. The Krillian energy pistol lay heavy and awkward in his hand. He'd lost his own smaller, lighter weapon in the skimmer crash. The piece was gone forever, like the rest of his Albian past.

With the back of his free hand he wiped sweat from his forehead and face. The hazed air stank of fear and blood and weapon after burn. Sunlight streamed through the one portico skylight, illuminating a shaft of dust and smoke. Along the east wall four of Gaer's raiders held more than two dozen Terran personnel under armed guard. Behind him, near the doors of the main elevator, huddled a few gravely wounded Albian soldiers.

"Bracquar!"

He wheeled in place at the sound of the guttural obscenity. Sindri's glare cut at him as surely as the hateful insult. Though honor demanded he answer the affront to his clan and heritage, he stifled the impulse. The lieutenant sat crumpled against a wall, guarded by a pair of Gaer's men, and disabled by a gaping leg wound. Calling out an already captured and wounded man conferred even less honor than letting the insult pass unchallenged.

In a simple gesture of disdain, he lifted his chin and began to turn away.

Sindri lurched forward. "A coward and a traitor!" he lashed out in Terran Standard for all to hear and understand. "Better that you ran off to the Krillians!"

Tynan forced a bland smile. "Insult me all you want, Lieutenant. I understand the psi-tactics. We learned from the same warfare manuals, after all. Maybe we even served under the same drill master."

His knuckles already strained white, Sindri gripped the blood soaked tourniquet tighter around his calf, then spat at Tynan's feet. A chill swept over him along with a new, terrible awareness of the clumsy weapon cradled in his palm. In his mind's eye he imagined pointing the barrel at Sindri's face and watching the lieutenant's smug expression freeze with terror.

There was no honor in making hollow threats, either. Sindri might believe him capable of cold-blooded killing like Gaer, but he had no stomach for it. He drew a deep breath, turned his back to the officer, and paced to the archway of the main corridor.

The hall lay empty. Nothing stirred, except a warning twinge in his chest. What was taking Gaer so long? With Kaljin leading the way he should have been in and out of Jarrit's room long ago.

Unless she did something stupid, like plead for Jarrit's life. Or worse, misdirect Gaer through the complex to waste the raider's time. Damn, she'd do it, too. She tested a man to the end of his patience with her principled compassion. She'd tested him enough over the past few days.

But didn't she have sense enough to understand thwarting Gaer was dangerous? Brutal and determined, the Krillian would use any means to bend her resolve.

"I swear, Gaer," he growled under his breath, "if you hurt her in any way you'll feel more than my fist in your face."

A low hum vibrated through his hand. Glancing down, he found his finger squeezing the trigger of his pistol with deadly intent. A fraction more pressure and an energy discharge would blow a hole in the stucco wall at the end of the corridor.

Stunned by the depth of his fury, he released the trigger and pointed the barrel of the weapon at the ceiling. New beads of perspiration broke loose from his forehead and sluiced down his face onto his neck. What kind of fool had he become? He agonized to the point of violence over Kaljin's safety when his own escape still wasn't certain.

The pounding of jackboots in the corridor cut into his boiling thoughts. He snapped his gaze upward to find a trio of Gaer's men herding several more Terrans into the holding area. The whimpers and wails of the new group sent a fresh current of muted panic through the portico.

His own anxiety mounting, he pivoted and scanned the room until he noticed movement out of the corner of his eye. He did a double take at the lanky figure sitting with his back to the floor. Jace Ugo beckoned him forward with a steady gaze.

He hesitated only a moment, checked the empty corridor one more time, then crossed the room.

As he approached Ugo, he glanced down at the clutch of people huddled along that section of wall. A nurse tended to Madame Bierich's broken arm. The chargé was alert enough to groan in agony.

"Is she badly hurt?" he asked the journalist.

Ugo replied without much empathy. "She'll survive to collect a commendation."

Tynan raised a brow. "What about you?"

"I had my teeth nearly blown out of my head, but I'm fine. No thanks to your friends. Can't say assaulting a neutral outpost is the best way to win support for the Krillians."

The journalist's scorn shredded the last of his already fragile patience. "You're not telling me anything I don't know. What do you want?"

Ugo jerked his chin up. "A word with you?" He looked left, then right. "Alone." It wasn't a request.

Tynan hesitated, but only a moment. Oddly enough, he trusted this Terran, Kaljin's friend, more than he trusted any of his Krillian rescuers. Without a word, he grabbed Ugo's scrawny upper arm and hauled the journalist to his feet. Two of Gaer's men turned sharply at the commotion, but lowered their eyes in submission when Tynan scowled at them and marched Ugo a few meters away from the rest of the captives.

When they left earshot of the others, Ugo cocked his head. "There's still time, Captain."

"Now that I hold a weapon I'm Captain, not boy?"

Ugo flattened his mouth into a grim line. "Shut up and pay attention."

Tynan raised his weapon and fingered the trigger mechanism. "You'd be wise to take this seriously, little man."

Ugo snorted. "You won't use that on me, not without good cause. Senseless violence is why you deserted your nation and your commission in the first place."

The journalist had nearly as much insight as he had audacity. Tynan raised his guard. The sharp command in his voice had less to do with anger than edginess. "Get to the point."

"Stay."

Tynan almost laughed. "What?"

"Stay, as in don't go back to a hopeless cause."

Tynan restrained his anger, but just barely. "The Krillian cause is less hopeless than you imagine."

"I know hopeless when I see it," Ugo gritted out. "Remember, I've been on both sides of the border. Returning with this bunch won't make or break the Krillian war effort, and you know it. Better you should stay here, claim the asylum you requested, and let me tell your story."

He did laugh at that, a low warning rumble that made the journalist blink. "You're amazing, Ugo. Nearly blown to extinction, your life dependent on a crazy bastard like Gaer, and all you really want is a story."

"I want this war to end, damn it!"

The desperation in Ugo's whisper took him aback.

Ugo pressed his advantage. "I've seen enough of it. I know too much about it. So do you. It should never have started. It has to end. You have a chance to help bring about that end."

As much as he wanted to believe the journalist's claim he knew better. "How could I tell what I know from an Albian prison? That's where I was headed. And after this raid, that's where I'll end up if I stay."

"Bierich might have been willing to turn you over to Sindri," Ugo agreed. "But the statement about your heritage and military status is now on record. I'll personally vouch for your credibility. The Terran ambassador in Timetsuara has no choice but to grant your petition for asylum until there's further investigation. In less time than it takes to file the bureaucratic requests I can have your story on every vid-terminal in the Planetary Confederation. No one can ignore you then."

Amused and disbelieving in equal measure Tynan shook his head. "I doubt your ambassador will look favorably on the petition. Even the patronage of an overbearing Terran journalist with more bluff than brains will be of little consequence."

Ugo let the insult go by without comment. "Riss will vouch for you, too."

He flinched before he could stop himself. "Helping me has cost her too much already."

"I don't think her career matters much at this point."

Something in the journalist's intense glare gave him the impression Ugo saw into his soul. To hide his disquiet, he waved his weapon in dismissal. "I used up her good will long ago."

"There's more than good will at work here, boy, and you know it."

When he opened his mouth to refute Ugo the lie stuck in his throat. Yes, there was something more than good will at work inside Kaljin— something that went beyond compassion or honor. He glimpsed it in her eyes, felt it when she responded to his kiss. Then she'd proved it by shielding him from Gaer's retaliation at the risk of her own life.

He fought down another ripple of guilt. "I will not be responsible for whatever motivates Kaljin," he insisted. "She made her own decisions and controlled her own actions. The consequences are her problem."

Ugo's glare turned ice-hard. "I know what happened after the explosion. I panicked when I finally got on my feet and couldn't see Riss anywhere. What I did see was you crawling over body parts and meter high piles of rubble to get to her. I suppose shoving Riss under that table then throwing yourself on top of her is her problem, too."

"I acted on instinct."

"You were driven to find her," Ugo insisted. "Otherwise you'd have found that big hole in the wall and hauled your ass into the desert."

He couldn't argue the point with any conviction. To avoid Ugo's penetrating stare, he slanted his eyes toward the long, empty corridor. "Think what you want."

"I think you've got the same problem she does."

He snapped his gaze forward again and scowled.

Ugo just stuck out his narrow chin, as if daring him to deny the charge. "I'm not the mystical type. I don't see great cosmic schemes in every coincidence. But for some reason Fate brought you and Riss and me together on this self-destructive rock at this particular time."

"And you think the reason is so the three of us can stop this war?" Tynan rolled his eyes. "I tried going through the proper channels, and contacting all the right people before I deserted my life and my career. No one listened then. Why should they listen now? If you think otherwise, I was right. You're delusional."

"As delusional as you were, thinking you could abduct Prime Minister Lares and Field Marshall Osten and make them confess their part in the Rising Sun incident?" Ugo baited. "Sounds like a crazy scheme, even to me. And why did you sacrifice your life, your family, your heritage if not to stop this war?" Ugo narrowed his eyes in speculation. "Or is the real problem that the Albians weren't paying you enough?"

The insult snapped his brittle control. "I'm not a mercenary!"

Ugo shifted his gaze side to side. Only then did Tynan realize the portico had fallen silent in the wake of his vehement denial.

"Prove it," Ugo taunted in a whisper. "Prove that an end to this war is what you've wanted all along. Stay and be witness to the truth."

"Truth is relative," Tynan reminded him.

Ugo held his ground. "Seeing and hearing is believing."

"You Terrans had a chance to believe," Tynan accused. "Your government claimed impartiality, yet favored Albia's claim that Krillia destroyed the Rising Sun. Trust me, Krillia receives no special favors, like the establishment of this neutral, humanitarian outpost."

"I know."

The two simple words hit Tynan like a blow to the stomach.

"I know all about it," Ugo repeated. "I know about the Terran economic stakes in the Albian mining consortiums. I know about the backdoor evasion of sanctions, and the one-sided Albian-friendly diplomatic mediation at the peace talks."

Ugo screwed his leathery face into a frown. "Why do you think I've put down stakes on this miserable pest hole-of-a-world and tried to swim upstream through bureaucratic shit these past two years? I may have lost half my brain cells to the excesses of my youth, but I'm no masochist, boy. Something's off-kilter on planet Serraine, and I intend to put it right. Isn't that what you want?"

Yes, that was what Tynan wanted. Now he also wanted to believe Ugo understood what so few others did or, worse, chose to ignore. So powerfully did he feel the need that his insides quivered with unfamiliar hope.

But before he could reply, the air stirred with ripples of tension, and the elevator doors opened with a soft sigh. He pivoted in place and gasped with everyone else in the room when Kaljin lurched across the elevator threshold.

He only glimpsed the crimson smears on her gray jacket and chalky face, and the fiery wreck of her loosened hair, before she stumbled and crashed to her knees in front of Lieutenant Sindri.

Rage blanked his mind. He stuffed his sidearm into the waist of his trousers and ran to her side.

***

Marista had tried to stay on her feet, but Gaer's sharp blow to the middle of her back propelled her through the elevator doors. She landed hard on her knees. Rubble pierced her skin through the folds of her skirt.

Breath-stealing pain shot through both of her legs. Her thigh muscles quivered then gave out. Groaning, she fell to the floor. With her hands bound in synthaflesh bandages behind her back, she cushioned the fall with her left shoulder. The impact sent another excruciating spasm through her arm and up her neck.

Yet, she welcomed the pain. It blanked her mind to the memory of carnage she had been forced to witness. When a pair of hands pulled her up and out of the protective huddle, she resisted the comfort with every bit of her waning strength.

Resistance proved useless. She felt herself lifted into strong arms and cradled with a tenderness that belied her rescuer's outrage. "What did Gaer do to you?"

She recognized the voice, and then the warm, musky scent that quelled the stench of weapons and death. Tynan.

She forced her eyes open. Tynan's features solidified slowly. His fearsome scowl didn't match the care with which he held her.

She tried to speak. Her tongue stuck to the roof of her mouth. Swallowing nearly choked her.

Tynan jerked his head up. "Why is she bound like this? What did you do to her, Gaer?"

The raider let out an incensed growl. "What did I do to her? Look what she did to me!"

She turned her head toward the solid familiarity of Tynan's chest as Gaer presented the right side of his face. On the raider's cheek, for all the world to see, lay a row of four gouges, her shameful retaliation for Jarrit's murder.

"She talks peace then tries to flay me alive," Gaer accused. "I bound her in self-defense."

Tynan reached around her body and fumbled in vain with the twisted synthaflesh bandage that immobilized her hands. "Kaljin doesn't believe in violence. She wouldn't have struck out unless she had a reason."

The spirited defense of her, though welcome, didn't lessen her guilt.

Gaer grunted a laugh. "She went hysterical when I finished Jarrit."

Tynan stilled his effort to unbind her wrists. His face smoothed into calm even as the muscles in his arms bunched with ready tension. "She was there when you . . .completed procedure?"

Procedure. She remembered the word. Jarrit himself had uttered it, though until now, she hadn't understood its true meaning. "Procedure" meant death in the face capture and interrogation by the enemy.

Tynan lowered his gaze to her face, scanned the length of her body once, and then glared back up at Gaer. "What did you do to Jarrit? Why is Kaljin so bloody?"

Safe in Tynan's custody, she dared look up.

Gaer stiffened and set his arms away from his body as if Tynan physically challenged him. "It was her fault. She couldn't turn off Jarrit's life support. I had to slit his throat. She stood too close to the pod."

"You did what?" Tynan rose from his crouch only a few centimeters before her weight brought him settling back down onto his haunches. "You deserve worse than a few scratches, Gaer."

Gaer didn't back away, though he glanced to the side as if unable to meet the impact of Tynan's glare.

A young raider diverted Gaer's attention, saving the oaf from further humiliation. "Commander, a signal from the shuttle."

Gaer snatched the communication handset from the messenger, spun around, and walked several paces away.

Marista released a shaky sigh of relief.

"Let me try to free your hands. Can you sit?"

When she looked up to answer Tynan's question, his expression conveyed the same serious but gentle concern as his secure embrace. Her heart gave a mysterious double beat, half-thrill, half-fear.

She nodded and allowed him to ease her forward.

"Let me through! No! Hey, let me go!"

Jace's indignant screech distracted her from wondering at the odd sensations Tynan drew from deep inside her. When she turned her head to look, she found the journalist struggling against the hold of two raiders half his age and nearly besting them.

"Let him go," Tynan ordered. When the raiders hesitated, Tynan sharpened the command. "Let him go!"

The raiders obeyed. Freed, Jace lurched forward and sank to his knees in front of her. "Damn, Riss, I hope you feel better than you look." His voice wavered.

"I'm fine." She tried to smile, but she had to bite her lip to keep her eyes from misting.

"Like bloody hell you're fine."

Swallowing hard she avoided looking at her stained skirt. "Jace, please don't say . . ." She took a breath. "Bloody."

"Sorry."

"I'm sorry, too." Tynan's words came from behind as he worked to free her hands. "Gaer should never have done . . ." He paused. ". . . what he did in front of you. He had to, though. Jarrit understood he faced the procedure imperative if we were captured."

The revelation revolted her. "In other words, you wouldn't have let Sindri take you out of here alive, either."

"That's right. Now hold still. I almost have the bandages loose."

The flat, factual tone of his voice angered her. "How can you be so indifferent to death? Of course, now you won't have to worry, will you?" she answered herself as emotion raised her voice. "You'll live to fight another day for Krillians like Gaer."

Tynan's fingers stopped working at the synthaflesh manacles. "Gaer had no right to mistreat you. But he has reason enough to hate. All of us have reason enough."

Next to her, Jace shifted in place. "Riss, there are things I didn't have a chance to tell you before the hearing started."

The hedging in Jace's voice grated her. "I think there's quite a bit you didn't tell me." She jerked her manacled hands out of Tynan's grasp and twisted halfway around to confront him, too. "I had to learn the hard way you're some ex-soldier who deserted then risked his life on a chancy assassination attempt . . ."

"It wasn't an assassination attempt," Tynan cut in.

"At this point I don't care," she snapped. "What else don't I know? Jace said you might be the key to ending the war."

"Maybe I am." He glanced at the journalist. "Maybe I'm not."

"You are the key, if you stay around long enough to let me tell the story for you," Jace insisted.

She widened her eyes in amazement. "Stay? Tynan, are you really going to seek asylum with us?"

He set his mouth in a stern line. "I didn't say that."

Jace stuck out his narrow chin. "Well, you'd better make up your mind fast, boy. The big guy's coming back, and I think he's ready to make a break for open air space."

Sure enough, Gaer stomped toward them. He flashed a series of hand signals to his men around the room. Immediately four of the raiders sprinted to the various portico entrances, dropped to their knees, and began unloading equipment from their rucksacks. The rest of the troops herded all the captives toward the elevator wall.

Tynan rose from his crouch and drew the sidearm from the waist of his trousers. With his legs apart and head high, he looked ready for action.

Jace circled her shoulders with his arm. Though her muscles cramped, she curled her legs beneath her and leaned forward. Her heart raced so fast she could barely draw air.

Gaer pulled to a halt in front of Lieutenant Sindri and glared down his nose. From the way the raider clasped his weapon, he appeared one moment shy of aiming and firing point blank at Sindri's head. "Call off the counterattack, or you die."

Counterattack?

Jace tightened his grip on her shoulders.

Sindri only smirked. "Did you think this outpost with its pitiful Terran security would be an easy mark? We Albians always have a backup plan." He slid his gaze to Tynan. "Or didn't the Bracquar tell you that?"

Gaer aimed and cocked his weapon. "I swear, Albian, I'll kill you."

"I'm ready to die, if it means death to my enemy."

Gaer bellowed and swept the butt of his weapon upward. The metal stock cracked into Sindri's jaw just centimeters from the end of his birth scar. Marista recoiled at the sound of breaking bone, but she couldn't tear her eyes from the sight of Gaer standing over Sindri's still body.

"I'm not as stupid as you believe, Albian," Gaer muttered to the unconscious man. "I have a backup plan, too." He slung the strap of his weapon over his shoulder and pivoted. Before she or anyone around her had time to react, Gaer seized her arm, and yanked her out of Jace's hold and onto her feet. When Jace flailed his arms in defense of her, Gaer kicked him below the ribs.

She cried out as Jace gasped for air and crashed to the floor. When she tried to go to him, the raider whiplashed her to his side, and clenched her arm with such biting force she yelped. "You shielded Tynan once today with you life, Madame Diplomat. Time to do it again. You're going with us."

Twelve

"What? No!"

Gaer cut off Marista's protest by flinging her backward. Unable to use her arms, she reeled and braced for another hard landing. Instead, Tynan stopped her free-fall and locked his arms around her shoulders.

Crushed to Tynan's chest, she felt as much as heard the angry words rumble in her ear. "You can't do this, Gaer. She's a Terran neutral."

"She comes with us."

She snapped her head up and stared into Tynan's face, pleading with her eyes as well as her words. "You can't let him abduct me!"

"He will if he wants to survive, Madame Diplomat," Gaer answered.

Tynan went rigid. "Kaljin is just a low-level aide. She's not worth the trouble."

"Unfortunately for her, she's more undamaged than the others," Gaer snarled, then cast the wounded Albian soldiers a hateful glare. "Besides, Albian commanders won't fire on us and risk killing civilians. Not again."

Again?

Now she understood Gaer's reasoning. He clung to Krillia's unproved contention that Albia destroyed its own civilian transport to provoke a war.

Was that Tynan's motivation as well? Was that why he sought to kidnap Prime Minister Lares and Field Marshall Osten? Did he and the Krillians intend to force some sort of confession from the Albian officials? But why? What exactly did Tynan know? Or think he knew?

Understanding motivations didn't lessen her panic. "Tynan, please make him understand. Taking me is politically and morally indefensible."

Tynan nodded. "She's right, Gaer. Using a Terran as a human shield will earn us nothing but contempt from the nonaligned worlds."

Gaer wasn't moved. "Damn the so-called nonaligned worlds!" He glowered at her. "And damn Earth ten times over! I want a clean escape. The woman comes with us."

Tynan's arm constricted tighter around her body. "Gaer . . ."

Gaer jammed the barrel of his weapon into Tynan's broad shoulder, just centimeters from her face. "Don't test my authority further, Albian. I lead here. She comes with us, even if you stay with Jarrit."

She recoiled from the weapon and the throaty warning. "Tynan, what does he mean?"

Tynan was still as death for a long moment. When he lowered his gaze to her, the cold resignation in his eyes made her shiver. "He means I go and live, or stay and die, like Jarrit."

Rage overrode her panic. "He can't do that!"

Tynan expelled his breath. "He can and he will. This is Gaer's command. I do as he says. For now."

Gaer sneered at the couched threat. "Yes, you do as I say, Captain."

Stunned, she gaped as the Krillian commander turned to the disarmed and disabled Albian soldiers. "Take care not to let any of these nice Terran neutrals leave the portico. My men rigged timed, motion-sensitive explosives to every door. After we leave, no one follows us for thirty standard minutes, or they risk death. Understand?"

As the soldiers nodded, Gaer tossed one of the less wounded Albians a communication device. "Alert your commanders not to interfere with our escape." He lifted the tip of his weapon toward her face. "Madame Diplomat will be our honored guest during the flight home."

She turned a pleading gaze to Tynan and tried to mute her voice. "You can't do this. The Interplanetary Code of Warfare prohibits the taking of civilian hostages. This is a criminal violation . . ."

"Shut her up, Tynan."

Gaer gave that last order, lifted his head in a signal to his men, and marched toward the main entrance.

She sputtered a few more words before Tynan tugged her forward. Astonished at first, she let him hustle her half-a-dozen steps past a semi-conscious Jace, then dug in her heels. "You can't do this. You'll be a war criminal, just like Gaer."

Tynan wrapped one arm around her waist and lifted her off the floor to keep her going. "Trust me, I'm far worse than a war criminal."

The dour confession startled her. "What?"

"Never mind," he snapped. "You're in no position to bargain. Can't you see all those idealistic laws are nothing but hollow phrases now? Assault weapons and death are the reality of war," he whispered and gave her another lift when she balked. "You have no control. Neither do I. Don't make me carry you to the shuttle. Move."

She yelped her refusal, but a wave of hot air took her breath as he dragged her outside into the desert. The sun's glare blinded her. She winced and missed the first two steps leading down to the paved transport driveway.

The awkwardness knocked Tynan off-balance, but he recovered before either of them toppled. Muttering a string of Albian words that sounded oddly similar to Terran obscenities, he scooped her up as if she were weightless and tossed her over his shoulder like a sack of laundry.

With her hands tied behind her back, she had only her voice to use in defense. She huffed out each word as Tynan's shoulder jabbed into her diaphragm with every step he descended. "You're . . . as . . . bad . . . as . . . Gaer. Put . . . me . . . down . . . it's . . . not . . . too . . . late . . ."

"Shut her up, Tynan, or I'll stun her into silence!"

Past the point of terror, she didn't heed Gaer's warning any more than she heeded the tightening of Tynan's grip across the back of her knees. She wiggled and harangued until the roar of engines drowned her out and sand swirled across her face.

She twisted her body just enough to see the gleam of an airship's outer skin. Over the sound of her own choking coughs, she recognized Gaer's muffled shouts as he gave his men orders.

With the raider distracted, she swallowed grits of sand and tried appealing once more to Tynan's conscience. "You say you don't have a choice, but you do. I don't know why you did what you did. But Jace and I will straighten things out. Please, let me go back inside. Go back inside with me . . . Oh!"

His grip on the back of her legs loosened. She seesawed on his shoulder a moment before he set his hands at her waist and pulled her forward. She slithered along the length of his body, the frisson creating ripples of unseemly yearning.

Once again eye to eye with her, Tynan held fast to her waist. The confusion in his eyes didn't match the ferocity of the words he barked over the engine noise. "I want to send you back inside. You don't know how much I need to send you back, and even go with you."

Her heart beat faster with hope . . .

Which he dashed in the next second. "I can't do either. Gaer trusts me less than he trusts you Terrans. If I tell him I want to stay, he will kill me. If I let you go and threaten our chances of a clean escape, he'll kill me then, too." Tynan searched her face, seeming to beseech her with his narrowed, dark eyes. "Try to understand. I've discovered I don't want to die."

Empathy and anger warred inside her. Anger, provoked by desperation, won. Though her knees wobbled and her vision danced with heat-haze, she wrenched from his hold. "I'm not getting on that shuttle! I'm going inside! Shoot me in the back if you want . . ."

Tynan snagged her arm. "Kaljin, stop!"

She whiplashed her body, but didn't free herself. "Let go! I won't let you abduct me!"

Tynan shifted his eyes left.

His inattention to her demand stoked her already white-hot anger. "Do you hear me? Let me go . . ."

"Gaer, don't!"

Tynan shouted the words over the top of her head. She opened her mouth to scream for his full attention.

The cold pressure on the back of her sun-heated neck startled her into silence.

Then she saw stars in a clear, blue Albian sky.

***

Kaljin's green eyes dulled and rolled back in her head. With a whimper of surprise, she collapsed forward. Tynan had half a second to decide whether to catch her limp body, or smash Gaer's smirking mouth with his fist.

His nobler instincts prevailed. He scooped Kaljin up, saving her from crashing to the paved surface. With her dead weight in his arms, he howled his rage.

Gaer laughed. "I told you to shut her up. I won't have my men distracted by her ranting." He leveled his weapon at Tynan. "You already wasted good men on a fool's mission, Albian. I'd just as soon execute you on the spot, so I suggest you don't irritate me further. Load up the cargo, or stay behind for the desert scavengers."

Seething, Tynan struggled to find a centered calm amid the roil of violent impulses. Not more than three days ago he might have called Gaer's bluff. But reckless heroics no longer drove him. He told Kaljin out loud what he suddenly knew to be true. He wanted to live, not merely exist.

And Kaljin needed him, alive and whole. Gaer would take her whether Tynan boarded the escape shuttle or died on the spot. She had risked not only her reputation, but also her very life to protect him. He would not abandon her to Gaer's brutality now.

He glared at the raider. "This isn't finished between us."

Gaer mocked him again with a sour laugh and charged up the boarding ramp into the shuttle. Grinding his teeth, Tynan slung Kaljin's lifeless body back over his shoulder and followed.

Bedlam met him inside. The stink of sweat and stale weapon's fire filled the cabin. Shouts of command and instant obedience drowned out the idling of the powerful engines. Men pushed and shoved and jammed combat equipment behind storage panels to ready for take-off.

The small craft was designed to carry no more than twenty people. He estimated nearly three dozen armed troops crowded the passenger compartment. In a scramble for available room against the bulkhead, three raiders jostled him aside, despite the woman draped over his back.

As he scanned the compartment for a clear space, he realized all the flight couches had been stripped out, probably to accommodate the extra personnel and equipment that had enhanced the success of the rescue mission. He had to locate a sheltered corner to keep Kaljin protected from the forces of take-off and acceleration.

Certain most of the men would try to find space mid-cabin, he headed aft. The further back in the fuselage passengers rode, the bumpier the ride. But comfort didn't matter. Expediency and safety did.

He edged through the milling troops and found a niche in the rear under a bank of flight data sensors. Red, green and yellow lights blinked cheerily at him as he knelt on the metal floor, leaned forward, and let Kaljin's body slide off his shoulder.

He tucked her in an alcove beneath the console reserved for a missing station chair. She didn't twitch, even when he rolled her to the right so he could work at loosening the synthaflesh manacles. Except for the rusty streaks of Jarrit's dried blood, her face lacked warm color. Her long, brown lashes lay dark against pale skin. Only the sluggish jump of pulse at the base of her throat indicated she still lived.

From the looks of it Gaer had stunned her with maximum force. She might be unconscious for a few minutes, or several hours. Chances were better than even that she'd suffer side effects when she woke.

A new burst of fury surged through him. He clawed at the synthaflesh with more vehemence than purpose. A strip of the bandage peeled away along with a narrow swatch of Kaljin's own skin. She jumped in reflex and moaned.

Horrified, he stared down at the slender wrist speckled crimson with beads of fresh blood. He had to calm himself and do it fast before he caused her worse injury.

Inhaling three times he shut his eyes, sat back on his heels, and untangled his thoughts. From beyond the reach of base emotions, he summoned forth his calm center. In moments, his hands no longer trembled.

The floor beneath him shuddered, a warning the engines were powering up for take-off. He lifted his eyelids, took one last cleansing breath, and renewed his efforts to unbind her.

At his gentler touch the bandages seemed to unfurl themselves. Kaljin's arms flopped free. She winced through her stupor as her shoulders resumed their natural position. Carefully, he propped her upright and folded himself into the corner next to her.

The shuddering beneath them intensified to a steady, deep vibration. Kaljin groaned, tried to lift her hand, and failed. Her head lolled side to side, and then came to rest on his shoulder. Silken red hair cascaded down the front of his shirt. The faint, floral scent of the coppery waves, infused with her unique feminine essence, overrode the stench of blood and desert heat. His mental wall of self-protective calm began to crumble.

Besieged with fierce, forbidden yearnings, he froze. How did this woman break through the barriers he'd erected around his emotions? Hunched into a corner against the bulkhead, with a hard metal floor pressed to his backside, he felt no discomfort, only the compulsion to bury his face in her hair and lose himself. Somehow, he understood the simple act would bring him the solace he could not achieve even through the deepest meditation.

Yet, he couldn't surrender himself. He wasn't free to give the depth of caring she needed and deserved. Neither was he ready to receive that gift himself. Honor and duty still demanded too much of him. He had to remember his warrior training, stay focused, guard against distractions. He had promises to keep, priorities to maintain. He couldn't fail.

Not again.

A more powerful vibration ran through the skin of the shuttle. The craft lurched, stilled a moment, and then lurched again. His stomach quivered with the gravitational forces of ascent.

As the shuttle lifted from the ground, he leaned his head against the wall behind him. The Borderlands lay only an hour to the south at best speed. Defying all odds, he'd lived through a catastrophic accident and evaded the ranks of the Never Born. His good fortune almost convinced him to believe Fate had further plans for him. Perhaps one day he'd even have another chance to give up his story to Jace Ugo and see Lares and Osten tried for their crimes.

Beside him, Kaljin stirred. He peered down at the woman, too aware he'd have to give her up in the bargain.

A klaxon blared for a count of three. In reflex, he pulled Kaljin closer. When the noise died, the ship's intercom crackled to life. "Incoming!"

An aerial attack? Impossible! Gaer had warned the Albians he'd taken a civilian hostage. Could the bastards in High Command still be that arrogant?

Or perhaps they were simply too sure of their nonaligned Terran allies.

A deafening explosion reverberated through the compartment. The massive shock wave hit a second later, pitching him forward then back against the bulkhead. He held fast to Kaljin, but couldn't prevent his own head from cracking against the wall behind him.

The sound of bone meeting metal echoed inside his skull until the klaxon screamed again. He shook his head to clear his senses. Though Kaljin wasn't fully aware, she twined her fingers into the front of his shirt. Without thinking, he curled his body over hers and braced them both against the second assault.

An even more violent tremor shot through the bulkhead. A sudden tilt to port wrenched him from Kaljin's side and sent him sprawling away from the alcove. He landed face down on his forearms in the middle of the cabin. Winded, he forced air back into his lungs before levering himself up on shaky arms.

Chaos whirled around him. Someone tripped over his leg, swore, moved on. Someone else shouted orders and boot heels hit the tilted floor. The odor of fried circuitry filled his nose and throat. Only then did he hear the sizzle and pop overhead, and feel the heat of flame.

Fire!

Coughing, he struggled to his knees and squinted into a smoky gray haze. Brilliant frenzied sparks showered down on him, stinging his hands before extinguishing to carbon ash.

Kaljin's shriek spun him around toward the alcove. She lay on her back staring up at the wall. Above her, the electrical panel shot out flame and fumes as it dangled forward trailing destroyed moorings.

Even as the panel swayed above, Kaljin didn't move. Terror widened her eyes. He realized the flames ignited painful childhood memories. Numbed by Gaer's stun, paralyzed by old nightmares, she did nothing to save herself. He had to get her back under the alcove.

Dropping to all fours he crawled to her. But a third jolt sent him sprawling backward. Past the buzzing inside his head, he heard Kaljin's scream over the grating whine and creak of stressed metal.

"Mama, don't go back inside! Mama!"

He flung himself back toward her, reaching the alcove as the panel broke loose and toppled forward. Still on his knees, he shoved her under the workstation, and then scrambled up next to her.

The panel smashed to smoldering, blackened bits on the floor, missing his body by centimeters. Tangled wires hissed and writhed like vengeful vipers. He swatted them away and suffered their sting, but kept danger at bay.

Within seconds three crewmen appeared and tamed the fire with a chemical mist, as he cradled Kaljin in his arms and waited for another jolt.

Instead, the turbulence died, and the craft leveled. He guessed they'd flown outside the range of Albian weaponry. When the ship accelerated with a jerk, Kaljin slumped against his torso.

He tucked his fingers under her chin and lifted her face upward. She was pale and wilted, like a bruised and battered sea flower that was her namesake. "Marista?"

The beautiful name slipped easily off his tongue. She didn't hear the unintentional intimacy. Though her eyelids fluttered, he doubted she was ever really awake, but only tortured by too real memories. How well he understood those haunting mind phantoms.

At least she breathed strong and steady. He'd saved her from further injury this time.

Yes, this time he hadn't failed.

He guided her head down gently to his chest. He could have settled her on the floor now that the danger had passed. She had no sense of time or place. She wouldn't feel the discomfort of hard cold metal beneath her cheek.

But holding her quieted the thunder of his heart and eased his labored breathing. How could this woman rile his emotions one minute and sedate his soul the next? How could he let it happen?

Thirteen

Tynan leashed his impatience with Colonel Alex Varden's measured strides. At this pace, the shuttle landing site still lay a good five minutes away.

Shadows lengthened on the mountain encampment's narrow dirt pathway. The temperature cooled as the Krillian spring afternoon stretched into evening. Nearly two hours had passed since a standard debriefing with Colonel Varden forced him to leave an unconscious Kaljin in the shuttle's tiny but private medical bay.

He controlled another urge to speed ahead. Kaljin's skin had been deathly cold and clammy when he carried her from the aft compartment to the closet-like unit. Worse, the medic, Lieutenant Sem Navarro, didn't inspire confidence. At least fifteen years Tynan's junior, he appeared less like a trained healer than a university student with his fuzzy beard and amiable grin. Tynan had balked at the prospect of entrusting Kaljin's care to such a neophyte.

But he had no choice. He left Kaljin with the youth to attend to his own duty.

". . . and Navarro has offered to find Madame Kaljin a bed in the med-tent, should it be necessary."

Tynan shook himself to attention. "I beg your pardon, Sir?"

If Varden had noticed his distraction he ignored it. "I said if you find this new responsibility too burdensome, Navarro has offered to find Madame Kaljin a bed in the med-tent. However, she would not sleep well there, especially with the number of burn victims who are, to put it mildly, restless."

"That won't be necessary, Sir."

The quick answer made Varden snap his head around.

Tynan surprised himself with the quick, earnest reply, but managed to meet the Colonel's infamous glacial stare. "What happened to Madame Kaljin is partially my fault. I accept my responsibility for her safety and comfort."

Varden measured him with cool precision, and then shifted his gaze forward. "I understand."

Tynan wished he understood the fierce protectiveness he felt toward the unsettling Terran woman.

Varden wasn't going to make it easy for him, though. "For someone who refuses to foist the duty onto someone else, you make the prospect of supervising this woman seem like a death sentence."

Not a death sentence, Tynan knew, but a life sentence of regrets and recriminations.

Varden cut into his ruminations. "I only hope Madame Kaljin will understand the crimes Gaer committed against her are not sanctioned by this command. That man has tried my patience for the last time."

"Yes, let us hope," he echoed as they finally reached the shuttle.

Varden raised a speculative brow, but forged inside. The two men stepped over debris and scattered gear as they headed for the medical bay. Once there, Varden pressed the intercom button outside the closed door to announce their arrival. The door slid aside and Sem Navarro came forward. The medic gave a brief salute to Varden and a formal nod to Tynan, and then moved aside.

One step behind Varden, Tynan looked past the Colonel's shoulder and was relieved to see Kaljin awake and rising slowly from a straight-backed utility chair. As she shifted her apprehensive gaze between him and the Colonel, he noticed the fresh color in her face. She also had showered. Her fiery hair lay loose and still damp about her shoulders. Thick tendrils teased her cheeks and forehead. She'd discarded her ruined uniform, save for the boots, and wore a regulation desert flight suit. The pale gold color was only a shade darker than her smooth skin.

To make the overlarge suit fit, she had cinched the waist tight, then rolled and pegged the excess material at her ankles. She also pushed the long sleeves to just above her elbows. Except for the Diplomatic Corps platinum bar pinned over her heart, and the delicate flower pendant that lay inside the suit's open neckline, she resembled nothing less than a shapely, self-confident rocket jockey.

His pulse thumped a little faster. He told himself he simply felt relief at seeing her revived. A surge of physical desire told him otherwise.

When he gawked too long, she tilted her head. To stem her curiosity, he stepped out of Varden's shadow and dipped his head in recognition. "You look better."

She returned the nod, and then inhaled sharply when she noticed his scorched knuckles. "Were you injured?"

He warned himself not to allow the sweet concern to touch him. Though it pained like fury he made a fist. "It's nothing."

She gaped at his abrupt dismissal of her worry, and he stood straighter. "Madame Kaljin, this is Colonel Alex Varden, our base commandant." He then turned to the senior officer. "Colonel Varden, Marista Kaljin of the Terran Diplomatic Corps."

With a dignified humility he had never before witnessed, the Krillian officer bowed his head. "Madame Kaljin, it is my honor to meet you. I am your contrite and reluctant guardian for, I hope, the short term."

She shifted her attention to Varden and smoothed her frown. "Thank you, Colonel."

When she extended her hand in the Terran gesture of friendly greeting, he noticed the bandage encasing her wrist and felt twin stabs of rage at Gaer and guilt over the abrasions he himself had caused.

Varden clasped her hand for a second. "You'll find our camp accommodations limited but adequate. Tynan informed me your father was a Terran general, so I am sure you understand the utilitarian nature of base life."

She smiled tentatively. "Yes, I lived on a few military outposts in my childhood."

Varden's posture relaxed. "Where did General Kaljin serve, if I may ask?"

"Henson," she corrected him. "My father's name is Anthony Henson."

From his vantage, Tynan thought he noted awe in the jump of the Colonel's brow. "Your father is General Anthony Henson?"

"Yes. Do you know of him?"

Varden flushed beneath his weathered tan. "Madame, fifteen years ago I served with an interplanetary peacekeeping unit on Yonar. Your father's exemplary duty as military governor and his pivotal role in the negotiations between rival Yonaran factions is legendary. His command methods are emulated to this day. His devotion to duty in the face of great personal sacrifice is no less admired."

Tynan knew what that "great personal sacrifice " had been—the lives of his wife and a daughter, not to mention the alienation of his one surviving child.

That survivor now stood rigid, with her mouth frozen into a flat line. "Yes, my father was that military governor. I admit I had no idea he's so highly regarded."

"Yes, Madame," Varden assured her. "Knowing as much now makes me doubly regretful that you have been mistreated by someone under my command. But I trust we've met your immediate needs and that you are feeling better?"

She glanced at Navarro. "I'm much stronger. The Lieutenant has been most attentive and kind. He even brought me a meal. In fact, I'm feeling well enough to return to the outpost at Timetsuara as soon as possible."

Damn, here it came. Tynan held his breath in anticipation of Varden's next words.

"I regret and condemn this situation, Madame," Varden began. "With his abduction and brutal treatment of you, Commander Gaer overstepped his legal and moral authority. On behalf of my government, I offer a formal apology. I assure you, Gaer will be disciplined."

She shook her head. "Colonel, I want no one punished for what happened. Just send me back to the outpost, and I'll consider the matter settled."

Varden paused, and expelled a breath of air. "You are, indeed, gracious. But I am afraid your leaving the base will not be possible at this time."

An uneasy silence enveloped the tiny compartment. Her eyes flickered with confusion, fear, and finally determination all in the space of three heartbeats. "But Sem told me I'm sufficiently recovered."

Navarro stepped forward and laid his hand on her shoulder with a familiarity that made Tynan's stomach seize up. "You are well enough.

You should have few, if any, aftereffects from the stun. But that isn't what Colonel Varden means, Marista."

Sem? Marista? How friendly had these two become in the past two hours? More irritating still, Tynan realized Kaljin avoided looking to him for any comfort or explanation. Instead, she moved closer to Navarro.

What could he expect of her? How often had he made himself accessible to her needs? Never. No wonder she now sought consolation elsewhere. Understanding, however, didn't soothe his bruised ego.

"What exactly do you mean, Colonel?" she asked.

Varden waved his arm at a chair. She looked down at it, then back to Varden and shook her head, declining his invitation to sit.

At her refusal, Varden stiffened. "What I mean, Madame, is that I would like to grant your request, particularly in light of the humanitarian efforts Tynan told me you made on his behalf after his capture."

She did glance his way then. Her surprise was as guileless as the flush that crept up her neck and face. "I did what my job required."

Varden pressed on. "According to Tynan, you went far beyond the limits required of any neutral diplomat. He claims you protected him from Albian extradition. For that, we are all grateful."

He wondered if she saw the gratitude in his eyes. As she slid her gaze away and fixed it on the Colonel, he doubted it.

"I assure you, Madame," Varden continued, "I would return you immediately if it were in my power. At this time, however, I have no such power."

Her eyes widened for one, stark second. Tynan readied himself to spring forward should her knees buckle at the unexpected news. Then he noticed Navarro already held his hand out.

The notion crossed his mind to move to her side and let Navarro know who really had command of the situation. But he dismissed the territorial impulse.

To her credit, she needed no one's help. In a soft voice, reinforced by inner strength he recognized well by now, she challenged the imposing Colonel Varden. "You have no such power? May I ask why not?"

Varden lowered his chin, as if considering his response to her deliberate, determined attitude. "To effect your return to Timetsuara, I would have to see you safely into the custody of the Terran ambassador in the Krillian provincial capital of Sarquis. At this moment, I have no means to transport you south to the city of Bethel, which is just beyond the nearest mountain pass, much less four hundred kilometers farther. I have tried to commandeer an airship from our base at Bethel, but the air guard cannot spare any resources at the moment."

Varden lifted his hand in apparent resignation. "The only other airship I have at my disposal right now is this shuttle. Unfortunately, it sustained enough damage from Albian offensive fire during the escape to strand you here for a few days while repairs are made."

The shock in her eyes didn't dissipate so quickly this time as she pressed her hand to her throat. "The Albians fired on the shuttle?" She glanced up at Tynan, as if begging him to tell her differently. "Gaer ordered Sindri's men to warn the command at Timetsuara I was on board. Was there a miscommunication?"

Tynan finally moved out from behind Varden. "The technicians are still analyzing the intercepted Albian transmissions. But we do know Sindri's guard contacted Timetsuara Command Center. It appears that Albian Command disregarded the warning that you had been taken hostage."

She made a tight fist around her flower pendant. "I can't believe it. Why would the Albians disregard the warning?"

Her inability to accept reality riled him. "Because the hard truth of it is, the life of one Terran diplomat wasn't worth letting Krillian infiltrators escape."

Varden raised his hand to cut off Tynan's angry lecture. Tynan obeyed, but he didn't cower from the horrible realization etched so clearly on her face. She was finally absorbing the truth—humanitarian conventions mattered little to the Albian High Command. Sindri's lack of concern for a captive's human rights was status quo.

It's time you understood, his thoughts railed at her. *It's time you paint over that sun-bright idealism of yours with a darker stain of reality!*

Yet it pained him to watch the glimmer of hope in her eyes dim. He had shocked her rock-solid beliefs as cruelly as Gaer had manhandled her physically.

Varden stepped into the void of stunned silence. "We are still studying the incident, Madame. I will apprise you of all developments. In the meantime, you are in no immediate danger. This camp is located inside Krillian territory, well south of the established demilitarized zone. We are a defensive reconnaissance station only. Our site is well cloaked from Albian ground or air surveillance. While attack is always a possibility, it is unlikely."

With a shaky sigh, she let go of the pendant and lowered her hand to her side. "I understand."

But Tynan wondered if she really did understand.

"I will instruct my men to treat you with all courtesy and respect due your station and neutrality," Varden continued. "Once again, I offer you my sincere apology."

She swallowed and replied in a steadier, more subdued tone. "Thank you, Colonel. Under the circumstances, I can expect no more. Actually, I do have two immediate requests. A friend of mine, Jace Ugo, was injured during the raid. I'd like to find out if he and my other colleagues at the outpost are all right, as well as get word to everyone I'm safe."

Varden nodded crisply. "I will do my best. We do not have such global communication equipment on base. But I will contact Sarquis command and insist on a quick response."

"My aunt and my father back on Earth should be notified, too," she hurried to say. "I know they'll soon learn about what happened and fear the worst."

Varden granted her a thin smile. "Captain Tynan has already taken that initiative, Madame."

Immediately she turned toward him and didn't hide her surprise, relief, and gratitude. The misty glimmer in her green eyes infused him with a heady pride. Had she asked anything of him just then, he would have granted it.

Varden intruded on the moment. "Since we have no formal diplomatic ties to the Albian government, the information is being transmitted through a complicated series of back channels. It may take a few days to contact your family."

Her shoulders sagged. "That long?"

"I can do no better."

She stiffened her back. "I understand. Unfortunately, my father's not a patient man. He may try fighting his way through the red tape with some verbal offensives of his own."

Varden chuckled, another rare occurrence. "A man of deeds, not words. May good fortune be with him. For my part, I will do what I can to speed the process. Is there anything else, Madame?"

She slowly shook her head. "Not at this time. Thank you."

"Very well." Varden made a quarter turn toward Tynan. "I'll leave you in the Captain's care. He has been charged with seeing to your safety and comfort."

Her mouth dropped open. "Tynan? But I thought . . ." Her quick glance at Navarro said exactly what she thought. She'd expected and preferred the company of the young medic.

Checking a surge of anger, Tynan stepped forward to redirect Kaljin's attention to him. "Navarro has other patients to attend. I willingly accepted this duty as repayment for your humanitarian efforts on my behalf."

At his clipped, inelegant words, her expression hardened to stone. Fortunately, Varden interjected himself. "Madame, if you object to Captain Tynan for whatever reason, I'll make other arrangements."

As she stared at him for what seemed an eternity, the air squeezed slowly out of his lungs. Moments before, he had dreaded taking personal responsibility for her. Now he dreaded relinquishing that responsibility if she wished it.

Finally she shook her head. "I have no objection."

But how could she not have objections? How could she trust him, after he'd withheld information from her? After she'd learned of his military background and desertion? After his confession about the plan to kidnap Albian officials?

And certainly after the folly in the storage closet.

"As you wish, Madame," Varden announced. "I'll take my leave and personally oversee your requests."

For a second time she clasped the officer's extended hand. "Thank you, Colonel."

After a smart nod to both Tynan and the medic, Varden turned on his heel, opened the panel door, and disappeared into the corridor.

Tynan fixed his gaze on Navarro. "Are you finished here, Lieutenant?" He didn't mean to sound harsh or dismissive, but managed both.

Amazingly, the young medic cocked his head as if in amusement. "A moment longer, Captain." Navarro turned to her and smiled with an irritating familiarity. "Come to the med-tent tomorrow morning. I'll run a few neurological tests to make sure all your synapses are firing properly."

At the gentle humor, she returned his smile.

Navarro set a vile of tablets into her palm and closed her fingers with his own. When she made no move to disengage herself from the medic, Tynan clenched his jaw until it hurt.

"This medicine is a relaxant," Navarro continued. "It tends to cloud the mind, so use it only if you can't sleep. Otherwise, the aftereffects might skew the tests tomorrow."

"I'll remember. Thank you, Sem."

The medic finally let go of her hand. "You're welcome."

Navarro made a quarter turn and gave Tynan a nod of respect. But Tynan swore he noted another wry crook of the medic's left eyebrow. "Good day, Captain."

"Navarro."

The moment the door panel closed behind the medic, Kaljin said, "You needn't have vented your frustration on Sem."

Already exhausted and soul-battered, he didn't need a scolding about his comportment. "What are talking about?"

She sank into the chair behind her. "I'm talking about your reluctance to take responsibility for me."

Glad she didn't suspect the real reason behind his snarl at the medic, he followed her lead. "The situation does present challenges."

"Well, please don't inconvenience yourself." She stuck out her chin. "I considered it my responsibility to help you, as well. I expect no repayment, sir."

Her scornful formality raised his hackles. "Don't turn stiff and self-righteous on me, Madame."

She didn't stand down. "Well, how am I supposed to address you? Quint, Heir of the Askanati Clan? Captain? How many other identities do you have?"

The truth of her pointed question nettled him. "Too many identities to list right now. Meanwhile, call me what you always have."

"Would that be what I called you to your face or behind your back?"

Her sarcasm surprised him. Then he noticed her rigid posture, not to mention the clench of both fists in her lap, and the tight line of her mouth. In spite of what she'd told Navarro, she hadn't overcome the shocks of the past day.

Stifling a sharp retort, he forced reason into his manner and voice. "After all that's happened to you on my account, I'm not surprised you assume the worst of anything I say or do. But I'm only doing my duty. I mean no insult."

She relaxed only a little. "I'm sure you don't. But I do not want payback for services rendered."

She was asking him to give from his heart, just as she had given to him from the beginning. That, however, he could not do.

"You might have told Varden you had objections to me."

"I might still."

He paced to where she sat and stared down into her upturned face. "The alternative might have been someone as hateful of Terrans as Gaer."

She lowered her eyes to her lap. "Oh."

Her weary resignation stirred his pity, and he crouched to become eye level with her. "You don't have the luxury of dictating how I choose to regard my duty toward you. Like it or not, for whatever reason, you're under my protection."

She lifted her gaze to meet his. "How ironic our positions are so reversed."

He shrugged. "Ironic and regrettable."

"Regrettable? Perhaps you misunderstand me, then. I don't want you to consider me just a duty, but I'm not displeased I'll be with you."

His retort slipped out with too much sarcasm. "How can you be displeased, given the alternative?"

She shook her head. "Given any alternative."

He sat back on his heels. "You can say that after all that's happened between us?"

Her honest gaze held him immobile. "I don't pretend to know what's going on here. After today, and the way the Albians fired on the shuttle . . ." She bit her bottom lip and swallowed hard. "I don't understand anything anymore. I'm almost afraid to try and understand."

Aware he wanted to shield her from any more pain, he shook his head. "This isn't the time . . ."

But she cut him off with a weak lift of her hand. "I'm starting to wonder if you don't have good cause to do what you've done, and feel the way you do about Terrans. In any case, none of this is your fault."

She lowered her eyes again. "And despite your overdeveloped sense of duty, your unwillingness to communicate, and all the clashes between us, I still think you smell right."

He scowled. "Now I don't understand."

A sad smile lifted one corner of her mouth. "Creation help me, neither do I."

He peered into her innocent eyes and wondered if she'd still trust him so unconditionally when she saw the billeting arrangements.

Fourteen

Marista lifted a battery-powered lantern she carried along with her grooming kit to light the path ahead. She felt the stares and heard the murmurings, as Tynan led her through the base camp. The troops were curious about her—the only woman in a men's enclave. A Terran in the midst of suspicious Krillians.

Strange and disorienting, as well, was the new lay of the land. Instead of pale yellow sand dunes beneath her feet, the ground rolled gently while the smell of damp brown soil filled her nose along with the smoke of cook fires. Vegetation had been cleared away to raise the camp, but tangles of stubby brush and wide-bladed foliage competed for space on the steep mountainsides.

The camp itself was confined to a narrow strip of ground between sharp slopes. Billeting tents that probably quartered six to eight soldiers, stood side-by-side, nearly touching. The shabby, patched camouflage material stretched over metal poles appeared barely able to keep out wind and rain. All in all, she guessed the enclave supported no more than a hundred or so troops.

Low, gray-black clouds scudded across the evening sky. Though the base camp lay under a natural rock ledge, in the windward shadow of the Barrier Mountains, cold wind swept down narrow pathways between tents and sliced through her hair as she kept pace with Tynan's long strides.

She snuggled further inside the jacket he had requisitioned from the supply tent. The warm comfort of the coat, however, didn't loosen the icy grip of a new truth. The Albians had fired on the escape shuttle. With her own eyes she'd seen the charred wreckage inside the main cabin, and the ragged scoring on the shuttle's hull.

If Albian High Command, knowing a representative of the Terran Diplomatic Corps was at risk, still used such ruthless and reckless tactics to capture a small group of Krillian commandos, that same Command might have been immoral and cold-blooded enough to shoot down an unarmed civilian transport to incite war.

For two years she'd harbored a secret revulsion toward the Krillian government for destroying the Rising Sun. Now, she couldn't ignore concrete evidence that Gaer, and the Krillians in general, really did have cause to hate.

She cast a furtive, sideways glance at Tynan's handsome profile. What drove him to defect and take up the Krillian cause? Was he a man of implacable conscience or mercenary convenience?

Conscience, she decided almost at once. He attended to duty with nearly obsessive determination, and he held onto his feelings and emotions like a miser with a stash of precious gems.

She had been able to draw a few snippets of information about the enigmatic Captain from Sem Navarro. He'd told her Tynan rarely interacted with anyone in camp. Neither had the Krillian command offered him a military commission commensurate with his previous rank and experience. Even now he wore dark brown civilian leggings, a heavy tan shirt, and a quilted black vest. Only his confident bearing and a new weapons belt at his side indicated he had a right to walk freely through the military camp.

Yet, Sem had said that most of the officers and enlisted men alike addressed him with respect as "Captain," and because of his familiarity with Albian fortifications and battle strategies, he participated in many of the most dangerous reconnaissance missions over the southern desert region.

Questions led to answers and led back to more questions. Who was this compelling, self-contained, and oddly vulnerable man who had spurned her help and compassion when he needed it most, yet now burdened himself with the responsibility for her care and safety?

His excuse was duty, but she knew he had issued orders for her sake above and beyond the call of that duty. The young medic had confided that Tynan insisted she receive Sem's full, individual attention and treatment in the shuttle's privacy.

Oblivious to her brooding silence, Tynan strode at her side, eyes forward, occasionally shifting the bedroll tucked loosely under his arm.

"Sem told me we're in the Borderlands, south of Zanfer," she finally said to divert her mind from frustrating questions.

He nodded without glancing at her. "The desert lays to the north and east. The Krillian continent spreads out to the south."

"This location seems adequate and defensible."

"It is."

When he glanced over and tilted his head in question she shrugged. "You forget. I've been around a few military installations in my life. I learned things I never wanted or needed to know."

"So the dirt, inedible rations, cold showers and hard ground will seem like home?"

She sniffed a laugh. "More than you'd ever imagine."

His smirk softened. "Your spirits are better. Good."

She smiled with a bravado she didn't feel. "You don't have to keep an eye on me. I won't sink into a depression or dissolve into hysterical tears."

He cast her a long, pensive look. "I didn't expect either from you."

Aiming the lantern light at the ground, she faced forward. "I think you're not sure what to expect. But I'm more of a realist than you believe. I go forward. I don't look back. And," she emphasized, "I do not become hysterical."

"No, I'm sure you don't."

He was cajoling her, something she didn't want or need. "I don't cry over misfortune, Tynan. I haven't since I was a child. Tears solve nothing and hinder reason."

"A very wise conclusion for someone to make when still a child."

"Don't patronize me. I had to grow up fast." A breath of air cooled her irritation. "Besides, it was simply a case of mind over matter."

He grinned almost sheepishly. "As in, 'If you don't mind, it doesn't matter?'"

Caught off guard, she let slip a smile. "Yes, my father used to say that all the time, especially after a transfer from one drab base camp to another even worse."

"I think it must be a universal military axiom, applicable in any or all difficult situations," he quipped.

Unexpected nostalgia gripped her. Perhaps the drift of the conversation triggered bittersweet memories, or perhaps the familiarity of sites and sounds and smells of a military base camp caused it. For whatever reason, and for only a split second, she yearned to see and touch her father again.

A shiver shook her body, one she couldn't blame on the snapping wind. Tamping down the ridiculous longings of a childhood lost, she lifted her chin. "I learned the lesson well. That's probably why I won't give up easily."

"Determination is a virtue."

"Really?" she bantered. "Weren't you the one who likened me to a kae-a-tek with its prey?"

"Only because you were determined to make me bend to your will."

He gave her an opening, and she walked through it. "Do you still believe I was wrong to help you?"

"In retrospect, perhaps you were right."

"Perhaps?"

He raised a brow. "Perhaps not."

She decided to take the jest in stride, since his lighter tone soothed her taut nerves.

"Did your father teach you anything about battlefield maneuvers?" he asked.

"Such as?"

His expression lost some of its animation. "Such as tactical retreat from a hopeless situation instead of fully engaging a better armed opponent."

"Gaer?" she guessed.

"Yes. Though he deserved what you did to his face, he isn't likely to forget or forgive."

Her cheeks heated. "I appreciate your defense of me, but I should have known better than to answer violence with violence."

"He pushed you beyond reason," he growled. "But if he runs true to character, he won't accept your apology or admit wrong. Make sure your path doesn't cross his any time soon."

The cold evening air fanned the sting of chagrin. "With one, angry swipe of my hand I made a lifelong enemy."

"Not just one enemy. Half the men in this camp are loyal to Gaer."

He answered her questioning frown with a scowl. "Gaer rose through the ranks to become a field commander. The men admire him for that. He's one of them. Not a politician. Not a schooled officer. He's suffered personal losses, like so many of the others he commands. Now he faces court martial and possible imprisonment for violation of Interplanetary Conventions. At the least, Varden will break him down two ranks. That doesn't set well with the troops."

"I meant what I said to Colonel Varden," she insisted. "I don't want retribution for what happened. I just want to go home."

He nearly strangled the sleeping bag under his arm. "You may not want Gaer disciplined, but I'm not so willing to forgive his reckless disregard for your life." He paused. "Or mine."

His righteous fury in her defense touched her heart. In a soft voice she said, "I'm not fit to judge what did or didn't happen to the shuttle or why. I don't remember much after the stun."

"Gaer probably had his weapon on maximum setting," he said, his tone as unyielding as his expression. "A jolt like that scrambles memory. Don't be surprised if you never remember what happened. That might be for the best."

The undercurrent of anger in his words deepened her curiosity. "Maybe, though, I'd like to know how you hurt your hand."

Tynan glanced over at her and shifted the bedroll from one arm to the other before answering. "The shuttle took a solid hit aft, where you and I were. An electrical panel blew, sparked, and flamed out before it fell down in front of us."

A rush of fiery color and sound whooshed through her mind, but didn't slow enough to root. She held her breath, listening to the tale, willing herself not to tremble. "And?" she prodded when he didn't continue.

"You were under a counter top against the hull," he said, measuring his words. "I didn't fit underneath all the way and pushed the panel out into the cabin to keep the fire away from me." He smirked. "I should have used my foot."

She tried to smile at the self-deprecating humor, but instead swallowed in a too-tight throat. "I'm sorry you were burned, but I thank you."

"For what? I shoved away falling debris."

"I didn't get under the counter myself," she reasoned. "You must have put me there, against the wall in the most protected position, and left yourself at risk."

"I didn't know I'd be at risk. I acted instinctively."

He refused to accept her appreciation. She refused to let it pass. "Then my thanks to your remarkable instincts."

"If my instincts had been sharper, I would have stood my ground and refused to let Gaer take you from the outpost," he argued. "I had hoped . . ." He gritted his teeth. "No, I should have known High Command would have no consideration for your safety. The Albians have conducted this whole damn war on the basis of shoot first, explain later." He frowned. "Remember, I was one of them."

"Perhaps one of them by heritage and profession, but not by character," she countered.

"Don't be so sure."

The warning lacked heart. She almost smiled, but she didn't want to insult the prickly pride of a man who had proven himself her protector more than once today.

"You definitely have information Jace wants," she prodded. "He doesn't chase fanciful leads."

"What I know may have been important once," he breathed out with a curious mix of sadness and frustration. "Now, it's old and stale and of little consequence. Nothing can be changed."

He evaded her probes with his clipped answers. Based on past experience, she knew a frontal assault would fail, and she decided to outflank his defenses with an indirect attack. "So, are you going to make another attempt to abduct Lares and Osten?"

"Another attempt would be futile," he retorted as if she should know better. "The first time we had an element of surprise. Now, all civilian and military High Command will have triple security. Lares and Osten will doubtless send their families off-world." A new tightness, neither anger or frustration, pulled at his jaw. "Such precautions are standard operating procedure."

She wanted to probe the terrible new tension in his manner, but she didn't really know what to ask. "Maybe after this attempt there will be questions."

He turned fierce dark eyes on her. "The Albians will deny the attempt happened."

"But Madame Bierich and the other staff at the outpost heard what you said . . ."

"Earth will instruct them to be circumspect in their analysis of the due process hearing and subsequent events," he cut in, his voice cold and analytical.

"Jace won't keep quiet," she argued.

"He'll find his sources dried up, and his reports dismissed, or denied, or both," Tynan answered, and searched her face. "The past will repeat itself." He drew a harsh breath. "Diplomatic ambiguity meant to deny an atrocity."

"You mean the destruction of the Rising Sun."

"Krillia has to answer for her own crimes," he stated. "But taking down the Rising Sun isn't one of them. Albia blew that shuttle out of the sky, just as Krillia always claimed."

After her experience with Albian disregard for civilian life, she had her own suspicions now, too. Yet she couldn't quite believe her government would sanction a lie about such a gruesome war crime.

"And you say you have proof," she pressed. "But why would Earth be a partner in such an awful deception?"

"I already told you this isn't the time . . ."

"This is very much the time," she persisted. "Explain yourself."

He glared at her. She didn't flinch. When he quickened his already brisk pace, she kept up, though exhaustion weighted her limbs. Her will finally overcame his reticence.

"All right, Little Diplomat," he snapped. "The truth. Your neutral government has reasons to accept Albia's account. The trade embargo Earth imposed on both sides is nothing but a cloak of respectability to conceal profiteering. Albia still ships its raw mineral wealth off-world. Surrogate agencies working on behalf of Terran industrial consortiums pay premium prices for the ores. Krillia has no such strategic resources to barter. Therefore Krillia had no influence at the bargaining table. It was all part of the master Albian plan."

She gaped in disbelief. "You're saying Earth sold her influence at the peace negotiations?"

He nodded once. "Ugo knows the truth. Ask him. Albia's war machine is primarily financed by Terran greed. Your Earth supports a government that kills its own people to steal land."

Her stomach turned upside down along with her most cherished beliefs. If she accepted what Tynan claimed, her neutrality was a sham, and the government she represented a fraud. No wonder he despised Terrans in general and diplomats in particular.

And Jace did know something about the transport incident. He had even wondered aloud "who the bad guys really are."

While her intuition accepted what Tynan said, her reason refused to believe she served the cause of dishonesty and avarice that had led to bloodshed. "But, Tynan . . ."

He stopped dead in his tracks. "Enough. I have no wish to debate further or justify myself."

She pulled to a halt beside him. "I have to understand."

"Then ask your friend Ugo for details."

Unwilling to be put off, she lifted the lantern higher and peered into his face. "I need to understand you."

His eyes flickered with surprise, and then hardened to black marble. "You understand as much as you need to understand."

"You know I won't accept that. But if you're bent on arguing, let's find someplace warmer."

He hitched a brow. Only then did she notice the apex of a pitched roof that rose a few centimeters above his head. She angled the lantern and let the light define the edges of the structure. Far smaller than the other tents, this one seemed at least sturdier and less patched.

Evening shadow concealed his exact expression, but he sounded vaguely triumphant. "As you wish, Madame." He grabbed one end of the front entrance flap and yanked it upward. As he did so, the faint odor of mustiness, dirt, and stale air wafted out at her. "Someplace warmer. Your quarters."

Fine particles of flying dust lodged in her throat. She coughed, and wondered for a moment if it wasn't time for one of those "tactical retreats."

He spoke over her sputtering. "We weren't prepared for distinguished company. This is the only shelter available." He scanned the sky. Encroaching darkness didn't fully obscure the baggy dark clouds. "I think we arrived just in time."

She wrinkled her nose. "I'm sure my aunt and I have camped for recreation in worse conditions than this. At the moment, however, I can't remember exactly when."

"Then you won't mind that the tent is even smaller inside than it appears on the outside."

She wanted to ask if it was dirtier, too, but decided she shouldn't mock her only protection from the elements. "Some shelter is better than no shelter at all."

"Another quote from General Anthony Henson?"

The barb renewed the ache of longing she felt earlier, but she cleared the emotion from her voice. "No, an original thought. I do have a few." She ducked under his arm and entered the tent.

The odors inside didn't hang quite so heavy. Perhaps opening the flap had let most of the staleness escape. Then she noticed a soft whistle and realized the tent had discrete vents for air exchange. Tynan relieved her of the lantern and hung it on a hook attached to the roof support pole. Slowly, she pivoted in place to scan her new quarters.

The tent had been pitched long ago, she guessed, since the ground lay trampled bare and smooth beneath her feet. The entire shelter measured no more than two meters wide by three meters long. The top of Tynan's head nearly touched the roof's peak.

At the back wall stood a mess-station, part food storage box and part cook stove. Next to that was a meter high water purification tank with a metal cup dangling from the spigot. A stored bedroll, similar to the one Tynan carried, along with a bulging rucksack and a small, oblong storage box, lay in the left back corner.

She sighed inwardly with relief and glanced up at Tynan. "There's more than enough room."

"Good." He then thrust the bedroll at her.

She juggled the bundle and her grooming kit, and then glanced to the left corner. "There's already one of these here."

He sauntered past her to the corner, grabbed the bedding and came back. "This one is mine."

"Yours?" Suddenly, she understood. "This is your tent? You've given up your quarters for me?"

He answered with a careless shrug.

Though grateful for his generosity, she frowned. "Where are you going to sleep?"

He dropped his bedroll. "Right here."

Fifteen

Tynan didn't know whether Kaljin would yell at him or pass out from holding her breath. Her eyes were liquid green and opened so wide her lashes nearly touched her brows. Slashes of red marked her pallid cheeks. In the same instant she appeared indignant and bewildered—a woman to be reckoned with and comforted.

He could handle her outrage with bravado. The fragility evident in the tremor of her lower lip, however, confounded his wits. Silently he begged her not to shatter.

Nothing she said or did would change the sleeping accommodations. He'd do his duty the best way he knew how, with the tools at hand.

As if she read his thoughts, she blinked away the worst of her shock. "Aren't you taking the orders to personally protect me a bit too literally?"

The grit in her voice relieved him of the need to treat her gently. "No more literally than you did at the outpost."

She clutched the bedroll tighter. "I never bedded down with you."

He smiled with honest amusement. "I offered."

Her face went scarlet, but she held her ground as she let out an exasperated breath. "So you did. But that's not what I meant. I simply don't see how this . . . this situation can work."

"Mind over matter," he taunted.

"Well I do mind. And it does matter." She tapped her foot on the dirt floor. "There's barely room for one person in here."

As if he couldn't see that for himself. He needed sleep. Plenty of it. Having to share a small tent with a woman whose mere presence shorted his mental circuitry made rest uncertain at best.

To disguise his uneasiness, he kicked his bedroll with the heel of his boot and sent it into the tent wall behind him. "I like the accommodations no better than you, but we'll make room. Otherwise one of us will have to sleep outside. With a storm brewing, I swear it won't be me."

As if to emphasize his point, a rush of wind set the roof snapping. Kaljin lifted her eyes and watched the tent's roof ripple frantically. When her shoulders sagged, he knew she'd accepted the inevitable. "Very well. We'll make room."

Setting her mouth into a prim line, she sank to the ground and began unfastening her bedroll. He suddenly resented her sullen resignation. He'd given her a boon, after all. Now he had a mind to tell her she could bunk in the med-tent and listen to groaning all night.

Then he remembered the easy familiarity that flowed between her and Navarro, and he bit back the retort. A stab of jealousy alarmed him more than the forced intimacy of the billeting arrangement. Bemusement shortened his temper. "You said you trusted me."

She didn't look up as she smoothed the length of the bedroll. "I do."

Her clipped reply wasn't convincing.

"If you're thinking of what happened after you took me to Jarrit . . ."

She snapped her head up. "I'm not."

But she tore her gaze away from his too fast and gave too much attention to the position of her thermal blanket.

He dropped to his knees in front of her. "Your eyes give you away, Little Diplomat. I think you need more assurance than just my words."

She rolled those innocent, beguiling eyes and sat back on her heels. "For Creation's sake, I told you . . ." She paused when he reached for the sheath that hung on his weapon's belt. "What are you doing?"

He unsheathed his long, wide combat knife and drove it into the dirt between them. She sucked in a breath, as if he'd plunged the weapon into her heart instead. "I'm setting a boundary. I behaved dishonorably toward you in the storage closet. Now I mean to repair that breach of trust."

While she stared at the few centimeters of blade that remained above ground, he lifted one knee, propped his arms on the pyramid, and then leaned forward. "There is an old desert tradition observed whenever Albian nomads make camp. Clans lay down their weapons between tents to mark boundaries. This is done not just as a warning, but as a vow of honor that one clan will not violate the possessions or territory of another. On the blade of my weapon, I swear I will not cross the boundary between us."

Her gaze still riveted to the knife, she gripped the edges of the thermal blanket so hard the skin over her knuckles went white. "The Albian nomads didn't invent that symbolism, Tynan. In Terran mythology two people named Tristan and Isolde did the same thing millennia ago."

He allowed her a skewed smile. "We are all human, after all. Perhaps my people borrowed the symbolism. You'll have to tell me the story sometime."

His good intentions obviously didn't ease her. The tremble in her hands matched the quiver in her voice. "I'll tell you this much. The story doesn't have a happy ending."

He shook his head. "We aren't mythical people."

"Neither are we desert nomads," she retorted. "This symbolic melodrama is pointless. Put the knife away. Please."

She struggled to breathe, and her body shook as if she'd taken a chill. Adrenaline overload, he guessed. He'd witnessed it often in the field, and been a victim himself many times. Neither the mind nor the body adjusts fast enough to trauma and stress. After a day of mental and physical upheaval this final shock of learning she had to billet with him had probably triggered her overreaction.

"Put the knife away, Tynan! Do it now!"

No, he suddenly realized, the reality of bunking with him tonight wasn't the trigger. It was the knife, so much like the one Gaer used to kill Jarrit.

He grasped the weapon by its handle and yanked it from the ground. When it gave, she started. He held out his free hand, palm side forward. "I'm sorry. I . . . I was thoughtless."

As he slowly sheathed and secured the weapon, she started at him as if he'd spoken nonsense.

"I didn't mean to upset you," he murmured, holding out both hands.

A warning from his soul held him in check. Stay back from her, you fool! Talk to her. Soothe her with your words, not your hands. Don't touch her!

Though she riveted her gaze on him, he knew she looked right through him. "I wanted to stop Gaer, but everything happened too fast," she muttered. "He took out his knife. I couldn't move. When he turned to Jarrit . . ."

Blinking away the daze, she tried to focus on his face. "The blood flew everywhere." She lifted two trembling fingers to her cheek. "It felt warm on my face. Jarrit died, quick and quiet. I think I screamed."

He ached for her—for the pain in her heart, and for the shattering of her control.

Don't touch her . . .

He leaned forward on both knees. "You couldn't have stopped Gaer. He had his orders."

"To kill in cold blood?" The words exploded at him through her clenched teeth.

Poor little Terran. She'd never witnessed such bloody violence.

He breathed slowly and evenly to keep himself calm. "To kill in mercy."

She shrank away from him, but he pressed his explanation. "Jarrit had only a few days at most to live. If Gaer had spared him, Albian command would have tried to prolong Jarrit's life to interrogate him. That would have been worse than a thousand deaths."

"One choice was no better than the other."

"No, Little Diplomat. But that's the reality of war."

Liquid pooled in her eyes and spilled onto her cheeks. She frowned, as if bewildered by the wetness tracking down her face. Yet, as soon as she swiped at the tears with the back of her hand more flowed. She drew in an impatient breath that sounded more like a dry sob.

Don't touch her . . .

He laid his hand on her shoulder. "Kaljin?"

She stared at her damp fingertips. "I never cry."

"Of course, you don't." Ignoring the whine inside his head, he cupped his hand over her cheek. Hot tears slicked his palm, and trickled over his knuckles. A jolt of fiery primal awareness shot up his arm, then through his body, heating him to the core of his soul. The voice of warning faded to a whisper.

"Marista?"

Her given name slipped off his tongue, surprising him as much as it did her. She peered up at him through a prism of tears and bit down on her quivering bottom lip.

Confused by his own reaction, he shrugged. "I . . . I don't know what to say or do. Should I call Navarro?"

She shook her head and closed her eyes. The motion pressed her smooth cheek further into his hand. Thick lashes fluttered feather light against the tip of his thumb.

His skin pulsed with a hot need that had nothing to do with compassion. His knees touched hers on the ground. With little effort and, he suspected, little persuasion, he could take her into his arms and finish what he had started in the storage closet. He could blank her mind for a while, and find a pleasing outlet for his own needs.

But was mind-numbing all she needed from him? And how much did he dare give without losing himself?

Push her away! Do it now!

As if she heard his inner voice, she laid her hand over his and pulled it slowly from her cheek. She blinked several times to expel the last of the wetness from her eyes and straightened. "I think everything that happened today finally caught up with me. I'm fine now. Thank you."

He drew back as she dried her face with the edge of the thermal blanket. Her innocent gratitude mocked his conscience. If she knew how he'd fantasized comforting her, he'd be wearing scars identical to Gaer's.

Clearing his throat didn't clear the gruffness from his voice. "Why are you thanking me?"

She laid her hands in her lap. "For taking on the responsibility for me. For trying to contact my father. For being here just now." She managed a shaky smile. "For finally calling me Marista."

His gut wrenched. He should have listened to the nagging voice inside his head. But no, he'd crossed into enemy territory ill-equipped and unprepared. Now he had to make a desperate retreat.

Setting his jaw and his will, he rocked backward, found his balance, and stood. The needle sharp pain of renewed blood circulation in his legs lent an edge to his words that he might not have otherwise managed. "Don't get used to it. A war zone is no place to strike up a friendship. I did what I had to do."

She stared up at him, her lashes still clumped by tears, but her eyes clear and searching. "Yes, of course, you did," she finally said with a touch of irony that stiffened his spine. "I'm sorry I lost control."

Too aware that some of her tears still clung to his palm he flicked his hand in dismissal. "Everyone loses control."

"Do you?"

She might have kicked him in the stomach, considering the rush of air from his lungs. If she only knew how close he'd come to losing control just minutes ago.

"I meditate," he snapped back.

After a pensive moment, she nodded. "Oh, yes, meditation. Perhaps I should allow you to teach me."

"There isn't time," he rushed to tell her. "I studied and practiced for years with a high master."

Shadowy images of placid blue eyes, long dark hair, and a knowing smile fluttered through his thoughts. He thumbed the narrow gold band circling the last finger of his left hand.

"Tynan?"

A froth of red curls came back into focus. The sudden realization that Kaljin was no mind phantom—that he could reach out just a little and caress her hair, then set his mouth to the curve of her lips—spurred him into action.

He retreated a step. The top of his head brushed against the pitched angle of the tent roof. "You should sleep. I'll go outside and give you privacy to settle in. I won't be far. Call if you need me."

He could no longer face her, the demons of his past, or the uncertainty of his future. Without waiting for a reply, he fled into the bracing night air.

Had he not promised to stay close to the tent, he would have taken a hard sprint around the camp's inner perimeter. He lifted his face to the sky, imagining the harsh flow of cold air over his heated face. The strain of his arms and legs as he pumped his muscles. The slow erasure of images from his overtaxed mind.

He glanced over his shoulder at the tent. A sliver of light leaked from a small tear in a front corner seam, but he saw no movement. The heavy tent material itself prevented the casting of shadows on the walls.

How he ached to pull Kaljin into his arms, cradle her, care for her. The rush of blood to his face warned him that his carnal desire hadn't dissipated. Caressing her cheek felt so good, so right. It had been too long since he'd touched or been touched by such tenderness.

Then he realized the fingers of his right hand tugged and twisted at the gold ring he wore. The past, solid and permanent like the ring, reproached his conscience, just as it determined his fate. Now that the Albians knew he was alive and possessed "special" information, he would become the target of Kill Squads. He was no more useful to a woman in need of compassion than to the Krillian war effort.

He trudged to a nearby stone ledge, scaled the meter high wall with instinctive effort, and lay face-up on the hard rock. Unbroken black hovered above him. The air felt oppressive with humidity. Wind cut through his heavy vest.

Closing his eyes he breathed deeply and found his quiet center. By degrees he grew impervious to the bite of the wind, the weight of the air, and the hardness of rock grinding against his spine. His heartbeat slowed. A foggy, gray ether damped his thoughts.

He languished in that blissful void until a raindrop plopped on his forehead. Reluctantly, he hefted himself up, slid off the ledge, and made his way back to the tent. Before lifting the entrance flap, he paused. "Kaljin, it's starting to rain. I'm coming back inside."

She didn't answer. Perhaps she didn't hear him over the wind. Yet, he didn't dare call any louder for fear of waking the men already bedded down in neighboring tents.

Cautiously, he lifted the flap. "Kaljin?"

A gust of wind sent the lantern swinging on the pole hook. Light and shadow chased each other over the walls and ceiling until he scrambled inside and secured the entrance. Only then did he look down. The sight of her undid his meditative calm.

The bedding swallowed her whole. She lay fast asleep on her side, facing the center, her knees tucked up to her waist beneath the drape of the bedroll. Only a frame of sleep-rumpled curls escaped the makeshift hood she'd made of her thermal blanket. Snug and warmed by her own body heat, her cheeks and lips glowed a rich, bright pink. The ridge of her brown lashes didn't quite hide the smudges of blue beneath her eyes. Neither his entrance nor the cold gust of air caused her lids to so much as flutter.

Beautiful. Trusting. Alone. Afraid.

The words clattered around in his mind as he gawked at her. He sensed he was violating her privacy, but he didn't have the will or desire to turn away. How in the name of common sense had he ever believed he could allow this woman under his roof and still have a good night's sleep?

The wind howled, and rain spattered the roof in a rapid-fire tattoo. She stirred and breathed out a yearning sigh that beckoned him. His pulse thrummed in time with the rainfall.

Turn away! Turn your back! Turn out the light and escape inside yourself!

Finally he listened to the voice, reached up and turned off the lantern. In pitch darkness he climbed into his cold bedroll.

Sleep eluded him. When the storm winds died and rain no longer pounded the roof, the distraction of Kaljin's soft sleep-sighs kept him tossing and turning.

Exhaustion finally claimed him.

***

Tynan started awake in the pre-dawn gloom to the sound of early morning camp noises, and with an urgent heat pulsing through his groin. Each breath he drew brought with it the heavy, warm fragrance of a woman.

He recognized Kaljin's scent at the same instant he realized her body was pressed against his entire length beneath their tangled blankets. Blinking the grogginess from his eyes, he gathered his scattered thoughts. The night had been cold. He supposed that, with less than a meter separating their bodies, both of them had sought out warmth.

The reason didn't really matter. As his mind focused and senses quickened, he became aware of her feathery soft curls snagged on the whiskers under his chin, and her face burrowed into his shoulder. Her fingers lay open and slack near his waist in the shallow valley between their bodies, hijacking the remains of his self-control. He stifled a groan, as a full erection strained for release against the front placket of his leggings.

He had to untangle himself before she woke up and screamed in defense of her honor.

He eased his torso up, but his arm, propped above her head, had gone dead and useless. Swearing to himself, he moved his fingers frantically to restore circulation.

She stirred, unaware in her sleep that her sinuous movement brought him to the edge of his already fragile willpower. She lifted her face from his shoulder and tipped her chin upward. For an instant before she turned to her back, her slumber-warmed, full mouth brushed his mouth, and he forgot to breathe.

How he wanted to take her under him, drive hard and hot inside her, and hear her cry of pleasure before he released himself. He'd spent too many nights alone with nothing but cherished memories. He craved the real, supple warmth of a woman's embrace—Marista Kaljin's embrace.

His mind whirled with possibilities. What effort would it take to coax her into willingness? He'd already seen desire for him flare in her green eyes, and he'd sensed the promise of surrender in the one kiss they'd already shared. With soft, seductive words and touches he could waken and woo her. When she gave her consent, he'd pleasure her in a dozen different ways before satisfying himself. Then . . .

Then what? Would she be content to share his bedroll until he delivered her safe to the Terran embassy at Sarquis? Would she smile and wave farewell as he resumed his quest for personal redemption and revenge? Could he leave once he tasted the richness of life again?

He knew the answers and muttered a curse. Marista Kaljin wasn't the kind of woman to give herself easily or cheaply. He wouldn't have wanted her if she'd been another way. She'd expect something of him in return, some deeper pledge of feeling, as was her right. He might have been pleased to oblige her, too.

But neither those feelings nor a future were his to promise. Not now. Perhaps not ever.

Prickles ran up his arm as he levered up on his elbow and slithered backward to his side of the tent. For several trembling heartbeats he watched her sleep on her back, her face turned toward him, her hand over her breast.

He couldn't let this folly happen again.

Scrubbing his face with the heels of his hands, he willed away the evidence of his desire and pushed off the ground. With fists jammed into his waist he drew in a shuddering breath and retrieved his harshest command voice.

"Kaljin, get up. It's daybreak."

Sixteen

The portable space heater's edge jammed into Tynan's left hip and seemed to weigh five kilograms more with every step he took. Worse, the rucksack slung over his shoulder felt poised to slip off any minute, and the fingers of his right hand were numb from gripping the two collapsible camp chairs tucked under his arm.

He ignored the discomfort as guilt drove him forward. He'd treated Kaljin badly this morning by ordering her to wake up, eat her rations, and hurry through the hygiene station as if she were some raw recruit under his command.

She bristled but checked her annoyance, then requested he take her to Varden so she could ask leniency for Gaer. Muttering something about soft-headed Terrans, he complied. Afterward he took her to Lieutenant Navarro for a follow-up neural examination. Before leaving her in the medic's care, he'd announced he'd posted a guard to escort her back to the tent and stay with her until he returned from his scheduled daily duties.

Then, like a coward, he'd turned and fled before she let loose the anger flashing in her eyes.

Neither the exhaustion nor the shame that lay at the root of his foul morning mood excused him. He had punished her out of frustration and self-loathing though she had almost been the victim of his rogue carnal impulses.

Sweat broke out on his forehead. He'd grappled with his conscience most of the morning, using every mind-relaxation technique he knew, and a few he hadn't tried before, to regain some peace of mind. As midday approached, his guilt still churned until he decided on a course of direct action.

Thus, he'd requisitioned the space heater, a luxury he'd never sought for himself during the cold mountain nights. If it meant keeping Kaljin on her side of the tent, he'd crank up the thermostat to produce mid-summer desert temperatures.

The other gear he lugged across camp were tokens of apology for his gruffness and the liberties he'd almost taken without her knowledge. The chair would keep her off the hard, cold ground. There were two extra changes of clothes for her in the rucksack, along with several book discs and a portable scan reader to fill daylight's long hours. He'd even managed to requisition a few pieces of fresh fruit from the mess tent to supplement his monotonous choice of rations.

Better yet, he could tell her Varden might receive word soon about Jace Ugo. Smiling in anticipation of her pleasure with his peace offerings and her forgiveness of his morning temper, he rounded the last corner and stopped dead in his tracks.

Where was the soldier he'd detailed to escort and guard Kaljin? Worse, why did the tent's entrance flap lay wide open and secured against the roof like an invitation for guests?

Despite the dead weight under his arms he lunged into the tent. But he skidded to a dusty stop before colliding with a footlocker from which spewed out three different sets of camouflage fatigues.

Kaljin knelt in front of the locker, her hands suspended in mid-air as she wove her hair into a single, long plait at the back of her head. Behind her, on his smaller storage box, stood the cup from his water purification unit stuffed with tiny purple and red flowers.

She jumped and pressed a hand to her throat. "Mother Creation, Tynan, you scared me! What's wrong?"

He tried not to gawk or raise his voice. "What's wrong? The tent's wide open."

She wrinkled her nose which, he noted, looked a bit sun reddened. "I'm letting in some air. It smells stale in here."

He glared at her sunburned nose. "Where is the guard?"

"I dismissed him."

"You what?"

She stiffened at his growl. "Actually Sem dismissed the guard. We didn't need him."

He dropped the chairs with a clatter, and the rucksack on top of them. Though he set down the space heater more carefully, it still hit ground with a thud. "Why didn't you and Navarro need the guard?"

The ridge of her cheekbones colored to match the bridge of her nose. "Because after my check-up I stayed in the med-tent talking to some of the patients. Then Sem had free time, so he took me to supply and requisitioned some things I might need during my stay here. He even found me some reading material."

The rucksack, stuffed with his peace offerings, seemed to lay heavier against his leg. "Really?"

She frowned warily. "Yes, really. I was perfectly safe with Sem. Besides, I don't see why I needed a guard in the first place . . ."

"What are those flowers doing in my cup?"

At his snarled interruption, she set her hand on her hip. "On our way back here to the tent I admired some wildflowers growing out of the rocks. Sem pulled a few out for me. Frankly they brighten up this place. But I'll find another vase if you wish."

"I'd appreciate that."

She raised a brow. "Very well."

Kaljin sprang off the ground so fast she loosened the bottom third of the braid hanging down her back. In a blur of motion she snatched the flowers in a stranglehold, grabbed the cup, and stomped past him to the tent entrance. After tossing the wastewater, she whirled in place and shoved the cup at him. "Happy?"

He stared at the cup. His anticipation from only a few minutes before now felt just as dry and empty. "No, I'm not happy!"

He ripped the cup from her grasp and threw it into the corner. "I told you to come back to the tent and stay here. You disobeyed me!"

Her green eyes sparked with fury. "Has my status changed without my knowledge, Captain? Am I no longer your guest but a prisoner-of-war?"

The sarcastic reference to his rank stoked his fury. "You're a cocky Terran diplomat under my protection, and you'll do as I say."

She threw her narrow shoulders back. "I think not. This cocky Terran diplomat has better things to do than sit around in a musty tent and wait for your arbitrary orders."

"Better things? Such as?"

"Such as collecting medicinal herbs down by the river this afternoon with Sem."

He shook his head, irritated more by the news of her planned activity with Navarro than her insolence. "Out of the question. Too far from camp."

"Guards patrol both the inner and outer perimeters, not to mention the sentries posted on the cliffs overlooking the river. The area is perfectly secure." She cast him a triumphant smile. "Sem assured me."

"I don't care what Sem told you. He's only a medic. I'm a trained soldier. I'm telling you no area is perfectly secure."

"I'll decide for myself."

"You'll do as I say."

Her expression went ominously blank. "Or what? You'll court-martial me?"

Actually he wanted to throttle her. "If it were within my power I would!"

She sniffed a humorless laugh. "How very military of you. Thank Creation, you have no such power."

On the verge of letting a retort fly, he heard an odd shuffling, shushing noises just outside the tent. When he glanced at the entrance, he spotted a half-dozen pairs of boots milling around in the dirt.

She noticed the impromptu audience, as well, and had the good grace to turn scarlet. Swearing under his breath, he lurched to the entrance and reached around outside. With a flick of his wrist he tore the door flap from its mooring and shut out the curious crowd. The whispers quieted, and the boots shuffled away.

Kaljin let out a disgusted sigh. "How embarrassing!" With that, she tossed the bouquet of wildflowers on her bedroll, grasped the end of her braid and finished plaiting her hair.

He snorted. "I take it that's an apology."

Glowering, she grabbed her outer jacket from the edge of her open footlocker and headed for the entrance. "No, it isn't. I meant how embarrassing it is for you. Now the whole camp knows you're an autocrat."

He snagged her arm as she pushed past him. "Where are you going?"

"To the mess tent. I'm meeting Sem there for the midday meal. Are you coming?"

"I eat alone." He released her arm and looked down his nose at her.

Tossing her head, she turned away from him. "Somehow that doesn't surprise me. Enjoy your solitude." She opened the flap. "I'll be back before dark. But, please, don't hold supper."

With that snippet of sarcasm, she deserted him.

"Fine!" he grated out as if she still stood in front of him. "Go have your meal with Navarro and then play down by the river!"

Reeling as if she'd landed a blow to the pit of his stomach, he expelled every molecule of air in his lungs, spun around, and kicked the rucksack to Kaljin's side of the tent. A hard thunk and muffled crunch told him the book disks had popped their cases and were probably no longer legible. He didn't even want to think about what his tantrum had done to the fruit.

"Damn woman!" he swore under his breath.

Lonely silence answered him from every corner of the empty tent.

***

Insufferable. Domineering. Overbearing. Inflexible . . .

Marista mentally recounted Tynan's shortcomings as she pulled up handfuls of a plant Sem called "river weed."

Curt. Uncommunicative. Arrogant. Obstinate . . .

Yet, none of the traits explained exactly why she allowed the enigmatic Albian to bruise her feelings and pride with nothing but a glare down his handsome nose.

Then the perfect word stood front and center: Soldier.

How could she respond differently to the petty dictates of a military man, an officer no less? She'd learned those responses at her own father's knee.

"You've been quiet this afternoon, Marista. Are you tired?"

Startled to find Sem crouched at her side, she sat back on her heels. The capricious wind tousled strands of his dark brown hair, giving him a rakish air. He peered at her with his kind, amber eyes and she couldn't help smiling. "No, I'm not tired, just lost in thought. Maybe I'm feeling a little guilty, too."

Sem took the river weed from her hand and stuffed it into a waterproof pouch. "About what?"

She watched the water run fast and white over the rocky river bottom for a moment before she had the courage to look back at Sem. "I think I may have gotten you into trouble."

Calmly he went about the task at hand. "How?"

In a few, short sentences, she recounted her confrontation with

Tynan. "I tried to make him understand the decisions were mine and mine alone," she finished with a sigh. "From the way he barked out your name, though, I don't think he listened."

Amazingly, Sem laughed. "Oh, he listened. The Captain just 'heard' something different."

When she frowned at his cavalier attitude, Sem laughed again, hoisted himself off the soggy ground onto a broad smooth rock, and then held out his hand to her. After she joined him and made herself comfortable, he swiveled to face her. "You can't see it, can you, Marista?"

"See what?"

His cheeks dimpled with a grin. "Tynan's afraid."

She sniffed. "Yes, afraid that I'll prevent him from efficiently discharging his duty."

He shook his head. "No, he's afraid of me."

"You? How could he be afraid of you . . ." She caught herself and flushed. "I didn't mean to offend you. But, really, how could you threaten Tynan? You're a decent, gentle, caring man, with the true soul of a healer. You aren't a warrior. Believe me, as someone whose father was the archetypal soldier, I know what I'm saying."

He waved away her babbled apology. "Most of us who joined the Krillian home guard aren't born soldiers. We despise this war. But we have personal reasons for serving. Mine is a brother, Declan. In the early days of the war he died in the field because his company had no medic to treat his wounds. I can't help him now, but maybe I can help someone else like him."

Her heart constricted with empathetic pain. "I'm sorry."

He accepted her sympathy with a brief nod and recaptured a sliver of his grin. "So, you don't offend me, because I don't pretend to be a warrior. I doubt the Captain confuses me with one. I threaten him not as a military equal." Sem's eyes twinkled with mischief. "But as a rival for your favor."

She paused to absorb the statement, and then rejected it. "That's ridiculous! Sometimes Tynan acts as if he can barely stand the sight of me, much less . . ." She broke off, made inexplicably breathless by the notion. "No, you're wrong about this."

"Am I?"

Could it be true? No, she decided immediately. Competition for her attention inferred a level of emotional involvement and a fear of loss. Tynan's feelings toward her were neither gentle nor deep.

"Yes, you're wrong," she finally answered, though her words wavered.

Sem chuckled. "Perhaps you would do me a favor in any case. Mention to the Captain that, while I enjoy your company, my heart belongs to another woman."

The diversion as well as the information delighted her. "Oh, Sem, who is she?"

"Her name is Dyani. She's a folk healer in Bethel, and the one who taught me about medicinal plants."

"Let me guess," she wheedled. "She's sweet, intelligent, and quiet but strong."

Sem's eyes softened with unmistakable affection and longing. "You describe her as if you've met her."

"I've met you," she replied. "I'd expect she'd be no less."

He accepted the compliment with a nod. "And she is beautiful. To me, the most beautiful woman in the world."

The sweet honesty of his words suddenly made her quite envious of Dyani. For one insane moment, she wondered what it might be like to see such devotion and affection for her in Tynan's eyes.

The notion hitched her breath. She dispelled the nonsense ramblings of her mind and flashed Sem a dazzling smile. "Will you marry this beautiful Dyani?"

Sem's kind eyes lost their luster. "Someday, I hope. Right now, the Krillian Sedition Acts forbids our marriage."

"How can marriage be considered an act of treason?" she demanded.

"Dyani is Albian. She and her family fled the Borderlands when Albian Command declared the area a strategic site in the first days of the war. They crossed the mountains to Bethel rather than let themselves be interned in relocation camps."

"Relocation camps?" She didn't hide her disgust. "The Albians do that to their own populations?"

"My government reacted no less offensively," he admitted. "Our officials didn't turn the refugees away, but neither were their motives humanitarian. In exchange for sanctuary, the Albians work for Krillian industries and on the farms to replace manpower lost to the war effort. The refugees receive shelter and food, but are not given wages. They have to take care of their own, with little intervention from the Krillian government. They are confined to guarded 'enclaves' within the city that are little better than the Albian camps they fled."

He waved at the bulging bags at his feet. "River weed is a stock treatment for Dyani's burn patients, not a convenient supplement. She is one of only three folk healers who care for Albian refugees in a medical facility that makes field medicine appear extravagant."

She gasped. "This all sounds like government sanctioned forced labor."

"The Sedition Acts permit it for security purposes," he agreed. "Dyani and I met before the laws were enacted. She was injured when she first came to Bethel. As a recruit medic for the home guard I was allowed the 'practice' of treating her wounds. We found we had much more in common than a love of healing."

Sem set his mouth in an uncharacteristic scowl as he bent over and tied the waterproof sack. "I can understand fear of the enemy. I feel it every day myself. But the Acts are excessive and cruel. I'm ashamed that as a soldier I'm sworn to uphold this injustice."

She understood. How many times in the past handful of days had her conscience warred with her pledge to uphold Terran interplanetary policy? And now, she even had grave doubts concerning the truth behind the Rising Sun tragedy. Yet, she still had no right to pass judgment on another government's internal affairs.

Suddenly, the diplomatic rationalizations galled her. "I wish there was something I could do for you. Maybe in my official report . . ."

He stopped her with a slow, sad smile. "Changing the law is not your concern. We Krillians must do that ourselves. If you truly want to help, tell Captain Tynan you and I are only friends."

The tease in his voice took the edge off her anger. "All right, I'll mention it to him next time we speak."

If he chooses to speak to me again, she added silently.

"I feel much better now," Sem joked as the sparkle returned to his eyes. "I don't know what it is, but there's something different about him since he returned from this last mission. In the past months, he's shown little or no emotion, and keeps his own counsel. I've heard others whisper he's somehow lost his soul."

He tilted his head toward the river. "Now, when I see the Captain with you, he reminds me of the water out there—restless, powerful, dangerous. Something . . ." He glanced back at her. ". . . or someone compromised his composure."

She wet her dry lips. "What happened to him at the desert outpost, and to the men with him, would have shaken anyone."

"I'd lay down a month's script that whatever drove him to betray his own heritage was much worse."

The comment surprised her. "I thought Tynan defected because of conscience."

Sem peered at her. "Perhaps. I told you, he keeps his own counsel. I suppose no one really cares why a high ranking Albian officer defects as long as the transfer of intelligence data is trustworthy and useful. To be honest, I thought if anyone would know about the Captain, it might be you."

She held back a humorless chuckle. "I knew Tynan for three full days at the Terran outpost, and he didn't even tell me his real given name until just before Gaer raided us. That is exactly how much he trusts me, Sem."

But Sem shook his head. "You are the one new variable since his last mission. You've shaken him, Marista."

She could have given him a dozen reasons why, starting with his disdain for her profession and her Terran citizenship.

"In a few days, when the transport comes to take me to Sarquis, none of this speculation will matter anyway," she told Sem out loud. "Tynan will have his precious solitude again." She squeezed Sem's arm. "And I will be missing my new friend."

Sem laid his hand over hers. "I will be sad, too, when that day comes." He sighed and glanced out at the river. "The duty officer will be missing both of us if we don't get back to camp. We can make it before watch change if we hurry."

She welcomed activity. Her brain hummed with enough new and conflicting insights to keep her thinking all night and into the next dawn. As she and Sem collected their harvest, she realized she'd be back to the tent well before the suppertime deadline she'd given Tynan.

The hike to camp took her and Sem longer than the hike to the river, burdened as they were with wet, heavy bags of plant life. By the time they arrived at the med-tent the Serrainian sun glowed orange-red low on the horizon.

"Give me a moment to drop these things inside, and I'll see you the rest of the way to your tent," Sem offered.

She waved him off. "I can find my own way."

He spread his hands and smiled. "Then a good night. Thanks for your help."

She took his hand between hers. "Thanks for your company."

Then she turned away and started down the well-trodden path, revived, renewed, and somewhat repentant about her quarrel with Tynan. With her thoughts focused on how she might soothe the tension between them, she didn't miss her jacket until a gust of wind chilled her to the bone.

Clutching her upper arms, she realized she'd left the jacket on the ground near the river and would have to go back to retrieve it. She could do without it for the rest of the night by wrapping herself in the thermal blanket. She could even withstand the cold morning trek to the hygiene tent in shirtsleeves if necessary. But rain or mist might soak the material through, and make it unusable for the next few days. After defying Tynan's orders about spending the afternoon with Sem, she didn't want to test the prickly Captain's patience any further by asking him to requisition a new coat.

Doing an about face on the path, she retraced her steps at a brisk walk. Without the burden of tools or heavy storage bags she reached the river bank in less than fifteen minutes. After slipping into the jacket, she turned and set her pace back to camp at a jog. She made it to the narrow rock wall passage that led to the camp clearing well before the gloom of dusk.

The camp was only five minutes away when a massive blur rushed at her from the tall stand of grass on the right. Blindsided, she skidded to a halt less than a meter from the human bulk that now blocked her path. She recognized the contemptuous features and froze. "Gaer!"

The raider sneered then made a tottering bow from the waist that conveyed anything but respect. "Madame. A fine evening for a walk."

He slurred the ends of his words. She suspected he'd numbed himself with drugs or drink. But his unsteadiness gave her an advantage. Aunt Mimi always said the best way to handle a bully is to call his bluff.

She pulled herself tall and set her expression as hard as the rock walls on either side of her, though her insides quivered. "Let me pass."

"Not before we speak our farewells, Madame." He advanced a step.

She retreated the same to keep him beyond arm's reach. "I'm not leaving anytime soon."

"I'm leaving!"

Curiosity overrode her anxiety for a moment. "Why?"

Gaer fixed her with a glare. "I've been told to pack up and leave."

Varden hadn't listened to her plea for clemency after all. "I'm sorry. I didn't know . . ."

He threw out his arm as if dismissing her apology. "I had a choice. Court-martial and imprisonment for the next three years. Or dishonorable discharge and exile. I did my job. I saved the Albian Bracquar, and it got me exiled." His eyelids drooped over a bleary stare. "You got me exiled."

Now she understood. Gaer blamed her, though she'd been his victim.

Hoping her voice wouldn't crack with tension, she tried to speak in even, soothing tones. "I wanted no one punished for what happened. I talked to Colonel Varden this morning . . ."

"I'm sure you did!"

As he spoke, he lurched forward and grabbed for her. She evaded him with a quick sidestep. But, the river lay at her back and the footpath passage narrowed in front of her to single file width. She had little room to escape. Even if she got a scream past the tightening in her throat, the guards posted high on the ridge above couldn't possibly hear her over the river's roar.

Her heart fluttering, she decided to do what she did best. She talked. "I'm sorry for what happened to you. But you don't understand . . ."

"I understand you owe me, woman," he ground out, fisting his hands at his sides. "You and Tynan both. The Albians kill for sport. You Terrans look the other way for profit."

She held up her hands, palm side out in a gesture of peace. "I know you have cause to distrust me . . ."

"Madame Kaljin, save your sympathy. You know nothing! You don't care about principle and justice." Gaer stumbled but quickly regained his balance. "You and Tynan are the whores of the universe! You owe me, woman. I can take my payment in many ways, but I will collect before I leave!"

As he worked himself into a frenzy, she realized he didn't want an apology. He was bent on retaliation.

Gulping, she lowered her voice with authority. "You aren't thinking straight. Consider what might happen if you harm me."

His mocking laugh sent a shudder up her spine. "You Terrans like to waste time negotiating. No more talk."

He stalked forward, this time with a measured, resolute gait that brooked no challenge.

"Stay away from me," she warned, shuffling backward. "I . . . I don't want to hurt you, but I know how to defend myself, and I will."

He laughed again, deep and chilling. "Yes, for someone non-violent you wield sharp claws. But I have a claw, too."

In horror, she watched as he drew from beneath his vest the combat knife he'd used to kill Jarrit. His eyes gleamed with murderous intent. "Maybe I'll cut you." He sliced at the air between them. "Maybe I won't right away."

Her head went light as blood pounded in her ears. With every ounce of will she resisted the panicked urge to turn and run toward the river, plunging into the water, if necessary. But she knew she couldn't outrun the stronger, enraged man.

She had nowhere to go, no weapon to use but her wits. "Gaer, listen. I'm a Terran with diplomatic credentials. The Council of Seven Planets will demand your death if you kill me. Leave now, before you condemn yourself!"

Rabid with anger, he ignored her and lunged. A strangled cry left her throat before she abandoned common sense and spun around to flee his grasping hands.

She knew the moment his fingers snared her billowing jacket. Her feet left the ground, and the gray rock blurred with the tall green grass for a whirling, sickening second. Then her heels and spine hit rock wall, and the air left her lungs in a painful rush.

"Terran whore!"

Gaer grabbed at her throat, but she managed to twist aside. Though he missed clamping on to her, one of his meaty fingers caught her necklace and ripped it off. The slender chain glimmered a moment in the setting sunlight, then dropped out of sight.

She didn't see where the necklace landed. In reflex she shut her eyes and raised her arms in front of her face. But, instead of fending off a blow, she found herself gripping the material of Gaer's shirt and straining to hold his forearm away from her windpipe.

Struggling for oxygen, she fought terror and the attack with equal force. "Let me go, or I'll make sure you never enjoy a woman again for as long as you live!"

His eyes widened for a stark moment, as if he actually took her seriously. An ear-shattering guffaw a second later crushed her hope.

Survival instinct took hold. She raised her right leg, hoping to strike a blow into Gaer's groin. Her foot barely got off the ground before her knee jammed into the burly man's muscular thigh instead.

Gaer's snicker stiffened her resolve. With all her strength, she let her heel crash onto the raider's instep. He hardly flinched. Too late she realized he probably felt no pain through his combat boot. But he did counter her meager efforts with even more brutal force. She gasped when the point of the knife pierced through the bodice of her flight suit just beneath her left rib cage.

So this was her end—senseless death at the hands of a frightened, bitter man. Her heart already seemed to have stopped beating. The air seeped from her open mouth in a steady, final stream. Her body numbed to the pain of rock grating against the back of her head and legs. A soul-deep peace enveloped her, even though she faced Gaer's hateful scowl.

She waited for the final thrust, the moment of searing pain, and the encroaching darkness. She wondered why her dying regret was that she'd never see Tynan again.

A bellow rent the air—a war cry of rage and doom. She glimpsed the whorl of gray and black as a shadowed intruder charged from the left. In the blink of an eye, she stood free. Her legs gave way, and she slumped to the ground. In front of her, Gaer grasped the back of his legs and hit the dirt.

Like death with a vengeance her rescuer swooped down, disabling Gaer with one knee to the spine and a combat knife to the throat. "Not again, Gaer! You won't hurt her again!"

Seventeen

Tynan's dark features, both savage and beautiful, were those once again of the warrior king. Marista's pulse hammered with relief and keen female awareness of her rescuer.

Bloodlust glinted in Tynan's obsidian eyes as he straddled Gaer's back and grasped the raider's matted hair in his left hand. With the point of his combat knife he drew a bead of blood from a fold in Gaer's stretched neck. "Varden ordered you to leave. I have the right to kill you for defying that order."

Gaer lay stiff and still inside the death grip. "No! No, wait! I'll go . . ."

Tynan pressed the blade closer to Gaer's neck and silenced the pitiful plea. "You beg for mercy, after you again brutalized Madame Kaljin? Perhaps I will listen to you as you listened to her."

The tremble of fear in Tynan's rumbling voice jolted her more than his threat of retaliation. Her mind flooded with memories, long suppressed by grief and anger. Memories of flame and smoke and her father kneeling beside her near the charred ruins of their home on Yonar. Anthony Henson bellowed with the same raging desperation against a Universe that claimed his wife and younger daughter.

Mother Creation! Just as her father must have cared more deeply than she remembered, Tynan cared for her more deeply than mere duty required.

Gaer whimpered, "I only wanted to scare her!"

"You should have groveled to her on your knees," Tynan growled. "She pleaded with Varden for leniency on your behalf this morning."

"You lie!"

A rush of air left Gaer's lungs as Tynan sunk his knee deeper into the man's spine. "I was there. I told her to save her plea for someone worthy. But she has a misplaced sense of compassion." His features blanked of any emotion. "I feel no such compassion for you."

Gaer screeched, and his face went white as the bead of blood on his neck became a slow trickle under the pressure of Tynan's knife. "I didn't know! I swear!"

"Ignorance won't save you." Tynan lifted his head and set his furious gaze on Marista. "Gaer's life is yours for the asking, Madame. Give me the word, and he will no longer threaten you or anyone else."

In that instant, she had no doubt he would carry out his threat. He'd kill Gaer at her feet without compunction—a warrior king's sacrifice to her honor, a pledge of his protection. The savagery of his offer clashed with her non-violent sensitivities. Yet, the seething ferocity of his desire to avenge and safeguard her life stole her breath and her heart in the same stroke.

As she struggled with her whipsawed emotions, Tynan held the blade poised for slaughter and awaited her decision. Finally, she braced her back against the rock wall and forced the words past her constricted throat. "I don't want Gaer's blood on your hands, Tynan. Let him go."

Tynan's expression lost none of its resolute intent as he set his glare back to Gaer. "Do you hear that? For the second time today Madame Kaljin grants you undeserved mercy. As for me, I'd just as soon cut out your heart. If I ever see you again, I will. Do you doubt me?"

The warrior king had passed sentence.

Gaer shook his head wildly.

Tynan glared at his captive a moment longer before he flicked his knife upward and wiped the bloodied edge on Gaer's shoulder blade. With powerful grace he hefted himself to his feet and stood apart from his defeated foe. "Get out of here. Run. Don't stop until you find a place far enough away that we will never cross paths again."

Tynan watched, seemingly unmoved, as a winded Gaer flopped over and scuttled backward on the ground. When he was well out of Tynan's reach, the raider lumbered upright and made a stumbling run toward the river. In seconds, he disappeared into the Serrainian dusk.

Relief washed over her in disorienting waves. So did the realization of what might have happened to her had Tynan not appeared. She expelled a long breath of pent-up air. Purple and gray spots danced in her vision, obscuring Tynan's rigid, battle-ready silhouette.

He must have heard her sigh, because he turned away from watching Gaer's retreat to look at her. Sheathing his weapon, he closed the distance between them in four long strides and dropped to his knees in front of her.

Leaning forward, he raised his hand as if to touch her. But he hesitated and frowned instead. "What in the name of common sense are you doing out here by yourself?"

Though he rebuked her, neither controlled rage nor bloodlust roughened his voice. As he let his frantic gaze travel over her face and throat, she recognized the truth in his eyes. Gaer's attack had terrified him as much as it had her.

She lifted a shaky hand to her neck where her pulse beat hard and fast. A dry mouth and lack of air made her voice a whisper. "I left my jacket at the river and came back for it."

He fisted his hands on his thighs. "I told you coming here could be dangerous. Do you have any idea what went through my mind when I didn't find you with Navarro?"

Blinking away her confusion, she bristled at the scolding snap of his tone. "Just why did you come looking for me? I told you not to wait supper."

His eyes narrowed. "What you do in your spare time and with whom you do it is none of my concern. I came looking for you as a courtesy. Varden received word that Ugo is well and recovering at your Terran outpost. I thought you'd want to know."

Ashamed of her pique against the man who had just saved her life, she sank against the rock and shut her eyes. "Yes, of course, I want to know."

"Did he hurt you?"

The question, gruff but soft, made her dare look back up at him. He held himself less rigid, and he tilted his head to one side, appearing sincerely concerned.

She shook her head. "I . . . I'm not hurt, just scared and winded."

His frown deepened. With his fingertip he traced a path along the left side of her neck, just below her ear. "What's this?"

His gentle touch left a sting in its wake. In reflex she flinched. "I don't know. Gaer didn't cut me, I'm sure . . . My necklace!" she remembered. "Gaer pulled off my necklace."

"He ripped off your skin, too, damn him!"

She only glimpsed the renewed rage in his face before he stood and scanned the ground left to right and back again. In less than five seconds he spotted her necklace, whisked it out of the dirt, and dropped to his haunches once again in front of her.

The chain lay mangled inside his wide, callused palm. From the day her mother had given her the flower namesake, she'd never taken it off. Now it appeared she'd never wear it again. She bit her lip to hold back tears.

"I think it can be fixed."

She lifted her gaze to meet his. His words of encouragement warmed her heart. "Really?"

He held her gaze a moment longer. Then he took her hand inside his, laid the necklace into her palm, and closed his fingers over hers. "I'm sure."

He could have released her hand then. He didn't. The proud, impassioned warrior king had retreated. Before her knelt a man who appeared awash in some great bewilderment that mirrored her own roiling confusion.

"Tynan?" She sighed.

He blinked lazily, as if coming out of sleep. "What?"

"Would you really have killed Gaer to protect me?"

"Yes."

The brusque, unhesitating reply brought searing affection to her heart. Without thinking, she raised her free hand and pressed her palm against his heated cheek. "Thank you."

Her touch seemed to clear his bemusement. He freed her hand from inside his, clasped her raised wrist and dragged her fingers from his face. "I . . . I did what had to be done."

His cool rebuff didn't fool her. She'd glimpsed in him a motive less rational than devotion to duty. "Yes, of course, you did."

Tynan scowled at her skepticism and freed her wrist, then stood. "Do you want to rest, or can you walk?"

"I can walk."

He reached down, grabbed hold of her upper arms, and drew her to her feet. "Then let's get you back to camp and cleaned up."

**

A cold but cleansing shower and a hot meal at the mess tent helped calm Marista's nerves. Afterward, Tynan delivered her to their tent, but he left immediately, muttering about reporting the incident to Colonel Varden. She didn't check, but she assumed he had posted a sentry nearby. The notion pleased her far more than it had earlier that day.

For an hour, she sat cross-legged on her open bedroll and pulled out military issue clothing from the rucksack she found upended on her side of the tent. One heavy, dusky green sweater made her grimace.

Guilt brought her up short. Tynan must have packed the clothing for her, just as he'd brought in the space heater and camp chairs. She'd vaguely noticed all the gear when they'd argued that morning, but she'd made her dramatic exit before letting him explain any of it.

Certainly her earlier inattention to his efforts must have stung his pride, especially after she'd practically flaunted the items Sem had given her. She had no right to disparage the clothes, or the three globs of crushed, inedible fruit.

With the care she might have given a length of fine silk, she folded the sweater into quarters and laid it aside. With the heater filling the tent with delightful warmth, she didn't need an extra layer of protection from the night chill. The long sleeved T-shirt and camouflage trousers she wore were comfortably heavy. After cleaning her boots earlier, she'd felt toasty enough to stow them and relax in her stockinged feet.

She reached for several reading disks that had tumbled out of the rucksack along with their broken cases, and shook her head. However in the world had the sturdy little cases shattered?

The tent flap snapped up, and Tynan blew in with a cold gust of air. She held down the edges of her bedroll until he secured the flap and turned.

A hearty ruddiness infused his cheeks. The muted overhead lantern light threw shadows on the angles of his face, lending it a dour cast.

Uncertain whether he actually frowned or just appeared in a foul mood, she offered a hopeful smile. "I see you showered."

When he squinted in question, she shifted her gaze upward to a tuft of hair that gleamed blue-black as it stuck to his forehead. "You're still damp."

He broke the spell when he ruffled the stubby ends with his hand. "I needed soap and water as badly as you did."

Foul mood it was, she decided from his clipped tone. Well, he had a right to be irritated with her. As long as he didn't drag it out forever.

"Here." He took a step toward her and thrust out his down turned fist. When she merely stared at his knuckles he crouched to her level. "Here. Take it."

Annoyed by the brisk order but curious, she held out her hand. He dropped the necklace, apparently intact, into her palm.

A laugh bubbled in her throat. "You fixed it!"

"It wasn't me," he countered. "One of our weapon's specialists found some tools small enough to make temporary repairs. He removed the damaged links and soldered the broken ends together. The chain is shorter. You'll have to replace it when you return to Earth, but the links will hold for now."

Feeling like a child with a new gift, she strung the necklace around her throat and fastened the clasp. "I don't know what to say!"

But when she looked up, he'd already risen, turned his back to her, and retreated to his side of the tent.

The silent rebuff hurt. She set her fingertips to the tiny metal flower on the end of the chain, a ritual that had always comforted her. The magic didn't work this time.

As she watched him remove his outer coat and weapons belt, her guilt, and the desperation to purge it, grew. She wanted him to talk to her, to accept her thanks and praise for his effort. And, by Creation, she'd keep at him until he listened!

She cleared her throat for another try. "Thank you for going to all this trouble to have my necklace fixed."

He growled something unintelligible.

"I really do appreciate the other . . ." She paused, unsure whether she should use the term gifts. "The other accommodations you arranged for me. The clothes fit me well. I'm wearing some of them now."

"Uh-huh." He grabbed his bedroll and spread it on the ground as if the job were far more important than responding to her.

His stubborn refusal to communicate challenged her to force the point. "The heater was an especially nice surprise. I probably won't have to use my blanket tonight."

Other than a quick, sideways glance, he showed no interest in her patter. Once he positioned his bedroll, he sat down on it and began unlacing his left boot.

She drummed her fingers on her thigh as he finished with the boot, pulled it off, and started on the right one. "The disks should keep me from getting bored," she continued, fighting to keep sarcasm out of her voice. "I've never read Psychological Warfare: Fighting the Enemy Within, but it sounds fascinating."

She wondered if the manual had any suggestions for tactical mental skirmishes like this one.

"The disk cases were broken, though. Do you know how that might have happened?"

He tossed the second boot alongside its mate at the head of his bedroll. The thump sounded for all the world like an, "I don't care."

She managed to keep the anger out of her voice by sheer will. "Tynan?"

He rubbed the back of his neck. Obviously the massage consumed too much of his energy, and he found it impossible to respond.

"Tynan, I'm trying to thank you."

He yawned.

"Tynan?" She paused, decided to use a different approach. "Quint?"

He jerked his body around as if he'd caught her sneaking up on him with a drawn weapon. "That's no longer my name."

Though shaken by his sharp reprimand she clung to her composure. "At least I got your attention."

He leaned toward her, bracing his weight on one arm. "You be careful how you get my attention, Little Diplomat. I buried Quint and my Askanati heritage. I can't resurrect either one. Understand?"

Instinctively, she uncrossed her legs and rose to her knees, ready to flee his sudden anger. "I beg your pardon . . ."

"You should. While you're at it, you should beg my pardon for what you did today."

"For what I did?" She clambered to her feet. "Gaer attacked me, remember?"

He rocketed off the ground, his glare dark as the moonless Serrainian night. "Yes, after I told you not to go to the river because of the danger."

She threw up her hands and then dropped them to slap against her thighs. "We've been through this. I didn't think . . ."

He closed the distance between them in two small steps and grasped her shoulders. "No, you don't think. You just feel."

She wiggled futility to free herself. "Sometimes I do. But my intuitions benefited you back at the outpost."

"Today they almost got you killed."

When she stared up at his face, her heart seemed to stop beating. He still glared at her, but the awful terror—the kind she once saw in her father's expression—augmented the anger in his eyes, just as it had after he'd battled Gaer.

She hadn't imagined it before. Beyond his duty, beyond his sense of responsibility, beyond any rational reason, he truly cared about what happened to her.

"From now on, Kaljin, you won't go anywhere without me or my express permission, is that clear?"

In spite of her new insight, his highhanded order sparked her indignation. "In case you've forgotten, I am a civilian, and an honored guest of this camp."

He ground his teeth and yanked her closer to him. "You are under military supervision, whether you want to be or not. That means following orders which might save your life. You can file a complaint when you reach the Terran Embassy at Sarquis. Until then, Madame Kaljin, you will do as I say."

She set her fists to his chest. "I see common gossip about the arrogance of Albian officers really is true."

His frown drew dangerously deep.

She rose to the challenge. "Yes, Sir, Captain Tynan. Since I'm now enlisted to serve at your pleasure, what is your first order?"

She expected him to toss her aside, and none too gently. When he dragged her so close she felt the warmth of his body, she let out a startled squeak and peered up at him with wonder.

He gripped her arms harder. "I want you to kiss me."

The words, low and rumbling with some indecipherable emotion, stunned her. "You . . . you want . . ."

He didn't wait for a coherent answer. Instead, with the sudden, scorching press of his mouth to hers, he sent a shock wave to her soul and back.

She went numb, then lightheaded as he let go of her shoulders and set his wide hands on either side of her face to hold her steady. Obviously, he meant to kiss her without restraint. Her pulse thrummed with wild, involuntary anticipation, but her emotions ricocheted between fury and lust, and lust and befuddlement.

He had no right to demand this of her!

Then why wasn't she battering against his chest? Why did she cling to the front of his shirt as if she were afraid he'd let her go?

Tynan sank his strong fingers into her hair. The sensation of his fingertips skimming over her scalp sent a shiver through her, and he groaned his satisfaction.

He would have killed to protect her, she reminded herself. She had nothing to fear from him. If she uttered one word of protest, he'd let her go.

But she felt no desire to protest anything he did. He taunted her lips with the tip of his tongue. The beseeching of further intimacy ignited a need so powerful she wound her fingers tighter into the folds of his shirt.

He wanted her. The knowledge of her power emboldened her. She slid her right hand over his shoulder, up his neck, and into the bristles of hair at the back of his head. With her left hand, she cupped his cheek, felt the heat gather beneath his skin. Did her skin burn so beneath his touch?

She let him part her lips with his tongue. As he circled and teased the tender inside of her mouth, a wondrous, terrifying dizziness blindsided her. A moan tore from her throat.

At the sound, he slipped his hands to the small of her back, fanned his fingers, and brought her body forward to meet his full arousal. Catching her breath, she let out a small cry of amazement.

He went still in her arms, lifted his face, and panted for air before fixing his gaze back on her. "Kaljin, this isn't really an order."

She stared up at him through passion-hazed eyes. Breathing in his clean, male scent, she felt the fullness of his desire against her inner thigh. "Well, this is, Tynan. Don't stop."

The need in her own voice frightened her. Perhaps it frightened him, too. He frowned, and then set her back at arm's length. "Do you understand what you're saying, Little Diplomat?"

"Of course I do!"

He narrowed his gaze, as if looking into her soul and forced her to do the same. Only then did she feel the wild, uneven thump of her heart, the weakness in the pit of her stomach, and the vague panic of uncertainty.

"Yes," she muttered, less surely.

When he lifted his hand to caress the underside of her jaw, she expected him to sweep her back into his arms. Instead, he worked his thumb over her mouth slowly, sending electric prickles along every nerve ending in her body.

Through a fog of bone-melting sensation, she heard him whisper, "Kaljin, I want you. I have wanted you for as many hours as we've been together. My gut has ached every one of those hours with needing you."

Her head cleared at the strange anguish in his voice. "Yes, I know."

He stilled his thumb on the tip of her chin, and his gaze centered on her lips like a man startled by an epiphany. "Perhaps you have understood all along."

He lifted his fingers and brushed a curl from her temple, before looking into her eyes. "But something else you must understand. I can make your body mine, give myself to you for tonight and all the other nights we have left together. Yet, I can't feel what you want me to feel. Emotions blur a man's focus and dull his sense of purpose. I cannot let that happen."

She searched his handsome, stoic face. "Why?"

The lines around his mouth and eyes deepened with stern determination. "Because of choices I had to make two years ago, I have no home, no clan, no future. My word of honor is all I have left, and I've given that in service to the Krillian cause. I will let nothing . . ." He seemed to hold his breath. ". . . not even a beautiful, willing woman distract me from that duty. So you see, I have nothing to offer you beyond this moment."

"But I don't care about clans and heritage . . ." she began to argue.

"You do care about honor, though," he interrupted softly. "You've shown me that from the moment we met. I'm only being honorable. Allow me that dignity. I cannot pledge you a future. I cannot allow myself to feel the emotions you want from me and still be true first to my duty. Trust me on this."

She had always trusted him. She had always understood, as well, that he was a proud man. He would not promise more than he could give. Stripped of his heritage, reviled and hunted by his own countrymen, he believed he had nothing of value to offer. Protests to the contrary would not sway him.

She marveled that he knew her so well, yet he seemed to know himself so little. Would he have risked his life to protect her if he didn't care? Would he have forced her to consider the consequences of passion without promise, or made this crucial choice hers and hers alone when he burned inside with need for her? He'd already sacrificed a piece of his heart to her. He just didn't realize it yet.

And she had no right to point it out. He had to come to that understanding himself.

She smiled with an inner certainty that seemed so rare of late. "I will accept what you offer me. Now, will you turn off the lantern, or shall I?"

He peered at her as if she'd spoken gibberish. But, when she opened her mouth to repeat herself, he whipped his arm out faster than a ravenous kae-a-teck snatching at prey. He grasped her waist and coiled his free arm around her back. Once again his arousal pressed hard and heavy against her willing, wanting body.

His hungry grin ratcheted her desire another notch. "Tonight you belong to me, Kaljin."

Tonight and always, Tynan, her heart whispered back.

He palmed the back of her neck and kneaded the tender flesh there with his callused fingers. "When I make you want to cry out in pleasure, remember there's another tent less than two meters away."

She widened her eyes with mock disdain. "I was right. You are arrogant."

Yet, when his roughened hand stroked the back of her neck, turning her insides molten, she suspected he had a right to his boast.

He brushed her temple with his lips. "I'll make you forget the rest of your lovers."

She smiled as his breath tickled the inside of her ear. "What other lovers?"

His low, throaty laugh sent ripples of anticipation coursing through her body. She memorized the sound like notes from a song, locking the melody deep in her heart before it drifted away.

He grazed her earlobe with the tip of his tongue, then caught the tender flesh between his teeth and gently pulled away.

She barely kept her knees locked. "Tynan, will you please just hurry and take off my clothes?"

"Patience, Little Diplomat," he cooed, then moved against her with a slow, easy grace that kindled her simmering need. "I'm going to make it right, not fast."

She let her head drop to his shoulder. "Don't I have a say in any of this?"

The tail of her shirt slipped from her trousers. His wide hand molded to the curve of her bare waist and slowly lifted until his thumb brushed the underside of her breast. She cried out weakly before her eyes fluttered shut.

"By all means, say something," he muttered, as he extended his thumb along the swell of her breast, but eased back before he touched the swollen, wanting peak. "Tell me what you want."

Somehow she found the strength to lift her head, slide her arms around his shoulders, and brush her mouth against his. "Make it right, not fast."

He laughed again, this time with impatience of his own, then bent to cover her mouth with his.

But she pressed her fingers against his lips. "One more request. Please."

He lifted a brow in anticipation.

"If you want to bed me you'll call me Marista," she whispered.

A shadow gathered in his eyes, obliterating the glimmer of passion for one, horrible moment. "You ask a great deal from me."

She peered into his hooded, hungry dark gaze, and her courage almost failed her. But she needed this concession from him, as certainly as she needed his hands caressing her body.

"I know that, but something has changed between us. You're holding me in your arms now. You're asking to be my lover. I want that, too."

His expression flattened as he listened.

Afraid she'd lost him with her demand she swallowed, her throat dry. "You say you have no freedom to offer your heart. Then I won't ask for it. But grant me this small concession, and I'll ask nothing more."

He hesitated, then released her from his intimate embrace and stepped a pace back. As the hem of her shirt shimmied down around her hips again, she stifled a chill of foreboding.

She would not retract her request. She could not, even if he turned and fled the tent.

Missing the heat of his solid body, she folded her arms under her breasts and waited, suffering five, erratic heartbeats until he shook off his paralysis.

She closed her eyes to the familiar hard determination she recognized in the set of his jaw. He had made his decision, and she dreaded hearing it.

Hearing him shuffle away, she drew her arms inward to check a groan of disappointment. She would be strong. She would not cry. Crying never solved anything . . .

The click startled her. She opened her eyes to pitch darkness and electric silence.

Only when she felt his hand caress her cheek did she realize he'd found his way back to her. When she felt the press of his mouth to her forehead she forgot to draw air.

His breath flowed against her face, banished the awful chill. "I will do what pleases you." He kissed her lips as if seeking permission. "Marista."

Eighteen

Tynan's raw whisper of her given name aroused Marista as much as the friction of his flesh against hers. She knew he had the strength to deny his desire rather than grant her request. She knew, as well, that honor prevented him from overwhelming her with physical pleasure at the expense of deeper needs. Instead, he offered this noble concession to please her heart as he promised to please her body.

"Marista?" His mouth hovered over her lips as he whispered her name a second time. "What is your wish?"

She wished to admit she loved him. Breath flowed from her lungs as the words formed in her mind.

A shred of reason, though, warned her this new bridge between them had little foundation. A rush of impatient words, or the weight of too much expectation, would destroy the fragile framework. She couldn't speak the secrets of her heart. She could only act on those secrets.

She set her hands on the front of his shirt. "This is my wish."

With quivering fingers she managed to find a gap in the front placket and pop open the top button. As she moved to the second button, she stroked his mouth with a light brush of her lips.

Pop. The second button came undone. Again she teased him with a fleeting kiss.

He groaned. "You test me, woman."

She slipped the third button free. "You said make it right, not fast."

"I didn't mean interminable."

Ignoring his own words, he grasped her elbows, pushed her arms skyward, and yanked up the tail of her shirt. She barely had time to gasp when she felt his thumbs slide inside the waistband of her trousers. Slowly, provocatively, he slid the trousers downward, letting his hands glide along the length of her legs, until he knelt at her feet, and the camouflage material lay wadded on the ground.

Though darkness enveloped the tent and the space heater pumped out warmth, the sudden surprise and chill of nudity brought a catch of surprise to her throat.

Tynan's deep chuckle rose up from the ground as he prodded her left foot, then her right foot with his hand until she stepped out of the crumpled trousers. "Modesty has its place in seduction. But not tonight, Little Diplomat."

Little Diplomat.

Once he'd used the name to mock her. Now he whispered the name with such sweet, husky promise that she had to quell a rise of emotion in her throat. "I'm not being modest," she denied. "I just didn't expect . . . Oh!"

The air left her lungs as his strong fingers molded around her ankles for a moment then began another slow progress, this time upward. As he rose from his knees, heat from his palms left a trail of fire along the back of her calves, behind the curve of her knees, and up her thighs before rounding her hips and settling at her waist.

"Your skin is as smooth and soft as I imagined," he murmured.

Trying to keep her knees locked and her wits clear, she grasped his arms to stay standing. "Did you wonder about it a great deal, Captain?"

"More than I care to confess."

The admission thrilled her, but no more than the sensations he created when he lifted his hands from her waist to the ridge of her ribs, continuing the sensual voyage over her body. "Did you wonder what my touch would be like on your skin, Marista?"

Her breasts ached with the anticipation of his caress. The tips bloomed and hardened, chafed by the simple current of warm, circulated air. "Far more often than I will confess. You're already too certain of your skills. I won't feed your vanity."

"Is that so?" He stopped mapping her curves just short of the swell of her heavy, aching breasts.

She refused to suffer the exquisite torment of his hesitation and leaned into his hands. "Are you going to make me beg?"

He brought his face down and pressed his cheek to hers, fire joining fire. "I would not have you beg for what pleases me to give."

When his hands covered her breasts she swallowed a cry of delight lest she wake anyone in the tent next door. He softly circled and stroked and taunted her flesh with his callused fingertips and palms. With his thumbs he brought the peaks to hard, throbbing nubs, and then he bent down and suckled the sensitized flesh.

The abrasion of his tongue on her flesh sent a spasm of pleasure through her. When the quiver settled warm and heavy and hot in her feminine depths, liquid heat gathered between her legs and flowed with every sensual lick. Already she felt the first contractions of release.

She'd never felt like this with Daniel!

Frantically, she took his face between her hands and brought his head up. "I concede your skills."

"I've not even started," he warned, slipping his arms around her back and up her spine.

She pressed her forehead to his. "You have no idea what you've started. I'm ready to take you inside me now."

"Now?"

She rewarded his sweet surprise with a lingering kiss as she pressed her hips into his hard arousal. "Yes, now. And you don't even have your clothes off."

She barely finished the playful observation before he set her free. Missing the heat of his body, she folded her arms, but smiled as buttons popped, snaps pinged open, and discarded clothing crinkled and whooshed to the ground.

Finally she heard only the whir of the space heater and the ragged catch of his breathing. "Am I more acceptable now?" he asked.

Although the dark concealed all but the outline of his strong, solid body, he loomed large. For a trembling moment, she felt afraid. This formidable man meant to satisfy her need for sweet intimacy. Yet, in all the important ways he remained a stranger. How could she so easily surrender her body and heart to a man who said he couldn't or wouldn't surrender his heart to her?

The air stirred with the musky essence of his male arousal, and the earthy but familiar odors of the tent. The heady fusion smothered her doubts. This time was right. This intimacy felt right. Tynan "smelled right," as Aunt Mimi would have reminded her. She had trusted him with her life. She would trust him, as well, with her body and even her hopeful heart. She had no desire to squander another minute.

"I suppose there's only one way to find out if you meet my approval, Captain," she baited sweetly, and reached out into the dark until her palm skimmed his solid, naked shoulder.

The heat beneath his skin scorched her flesh. His muscles bunched hard as she ran her palm down his chest. Crisp, curly hair tickled, the sensation prickling up her arm and traveling to the pit of her stomach. When she grazed the point of his taut nipple, he sucked in air and threw his head back.

Feminine satisfaction made her smile. "Yes, now you're much more acceptable."

"Yes. Much," he ground out.

Without warning, he snatched her off the ground and into the cradle of his arms, and then sank to his knees. He set her down gently in the center of her bedroll and, with a sweep of his arm, cleared the thin mattress of reading disks and stray bits of clothing. Kneeling still, he lowered his head to claim her lips.

She opened to the intimate probing of his tongue and allowed him to ease her slowly onto her back. She clutched at his shoulders, and he came down with her, hovering just enough above her to continue the erotic exploration of her mouth.

As he traced the outline of her lips with his tongue she teased his sensitized nipple a few thundering heartbeats longer. The furious press of his mouth made it clear she excited him. Seeking to intensify his pleasure, she slid her hand across the scarred flesh on his left side and across his abdomen.

The back of her hand brushed the tip of his erection. In reflex she opened her hand wide to caress his hard, hot flesh.

But he suddenly clamped his hand around her wrist and broke the magic of his kiss. "No, Marista. It is not your duty to make me ready."

She opened her eyes wide in the dark. "You're more than ready. I only wanted . . ."

He shook his head and tightened his grip on her wrist. "In my tradition, a man brings himself around to the edge of completion after he has satisfied the woman who shares his bed. I have not yet begun to satisfy you, Little Diplomat. Afterwards you need do nothing but take me inside."

She smiled at the boastful pride in his voice. "I admire a tradition in which a man places the needs of his partner before his own. But, in my tradition, a woman draws satisfaction and pleasure from touching a man as I wish to touch you. I want to feel responsible, as well, for your excitement."

"You are responsible for all the excitement I feel."

"Then let me take pride in it. Let me take pleasure in pleasuring you this way."

He held still for a long moment. Tradition ran deep and strong in Albian society. Violation of ingrained behaviors and mores caused deep self-reproach. He had already withheld commitment of himself because he felt unworthy or unable to offer her anything beyond a brief interlude of passion. Perhaps she had no right to ask this breach of intimate, sexual custom.

Unsettled by his lengthening silence, she prepared to withdraw the request.

But he loosened his grip on her wrist before she had the chance. His warm breath held an uncertain sigh. "This touching will please you greatly?"

"Yes. Greatly."

He lifted his hand away, giving tacit permission.

Imagining his expression to be somewhat worried, she grinned up at him. "Will I be the first to touch you in this way?"

"Yes."

A new rush of urgent desire assailed her. "You honor me, and that heightens the pleasure I'll take. Now kiss me, please."

He obliged, his lips warm and sweetly tentative. She let him work his way back into a powerful, pressing urgency before she captured the swell of his arousal.

The hard flesh throbbed under her eager but gentle hold. The tip beaded with moisture and slicked her course down the rigid shaft. He gasped helplessly and buried his face into her shoulder.

"Shhh. Remember the tent next to us," she teased.

He answered with an impatient but muffled groan that rumbled from deep inside his chest.

She molded her fingers around the precious flesh, flexing and contracting her hold, working into a slow rhythm. "This isn't so bad, is it?"

Short, ragged gasps of air answered her question. So did the movement of his hips in time with the stroking.

Ending all resistance he gathered her closer, his whole body sweat-dampened from the pleasure of her ministrations. She continued the rhythm, down and up, down and up, then up and over the swollen tip, and down to the softer mound of flesh between his legs.

"Stop!" He captured her wrist again. Only this time, he drew her arm to his chest and held fast. "Enough," he ordered through broken breaths, "or I will disgrace myself, my clan, and all Albian traditions."

She laughed at his exaggeration, aware her giddiness stemmed from the knowledge she had excited him to the edge of physical self-control.

"You will lie still for me now," he commanded.

"You didn't hold still for me," she countered pertly.

"For that matter, neither will you."

His sensually wicked laugh filled her with anticipation. He arched his torso and slid the solid planes of his chest over her aureoles. Sensations both sleek and coarse assaulted every nerve in her body as he kissed her lips, jaw, neck and the aching swell of her breasts. He captured one aroused peak with his lips and slicked it with the tip of his tongue.

Her insides clenched and another rush of hot moisture flooded the core of her womanhood. In primitive reflex she bent her knee, lifted her leg with invitation, and pulled him forward. "Come into me."

He answered through set teeth, "Not yet."

When she tried to snag his leg with hers, he once again resisted the seduction and gently pushed her flat on the bedroll. But instead of returning to his erotic suckling he laid his face against the pillow of her bosom and slid his palm downward until his hand rested snugly between her thighs.

She gasped at the new, more potent intimacy. Then she gasped again when he slipped a finger inside her depths and drew it out and up over the small, sensitive nub at the apex of her womanhood with slow, deliberate care.

"You are ready for me, Little Diplomat," he marveled. "But I'll make you readier still."

"Tynan . . ." she rasped.

"Shhh. Remember the tent next to us."

The echo of her own teasing did remind her. But another thrust and sweep of his finger filled her with such a deep, wonderful, aching sensation that she had to bite down on her lip to keep from crying out.

Feeding that need, he worked magic into a tender but relentless cadence with his palm and fingers. She suddenly realized she moved instinctively beneath his touch, the erotic dance heightening the pleasure. Her womb clenched tighter with every thrust and retreat he made.

The tremors of release took her by surprise. She gripped his shoulders, burying her fingernails into his flesh, thrashing wildly and swallowing cries of ecstasy.

"Open for me now, Marista."

Her insides still convulsing, she obeyed. Tynan levered himself up and clasped the crest of her hips with his strong hands.

He filled her warmth in three easy thrusts, letting her narrow channel adjust painlessly to his full length. His slow restraint and his building rhythm reignited her need. She wrapped her legs around his hips, urging him to penetrate deeper.

He groaned, held his breath, and groaned again. Then suddenly he convulsed with his own release, catching a strangled cry in his throat as he poured out his fluid.

Gripping him hard, she let the soul-shaking tremors take her a second time.

He finally collapsed forward, using a brace of his arms on either side to keep from crushing her. "I think I would be pleased to learn more of your Terran sexual practices, Little Diplomat."

A weary laugh bubbled in her throat. She stroked his cheek with trembling fingertips. "I'll be happy to teach you, Captain."

Then he set his mouth to hers in a long, languid kiss that seemed to seal that promise. Afterward he rolled away and groped around in the dark. A moment later, he cocooned them together in a single thermal blanket.

The concern of his gesture, his desire to keep her close even though they'd spent their mutual passion brought moisture to her eyes. She dared not look for deeper meaning in his kindness. Yet, his tender, protective embrace quickened the hope in her heart.

***

Peace swallowed Tynan whole. In all the hours he'd spent meditating, he'd never achieved such inner calm.

Snuggled in the hollow of his shoulder, Marista dozed. Her warm breath skimmed over his chest. Beneath the blanket her slender curves molded to his body.

This woman was the source of his inner tranquility. And he discovered her healing magic in the throes of magnificent passion. He had no desire to let go of the wondrous contentment any time soon.

She'd felt so small and vulnerable between his hands, and under his body. His palms covered her breasts entirely. The span of his fingers nearly cinched her waist. A surge of desire to coddle and comfort her compelled him to pull the end of the blanket over her exposed arm.

Even as he readjusted the cover, he knew Marista Kaljin's delicacy camouflaged the real woman. She might be too trusting and soft-hearted, but she possessed an inner strength that would have humbled most combat-hardened soldiers he knew. Her tenacity and sense of honor had captured his grudging admiration. Her fiery kisses and wanton sighs had satisfied his long denied need to find comfort in a woman's arms.

But he realized he had sought more than satisfaction for his lust. If he'd wanted mere physical release, he could have swallowed his pride and hired one of the camp followers who were allowed inside the perimeter every ten days or so. He might be an Albian, but none of the Krillian girls would have turned away his military script.

No, he'd wanted this one woman. He had wanted her from the moment he'd opened his eyes to her image in the treatment room. The need to have her surrender in his arms had overwhelmed him so that he had lowered his inner shield and agreed to her request that he call her by her given name.

In the end, he had surrendered himself completely. Marista Kaljin had conquered his body and mind with her tender passion and quiet will.

He could not allow her to claim his heart, as well.

She stirred. "I think there's a stone in my back."

Though groggy he reacted at once. In a quick, easy motion he snagged her waist with his arm and hauled her on top of him, being careful to drag the blanket along.

She gave a brief squeak of surprise, but settled against him—shoulder to shoulder, chest to full, smooth breasts, hips to the feminine depths he yearned to explore again. Her tousled curls dragged over his face. The silky tendrils teased his skin and heated his desire.

She had such beautiful hair. He threaded his hands through the luxurious mass, captured her face and bent it forward until he could kiss her nose. "Displaced by a little stone? Didn't you brag once about the uncomfortable places you've bedded men?"

She sniffed, but the disdain evolved into a breathy laugh. "I didn't brag. I told the simple truth." She laid her face on his shoulder. "And there was only one man."

"One?"

He almost bit his tongue. He didn't want to know of her past lovers. He wanted to know nothing about her but that she writhed gloriously in his arms and drove him to the brink of mind-numbness.

"Who was he?" he heard himself ask.

She wound her right hand over his left and clutched it to her breast. Then she stretched one leg to cover his and slid the other leg over his hip, the movement both innocent and erotic.

As new pressure built in his groin he fingered the cape of hair that lay on her back. With blood rushing in his ears he almost didn't hear her answer.

"His name was Daniel. We were classmates at the Mitterand Academy of Diplomatic Arts. He wanted to marry me."

Her pause gave him the choice—let the conversation die, or pursue it. He decided to let the conversation die.

Unbidden, the question rolled off his tongue. "Did you love him?"

Her reply came just as readily. "Yes."

"Why didn't you marry him?"

Obviously, his self-control had fled along with his better intentions.

"Daniel became impatient because I put off our marriage plans too many times. He accused me of loving my career more than I loved him."

"Did you love your career more?"

Beneath his hand the muscles in her back tightened. "No, but I wanted my career more than I wanted him. I realize that's a narrow distinction, and I hurt Daniel all the same."

He let his hand glide back and forth over her taut muscles. "Did you want the career more because of your father?"

She sighed. "In part, yes. But I truly wanted to be a diplomat. Maybe because of what happened on Yonar, I believe that war is nothing but failed diplomacy."

"Do you regret your decision?"

He wondered why he found it so important to know such a personal fact. He held his breath and stopped the rhythmic kneading of her back as she lifted her head. In the gloom he discerned only the vague outline of the familiar delicate features, not the cast of her expression.

"No, I don't regret it," she finally answered, her voice edged with a hint of surprise. "I've always gone after what I've wanted, straight and sure. I suppose in that way I'm a little like my father. If I had loved Daniel enough, I would have found a way to keep him interested before he gave up on me."

The words sent a rush of exhilaration through him, as if he'd vanquished an opponent. The notion that her past relationship sparked any sort of jealousy niggled, but not enough to make him suppress a relieved grin.

Glad, at least, that she couldn't see his expression in the dark, he untangled her hair with a comb of fingers. "What is it you want now?"

She tightened her grip around his loose fist. "I want you to call me Marista from now on. Beyond that, I don't know what I want."

Her uncertainty prompted a moment of doubt in his own mind. He forced a teasing tone into his voice. "I knew a drill master who told his recruits a hundred times a day that it's never wise to be sure about anything."

"Then right now I'm the wisest person in the universe, because I'm sure of very little. I feel like I'm out of control, but I don't really care."

He cradled the back of her head and guided it down to the resting place on his shoulder. "Perhaps you should have allowed me to keep my knife staked between us."

Her lips curved against his skin. "That trick didn't work for Tristan and Isolde."

"Ah, yes, the two mythological Terrans. You said their story didn't end well."

"It ended tragically."

"Tell me what happened."

She tilted her face upward so that her forehead touched the tip of his chin. "I'm sure you'll appreciate this story. It revolves around strict adherence to duty."

He groaned a protest, but she went on. "Tristan was a knight on a mission to escort Isolde to the castle of her intended husband, King Mark. As in any great epic, complications arose from the start. On his way to Isolde, Tristan was wounded, and she nursed him back to health. During Tristan's recovery the two fell in love which, of course, defied the convention of arranged marriages."

"Did they run off together?"

"No, they were ashamed of themselves for daring to fall in love. So they kept their feelings secret and promised not to act on their emotions for the sake of honor. When Tristan finally had to take Isolde to Mark, he put his sword between them at night as a barrier against temptation."

"So it is with the desert nomadic traditions," he reminded her.

Beneath the caress of his hand she shook her head. "Well, your people may honor the symbolism. But these two Terrans had a few problems with it. One night, they drank some wine which was actually a love potion meant for Isolde and King Mark. After that a wall of swords couldn't keep them apart."

"I see."

"So did the king. Mark figured out what had happened. Maybe Tristan and Isolde couldn't hide their love."

At the mention of that tender emotion, a chill of discomfort snaked up his spine. "Or their guilt."

She nodded. "Or their guilt. Mark did marry Isolde, but banished Tristan forever from her sight. A tragedy."

"A predictable tragedy. Your mythological Terrans should have known better than to choose love over duty."

"Didn't I say you'd appreciate the myth?" she teased. Then, however, she paused, as if considering her next words carefully. "But maybe doing right isn't always doing good. I think Tristan and Isolde made the only choice possible for them and acted on their feelings when they had a chance. Maybe that's part of the story's lesson."

"What good came from their dishonor?"

"They had each other for a short time," she replied in a soft, faraway voice. "They had the joy of experiencing a love neither experienced again."

"What of the grief they experienced at loosing each other forever?"

The leashed anger of his words stunned him almost as much as it seemed to stun Marista. She brought her head up. In the dark he felt her gaze ask questions he wasn't prepared to answer.

"You're right. It is a tragic story," he agreed, forcing a false calm into his voice. "But I think you take the lessons of this story too seriously. Myths and legends are cultural remnants of less rational, non-technological societies."

"Myths and legends are wonderful, romantic stories," she argued quietly. "They help explain who we are, what we believe, and what's good and bad in all of us. Albia has its own heroic literature."

"Camp stories told to amuse children," he scoffed.

"Really? Does that include the Albian creation story? Remember, the one about the God of the Sun and Goddess of the Desert?"

He chuckled. "Yes, I remember the story. It reads like an adolescent boy's erotic fantasy."

She sighed with exasperation. "I read the classical version during my background preparation for this posting. There's more to the story than sex."

He slid his hand down the swell of her backside. "Not when I was an adolescent boy."

His attempt at distraction elicited a playful jab of her toes into his calf.

"It is not a childish story," she insisted. "The tale is a beautiful metaphor of life and the theme universal. The Sun and Desert give meaning to each other. Without the sun the desert and its creatures would not exist. Without the desert, the sun would have no reason to shine. They give purpose to each other. All of us need a higher purpose."

"Is that what the story means?" he teased. "After years of ignorance a Terran diplomat explains it to me. What enlightenment."

"I'm serious!"

But she didn't completely hide her amusement, and he laughed at the feigned indignation.

"Tynan, I've never heard you do that."

"Do what?"

"Laugh. At least not like you just did, with so much happiness."

He blinked in the darkness. Happiness? He dared not believe it possible.

Her fingertips explored the small ring he wore on his left hand. "There's so much I don't know about you."

His brain flashed a warning. He dragged his hand from her hold, trailed his fingers down along her side, and cupped her bottom. The feel of soft feminine flesh and muscle in his grasp brought his desire to full roar, and he pressed his cheek to hers. "This is all you need to know right now, Marista. This moment is our only higher purpose. Let it be enough."

He thrust his lower body upward and, with both hands, guided her toward his waiting arousal.

She offered no resistance to his prompting. He entered her and felt the immediate quiver of warm, moist flesh welcoming him.

Waves of heat rolled through him, igniting the still glowing embers of desire. Marista moaned against his thundering heart. He worked his hips until she shuddered with completion. Then he abandoned himself to the same wild pleasure.

Before his mind blanked with ecstasy, he heard his own words ricochet around his brain. *Let it be enough.*

For both of them.

Nineteen

Marista looked up from the portable scan reader and confirmed what she already suspected. Despite the commotion and undercurrent of voices in the med-tent, the young, wounded soldier to whom she read had drifted off to sleep.

She started to stretch her cramped back muscles, when she felt a prickle of recognition warm her skin. Even before she glanced toward the entrance of the tent, she knew he would be there.

Tynan stood at parade rest as he spoke to Sem. She smiled to herself. Now that he claimed her body, he no longer viewed the medic as a rival for her attentions. After one night of passion, he had the unmitigated gall to believe her bound to him.

Not that he didn't have every right to believe it.

The inner smile spread to her face, and the prickle of warmth became a rush of heat as she remembered last night. His skilled touches were bold but tender, urgent yet unselfish. He seemed to take pleasure in pleasuring her and giving before he took.

She had known with a woman's instinct that she would find satisfaction in his arms. She never expected the wild joy and the wonderful certainty that she'd found a missing piece of herself.

Yes, she did feel bound to him, body and soul.

He seemed to sense her gaze as she had sensed his presence. Turning from Sem, he locked his dark eyes on her. For a moment, he only stared. Then, amazingly, his military bearing cracked and he allowed her a slow grin full of secret meaning and promise.

She knew then that he recognized the memories in her smile and recalled them, as well. Wanting to run to him, but restraining herself for the sake of appearance, she rose from the camp chair and, with measured steps, made her way down the aisle of cots.

From the lift of Sem's brow, she imagined the medic saw through her façade of dignity and Tynan's new congeniality. Her skin heated with embarrassment, though Sem greeted her with a gentle grin. "Thank you for staying with Faolan this afternoon, Marista. You helped calm him with your conversation and attention."

"Or maybe I bored him to sleep," she demurred at the compliment.

Sem laughed. "Not likely. But I'll let you go now that your escort is here." He nodded at her, and then turned to Tynan. "Captain, a good evening."

As she looked after Sem she wondered if she detected innuendo in his wish for Tynan's "good evening."

"If you sat next to my cot, I wouldn't fall asleep."

She whirled in place to find him stifling a smirk. "Why, Captain, are you flirting with me?"

He shook his head, but his smirk became a smile. "Albian men don't flirt, Madame. We speak plain fact."

Flattered, she managed to keep her voice steady. "If you're complaining I deprive you of sleep I'll request a separate tent."

"Then I would have to refuse the request. I'd rather be denied sleep than your company." With a roguish tilt of his head, he pushed open the door flap. "Shall we go?"

"I think we'd better before someone overhears us."

He replied with a low chuckle as she ducked under his arm. The brisk, late afternoon air stung her overheated cheeks.

"You came earlier than I expected," she commented as he stepped up beside her and they started to walk.

"I'm glad I did. You look tired."

"I just sat a little too long. I'll be fine."

"Navarro claims you boost the morale of both the wounded and the staff."

Lifting her face to catch more of the refreshing breeze, she smiled. "Sem's been patient in helping me find a way to be useful. He offered to teach me some basic nursing. But even after working with wounded refugees at the outpost I still become queasy at the sight of blood."

He crinkled his forehead. "What did you expect from your posting in humanitarian services?"

"I didn't expect to be working side-by-side with med-techs," she assured him. "I figured I'd be issuing orders from behind a computer terminal."

"Yes, you're very good at issuing orders, Madame. I haven't found a way to keep you quiet."

"You did last night."

At her sauciness he grinned wider. "Perhaps you would like to share another quiet evening with me?"

As if having to consider the invitation, she bit her lower lip but couldn't suppress a pleased smile. "Perhaps."

But instead of turning toward their tent he strode straight ahead.

"Where are we going?" she asked.

"I'm taking you to the com-station on the shuttle," he replied. "Late this afternoon we received a recorded video message from your father."

"My father?"

He must have heard her apprehension. "I thought you'd be pleased."

"I . . . I'm just surprised the communication went through so fast," she hedged. "I wasn't even sure the authorities would find my father on Earth."

She winced inwardly at his puzzled frown and felt compelled to explain further. "He travels quite a bit now that he's retired."

"Doesn't he tell you where he's going?"

Unwilling to deceive him, she let down her defenses. "We don't communicate directly very often. My father and I usually relay messages through my Aunt Mimi."

"Then you and your father are estranged."

She'd never thought of the strained relationship with her father in those terms. "No. No, estranged is too harsh a word. We . . . we simply have our differences."

"You blame him for the deaths of your mother and sister."

"No, I never blamed him for that," she countered. "I blamed him for sending me away. I needed to grieve with him. He was all I had left of my family, but he set me aside and carried on with his duty to the military."

"What about your aunt?"

She struggled against the rise of old pain and resentment. "Mimi was my mother's sister on Earth. Since my father was rarely stationed at home I hardly knew her before she took me in. Mimi's wise and wonderful, and I grew to love her."

"But you missed your father."

Realizing that she'd lapsed into self-pity, she shook herself. "Of course, I missed him. I thought he'd abandoned me. But that's all in the past."

His silence didn't reassure Marista that he believed her. "Do you miss your family?" she dared ask to divert his attention.

"I can't miss something that no longer exists," he replied in a flat voice. "When I died in the field I abandoned the life I knew. I'm a man without a country or a heritage. Now that there's proof I betrayed my people, no one, not even my mother will speak of me again. What I had is gone forever. Missing it is a waste of time."

Though he sounded stoic, he didn't meet her gaze as they slowed in front of the shuttle doors. "You sacrificed a great deal for your conscience," she ventured.

His expression remained shuttered as he opened the door for her. "I'm not as noble as you believe. Now, if you prefer to view the recording tomorrow, I'll understand."

Once again, he'd withheld the whole truth. Yet, she had promised to ask no more of him than the present moment. And her word was her bond.

Listlessly, she waved him forward. "Lead the way."

Tynan took her into the com-station and sat down with her. After giving brief instructions on the use of the viewing equipment, he stood. "I have a conference with Varden. When you're finished, stay here and I'll come for you."

She nodded. "Thanks."

He stepped into the corridor and smiled briefly before closing the panel door and leaving her alone.

Minutes passed as she stared at the blank screen. Some long ago sealed and empty corner of her heart waited to be opened and filled with Anthony Henson's voice and face. That same empty corner needed to feel his presence, however distant and delayed it might be, as much as the girl had needed the comfort of her father nearly twenty years ago.

Yet, she feared rupturing the protective seal she'd set in place as a child. What if she again fell headlong into the dark and endless depths of despair that once nearly swallowed her spirit whole?

Or worse, what if her father's manner was, as usual, dutiful and controlled, when she needed and still missed a parent's warm, loving support? How sad she didn't even know what to anticipate from her closest kin.

Suddenly impatient with self-pity, she flipped a switch and set the recording in motion. The viewing monitor crackled to life, rolled three times, and finally went blue.

Anthony Henson's face came into sharp focus. He seemed so much older than she remembered. The short tufts of his deep brown hair had gone mostly gray, and the crinkle of lines around his mouth and eyes had deepened with the effect of sun and gravity. His strong, square face, still uncommonly handsome, had fleshed out noticeably at the jaw line and below his chin.

But his sharp, calculating eyes were unchanged. She stared into those eyes, noting they were hazel shaded to green. She'd always assumed her own eye color was the quirk of a recessive gene. Now she realized they were a gift from her father.

In reflex, she lifted her fingers to touch the screen as if she could really touch his face. "Dad?"

Anthony Henson cleared his throat. "Marista, I don't know when this will get to you. I hope soon. I used some old contacts to put this message on priority com-link . . ."

Her throat constricted with emotion and she answered him with her thoughts. Of course, you did, Dad. The old Network came through as usual. Maybe Bierich was right about how I received my posting.

"Mimi contacted me in Anchorage two days ago to tell me what had happened at the Terran outpost. We didn't find out you were safe until later that day. Damn, Riss, I wish I could see for myself that you're all right. No offense, Baby, but I just don't trust diplomatic double-talk."

He hadn't called her Baby since that terrible day on Yonar. The quivering indignation of his words brought tears to her eyes.

"The Secretary of Interplanetary Affairs told me Krillia promises to return you to the Terran Embassy in Sarquis. But right now the authorities can't arrange transportation for you. Don't let them stall, Riss. You know better than anyone what bureaucratic promises are worth in a war zone. I want to get you out of there, fast."

Her stomach lurched with sudden panic. She didn't want to leave the camp. She didn't want to leave Tynan . . .

"I know you don't want me to interfere in your life, Riss, but you're going to have to put up with me this time. I'm coming to Serraine to bring you home. I've made some preliminary inquiries. Been told to shove it . . . well, you know where. But I'm not going to give up."

He extended his hand as if to reach for her, then seemed to remember himself. "You're all I have left, sweetheart. I . . ." He swallowed hard. "I won't make the same mistake again. I'm coming for you, whether you want me to or not."

Her composure shattered. She covered her face with both hands and held back the worst of her tears by sheer will.

"I love you, Baby. I won't let you down. Not this time."

She looked up just as her father's image faded to blue. Was that an apology? And why now, twenty years too late?

Yet, she recoiled from the lingering resentments. She still judged him through the prism of childhood loss and pain. But who was she to judge him at all? How often did she give total strangers the benefit of the doubt concerning their actions? Tynan alone had used up her lifetime allotment of dispensation, and she still knew little about what motivated him. How could she be so ungenerous toward her own father?

With trembling fingers, she flipped off the monitor, leaned back in the chair, and stared at the blank screen. "I love you, too, Dad. But I'm sorry. I need time. I can't forgive you just yet."

***

The remnants of the evening meal still littered the footlocker they'd used as a table. Marista knew she and Tynan should clean the dishes before the leftover food dried hard.

But she didn't stir, and instead stared ahead as she sat on the conjoined bedrolls with her back to Tynan. Her arms circled the pyramid of his right leg. As she propped her chin on his raised knee, he set about undoing her braid and combing the loosened hair with his fingers. Each smooth, downward stroke hinted at sensual purpose and sent ripples of delight shooting from her scalp to her toes.

"You're quiet tonight, Marista. You have been since I came for you at the com-station. I think that should worry me."

His gentle teasing cut into her mental fog. But how could she explain her conflicted feelings about her father to him when she hardly understood them herself? "I'm sorry. I don't mean to worry you."

"You seem sad."

"What you're doing makes me drowsy," she excused herself.

"We can't have that."

When she felt his warm lips press to the exposed left side of her neck, a lick of desire coiled in the pit of her stomach. "Are you trying to tempt me, sir?"

"Not when you're sad."

"Then tell me something that makes me happy."

"Your beautiful hair excites me. It smells good."

He gathered her unruly curls in his hands, and then pressed his lips to her nape. She imagined he'd buried his face in her hair and breathed deeply. The coil of desire tautened, and she laughed softly. "My hair smells like military issue soap."

"No, it smells like you. You excite me."

She closed her eyes, tightened the circle of her arms around his leg, and let his words seduce her. "Yes, that does make me happy."

He slipped his arm around her waist, and set his cheek into the curve of her neck. "I have news that should make you very happy."

His breath wafted inside the "V" of her open collar. Her breasts peaked hard, and she stirred with mounting restlessness. "Hmmm? What news?"

He kissed the ridge of her collarbone. "While you were at the com-station Colonel Varden informed me that he has commandeered two ground shuttles. You'll be on your way to Bethel by tomorrow morning."

"What? No!"

She lifted her head so fast he whiplashed to move out of the way. She twisted herself within the boundaries of his arms and legs and peered up at his shocked expression. "I mean," she backtracked, "I wasn't expecting to leave so soon."

He narrowed his eyes. "Neither was I. But yesterday's reconnaissance indicated there's new Albian troop movement and weapon's deployment on the other side of the mountains. Officials in Sarquis don't want a Terran diplomat at a frontline outpost. They ordered the Command Center at Bethel to dispatch transportation for you immediately."

Irrationally alarmed by the prospect of leaving the camp, Marista reached for excuses to stay. "The wounded should go out first. That boy, Faolan, needs care in a real hospital."

He nodded. "Navarro has permission to escort some of the most seriously wounded to Bethel." He smiled and threaded his fingers through the ends of her hair. "The vehicles aren't very big, and space will be tight. But there'll be room for all of us."

"I'm not worried about my comfort."

The snap in her reply brought a frown to his face. "What are you worried about then? You'll be safe. The country is rough forest terrain, but the trip won't take more than a day-and-a-half. Our forces have marched through the area scores of times without incident."

When she didn't answer for lack of a sound explanation, he set his hands on her shoulders and gave a light squeeze. "I thought you'd be glad to leave camp. You'll have lodging at the Provincial Government House, along with good food, hot showers, clothes that don't hang off your body." He grinned, and traced a line along the exposed crest of her shoulder with his index finger. "Though ill-fitting clothes have their advantages."

When she didn't laugh at his flirtation, he frowned. "What is it, Marista?"

The vague fears and chilling apprehensions would not crystallize into anything she could name. She grasped the first, most logical reason that came to her mind. "Bethel brings me one step closer to Sarquis . . ."

"And?" he prodded at her pause.

She almost answered, *And takes me one step farther from you.*

But she locked away the truth in her heart and reached for the second most insidious dread. "And my father, in his usual no-holds-barred way, is trying to find passage to Serraine so he can take me back to Earth himself."

"That worries you?"

"Let's say I have mixed feelings about seeing him."

"Because he left you alone when you were a child?"

"I'm beginning to think I haven't moved as far beyond the hurt as I want to believe." She cringed. "I'm feeling guilty, too, I suppose. Over the years I've tried consciously to separate myself from Dad. I even legally assumed my mother's surname."

"It isn't uncommon for Terrans to do that."

"No, not uncommon," she agreed. "There are plenty of economic, social, and political reasons. But I wanted to obscure my connection with General Anthony Henson. I wanted to succeed on my own merits, not because I was his daughter."

She shrugged. "Maybe I was rejecting him like I imagined he rejected me. I've always thought of myself above vindictiveness. Now I'm not sure, and I'm almost ashamed to face him."

"You aren't vindictive."

His encouraging words pleased her, but she shook her head in doubt.

He set two fingers against her chin and held her still. "It is not part of your nature to retaliate."

"Madame Bierich would disagree."

"Would Gaer?"

His dark gaze, soft with kindness, challenged her to look deep inside herself. "Maybe not now."

"What about Colonel Varden and Lieutenant Navarro?" he pressed. "Or the wounded men you comforted this afternoon. They were all members of the raiding party that took you from the outpost. Yet you treat them as if they were your own people."

His sincerity demanded the truth. "Oh, Tynan, don't you understand? It's so much harder to forgive someone you love."

He winced, a fleeting but pained expression. "Yes, I do understand." Then, he set his cheek to hers and whispered, "But I believe you chose your surname to honor the mother you lost, not to spite the father who still lives."

Perhaps he did understand. From the comforting way he pulled her into his arms, she was certain he believed she had noble intentions.

The forgotten coil of desire wound itself unbearably tight. She raised her hand to his face and shivered as the stubble of his beard raked her palm. "Tynan, take me under you and make me want to cry out."

A sound of eager and impatient consent rumbled out of his throat. He wasted no time stripping their outer clothing. Only when he slipped his hand inside the waist of her briefs did she realize the lantern still burned from its perch on the end of her footlocker.

But when she reached around to damp the light he grasped her arm. "I've seen your body only in shadow, Marista. I've touched the flush of your skin and the soft readiness of your secret places. But I've never seen you with my eyes. Don't hide yourself tonight. Let me watch my hands heat your skin. Let me see your face when I bring you pleasure."

Spellbound, she held her breath as he grazed her fingertips with his teeth, then traced her palm with the tip of his tongue before setting her hand unabashedly against the bulge of his own arousal. "Last night you convinced me to try this new touching that pleases you. It would please me to see our bodies joined. Wouldn't you like to see my eyes when I lose myself inside you?"

She might have played cool and coy to make him convince her further. But the erotic images he stirred with his bold words inflamed her desire as surely as the feel of his wanton flesh cradled in her palm.

She fell against him and acquiesced with a fiery kiss. In a few breathtaking minutes, he brought her to a frenzied arousal with his hands and mouth and sensual murmuring.

Indeed, the sight of his lean hips thrusting against hers, his sun bronzed skin glistening with sweat, and his muscles straining to assure her release before achieving his own did heighten her excitement. He wanted her. He needed her. She was the reason his eyes shimmered with desire and his body moved with erotic purpose.

In the seconds before she came to completion, she gazed into his tautened face. Once again she beheld the warrior king, now a lover king as well. His dark eyes were glazed with passion, and his smile was triumphant in victory as he moved his length inside her to the rhythm of her mounting excitement. She arched against him.

And then she lost herself to the ecstasy. His hips worked furiously against hers, enhancing the already overwhelming sensations. As her passion crested, he let out a groan of his own. She opened her eyes in time to see him throw back his head and open his mouth in a silent cry to the heavens as he spilled himself into her depths.

Spent, he sagged forward and braced his weight on both arms as he hovered over her. "I have other suggestions," he panted. "Would you like to hear them?"

She kissed the self-congratulatory grin from his mouth. "Does that answer your question?"

He drew himself out of her depths, gathered her to his side, and pulled the two blankets over them both. He made no further effort to talk, but she doubted she could muster the energy to answer him anyway.

Their passion held old fears and resentments at bay a while longer. Cuddled against Tynan's body, she drifted into a peaceful, dreamless sleep.

She woke, however, with a start, and sensed light through her closed lids. Mother Creation, did the lantern still burn?

Struggling to open her eyes, she ran her tongue over dry lips and tried to roll over on her back, but Tynan's arm locked her in place on her side, facing him.

Though she didn't want to leave the circle of his embrace or the warmth of the blanket, muted footfalls somewhere in the distance alerted her that the perimeter guard was changing. Dawn would break in less than an hour, and exhaustion still dragged on her body. She knew the light would distract her from falling back to sleep.

With reluctance, she laid her hand on Tynan's shoulder and gave a gentle push. His eyelids twitched but didn't open. Instead of releasing her, he drew her closer. A bristle of his hair brushed her nose. The scent of lovemaking still clung to his skin.

Her own skin tingled in response to his physical nearness, though she realized he hadn't even wakened. His power over her body amazed her, and she laughed softly with pure delight.

He groaned, shifted his legs. "Near. Ri?"

A flicker of memory went off inside her brain. She'd heard him utter something similar before, that first night in the treatment room at the outpost.

Though certain he didn't really hear her, she answered. "Tynan, I'm here. Wake up for a second and listen. Let me go turn off the lantern."

"Near . . . Ri? Stay . . . Don't leave. Don't . . . go . . . Can't let you go . . . not this time . . ." His features creased with anger or fear or both, and his arm tightened around her with a fierce possessiveness.

Apprehension sent her pulse fluttering. Behind his closed lids, his eyes moved rapidly side to side, a sign he was dreaming something vividly enough to make him talk in his sleep. The mind phantoms compelled him, as well, to reach out and command her to stay close.

She sank her fingers into his shoulder and shook him hard. "Tynan, wake up."

"Neari, come back. Don't go. Neari!"

He spoke clearly this time, and she realized he called a name, not an order. He hadn't slurred his words here as he lay beside her or in the treatment room. He hadn't asked for anyone to stay close. He'd asked for someone to stay close.

Neari.

Burying his face in the crook of her neck, he let his hand slide over her breasts before resting it on the flat of her abdomen. "Neari? You're . . .here . . ."

The intimacy of his touch froze her. Her plea for him to wake stuck in her throat, caught on the hooks of an intuition so acute she gasped aloud. Neari was a woman. And not just any woman, but someone upon whom he'd bestowed intimate caresses of the kind he now bestowed on Marista's body while he dreamed.

Her heart beat ragged and fast. Stone cold jealousy and hot fury met, clashed, and struggled to dominate her soul while Tynan slumbered and dreamed.

She clenched her fists, but fought the urge to thump his chest. Horrified by the violent impulses, she grasped his hand where it lay sprawled over her belly and pushed it aside. Once free, she scrambled to her knees, dragging her thermal blanket along.

She had to get away from him, gather her wits.

He sucked in air and rolled to his back. His eyes flew open and fixed blankly at the tent roof for a handful of seconds before he bolted upright. "What . . . what happened?" He scrubbed his eyes with the heels of his hands then squinted into the weak lantern light. "Marista, what are you doing over there? What's wrong?"

She clutched the thermal blanket to her breast. Beneath her fist, her heart quivered. That same quiver shook her voice. "Who's Neari?"

His grogginess cleared instantly. Bleak dismay flickered in his wide eyes. "How do you know that name?"

"You said it in your sleep. You . . ." Her treacherous voice cracked. "You called to her in your dreams."

Without answering, he snapped his head around and gave her his profile.

She lowered her voice to hide the awful desperation of her demand. "Who is she, Tynan? I think I have a right to know that much about you."

After a moment of wrenching silence, he turned to her. "Yes, you have a right to know."

The cold desolation in his glare panicked her more than her own wild imaginings. "Neari . . ." He paused, steadied his voice. "Neari is my wife."

The air left Marista's lungs . . .

"She's dead. I killed her."

Twenty

The words ricocheted inside Marista's head, making no sense yet explaining everything. Another woman. Another life. Another love. The reason Tynan couldn't give his heart.

She wanted to pick herself up off the ground and flee. Shock immobilized her.

Tynan angled one knee up and rested his arm on top. "What words don't you understand, Marista? I can say the same thing in four languages. Neari is my wife. Was my wife," he corrected harshly. "She's dead."

She clutched the blanket tighter to her breast, but still couldn't move as he twirled the tiny gold ring with the thumb and forefinger of his right hand.

"Say something, Marista," he demanded. "Say anything. Scream. Cry. Hit me." He arched a brow. "Forgive me, I forgot. You make love, not war."

Anger overran shock. "Don't turn this back on me, Tynan. Just explain yourself. Any language is fine. What do you mean, you killed your wife?"

He clenched his jaw. She knew he was struggling with his emotions. But so did she. Grief overwhelmed whatever compassion she might have felt for him.

"I killed Neari," he repeated. "Not with my own hands, and not on purpose. But I am responsible for her death."

She heard the bone-deep sadness and longing despite his clipped words. "Mother Creation, Tynan, she isn't dead."

That brought him up to his knees. He loomed over her, hands fisted at his side. "I've done many questionable things in my life, but committing adultery is not one of them. I wouldn't have bedded you if she were alive."

He'd misunderstood. Perhaps he didn't even fathom the depth of his own feelings. She shook her head, slowly at first, then more certainly. "No, your wife isn't dead. Not when you still keep faith with her in your heart."

He narrowed his gaze. "You think that because I dream about her? She was part of my life for five years. I can't just forget her."

"Is that her ring you wear?"

The question caught him off guard. "What?"

An eerie calm settled over her, the sort she'd felt when Gaer threatened her life. Even to her own ears, her voice sounded flat. "I know the ring is special to you. You touch it whenever you're tense, as if it has the power to calm you. I do the same with my necklace. I also know Albian men don't wear jewelry, not even as a talisman or . . ." She took a quick gulp of air. "Or as a marriage band. The ring is so small it fits only your last finger. It must be hers."

He raised his left hand and turned it sideways so she could see the gold band. "Yes, the ring belonged to her. I wear it and use Neari's family name to honor her memory." He let his hand fall to his side. "And to remind me of my duty to her."

Tears climbed up her throat. She swallowed them. "If Neari's dead, what duty can she demand of you?"

"The duty that compelled me to renounce my heritage."

"Explain," she commanded softly.

He started to turn away. "What happened isn't important."

"Yes, it is important!" Her calm facade crumbled, and with it her reason. "I've trusted you with my life, my honor, and my body. Now, I ask—no, I demand—you return that trust. Tell me!"

She hated the frantic tone of her ultimatum. Yet she would not let him deny her an explanation. Not again.

Raking the bristles of his coal-black hair, he sat back on his haunches. "I don't know where to start."

"At the beginning."

He frowned. "This is a long story."

"I'm not going anywhere until I hear it."

He sighed, reached past the head of the conjoined bedrolls to grab her discarded clothing, and shoved the wrinkled wad at her. "Why don't you dress first?"

She jutted her chin. "Don't put me off."

"I won't."

Though he sounded resigned, Creation knew she'd misjudged him before. She hesitated only a second before snatching the clothes from him. "If you'll turn around and give me a moment, please?"

He scowled. "Don't you think it's a little late for coyness?"

Buried in the sarcasm was a stark truth. With her eager permission, he'd explored every plane and crevice of her person with his eyes and hands and mouth. In turn, she had committed to memory the sight of his body joined to hers, the feel his hands bringing her to fulfillment, and the taste of his passion-slicked skin.

Yet, as much as the sudden need to shield herself from his gaze defied logic, she could not ignore it. Unable to answer for the tightness in her throat, she twisted in place and put her back to him.

He grumbled a curse. Out of the corner of her eye, she saw his clothing disappear from the head of the bedroll. Seconds later she heard the rustle of legs and arms beneath his blanket as if he felt less comfortable with his nakedness, too.

As she slipped into her shirt and pants, conscience and reason berated her. She'd lost her head and her heart to a virtual stranger, and now she faced the consequences.

Finished dressing, she pushed off the ground and glanced over her shoulder just enough to see he still struggled beneath his blanket. Quickly, she moved to her footlocker and took a seat next to the lantern.

He finally hefted himself up and, still facing the tent wall, waved his arm in her general direction. "If you need more time, I'll leave."

"I'm ready."

She'd have her answers and have them now. Even if it ripped both their souls to shreds. With every bit of willpower she had left, she folded her hands primly in her lap and set her expression with a blandness that belied the tumble of her emotions.

He pivoted and dropped into an empty camp chair well out of touching range. "How much did Ugo tell you about his research?"

"Very little. But I don't want to talk about Jace."

"I'm not. I'm talking about his research. Did he tell you about it?"

His weary tone blunted her impatience. "He never told me anything specific. I know now it concerns the destruction of the Rising Sun."

He kneaded the back of his neck. "Ugo discovered the Albian government falsified the reports of the weapons placement and military base construction it presented to the Council of Seven Planets at the official inquiry."

For a moment she forgot her anger. "Jace told you that?"

"I already knew it."

"How?"

"I falsified some the information myself before the crash."

Her head spun. "What?"

"I didn't know I was falsifying the data," he went on. "I was a mid-level intelligence officer, so I processed and disseminated the information I received from my superiors. I did what I was told to do like any good Albian soldier, even though so much of the data was contradictory to other intelligence files I had read, and to what I knew from my own field experience. It was all there in black and white. Albia was preparing for an offensive war along the Borderland frontier."

Resting his arms across his legs, he cast his gaze to the ground. "If I had raised questions or voiced concerns, Neari wouldn't have died. None of those people would have died."

The despair in his voice made Marista almost hesitant to prod him. "What people?"

He fixed her with dark, infinitely sad eyes. "The people who died on the Rising Sun."

The enormity of the revelation overwhelmed her. "Your wife? Mother Creation, she was aboard the Rising Sun? That's why you tried to kidnap Lares and Osten. That's part of your . . ." She nearly choked on the word. ". . . duty to Neari's memory."

He bolted from the chair, but pulled up short of the tent entrance and made a quarter turn. The lantern light cast deep shadows on his face as he fixed his stare on the tent wall.

"I didn't know all the pieces of the grand scheme," he continued. "But I had enough access to strategic planning that I should have guessed something was about to happen. Map projections showed missile installations where field reports stated the sites didn't exist. There were troop deployments to bases that had no official designations. Then there were the 'unofficial' visits to High Command by civilian leaders, and heightened security measures."

He rubbed his eyes with the heels of his hands. "All pieces of a giant battle plan. Maybe I didn't want to see the whole, ugly picture. Maybe I didn't want to believe it."

Part of her, the cowardly part, wanted him to stop his narrative, and leave her in ignorance. Another part of her, the honest core, knew she needed to hear the rest as much as he needed to tell her.

When he finally spoke again, she held her breath. "I heard rumors High Command was about to impose travel restriction on the Albian populace. Some intuition clicked inside me. I decided to send Neari out of harm's way before the restrictions became a ban."

"Standard operating procedure," she echoed his words.

He nodded. "Neari was a Malvian national, a professor of Interplanetary History. She didn't want to take leave of her position at the Multi-Cultural Institute in Timetsuara and argued that if the situation deteriorated, her own world would evacuate its citizens. I went ahead and bought passage for her anyway."

He lowered his voice until it matched the faraway cast of his stare. "She didn't speak more than ten words to me all the way to the transport dock. Then, just before boarding, she took off her ring and put it in my hand. She called me a stiff-necked Albian, told me to damn tradition for once and wear the ring until she came back to claim it. We kissed. She left. An hour later the Rising Sun exploded near the Borderlands. Albian artillery shot it down. They had an incident to start a war the government knew it could win."

She stifled conflicting pangs of jealousy and sympathy. "I'm sorry," she finally managed to croak.

Tynan faced her. "With all due respect, Marista, you don't know the meaning of the word sorry. For weeks I drowned in grief and self-loathing because I sent Neari to her death. I went home on medical leave and set out on Medan's Ocean with the bi-sail we owned. I sat for hours on the water, trying to blunt the pain with the meditation techniques she taught me."

Medan's Ocean. The bi-sail. The roll and pitch of the water. Learning meditation from a master.

He had spoken of those things at the outpost. In rare moments of reverie he still sailed Medan's Ocean with the woman he loved. He still employed the Malvian meditative arts his wife had taught him to calm his spirit. Neari did live in the recesses of Tynan's beating heart.

His gravely voice broke into her bleak epiphany. "When I finally dragged myself out of depression, I began to understand the enormity of what I'd done, or at least allowed to happen. I helped kill all those people. I killed my wife."

"You didn't know." She stretched out her hand. "You can't take responsibility for decisions beyond your control or knowledge."

"I should have known." He ignored her gesture and dropped back into the camp chair. "I was part of the system. I knew how it worked. But I closed my eyes. I divided my attention and loyalties. I wanted career advancement and prestige, honors Neari tried to tell me were without real substance. But I wanted her world, too. I studied mediation with her, gentled many of my 'harder' qualities, the qualities that made me a good Albian soldier. I numbed my instincts when I needed them most."

He lifted his face to the tent roof. "I wanted it all, and I ended up with nothing. I let the happiness I found with Neari distract me. In the end I failed myself, my duty . . ." He clenched his hands. "And I failed Neari."

His terrible frustration finally stirred her compassion. "Is that why you deserted, because you lost faith in yourself and your government?"

"Nothing so noble," he answered, with a contemptuous smirk. "I started asking uncomfortable questions. When I found no answers, or worse, deceit, I went rogue. I accessed records beyond my clearance, pieced together telemetry data from different agencies. I even visited some of the bases that officially didn't exist.

"By that time, much of the information that had triggered my first suspicions was destroyed, or altered and useless. I became reckless. A close friend from internal security warned me I had drawn the attention of her superiors. I compiled as many secured documents as I could compress on a few data chips and then staged my death during a routine training exercise. Had I stayed, the military would have found cause to court-martial and execute me for dereliction of duty."

"Dereliction of duty?" She rolled her eyes. "You did everything they asked at the expense of your own happiness!"

His eyes softened for a brief moment. "You would still defend me, Little Diplomat, after all I've told you?"

While he seemed honestly surprised, she couldn't be sure he wasn't baiting her. She gave him a measured reply. "You were unaware of your nation's deceit. Creation knows, if half of what you told me about Earth's complicity in all this is true, I've served corruption no less than you did."

His eyes narrowed in an odd questioning way that melted some of the frost in her heart. "You astound me. How can you ever make a decision about what's right when you consistently see the validity of all situations?"

"I listen to my heart."

She arched a brow, expecting ridicule that never came. Instead, he sank back into the camp chair and regarded her with wariness.

When she looked down at her lap, she found her hands steadier than her frantic pulse. "After what you just told me I think Jace is right. You might be the key to ending this war. When we reach Sarquis I'll try to contact him through the Terran Embassy."

The camp chair groaned when he shifted his weight. "No."

She snapped her gaze up to him. "Why not?"

"I tried all the official channels two years ago when I defected," he grated out. "The Yonarans were sympathetic. The Malvians were outraged because of Neari, but powerless to act decisively. The Terrans didn't even grant me an audience."

Shame, then anger, washed over her. "But you said you had proof. Hard data."

"Not enough," he muttered. "Your world had already taken sides. Unofficially, of course."

"What about now?" she insisted.

He laughed harshly. "Am I more credible now? A Bracquar, risen from the grave, who actively hunts down Albian officials for personal vengeance. At best, I'd be declared mentally unstable."

"I'll vouch for you, then."

He groaned a sigh. "No offense, but you're only a low level diplomatic aide. You'd burn and bury what's left of your professional reputation."

His stubbornness raised her hackles. "I'm willing to do that. I believed in you from the beginning. I believe you now."

"Your heart speaking again?"

She slid forward on the footlocker. "Yes. You're a good, decent man with honorable intentions."

He gazed heavenward and threw up his hands. "You still don't understand. I left my honor behind when I defected from Albia. I killed Neari and all those people."

"No, you don't understand," she argued through set teeth. "I think pity has become too comfortable for you."

His eyes hardened. "What?"

She didn't flinch. "You wear guilt like a shield around your heart. It lets none of the pain out and none of the healing in. But the pain is familiar. You can tap it whenever you need to remember how not to be hurt again."

He shot up so fast the chair tipped backward. "I warned you not to try and get inside my head."

She pushed off the footlocker. "I don't have to go rummaging around up there. That dream said it all."

His glare narrowed. "That is?"

"You won't let Neari go," she obliged him, though her voice wavered. "All that nonsense about having no clan, no identity, nothing of yourself to give, is camouflage for the truth that you've made repentance for her death the reason for your life. You've locked out everyone and everything except this destructive, self-appointed duty to bring the real criminals to justice!"

He hardened his gaze. "Didn't you say we all need to have some higher purpose?"

The mock seared her already wounded heart. "Revenge and absolution from guilt are not my idea of a higher purpose!"

He pulled back a step as if she'd struck out at him. "You don't know anything about what I feel."

"I know you still love her."

Hurt forced sharpness into her tone. She pressed her fingers to her mouth and exhaled her frustration and regret. But apology died on her lips when she noticed a sheen of moisture soften his eyes. In that moment she realized she'd uncovered a wrenching truth.

The pained rasp in his voice confirmed her fears. "Yes, I still love Neari. I will always love her. She shared my life and my dreams. She taught me to look beyond who I am, where I came from, and deep into my soul." His voice hushed. "She carried our child."

Grief sucked her into its black depths. A wife and a child. No wonder he couldn't forget. No wonder he couldn't forgive himself or give his heart to her.

"I warned you, Marista."

Had he read her despairing thoughts so easily? She swallowed the thickness in her throat. "So you did, Tynan. In that regard you've always been honest."

She stumbled backward against the footlocker and sat down on it hard.

Immediately he dropped to his knees in front of her, his frown now one of gentle concern as he reached out to steady her. "Marista . . ."

She held up her hand to stave him off. "Be honest with me now." She slid her gaze to the wreck of blankets at their feet, and spoke past an unwelcome sob. "Was it me you bedded, or was it your memory of Neari?"

"Marista, look at me."

She shut her eyes. "Just tell me . . ."

"Not until you look at me."

She wasn't sure how she made her eyes lift to his face. She found few answers in his bemused expression.

He drew in air. "I could never confuse you with a shadow of my mind. Your life force is too strong. I knew that back at the outpost from the moment I opened my eyes and saw you hovering over me."

A wan smile lifted his mouth. "You were so serious and kind." He lifted his hand, almost touched her hair but refrained. "I didn't think of Jarrit, or the failed mission, or my injuries. I could think of nothing else but how beautiful you were."

She wanted to bask in his wonderful admission, but didn't dare let herself hope. Instead, she bit her lower lip to keep it from trembling. "You looked at me as if I were death come to claim you."

"You were worse than that. You were life."

When she frowned her confusion, he nodded. "I was more afraid of living than dying. After Neari died I shut myself down. I reasoned and reacted, but I didn't want to think, or remember, or feel. So my subconscious took over and the dreams started. I thought I'd tamed them with meditation."

He raised a brow. "Then you appeared, in a place you shouldn't have been, at a time when I didn't care what happened to me. You set about saving me, surrounding me with all your energy and emotion. I tried to block you out. You just found new ways inside."

He sat back on his heels. "Then, Gaer threatened me when I defied his orders, and I realized I could no longer be reckless. Because of feelings you brought back to life inside me, I cared enough again to fear dying."

The words of praise slashed at her heart, and she waved at the blankets. "This was nothing but payback for services rendered?"

His shoulders stiffened but his voice remained level. "Did it feel like nothing but payback?"

Tears burned her eyes. She closed her lids to hold them in check as she answered with her heart. "No."

"I never promised you a future," he whispered. "I can't. That would distract me again, this time from my duty to Neari's memory. Somehow I will find a way to bring Lares and Osten to justice."

She opened her eyes to find him scanning the rumpled bedrolls. "I know you want more from me, Little Diplomat," he murmured. "You deserve more. But I loved once, and I lost that love. I've given you as much as I can without giving too much again. I'm sorry."

She nodded once, and forced air past a painful lump in her throat. "You warned me. I didn't listen. The fault is mine."

He hung his head. "Oh, Marista . . ."

She recoiled from his groan of regret and bit hard on her lower lip to hold it steady.

He rose and hovered over her. "I'll check to see if the ground transports have arrived. Eat your morning meal, take your turn at the hygiene station, and gather your things together. I won't be away too long."

She managed another weak nod. After a pause, she heard him pivot and leave. When the tent flap snapped down her will finally failed.

For too long she'd blanked her mind to the consequences of falling in love with Tynan. Now she had to pay the price for her risky gamble.

She bent double, covered her face with shaking hands, and muffled a sob that drained the air from her lungs.

***

An early morning mist clung to the damp ground, and thin clouds blotted out the weak sunlight. The odor of forest rot and wet stone rode a cool breeze.

Tynan lingered at the edge of the campsite, watching Navarro supervise the loading of his wounded patients into the ground shuttles. In less than thirty minutes the small caravan would be ready to depart for Bethel. He should backtrack the few paces to his tent and collect Marista. He could no longer avoid his duty.

Duty. His guilt hitched several notches at the impersonal sound of that too familiar word. Yet he accepted what had to be done. He had to do right by Marista, not only for her sake but for his own peace of mind.

He headed toward the tent, his pace sluggish with self-reproach. He had been a fool to believe he could find contentment in the arms of a good and decent woman and not involve his emotions. His jealous memories called out to remind him of that folly.

Yet, the dream of Neari was not the same one that usually woke him aroused, needy, and frantic to release his seed. Neari had appeared to him this last time awash in soft light. She'd taken his hand and laid it over her belly where their boy-child grew, and then she'd pressed her ring into his hand and stepped back into the light until her placid features merged with the glow. A stab of loss and longing had jolted him awake. But as he'd stared at the tent ceiling, a strange peace had engulfed him.

Then he'd looked into Marista's wide, uncomprehending eyes, and guilt crashed over him again like a mountain avalanche. She'd demanded the truth. How could he have denied her? She had given to him selflessly. He was alive because she'd shielded him from Sindri's machinations and Bierich's blind deference to diplomatic entente. He'd found blissful release inside her body and comfort in her company. Yet she'd demanded little in return.

And he'd repaid her generosity by breaking her heart, then fleeing like a coward. It didn't matter that he'd warned her of his limitations. Hearing her try to deaden the sound of sobs as he stood outside the tent almost cost him his own self-control.

Though loath to commit this unpleasantness, he was eager to be done with it and he quickened his step. When he reached the tent he pulled up before charging inside and cleared his throat. "I'm back."

"Come in."

The strength in Marista's voice relieved him. Perhaps her tears— the ones she swore she never cried – had cleared her mind. Perhaps she would understand the wisdom of his decision. His determination renewed, he ducked inside.

She stood in the middle of the tent with her hands clasped together, and her shoulders straight. She'd worked her beautiful, sunset red hair that he loved to hold and smell into a tight braid at the back of her head. Only a fringe of the silky wisps grazed her forehead and cheeks. Her eyes were luminous green and far too large.

Camouflage fatigues and a bulky jacket concealed her womanly curves. With her chin tipped up and her mouth set in a straight line, she appeared innocent and yet self-possessed. Surges of need and desire and fierce protectiveness almost quelled his resolve.

"I saw the ground shuttles on my way back from my shower," she said into the awkward silence between them.

He nodded stiffly. "They're ready to leave."

Looking at the ground, she tapped her rucksack with the toe of her boot. "I packed just what I needed for a day. Should I take my bedroll?"

The question galvanized him. He blinked away the haze of emotions. "No, the shuttle seats convert to bunks."

She shrugged and started to crouch. "I'd better hurry then and get the rest of this gear back to supply."

His mouth went dry. "I'll take care of it later."

She snapped herself straight. "When later?"

He fought the urge to take her into his arms and hold her one last time. "Later, after you leave camp."

"You . . . you aren't coming?"

"No, I'm not."

"But you said . . ." She pressed her fingers to the namesake flower pendant at her throat. "Why?"

He forced a reasoned nonchalance into his voice. "There isn't a need for me to go along. The shuttles are swift, well-armed, and heavily guarded. You won't be without company, since Navarro and one of his aides are traveling with the wounded. Once you reach Bethel, the authorities will arrange suitable quarters for you."

Her bewildered frown tested his will. "But you're responsible for my safety. Varden gave you orders."

"Technically, my responsibility for your safety ends when you leave camp," he replied, though his mind protested. "I spoke with the Colonel, and he agrees I'm needed here rather than escorting you through secure territory." He angled his head. "We both know you can take care of yourself."

Anger glimmered in her eyes. "You're sending me off, by myself, and you didn't have the courtesy to so much as consult me?"

"I made the decision myself to avoid this sort of debate."

"A debate isn't what you feared. You feared not being able to get rid of me fast enough."

"That's not true."

An eerie composure settled over her. "Yes, Tynan, it is true. This is history repeating itself because I never learned the first lesson well enough. A soldier does his duty first and foremost."

The glimmer of anger in her eyes faded to a flat indifference so utterly cold that he hardly recognized her. "Attention to duty can justify causing a great deal of pain. My father used the same excuse. Both of you shut yourselves down so easily. I never learned how. I'll never understand why."

Intuition hit him like a blow to his gut. In trying to protect her from further hurt, he'd reawakened the pain of childhood abandonment and loss of control. Like her father, he'd decided to send her away. His stomach did a hard flop, and he reached for her arm. "Marista, this isn't what you think."

She recoiled from his touch. "I know what to think. You're a soldier. You travel light, taking only what you can carry on your strong, broad back. You don't need extra weight in your heart to slow you down. You can't take the time to deal with your own pain, much less someone else's pain. The bodies you leave behind are nothing but collateral damage."

"Marista . . ."

Once again she dodged his grasp, scooped the rucksack from the ground and slung it over her shoulder. As if he'd disappeared into thin air, she marched past him and out of the tent.

He should just let her leave, the less said the better. Instead, he flew out behind her and managed to latch her elbow before she went five steps. "Marista, we can't part like this, not when I'm indebted to you for my life."

She wrenched free of his hold. "I only did my job. A thank you will be sufficient, Captain."

Her sardonic formality insulted him. But, like a censured recruit, he simply nodded. "Then, thank you."

Her chin quivered, but she quickly restored her cold demeanor and resumed her progress. When he fell into step beside her, she stopped and raised her hand. "You don't follow me, and I won't look back. Take it from someone who knows. It's the easiest way."

She spun around and left him behind. With every step she retreated, he felt a twinge of frigid emptiness. By the time she launched herself into the transport, the emptiness had grown into a breath-stealing ache.

Twenty-one

Marista grinned with self-congratulation as she threaded the last of the jubinda through the arch of the wedding bower. Though working with care and patience, she snagged one of the vine's delicate four-petal pink flowers. The blossom released its potent perfume into the air, and the fragrance briefly overrode the dank odor of the nearby Narquat River.

Strange, she thought, that an uncomplicated, physical activity could bring with it such a sense of complete satisfaction. But, then, lately she'd had to find reward in the little joys of life. For most of the thirty days she'd been stranded in Bethel, she had waged a pitched battle against the Krillian bureaucracy over their shameful treatment of Albian refugees. She'd finally just acted on her own and moved herself into the refugee enclave outside Bethel city limits.

The city officials reacted with diplomatic but stern words of warning that she threatened her own safety. But she didn't care, because she'd found a new purpose when she'd needed one the most. The plight of the Albian refugees filled a gaping black hole in her heart that had threatened to swallow her completely when she'd left the Barrier Mountains base camp. It gave her the energy to rise at dawn, despite a persistent dull ache in her head, and a constant churning in her stomach. Her work left her too busy during the day to think about personal loneliness. At night, she was too tired to dream.

That suited her just fine.

Tilting her head, she leaned back enough to critique her work but not enough to lose her balance on the top step of the ladder. "What do you think, Dyani? Should I add more razzle-dazzle, or are we just about finished?"

The young woman on the pavement below giggled, and Marista glanced down. For a moment breath caught in her throat, as it always did when she looked into Dyani's face—a once wholly beautiful work of nature now half-shattered by the senseless violence of war.

A raw vermilion scar ran diagonally from the left side of Dyani's forehead to her right jaw line, the remnants of a nearly fatal wound that had healed unevenly. Her left eyelid drooped helplessly, her upper nose was flattened at the bridge, and the cusp of her upper lip didn't quite meet in the center.

Yet, Dyani held her chin high and peered up at Marista with laughing, sky-blue eyes. "To me she is beautiful," Sem had claimed. Now she understood that those words expressed more than a man's pride in the physical appearance of the woman he loved. Sem spoke of Dyani's quiet dignity, and her gentle, generous nature. Dyani of the Qaletaqa Clan was beautiful in all the ways that really mattered.

"I think you've razzle-dazzled enough," Dyani answered, giggling

again as she repeated the unfamiliar phrase. "It looks perfect. Here."
She grinned with the good side of her mouth and handed Marista an old-
fashioned, wick-burning hurricane lamp. "Is lantern light part of the
Terran wedding tradition like the arch and flowers?"

"Actually the tradition calls for light from beeswax candles,
especially during an outdoor, evening ceremony like this," Marista
answered as she hooked the lantern in the center of the bower. "But
since we have no candles, beeswax or otherwise, flickering light from
the wick will do."

"I think it will be very romantic," Dyani said with obvious
anticipation.

Marista grinned her agreement as she descended the ladder. "That's
the idea. Sem will fall in love with you all over again."

Once on the ground, she looked across the open-air courtyard and
surveyed the results of their efforts. The cobblestone pavement, though
still gray with age, was swept and scrubbed. Long tables rimmed the
back and left side stone walls and were strategically placed to cover
dangerous ruts. Tonight those tables would be laden with community
donations of food rations and handmade tokens of congratulations.
Garlands of pink, yellow, and periwinkle wildflowers spanned the trefoil
arches of the courtyard's main entrance, concealing the chipped and
crumbling masonry.

"You know," Marista said with a satisfied nod, "tonight, when we
light all the lamps, this whole place will look romantic."

Unexpectedly, Dyani's eyes filled with tears, and she pulled Marista
into a tight hug. "Both Sem and I are so indebted to you. You have risked
much for our sake, and for my people."

Marista felt moisture sting her own eyes and drew in a shuddering
breath as she held Dyani close. "You can thank incredible timing and
luck. The Krillian government is a victim of its own ineptitude. They
can't get me to Sarquis, as they promised. And I'm not one to sit around
getting bored. My Aunt Mimi always said it's good to stir the pot once in
a while, just so all the good stuff doesn't settle to the bottom."

Though Dyani laughed at the joke, she shook her head as she pushed
away enough to look into Marista's face. "Your generosity has far
surpassed what we might have expected from . . ."

"From a Terran?" she finished when Dyani stumbled in
embarrassment. Then she grinned. "Don't be too critical of your adopted
world. Neither of us would want the Krillians to believe my sponsorship
of your Terran citizenship was nothing more than a legal maneuver to
evade the Sedition Acts. That would get me into trouble."

Both of them laughed again until Dyani looked past her shoulder
and broke from her embrace. Even if Marista hadn't heard the uneven
rhythm of a walking cane and boot steps on the pavement she would
have known Sem approached them from behind. Nothing else brightened

Dyani's face so, or brought such a lovely blush to her cheeks.

Her chest tightened with both an ache of joy and a pang of envy. Seeing her two, dear friends together never failed to push her too close to the emotional abyss she had tried to avoid for the past month. Mother Creation, how she longed to feel the wonder and thrill of such love again!

Dragging his injured leg heavily on the pavement, Sem moved alongside of them. He'd received the wound less than three weeks before at the front lines, and it had made him unfit for further military duty. Chances were great he'd never walk again without a cane.

Marista tamped down a surge of pity and slid her gaze toward the bridal bower as Dyani fell into his welcoming arms. She didn't—couldn't—turn back to the couple until she heard the bride-to-be cluck her tongue.

"You aren't supposed to see me before the ceremony," Dyani lightly scolded Sem.

Sem glanced at Marista and raised a brow. "Another Terran marriage tradition?"

"Actually," Marista said with a grin, "the groom isn't supposed to see the bride in her marriage gown before the ceremony. So technically, you're still on the right side of good fortune."

"I have a great deal to learn about my new heritage," Dyani joked.

Marista shrugged and had the decency to blush. "Yes, well, I didn't have time to teach you the finer points of the culture."

Sem peered at Dyani and sighed. "I must confess, I did not come early just to see you." He turned to Marista. "I brought someone to see you."

She closed her eyes and leaned toward Sem in confidence. "If it's Vice-Magistrate Ouray again, she can just turn around and go back to the city. I have no more business with her."

"But I have business with you."

The ghostly familiarity of the rich, male, Albian-accented voice rose from her buried, secret longings. Disbelief, then panic, weakened her knees and caused her heart to skip several beats. When her lungs refused to work, she grasped Sem's arm and shut her eyes tight to control the sensations.

"Marista?"

He stood at her shoulder now. Her name floated on currents of his warm breath, ruffling the hair on the back of her neck. Blood pulsed in her ears. Was she finally hallucinating from lack of food and sleep and too much worry?

"It can't be," she whispered. "Tynan?"

"Yes. I'm here."

She opened her eyes to find Sem frowning. "I think you better sit down, Marista."

Instead, she composed her expression and gathered her scattered wits. Then she released Sem's arm and turned to face Tynan.

The sight of him nearly undid her a second time. More than a standard month on the battlefield had taken its toll. The planes of his face were sharper. The sun-weathered lines around his mouth and eyes were cut deeper. Weariness weighted the edges of his frown, and his obsidian eyes had lost some of their fierce luster. No longer did his hair stand bristle-straight, but laid in gentle waves to the left side of his crown. Thick, black strands curled around the rims of his ears.

His trousers fit snug, outlining the powerful muscles of his legs and thighs, marking a contrast to the loose, roguish fit of his pale blue shirt.

She simply stared at him for a long moment, remembering words and caresses that even now filled her with desire.

Perhaps she stared too long. Tynan finally reached out and clasped her forearm. "Navarro's right. You should sit down."

A spasm of sensual recognition shot through her. Infuriated rather than soothed, she shook him off and braced her hip on the second step of the ladder. "I'm just startled." She quelled a new tremor in her voice. "I didn't expect to see you again."

Tynan pressed his mouth into a thin line. "Nor did I expect to see you. Certainly not in a refugee station."

Hoping to disguise her discomfort with nonchalance, she shrugged. "Fortunes of war. And speaking of such things, what business could you possibly have with me?"

His frown deepened. "Perhaps we could speak in private?"

Sem immediately grasped Dyani's arm. "We'll leave."

At that, Marista shot off the ladder step and grabbed Sem's sleeve. "No, please stay." She turned to Tynan. "I really have no time to talk. In less than two hours I have a marriage to oversee. As a matter of fact, Dyani and I just finished the decorations and are on our way to dress for the ceremony."

"I'll take you to where you live," Tynan suggested reasonably. "We can talk on the way."

The lift of his chin and the gleam in his dark eyes challenged her. She couldn't refuse without appearing a coward, however cowardly she felt, so she gave a crisp nod. "Very well. I live five minutes from here. I hope your business doesn't take longer than that."

"I'll explain myself quickly."

After mumbled farewells, Sem and Dyani made a hasty retreat. She watched them leave and, without a glance at Tynan, started to walk out of the courtyard.

He followed silently until they had gone several paces along the narrow, congested main street. "You aren't happy to see me," he finally said.

She considered the conflicting emotions rocking her soul. "As I said, I didn't expect to ever see you again."

"Is that the same as not being happy I'm here?"

She felt his gaze on her but didn't meet it. "No. At least I know you're well." She gave him a quick sideways glance. "You are well, aren't you? I mean, you haven't come back because you were wounded, like Sem?"

"Would my being wounded concern you, Little Diplomat?"

His use of the affectionate nickname he'd given her bemused her. She tensed and set her eyes ahead. "Of course, I would be concerned. I didn't keep you out of Sindri's grasp just to have someone like him blow you apart on the front lines."

Her voice shook with too much emotion. She bit down hard on her lip and turned her head to greet a clutch of laborers returning from their workday in the fields outside Bethel.

"I'm still intact," he answered when the laborers passed. "Mostly."

What did he mean by "mostly?" At the hint of sadness in his strange words, impulsive curiosity made her look at him. "Why aren't you at the front lines, Tynan? I would think Krillian Command couldn't spare a single soldier right now."

He fixed her with a stern, quizzical stare. "Right now? What have you heard about the war?"

"Not much," she admitted. "But General Ravid has exerted martial law over the civilian population, restricted travel, and imposed communication blackouts. All those measures speak volumes to the daughter of a retired officer. The war isn't going well, is it?"

He wasn't ruffled. "Not well at all. But I'm needed less at the battlefield front lines than at the front line here in Bethel."

When she frowned her puzzlement, he gave her a half-grin. "I've been told you declared a rearguard action against the Krillian government. Since you and I had established . . ." He paused, started again. "Since we have a history together, Colonel Varden and Vice-Magistrate Ouray thought I might be able to negotiate a truce. I've been ordered to do something about you."

She raised her eyes toward the sky and almost laughed. "Thank Creation! At least I have their attention." Then she looked back at him. "I suppose Ouray detailed my skirmishes with her."

His expression softened to one of patient amusement. "Slipping away from your personal guard."

"None of them would take me where I wanted to go," she explained.

"Leaving your residence at the municipal complex to come live here at the refugee station."

"Because the guards refused to take me where I wanted to go, which was here," she repeated, waving her arm to encompass her surroundings.

He glanced around with obvious disdain. "You left clean, comfortable, safe quarters for this?"

Her defenses went up. "Believe me, I'm safe here. These people are honest and hardworking. How could I have been comfortable at the complex knowing this sort of xenophobic inhumanity existed right outside the city?"

"Marista, there is nothing here but rot and ruin. Most of the buildings are ancient."

"Yes, they were built during the first days of Bethel's existence," she agreed. "The river floods the streets almost every spring so the Bethelites abandoned the area decades ago. But they thought the site suitable enough for an Albian refugee enclave."

"The air is rank," he went on stubbornly.

"Only when the west wind blows. Now that the river has receded the air doesn't smell nearly so bad."

"These buildings appear ready to crumble."

"Actually, the basic structures are quite safe. I agree the façades are ramshackle. But within hours after I moved out here the magistrate himself ordered repairs to the deplorable infrastructure."

She smiled with satisfaction. "Amazing what a bureaucracy can achieve when given incentive. Now every run-down hut has unlimited power, running water, and decent sanitation."

"You backed the government into a corner," he translated.

"I did what I had to do."

"That is always the case with you, and damn the consequences."

She ignored the exasperation in his voice and picked up her pace. "You should be happy. These are your people, after all."

"I no longer have a people, Marista."

The snap of his voice didn't reprove her. "Well, these refugees aren't my people, either. But that doesn't mean I'm blind to their misery."

Perhaps because she wouldn't capitulate the point, he switched subjects. "What about Dyani's abrupt change of citizenship from Albian to Terran?"

"A valid exercise of my diplomatic powers."

"Ouray termed it a gross abuse of power."

She rolled her eyes. "The Vice-Magistrate perceives the situation that way because my actions undermined those stupid Krillian laws preventing people like Sem and Dyani from associating, much less marrying."

He raised a dark brow. "You granted Dyani Terran citizenship rights in less than a week."

"I taught her the condensed version of Terran history and language," she countered. "Dyani's a quick study."

"She must be brilliant."

Marista tried unsuccessfully to hide her smile.

"What about the charges you consorted with the black market?"

Uncomfortable now, she hedged, "I'm sure there are plenty of outrageous accusations against me."

"Where's your platinum bar?"

Unconsciously she covered her heart with her hand. She hadn't missed the little strip of platinum in many a day. "Oh, I probably misplaced it somewhere . . ."

"Marista?"

She looked up into his face but surprisingly found his expression gentled with concern. "Well, I couldn't trade the damn thing for influence with the Krillians, so I traded it for food and medicine."

"Dealing with the black market is illegal."

"I know. I crossed the line. But I had good reason. Because the folk healers now have good, plentiful supplies, our cases of river fever are down by a third."

"Black marketers are dangerous. What were you thinking?"

His quiet anger didn't disguise the fear in his voice and eyes. Her heart leapt in the same instant her pride rebelled. "I didn't go alone."

"Yes, Navarro admitted he went with you."

That made her laugh softly in spite of the tension. "Dyani's often said if Sem doesn't learn to keep his own counsel, he'll find trouble one of these days."

"That's not all Navarro told me. He said you were damned good at negotiating with those thugs."

He stopped in the middle of foot traffic and waited until she did the same. His glare castigated as much as it seemed to blanket her with protective worry. "That scares me, Marista. Engaging in criminal activities could jeopardize your neutrality and your diplomatic immunity. I think Ouray's right. You do need a guard. A full-time keeper, for that matter."

Her anger flared. "Is that why she sent you here? To be my keeper? Well, I'm sorry you were called away from your important duties at the front, because you've wasted your time."

"I told Ouray you wouldn't listen."

"But she insisted," Marista guessed. "Didn't you explain how you'd already determined I could take care of myself and shut me out of your life?"

The bitterness of her words shamed her and seemed to take him off guard. She peered into his wide, troubled eyes and clamped her fists tight, hoping it would help her maintain her control. "I'll fight my own battles, Tynan. Go back to the front lines and fight yours."

"There are no more front lines."

She clutched at her flower pendant. "What?"

His gaze followed her hand to the pendant and lingered there a moment, then lifted to her throat, her lips, her hair. She felt exposed under his slow examination, but hypnotized as well by the barely concealed need clouding his dark eyes.

When he spoke, he did so with urgency. "You guessed right. The war is going badly. Albian advance forces are on the verge of overrunning our fortifications at the Barrier Mountains. We abandoned our base camp days ago and retreated into the forest across the river. We're holding our own right now, but the enemy numbers are too great against our smaller units. Within days, Bethel will be the front line."

The air left her lungs, though his news shouldn't have come as a shock. For several nights now the skies had been lit with the explosion of artillery fire just beyond the mountain pass. The sound and fury of warfare disturbed the city's slumber. General Ravid even ordered all fields and orchards to the far north of the city abandoned.

"The Albians won't attack the city," she assured him as she tried to assure herself. "Targeting civilian population centers is contrary to the Interplanetary Code of Warfare."

"A code the Albians have ignored at their convenience."

As she considered this latest shock to her system, he held out his hands as if to grasp her shoulders, but he let his arms drop to his sides instead. "Within the next two days the magistrate and General Ravid will begin a voluntary evacuation of the city. You will be a part of that evacuation."

She retreated a step and shook her head. "Don't think you can rid yourself of me so easily this time. I have a purpose here. I'll leave if and when I decided evacuation is necessary."

Her anger didn't seem to faze him. "This isn't personal, Marista. The Krillians don't want responsibility for your continued safety, especially when you defy their recommendations. They'll force you to evacuate, if necessary. And what about your father? Isn't he in Sarquis by now, waiting for you?"

His detached manner was irritating. To her, this damn well was personal. "I haven't heard from Dad in over twenty days," she retorted. "I'm not even sure he hasn't been evacuated off world himself."

"Marista, be reasonable . . ."

But she held up her hand, stopping him mid-sentence. "Your responsibility for me ended when I left the Barrier Mountain camp. You cut me loose. In doing so you gave up your right to worry about me, along with your authority to shove me out of the way in deference to your duty."

"It was my duty to protect you!" he rasped.

"You protected your heart and your conscience!" she fired back.

"Then I failed!"

His vehemence, and the flicker of pain in his eyes, silenced her. Yet, she seethed with so much unrequited pain she could find no measure of sympathy for him. Instead of reaching for him as her intuition prompted her to do, she waved her hand in dismissal. "You'll get over it, Tynan. We both will."

Unable to face his reaction to her lie, she turned and strode ahead, desperate to reach the refuge of her decrepit stone cottage. To her dismay, he followed.

When she opened the slatted wooden door with a twist of the ancient knob, he let out a groan. "You don't have a lock?"

She swiveled to look up at him. "I trust these people. They trust me. They need me."

All anger and frustration lifted from his expression. "I needed you, too."

The soft plaintive quality of his words pumped a surge of powerful longing to her already flooded emotions. She fought the yearning to throw her arms around his neck. "You sent me away, Tynan. You didn't need me enough. And you couldn't give your heart at all."

He fell back a step, unwilling or unable to answer her accusation. She felt too drained to care which.

"Your mind is set."

"You stated the obvious, Captain."

A little of the tension eased from his shoulders. "Then I'll leave and let you prepare for the Bonding Ritual. You must feel honored to officiate at such a happy event."

The sudden change of subject surprised her, but she nodded. "By Krillian law, Sem and Dyani are already married. They signed the legal documents yesterday." She quirked her mouth into a weary smile. "But both of them wanted all the wedding rituals as well. A celebration like this gives everyone reason to hope for the future."

His brow pinched into a pensive frown. "Perhaps."

The question slipped out before she could catch herself. "Will you be staying for the ceremony?"

He started to shake his head, but stopped abruptly. "I . . . I should report back to Ouray."

She hoped to disguise her deep disappointment behind a sardonic sigh. "Of course. Duty calls. Our business is finished then."

His expression was unreadable. "Yes, finished."

Steeling herself, she held out her hand. "Good-bye."

He peered at her outstretched fingers, hesitated a moment, but then slid his palm inside hers. The friction of his skin against her skin ignited warmth that shimmied up her arm, through her chest, and into the center of her longing. Her heart set to hammering, and her blood boiled with terrible need. If she held on one second longer she'd drown in the tide of desire washing over her.

Yet, hold on she did, searching for any sign that her touch provoked the same response in him.

While he didn't shake her off, he wore the mask of the stoic warrior king and seemed oblivious to her inner turmoil.

With soul and body spent and hurting, she spoke from her heart before her head could stop it. "Mother Creation, I missed you, Tynan."

Twenty-two

I missed you, Tynan.

Marista's final words echoed inside his skull. Had she been merely polite in asking if he intended to stay for the Bonding Ritual? Or did she wish to see him again?

He damn well wished to see her again, if only at a distance.

Was that why he had dawdled for two hours in the stinking alleyways of the refugee station? Is that why he now skulked in the shadowy lee of a massive support arch, like some unwelcome guest, waiting for the marriage ceremony to end?

He had hidden himself off to the left of the wedding bower. The scent of flower garlands strung overhead mingled with the aroma of steaming food and the faint mustiness of old masonry. The surprisingly pleasant fusion of smells wafted on currents of warm, night air.

Unsteady light from at least three-score strategically placed wick lanterns cast flutters of amber brilliance and dancing shadows on the courtyard walls. The ethereal effect transformed the decrepit courtyard into an open-air temple. Had he not seen the wreck and ruin in broad daylight, he would never have believed such a change from mundane to magical was possible.

But there was nothing magical about the way his heart pounded with need and his arms ached to hold Marista again.

I missed you, Tynan.

Remembering how she'd appeared that afternoon—too tired, too thin, and too skittish—he winced. He had caused the hurt he'd seen in her ocean-green eyes when she'd turned to look at him for the first time after so many empty days.

I missed you, Tynan.

"How could I have sent you away?"

The murmur left his throat as a hornpipe began playing a sweet melody. He straightened, careful to stay within the shelter of the arch. Unlike the other hundred or so guests, he gave his full attention not to Sem and Dyani, but to the woman who presided over their wedding.

Marista. The magic of light and shadow transformed her as it did the courtyard. In place of the careworn waif stood a poised woman, her profile lovely, her smile generous and sincere. She'd gowned herself in a traditional Albian sari the color of her eyes. The gauzy material caressed her body as his hands once did. She'd drawn the wrap over her head in keeping with the formality of the occasion, but tendrils of her sunset-red hair frothed around the gold-trimmed edges.

Never had he been so keenly aware of her grace and beauty. He could have mistaken her for an Albian gentlewoman. As a clansman of high rank, he would have been honored to bond such a woman to the

Askanati's.

Where had the notion of bonding with her come from? A tremor shot through him, but one that left contentment, not regret or panic in its wake. Perhaps the shimmering, shadowy magic of this place, of this night, of this ritual overwhelmed his weary mind and battered will.

Yet, even as he shook himself free of the reverie and focused on the ceremony, the idea buoyed him.

Navarro and Dyani faced each other and spoke words, once in Albian and once again in Krillian. Though Tynan barely heard their voices he knew they vowed mutual honor, love, and loyalty endless as the desert sands, unyielding as the desert sun. They pledged to become one, to give each other purpose and meaning.

Purpose and meaning. In spite of the gold band on his finger, he had had little sense of purpose or meaning in the past thirty days. He no longer dreamed of his wife. The last apparition, the one Marista witnessed, had been Neari's farewell to him. With the end of the dreams came a lessening of his grinding guilt.

But now he woke longing for Marista, breathing in her sweet, feminine fragrance that still clung to his bedroll despite rain and dirt and the stench of battle. Without the beautiful Terran woman at his side, he felt only loneliness.

Navarro and Dyani finished their vows, then handed Marista the cords of jubinda vine they had carried to the bower. In strict Albian tradition, the lengths of cord were fashioned of beaten gold or silver to signify the material worth each partner offered to the new clan unit. Once, as the son of a highly esteemed clan, Tynan could have offered a woman status and wealth. Now he had nothing to offer.

Marista handled the cords as if they were precious metals instead of interlaced greenery. Her smile became radiant as she turned to the assembled crowd and held the vines high over her head for all to witness. Then she faced the couple again and nodded for them to join hands.

With all due solemnity, Marista laid the vines in the cradle of the couple's hands and lapped each trailing end one over the other. Symbolically, the two were now one.

Reverence forgotten, the audience gave up a cheer and converged on the bower with a rain of flowers. For a minute, he lost sight of Marista in the commotion.

Then, like the fragrance of crushed petals floating on the warm night air, she emerged from the melee not more than two meters from where he lurked in the shadows. With one hand she clutched her namesake pendant. With the other, she swiped at a sheen of moisture on her face.

This woman who claimed she never cried now tried to hide her tears, just as he tried to hide his presence.

His thoughts reached out to her. What are you feeling, Little Diplomat? Happiness for your friends? Grief for your own losses? Bone-chilling loneliness?

As he hid in the dark, listening to the rattle of his heart, he realized he might have been asking those questions of himself.

The hornpipe took up a more rousing melody in concert with a drum and mandolin. Marista glanced furtively toward the back of the courtyard where most of the crowd surged in anticipation of the wedding feast. She drew in a quivering breath and turned to join the celebration.

He could no longer conceal himself, or his emotions. "Marista, wait."

Startled by his emergence from the shadows, she fell back three paces. "What are you doing here? I thought you said . . ."

"I know what I said," he cut in. "I also heard what you said. You missed me."

A soft cry left her throat, and she turned her face toward the celebration at the other end of the courtyard. "Please, don't take pity on me."

He closed the distance between them and grasped both of her cool, trembling hands before she could retreat again. The capture forced her to look up at him. Her eyes, the mirrors of her soul, reflected such panic he fought the urge to fold her into his arms then and there.

"Tynan, I mean it," she warned.

"If I pity anyone, I pity myself."

She scowled. "Then don't use me to replace Neari."

"I never confused you with Neari," he insisted, letting his heart speak for the first time in a long time. "When I held you I held Marista Kaljin, not some ghost from the past. Your kisses excited me. Your body moved beneath mine. Your memory kept me awake at night in the field."

Her chin quivered. "Tynan, don't . . ."

"I missed you, too."

Her wide eyes shimmered amber and green in the flickering lantern light. He couldn't say whether she stared at him with disbelief or astonishment.

He slid his hands beneath the silky material of the sari and up her arms. Her skin, smooth and already warm, heated with his touch and radiated her unique feminine essence. Her eyelids fluttered twice before she caught herself. When he leaned close enough that his cheek grazed hers, she drew in a sharp breath and held it.

"Neari no longer haunts my dreams," he whispered in her ear. "You helped put her to final rest."

Temptation overwhelmed him. He brushed his lips against her cheek. She responded with an encouraging shudder of pleasure.

But when he drew closer she stiffened. "I don't want your gratitude, either."

If he weren't afraid of insulting her, he might have laughed at his own expense. "Gratitude is not what I'm feeling, Little Diplomat. I'm not even sure I can tell you how I feel." He backed away enough to peer into her bewildered gaze. "Albian men speak better with actions than with words."

Her eyes softened with pleading. "Then what are you doing?"

"You tell me."

He swept her into the shadow of the trefoil arch. Bracing his back against the stone, he drew her into his arms and kissed her with gentle, but urgent, passion.

He expected resistance. Instead, she melted against him at once. Emboldened, he slanted his mouth over hers, teased her lips apart with the tip of his tongue, and moaned when she granted him entrance.

She slid her hands over his shoulders and up the back of his neck. He shivered as her slender fingers twined into his untrimmed hair. In answer to her erotic tenderness, he combed the fingers of his left hand through the fiery silk of her hair. With his right hand, he pressed the small of her back until she leaned into his hard arousal.

She didn't flinch from the evidence of her power over him. Indeed, she moved her body against his groin and brought him to the edge of control. A moment later, though, she broke from his kiss. The shadows cloaked her expression, but he heard the apprehension in her voice. "I don't understand."

"Neither do I. I meant only to stay in the shadows and watch you tonight. Damn it, woman, you drive me to act against my will."

She sighed and rested her forehead against his. "You drive me, too. Sometimes to the point of insanity."

Lifting her chin with his fingers, he smiled down into her green eyes, hazed with passion. "I did miss you, Marista. Come away with me, back to your cottage. I want you. I need to have you. Now."

"Want?" she whispered into his urgent prodding. "Need? Oh, Tynan, I want and need you so much it frightens me. But I'm more afraid of having you for awhile, then losing you again."

He pulled her tighter against him. "You said the lesson of the Tristan and Isolde story was that they acted on their feelings. They had each other for a short time, but they had each other for awhile."

He kissed the crown of her head and breathed in the perfume of her hair. "Our destinies are bound to part us. You're a peacemaker. I'm a warrior. You talk. I act. We have different obligations and responsibilities . . ."

"Duty," she cut in, her voice a ragged whisper.

"Yes, duty," he repeated, though the word almost stuck in his throat. "We can't abandon what we believe or who we are, Little Diplomat."

"Can't you see there's so much more to life than cold, uncompromising duty?" she pleaded.

He brushed his lips to her temple, then her cheek. "That may be true for you. But you have a future. I have nothing but the present, a stolen name, a borrowed cause, and a price on my head. I can promise you only these few hours of time, right here, right now."

"Now, yes," she murmured against his shoulder. "But why can't it be forever?"

"I don't have forever to give."

She stiffened in his arms and whimpered with dismay. For a bleak minute he feared he'd never again find peace and joy in her arms. When she pulled back enough to look up into his face, he trembled as much from anxiety as from building arousal.

Her eyes were troubled, but her voice was stronger. "You're wrong. We can be together and still be who we are. How can I make you understand . . ." She broke off and blinked back tears. "Here and now will never be enough for me, but I'm willing to compromise even if you aren't. Yes, I'll go with you."

He caught a relieved breath and pushed away from the arch. Before he swept her more than a few paces along the pavement, however, she dug her fingernails into his arm and pulled him up short.

"I'm giving this party," she reminded him. "I can't just walk out now."

He gaped at her, and then lifted his face to the star-dappled night sky. "No, please no!"

Marista's tremulous laugh pulled his attention back to her. With the tips of her fingers, she dashed away the last of her tears and peeked up at him through her damp lashes. "You really don't know how to flirt, do you?"

"What?" he croaked. "Flirt?"

"You're far too impatient."

"Yes, I'm impatient," he agreed, and swung her around again until her hips met the physical evidence of that impatience. "I'm a soldier. I don't talk around the subject. I simply ask for what I want."

"I suppose I should admire your blunt honesty," she teased. "But sometimes a woman wants a man to flirt before she gives up her favors. And considering this celebration will last at least three or four more hours, I'd say you have lots of time to practice."

He gritted his teeth and pushed her to arm's length. "Very well, Madame," he ground out. "I'll learn to flirt." Then he added when she laughed behind her hand, "First show me where I might find a drink to ease this ache you caused me."

"First," she corrected, "we'll find Sem and Dyani to wish them good fortune. Then we'll find relief for your . . . ah, problem."

"Temporary relief."

She laughed again and pulled him into the courtyard. He blinked hard in the flickering light, as if coming out of a deep slumber.

***

As Tynan opened the slatted door and let Marista walk ahead of him into the ramshackle cottage, desire and guilt nearly ripped his conscience in two. He wanted to steal a precious few hours in her arms and inside her body. But she had to be exhausted after overseeing the preparations for the Bonding Feast that had lasted well into the new day. He should let her sleep.

To his surprise and relief, she preempted his need to make a noble choice and say good-night. She hardly let him close the door behind them and switch a table lamp on low before she flew into his arms and kissed him with passionate demand. He didn't waste time with insincere excuses of why he shouldn't stay, but gathered her hard against his willing, aroused body.

Wisps of her hair tickled his nose and neck. Her womanly scent stoked his passion. But freeing her from the beautiful sari confounded his wits and his suddenly clumsy fingers.

"I never did understand how or why women wrapped themselves in so many meters of material," he grumbled through set teeth.

She laughed at his fumbling, frustrated attempts. "Perhaps the purpose of the gown is to distract and discourage a man's lust."

But she stopped laughing when he untangled the last gauzy meter and the material pooled at her feet. She stood before him clad in only the short, white shift women wore beneath the traditional gown. Beneath the filmy sheath her breasts peaked hard with evidence of her own anticipation. She smiled, a secret female smile, the final invitation he needed to sweep her off her feet and carry her into the sleeping room.

With determined focus, he set about pleasuring her in every way he knew, and some ways he invented in the heat of the moment. She gave him leave to use hands and mouth and tongue to tease and taunt her breathless, then bring her to rapt completion.

She never questioned or objected. No magical aphrodisiac could have heightened his arousal more than her implicit trust in his care and consideration of her needs.

When he finished with her, she proved equally willing and able to shatter his senses. She provoked his body with feathery touches until he burned inside and out. She suckled his nipples until they became as pebble hard as hers, then she tracked kisses down his chest and abdomen. He clutched the mattress to maintain control.

Then she took his arousal into her warm mouth and set a heated rhythm with her lips and tongue. He cried out his startled ecstasy. In his tradition, women did not pleasure men in this way. Such bold, exotic intimacy brought him to the edge so fast he bellowed a warning only seconds before release. He barely managed to pull her up, over, and finally beneath him before he spilled his seed into her tight, moist depths.

The last thing he remembered before exhaustion claimed him was folding Marista into his arms and feeling her heart beat in double-time syncopation with his.

Hours later, the quiet woke him. Disoriented, he stared into the dark and waited for the scream of an aerial barrage. When he heard nothing but Marista's soft slumber-sighs, he caught a deep breath and let it out slowly.

The past three hours hadn't been just a sweet dream triggered by her scent on the bedroll. Marista did lie next to him. Her head rested in the crook of his arm. Her back fit against his chest, and her bottom burrowed into his lap. "Spooning" she'd termed this practice of couples sleeping in such an intimate fashion.

Dangerous, he called it, especially if flesh met flesh the way her naked body met his now. More dangerous still, she held his right arm in the valley of her bosom so that his hand cupped the soft mound of her breast. Beneath his palm her heart beat a steady slow rhythm in contrast to the sudden agitation of his own pulse.

Groaning his need while his erection pressed into her bottom, he nudged into her soft warmth.

She squirmed, buried herself further into his lap. "Tynan?"

Her sleep-scratchy voice touched a chord of tenderness. Forgetting his desire for the moment, he laid his cheek on hers, kissed her nose, then her lips and shut his eyes to the sting of unbidden tears. He could cherish this woman who trusted him so. He could live a life devoted to her happiness. He could give her all of himself . . .

If he only had something left to give.

"Is it morning already? Is it time to get up?"

Her question mercifully cut short his dour ruminations. He slid his hand over her breast and smiled when the tip peaked in anticipation. "Not morning yet. But I'm up."

She slid her backside against him. "Hmmm, yes, I see . . . I mean I feel. But I'm hungry. What about some breakfast?"

"I can think of better things to do with my mouth."

To demonstrate, he kissed her and let his hand wander across her stomach, over her hip, and finally come to rest over the froth of curls at the juncture of her thighs. When he nipped her ear, she dutifully opened her legs.

"You make my imagination run wild, Captain," she whispered, arching her hips with encouragement. "Are you endlessly creative?"

"Endlessly willing to please you, Little Diplomat."

Her sigh transformed into a needy moan. "Please, then, please me."

He had just eased her to her back and shifted his leg to straddle her body when someone pounded on the front door.

She jumped and clutched at his arm. "Who could that be?"

He lowered himself over her protectively, his warrior instincts overriding his desire. "You don't have to answer. It's the middle of the night. Whoever it is can wait until dawn."

But the sexual tension drained from her body. "I should see who it is. No one disturbs me unless it's important."

The pounding jarred them a second time. He exhaled his frustration, but he freed her from the fortress of his arms and legs. She turned up the wick lantern on the bedside stand and slipped out of bed.

Her skin took on a golden hue in the flickering light. Those same sparks of gold threaded through her flame-red hair. He stared at her naked body—so beautiful, so delicate, so perfect a fit for his own body. Without the least bit of conceit, he knew that no other man would ever again make her cry out with such joy the way he did.

Neither would he find such contentment in the arms of another woman.

Unaware of his musings, she wiggled into the short body-hugging sheath she'd worn under the sari.

At the sight, he shot up straight in bed. "You can't go out there dressed like that!"

She gave him a tolerant smile and leaned across the bed to kiss his lips. "I'm only going to peek around the edge of the door. Don't worry."

But when she stood, the hem of the sheath had crept upward. With a wiggle of her hips, she coaxed the material back down over her thighs.

He shook his head. "Marista . . ."

The intruder pounded a third time.

"I'll be right back," she assured him. "Keep my place warm." With a teasing grin, she turned and left.

Grumbling a curse, he threw back the thin coverlet. When had he ever talked Marista Kaljin out of anything? Well, he wasn't going to let her go alone to greet visitors in the middle of the night dressed for seduction.

Swinging his legs over the edge of the mattress, he ran a fan of fingers though his hair, vaguely aware he needed to see a barber soon. As he reached for the tangle of his clothing on the wooden floor, he heard the entry door squeak open on rusty hinges.

When he heard Marista's strangled cry, he barely had the presence of mind to shimmy into his briefs before he bolted into the front room.

The brighter light made him squint for a moment before his eyes adjusted. That didn't slow his forward momentum toward the door. "Marista! What's wrong? Who is it?"

He stopped dead less than a meter from the doorway where she hung suspended inside the tight embrace of a strange man.

In a blink, he took stock of the intruder. Though gray shot through the stranger's dark hair and deep lines creased his rugged face, his flinty glare challenged Tynan as an equal. The man stood as tall as he and measured almost as wide at the shoulders. A jacket hid his arms, but large hands and blunt fingers were roughened from hard use.

The stranger certainly handled Marista's weight with little effort. Though she seemed to return the man's embrace, Tynan gave a growl of warning and prepared to launch himself in her defense.

"Who the hell are you?"

The stranger's barked question held Tynan in place. He suppressed an overpowering urge to draw to attention and salute. Instead, he lurched forward to position himself directly at Marista's back. "Who the hell are you?" he barked back.

Marista let out another cry, this time one of distress.

The stranger glanced down at her, and then loosened his hold enough to let her tiptoes touch the floor. "Riss, who is this man?"

Riss? The sound of the familiar pet name made his stomach do a queasy flop. Even before Marista turned inside the man's proprietary embrace and looked up at him, he knew what she would say.

"Tynan, this is Anthony Henson, my father."

Twenty-three

Marista stuffed her arms into the sleeves of a tan jumpsuit and zipped up the front placket so fast she caught the skin at her throat. Ignoring the sharp bite, she ran trembling fingers through her hair until she tamed the strands enough to plait.

At least she didn't hear any furniture crashing in the front room, though the ominous silence might mean the two men had already dispatched each other with the shear force of their deadly glares.

The open suspicion between Tynan and her father should have made her feel wanted and secure. She almost understood why her father had kept his arm around her shoulder until Tynan reemerged from her sleeping room fully dressed.

She understood, as well, that Tynan might feel defensive and embarrassed after having been discovered by the master of intimidation himself, General Anthony Henson, running from her bed, nearly naked, in the middle of the night. Perhaps if she had one gram of wit and humor left, she might have found the absurd situation worthy of a belly laugh.

Instead, she seethed with irritation at both men who seemed cut from the same stiff and indestructible camouflage fabric. When would they both realize she was nearly thirty years old and could run her own life without their direction?

Nervous energy propelled her off the bed. She should take a moment to rinse her face before confronting certain doom. The after scent of lovemaking clung to her skin. Maybe her father wouldn't notice.

Of course, he'd notice, dammit!

She passed up the lavatory for expediency's sake and flew to the front room. Standing in the arched entry, she quickly became the focus of the two, dour-faced men sitting across from each other at her rickety dining table. They glared at her like two ravenous predators coveting the same piece of prize carrion. The air crackled with competitive antagonism and rampaging testosterone.

"Tea anyone?" she asked sweetly, forcing a smile.

Neither man so much as broke a grin. If she didn't love the two of them so much she would strongly suggest they both take an early morning plunge in the cold Narquat River.

Her father pulled out a chair next to him. "Come sit down, Riss. We have to talk."

Tynan glanced at a chair closer to him.

She crossed her arms beneath her breasts. "I'll stand, thanks." Then she cast her father a worried frown. "You look tired, Dad."

The General let down his guard and scrubbed his salt-and-pepper stubbled face with both hands. "I'm fine, Baby."

Marista strode to him and laid her hands on his shoulders. "Then let me get you something to eat."

"There's no time, Riss. I've got to get you out of here."

She dropped into the chair near her father. "Dad, I can't leave now . . ."

"Listen to me!" the General bellowed. When she started, he leaned forward and reached for her limp hands in her lap. But then he reconsidered and drew a breath. "This is serious business here. I didn't spend the last fifteen days in a caravan of smugglers and blockade runners just to come say hello and go back without you."

"Smugglers?"

At her shocked expression, he allowed her a weary grin. "They were the only ones willing to guide me from Sarquis to Bethel. No offense, Baby, but your colleagues at the Terran Embassy are a bunch of candy-asses. I nearly coldcocked the ambassador twice before I took matters into my own hands."

Tynan let out a low chuckle. When the General raised his head in question, Tynan slanted his gaze at her. "That determination runs in the family, Sir."

"I know."

Her father's soft-spoken agreement sounded like high adulation. When she looked into Anthony Henson's hazel eyes, she saw the same pride she'd heard in his voice.

Then he repeated, "I know," and reached for her hands again. This time he grasped her stiff fingers and cradled them gently. "You do take after the old man a little bit, Baby, whether or not you want to admit it." He shook his head at her puzzlement. "I know why you entered the Diplomatic Corps. After what happened on Yonar a fool could have figured it out. And I'm no fool."

Tears of guilt filled her eyes.

"I understand," he soothed. "I admire that you didn't spend your life chasing after my attention and approval." His eyes softened as she rarely saw them do. "You always did have my attention and approval anyway, Riss. You've done well for yourself."

She had to ask. "Have I done it all by myself?"

The General scowled. "Talk straight, Riss. What do you mean?"

She steeled herself. "I mean, did you put in a good word about me to one of your influential friends?"

Her father's craggy face lost all expression. She once feared that solid granite demeanor. But not now, when there was a definite glint of hurt in his eyes. "Why the hell would I insult you by doing something like that?"

She sighed in relief and gripped her father's hard hands tighter until he glanced down in surprise.

"Don't get too arrogant, young lady," he muttered. "You may end up needing my help yet."

She disengaged her hands and sat straight. "Now, you speak plainly."

Her father rubbed his spiky beard. "You made some enemies in high places. Don't know why. But that's the reason authorities in Sarquis weren't too cooperative with me."

Mystified, she lifted her shoulders.

The General cast Tynan a quick glare, then went on. "Seems there's some controversy about the circumstances under which you left the Terran outpost."

The news startled her. "I was in the wrong place at the wrong time, and I was abducted in a raid."

The General shifted his attention to Tynan and his eyes went hard and cold. "No thanks to him."

She leaned forward so her father could only see her. "He had no choice. The commander of the raid would have killed him if he prevented me from being taken as a human shield. As a matter of fact, Tynan later took me under his personal protection."

"How far under his protection?"

Tynan nearly sprang from the chair. "Begging your pardon, Sir, but that's none of your damn business."

"The hell it isn't . . ."

With a tug on her father's hands, she held him in place. "Dad, I think it's obvious Tynan and I are more than passing acquaintances."

The General wasn't pacified. "What if he's taking advantage of your situation?"

"He hasn't, and he isn't."

Her declaration got both men's immediate attention. But while the heat in her father's glare could have melted lead, the warm gratitude and flicker of joy in Tynan's dark eyes melted her heart.

Wanting to bask in her lover's gaze, she reluctantly turned back to her father. "All that is beside the point right now. What's this about a controversy?"

The General braced one arm on the table. "Some Albian lieutenant named Sindri claims you might have conspired with Tynan to make the break."

She nearly shot from the chair. "That's not true! Didn't Bierich contradict him?"

"Bierich did a fine job of saying nothing with too many words," the General snarled. "She gave the facts that lent credence to Sindri's version of events."

She could hardly speak. "I don't believe it!"

Tynan leaned into her line of sight. "Believe it, Marista. Earth's long term interest in Planet Serraine is more important than the career of one diplomatic attaché."

"But what about Jace's side of the story?" she sputtered.

"Jace has burned too many bridges," her father pointed out. "No one likes him much in the first place. And his credibility is suspect because of his ties to our family."

Her father jerked his chin in Tynan's direction. "Frankly, Riss, this guy is a millstone around your neck. The Albian High Command wants him bad. If you're caught associating with him . . ." His jaw twitched. ". . . in any way, you won't have much of a defense against Sindri's suspicions, or Bierich's attempt to undercut your credibility."

Her heart seemed to freeze in place. "I knew my career was in jeopardy, but now my reputation, too? What am I going to do?"

Anthony Henson shifted his gaze. She followed her father's line of vision and tensed when she glimpsed the hard resolution in Tynan's obsidian eyes.

She jumped when Tynan laid his hand softly on her arm. "Marista, your father thinks you should cut me loose."

"No!"

Wrenching her arm from his gentle hold, she snapped her gaze back and forth between the two men. "I won't do that!"

Tynan's gaze softened with what seemed to be gratitude. "They have you on the defensive, Marista. You can't let sentiment or loyalty dictate your battle strategy now."

"This isn't a war . . ." she started to object.

"The hell it isn't!" her father argued. "You're fighting for your honor. Not to mention your career. Maybe even your freedom if someone decides to charge you with aiding and abetting criminal activity and revokes your diplomatic immunity. You have no choice."

For one, thunderstruck moment she went still. When she regained her poise, she glared at her father first. "I do have a choice this time, Dad." She turned her glare to Tynan. "I won't abandon you. I'm innocent, and your cause is right, even if you insist on using force to achieve justice."

Tynan sank back into the chair. "Marista . . ."

"No," she repeated and turned back to her father. "That's final."

Anthony Henson drew a hand over his scruffy beard. From the hard glint in his eyes, she knew he wasn't entirely defeated. "All right, fine. Loyalty to Tynan aside, think of your physical safety."

She didn't stand down with him, either. "So far, Commander Ravid has issued instructions for voluntary evacuation only."

"Take it from an old military man," her father said with a scowl, "the brass-asses behind the lines don't know a tenth of what's really going on in the battlefield. The people I traveled with on the caravan may not be the sort you want to welcome into the family, but they've been back and forth across the demilitarized zone. They know more about troop movements, supply lines, and weapons placement than some desk-jockey who stares into a terminal all day and reports statistical analyses."

His sneer dissolved into worry. "The evacuation plan may be voluntary now, but it won't be much longer. Krillian defenses are collapsing. Albian forces are headed this way as we speak." The General jerked his head toward Tynan. "We had a little chat while you were making yourself decent. He claims he told you almost the same thing."

She glanced at Tynan.

He affirmed the General's contentions with a nod, and then added his own assessment. "The evacuation force is massed at the south edge of Bethel. I didn't know the front lines had deteriorated to the point of collapse in the past few days, but I trust what your father says. You should, too."

Her chest constricted as her mind clicked. "Then I have to notify the station elders so they can prepare the refugees for evacuation at once. The infirmary wards are still jammed with cases of river sickness, so I think we should concentrate our first efforts there."

Tynan leaned forward and gripped her arm. "Marista, the Krillian government isn't going to make room for Albian refugees aboard the evacuation transports."

She glared at him. "There are only two hundred or so refugees, mostly women, children and old men. If they don't go, I don't go."

"Riss, are you crazy?" her father asked.

"You'll go!" Tynan ordered.

She glanced back and forth between the two men who shouted over each other to be heard. Well, at least they agreed on something, even if it was at her expense.

She pushed off the chair and stood over the two men. "Both of you understand this right now. I will do what I want to do, when and with whom I want to do it. Clear?"

A low rumble and a flash of light answered before either man had a chance. In the next second a roiling tremor pitched her off her feet. A deafening blast followed, like a rip of thunder follows a slash of too close lightning.

Reflexively, she rolled to her stomach and covered her face with both hands as the floor beneath her shivered like quicksand. The joints of her cottage groaned and creaked. Shards from the window near the front door pelted her back.

Through closed eyes, she sensed a second streak of brilliance, and braced herself for the follow-up trembler that sent the floor into convulsions.

Her ears rang from the din of the blast, but she heard the muffled cry of her name as if it came to her through water. She tried to answer, but choked on powdered masonry shaken loose from the walls and ceiling. Then Tynan's scent cut through the smell of destruction as he coiled his arms around her body.

"Dad?" she called, and choked on debris dust.

"I'm here. I'm fine." Anthony Henson appeared through the haze, crawling on his belly.

She gave him a quick hug. "What . . . happened?"

"Felt like an aerial assault," her father answered. "Surface-to-surface weapons. It hit close."

"Close? That felt like it hit the house!"

Tynan helped her sit up. "The missiles probably hit no closer than the orchards on the northern hillsides."

Her father nodded in agreement. "Hell just broke loose. Time to get out of here."

She scrambled off the floor with only a little help from Tynan. "You're right, but I'm not going anywhere without the refugees."

Tynan grabbed for her arm. She sidestepped him and went for the front door.

Behind her she heard the General complain, "Might as well follow her, son. She'll damn well go without us anyway."

***

The sky glowed eerie yellow-orange in the pre-dawn gloom. The five minute aerial assault spawned fires fanned by a stiff easterly wind. Blazing destruction devoured the hillside orchards and terraced fields like some roaring, vengeful beast. Only a rain-swollen tributary of the Narquat River lay between perdition and the northern edge of the refugee station.

Ironically, the flickering menace provided light for Marista and Dyani to coordinate the evacuation of sick and infirm refugees from the station medical center. Meanwhile, the General and Sem made a house-to-house search for anyone not already driven into the street by caving roofs. Tynan had run back to Marista's cottage to collect her personal belongings and retrieve the ground car he'd driven to the station the day before.

As the odor of flaming destruction encroached, Marista dashed from floor to floor, ward to ward, inside and outside. She moved with mechanical precision, giving orders, lifting stretchers, packing supplies for transport. But her fingers were numb and her palms felt clammy. Her heart slammed against her ribs. Her throat tightened and her mouth tasted bitter.

She paused in the middle of the third floor ward and peered up at the wide expanse of skylight. Heat and flame infused the billowing ash and haze with a deep russet glow. In the past she'd dispatched her fear with flight and distance. Now she didn't have that choice. Today she couldn't run or hide her eyes from the fire and smoke. She couldn't shut her mind to the onslaught of memories.

"Marista?"

She spun around, nearly dropping the crate of supplies she carried.

Dyani retreated a step. "Marista, you're pale as a winter sun. Perhaps you should rest."

"I'm fine," she lied. "There's no time to rest."

Gently, Dyani took the crate from her arms. "I came to tell you Tynan's back. He's on the street helping to load the rest of the second floor patients. Go to him. I'll finish here."

Marista nodded her thanks and rubbed her stinging eyes with the heels of her hands. "I was just about to start distributing the portable oxygen masks. If the air gets any thicker we'll all have trouble breathing. I'm sure some of the elderly and many of the children will need help sooner."

"I'll see to it." Dyani tilted her head toward the exit. "Go now."

She gladly obeyed the quiet command. On wobbly legs she stumbled down two flights of stairs and rushed into the street. Tynan saw her coming, opened his arms to receive her, and pulled her into the privacy of a nearby alleyway. His fierce embrace warmed her through.

When he let her go, though, his scowl tempered the moment of relief. "I did as you suggested, Marista. I telecomed both the Magistrate's office and Commander Ravid's headquarters. I was told all emergency fire-fighting equipment is being used to protect the city proper. Unless we can get that old water pumping unit repaired, we'll have no defense if the fire jumps the river."

Cold dread seized her, but she focused on her other concerns. "What about the evacuation of the refugees?"

"Ravid is allowing the refugees to enter the Bethel evacuation area for transport to a retention camp north of Sarquis, but only under escort of the guards already posted here at the station. Your father and Sem are sending out groups of thirty people with three guards each. Within fifteen minutes everyone should be clear of the station."

He shook his head. "The government can't give us more personnel carriers, though. Most of the refugees will have to walk to Bethel since we have just the three labor transports out front here."

"Fine. We'll make do," she snapped, temper flaring. "But these people will not be confined to a retention camp. Sem tells me those places are no better than outdoor prisons."

A muscle in his jaw quivered. "This isn't a good time to negotiate a better offer."

"I'm not negotiating. I'm demanding."

He smiled grimly. "Then I suppose I shouldn't bother telling you Ravid and Ouray both ordered me to load you and your father into the ground car and return you to the government complex for immediate evacuation."

"I won't go, not without the refugees," she declared, stepping away from him. "And not without assurances that they'll receive fair treatment and decent accommodations." She narrowed her gaze. "Don't even try to convince me otherwise."

His smile softened, and he brushed pieces of charred matter out of her hair with a gentle sweep of his hand. "I already told Ouray and Ravid you'd never compromise on this. Since neither of them wants trouble with the Terran government over your safety, you have the upper hand. By the time you and the refugees overrun the evacuation site, the bureaucrats will have agreed to your demands."

Managing a weary smile, she snuggled back into his embrace. "I'm not sure which side is worse—the Albians for attacking a population center, or the Krillians for exploiting these refugees."

"Technically the Albians didn't attack a population center," he said while stroking her nape. "They attacked the rural perimeter of the city and let the wind do the rest."

"A treacherous strategy," she snapped.

"But a cunning one, and a valid claim should the Krillian government file a charge of war crimes with the Council of Seven Planets. All part of a grander strategy."

He glanced up at the low, thin clouds of black and gray smoke. "Even if the fire doesn't take this area, the air will soon become unbreathable."

A fresh wave of anxiety rolled through her body. She failed to suppress a shudder.

He held her closer. "Let me take you back to your house. You can wait for the rest of us there."

Summoning her will, she pushed away from his support. "I'll be fine. I won't become hysterical."

He frowned with unconcealed annoyance. "I didn't consider that a possibility."

Before she could reply, screams rent the thick air. Tynan dragged her back into the street. One glance into the sooty dawn sky made the cause of the alarm apparent. Scraps of fiery wind-driven debris floated through the heavy haze and flamed out like meteorites before touching ground. Larger chunks still burned after hitting the stone pavement.

She watched in horror as people ran to the glowing piles and stamped them out with nothing but the soles of their boots or articles of clothing. The mere thought of standing so close to an open flame stalled her breath.

Tynan tried to fold her back inside his arms. But another panicked scream froze them both. A woman she recognized as one of the Albian folk healers pointed to a stand of tall yubic fern trees that grew wild alongside the medical center.

The entire grove disappeared in a whoosh of bright red and yellow flame. Tongues of fire leapt skyward and cracked like whips in the dense air. Blazing yubic fronds rode gusts of wind and spun in crazy, off-center circles before landing on the medical center's roof.

She clutched Tynan's sleeve. "Dyani and some of the patients are still on the third floor!"

Another violent pop and snap sent a glittering shower of sparks high into the air. Tynan whisked her to the opposite side of the street before any of the ghastly fireworks floated to the ground.

Terror rolled over her in tsunami-force waves as the flaming debris tumbled across the center's roof and leapt to another building. A numbing, inner-cold battled with the hot wind swirling around her. In the circle of Tynan's arms she covered her mouth and squinted against the heavy, smoke, waiting for Dyani to emerge with the others who fled the building.

Yet, when the frantic exodus was finished, Dyani was not among the coughing escapees. A new dread built inside her chest as the blue and white flames leapt higher in the sky. A second violent explosion and a shower of molten plastiglass announced that the skylights had melted and burst.

"Dyani!"

Tynan gripped her arms and shouted at her over the human shrieks and the grinding death throes of the building. "I left the ground car halfway down the street. Get to it. Use the telecom to contact your father and Sem at the guardhouse. The transmission code is six-three-zero. Got that?"

She nodded. "Six-three-zero."

"Have them come back here right now and help get these transports out of the station," he ordered. "Then I want you to stay at the ground car and wait for me."

She tried to swallow. Couldn't. "Wait for you? Where are you going?"

When he glanced at the inferno across the street, her heart gave a frantic double beat then seemed to stop.

Mama! Don't go back inside again . . . Please!

She gripped the front of his jacket with her numb hands. "Tynan, don't go inside. Please!"

His scowl belied the gentleness of his touch as he untangled her stiff fingers from his clothes. "The building is stone and masonry. I'll have plenty of time to get in and out before the fire spreads."

"But the skylight . . . the oxygen units . . ." she tried to warn him.

"Do as I tell you, Marista," he repeated, in a slow, stern voice. "Dyani and I will meet you at the ground car."

"Tynan, please . . ."

He set her away from him and gave her a push. "Go!"

Her chest and temples throbbed. She wanted Dyani safe, but she couldn't let him risk his own life. "No, please!"

"I want to see you go, dammit! You have your job. I have mine. You're wasting time keeping me here!"

The fierce command galvanized her. He knew what was right, she told herself as she turned away and flew along the pitted walkways. He didn't have time to deal with her panic. He needed her gone, out of harm's way, before he risked his own safety.

Though part of her demanded she stay and try to prevent him from entering the inferno, another part—the terrified child—wanted to be far away from the flames and memories.

With every step and gasp of air she repeated her reasoning—he needed her to follow his orders. He needed her gone to do his job. He needed her out of harm's way.

As the ground car came into view, a third explosion rocked the pavement and slammed her against a stone retaining wall. Before her head stopped spinning enough for her eyes to focus, a rumble of disintegrating masonry warned her some part of the medical center had caved in. With terrible certainty she knew it was the third floor.

"Tynan!"

His name ripped from her throat in a scream or grief and anger. Not again. Please, Mother Creation, not again!

She couldn't stand paralyzed while someone she loved died before her eyes. Without thinking, she propelled herself back toward the medical center.

"Tynan!"

Her shriek cleared a path through the roiling crowd. Ignoring the painful thrust of her heart against her ribs she shoved bodies and restraining hands aside and lurched toward the main entrance. The entry doors flew open, missing her face by centimeters. Two men carrying a woman on a stretcher and three ambulatory patients pushed past her.

As smoke belched out, watering her eyes and stealing the air, she grabbed the last person through the door, a woman who wore an oxygen mask. "Where are the others?"

The woman's eyes widened at her screamed question. Only a step from safety, she struggled to free herself. Marista hung on until the woman mumbled something past the mask and tossed her head backward.

"Dyani?" she pressed.

The woman nodded, pointing toward the building.

"Tynan?"

This time, the woman shrugged and shook her head.

She had to find him. She couldn't let him die. She made ready to plunge into the murky gloom.

Suddenly, the woman she'd accosted tore off her oxygen mask and yanked Marista to a stop. "You're not going in there?"

Marista jerked away from her. "I have to."

"Then here!" The woman jammed her oxygen mask into Marista's hand.

The building lurched with another muffled explosion. Marista wobbled but maintained her balance, then slipped the mask around her face.

"Mother Creation," she prayed, "help me!"

Twenty-four

Smoke obscured the emergency backup lights mounted in the ceiling. Marista groped her way through an obstacle course of overturned gurneys and equipment. The central stairway, she knew, lay somewhere ahead and to the right.

At least no fire leaped out at her from the hot, smothering grayness. But overhead the inferno's rumble vibrated the thick air. She prayed Tynan and Dyani had reached the second floor before the roof collapsed.

Kicking and pushing her way through the debris, she battled both time and a seething compulsion to turn and flee. Her arms seemed weighted as she swung them wildly to clear a path. Though she drew in gulps of pure oxygen from the mask, her ears buzzed and her vision liquefied.

After the first surge of adrenaline-charged courage, her childhood demons again seized her by the throat and tried to throttle her into whimpering submission.

No! Not now! she commanded the mind-terrors. I will not give in to you now! I have to find Tynan and Dyani!

Scorching air and smoke forced her eyes shut. Overhead the rumble of ravenous flames deepened, and stressed metal keened a warning. Tynan had misjudged the situation. Once admitted through the destroyed skylight, the flames had set a hungry, harried pace through the old converted warehouse. There were no fire-breaking walls in the wide-open wards. Wooden and cloth cots were as good as kindling. Soon, the oxygen units would add their volatile fuel.

From the mounting overhead roar she reckoned the flames had breached the second floor. She sobbed her grief, and clutched the flower pendant at her throat. Tynan and Dyani had not escaped. Was she to die, too, standing in the middle of the hellish tableau of her worst nightmare come true?

Her head went light. Perhaps she was hyperventilating on the pure oxygen. You have nothing to fear. The nightmare will end, a murmuring inside her head comforted. Stay where you are . . . stay where you are . . . stay where you . . .

". . . are! Marista, stay where you are!"

The command sliced through her mental haze. She sucked more oxygen from the mask, whirled toward the sound of the voice, and squinted into the dense air. Figures were bunched in a protective huddle halfway down the stairs, not more than ten meters distant.

Tynan was in the lead! With one hand he lifted an oxygen mask from his face to call to her. His other arm gripped Dyani's shoulders.

"Tynan!" she called, and lurched toward him.

"No! Stay back! The ceiling . . ."

The hellish creak of crumbling mortar and melting metal cut off his warning. Something hot flew past her face.

She dodged the flame and threw her arms over her head. Moments later the section of the second floor between her and stairway surrendered to the fire.

The shock wave hurled her backward. She landed on her tailbone and lost the air from her lungs. Stunned, she gasped and tried to clear her vision.

Carts and equipment mounded around her at odd angles. The mattress side of an overturned gurney pinned her against a wall. Bracing both her feet against the soft pile, she shoved. The gurney shifted enough to let her climb out.

"Tynan!" The oxygen mask muted her scream.

Heat pressed in from all directions. So did the stirrings of a powerful, deadly back draft rushing in through collapsed sections of the walls and roof. Soon the whole floor would be ablaze.

Wavering, disorienting orange and red flame blasted out of the pile that had seconds before been the ceiling. She peered through the fiery curtain, and her heart wrenched. Tynan crouched low with the others on the steps. Semi-molten support rods and a mountain of burning debris dammed their escape route. Worse, the low rumble of combustion ratcheted to a roar.

"Tynan!" She screamed his name from the depths of her fear. He would die in a pit of fire, just as her mother had, only meters from where she stood.

No, she wouldn't leave him and Dyani stranded on the stairs. She had to get through the fire and debris. She had to clear a path for them, or die herself in the effort.

She focused her mind, and smothered the panic with desperate resolve even as the flames built higher. Her heart no longer slammed into her ribs. Indeed, it hardly seemed to beat at all. As if suddenly detached from herself, she gripped the metal frame of the overturned gurney and yanked the heavy piece upright. Ignoring the pain in her arms, she groped her way over jagged masonry and flaming embers to the back end of the gurney.

She drew air deeply from the oxygen mask and gripped the foot rails. Gritting her teeth, she propelled her entire weight forward. The metal frame jammed into her stomach. In spite of the knife-like pain registering at the edges of her mind, she hurtled herself ahead.

The gurney pitched and rocked as it plowed over chunks of collapsed ceiling. She held it steady and upright, using her last gram of strength. By luck or will or both she navigated to a section of open floor and accelerated her pace to a near run.

She had to ram the debris away from the stairs. She had to clear an escape path. She had to save Tynan. She loved him and would not let him die.

The blazing pile clogged the last few meters. Screaming her rage, she smashed the front end of the makeshift battering ram into the implacable blockage.

Sparks and pellets of masonry flew up. For a second she felt the mass buckle and heard the crunch of displaced rubble. Then the gurney bucked to a halt. The railing drove into her ribs, and sent her flying backward onto the floor.

Dazed, she huddled into a protective ball. Hot tile seared her arms. Tears evaporated as she shed them. Mother Creation, she'd failed. She would never again see Tynan, hear his voice, or feel his hands possess her body.

She would never be able to tell him she loved him.

The din of fiery destruction was only white background noise against the shrieking grief inside her head. She tried to rise, but her arms refused to support her weight. She sobbed and gulped the last of her oxygen supply. In seconds her heart would slow and stop . . .

A vise snapped over her wrist. Her eyes flew open. Through a blur of tears and smoke she saw the familiar large hand and the small band of gold circling the smallest finger.

Tynan!

He hovered for a moment, and then he scooped her into his arms and pulled her to her feet. The coil of his arms around her back, and the press of his shoulder against her cheek assured her he was real, not some hallucination of an air-starved brain. He clamped his arm around her waist and dragged her toward the entryway.

Dyani and the others forged ahead through the debris. Behind them all, the rest of the ceiling whined and creaked, and finally gave way with thundering finality. She knew without looking back that the place where she'd crouched seconds before had been buried by fiery wreckage.

She wrapped her arms around Tynan's ribs and felt his strong heartbeat beneath her hand. Each of his labored breaths celebrated survival. She'd faced the fire, her demon incarnate, and escaped with both her life and her love.

Weak daylight cut through the haze of smoke and ash. The menacing roar of flames and the moans of a dying building faded in the distance. Cool dawn air caressed her as she emerged from the gates of hell. Tynan's strong arms held her steady. He whisked her across the pavement and down the street where the sounds and stench of destruction didn't hang so heavy.

The ground transport came into view. Once beside it, Tynan guided her into a sitting position on the ground. When he ripped the empty oxygen mask from her face and tried to replace it with his own, she pushed the mask away and struggled to sit up. He allowed her to right herself, but would not free her from his arms.

Soot embedded the tiny lines around his obsidian eyes and mingled with his sweat. Charcoal streaks ran down his face. How wonderfully stoic and noble he looked just then. And never more handsome, she decided. In that moment, she loved him as she had never loved another. "You saved my life, Tynan."

His gaze softened with wonder. "No, you saved us. You pushed away enough of the fallen ceiling so we could climb past it." His eyes glimmered with a different, indecipherable emotion. "You feared the flames, but you still came into that building."

Tears burned as they washed through the grit in her eyes. She no longer cared if he saw her cry. She wept not from weakness, but from the strength of her feelings. "I did what I had to do," she said. "I couldn't let you die."

Did he finally understand she loved him?

Even if he wouldn't love her in return.

He pulled her back into his arms and rocked her gently. Beneath her cheek his chest heaved in and out.

Yes, she realized, he did feel something for her. Perhaps not love, but a measure of deep affection. When they finally parted he might even feel some regret.

"You're all right!"

She tried to focus on Dyani's face, but it blurred with the images of Sem and her father.

"Riss, baby, what the hell happened?"

"Tynan, let her go. I should check her for injuries."

Tynan responded to Sem's practical suggestion by tightening his hold and laying his cheek to the crown of her head. She pushed gently on his chest. His heart slammed three times against her ear before he loosened his arms and allowed her to straighten, but only within the circle of his embrace.

"I'm fine, Sem," she told him and rubbed her solar plexus. "Bruised, but not broken."

Dyani crouched to eye level. Her face and clothes were smudged with tears and grime, but her smile was glorious. She took Marista's right hand inside hers and brought it to her smooth left cheek. "You gave me my future, Marista. You are the sister of my soul, now and always."

An Albian woman could speak no higher words of praise and affection to another woman. She eased from Tynan's embrace and pulled Dyani into her arms. "Sister of my soul," she repeated. "Now and always."

The rumble of transport engines broke them apart. Sem grabbed his wife's shoulders and drew her up to him.

Tynan craned his neck to see past the fender of his vehicle. "Time to move out. Everyone inside the car." He set his hand under her chin and waited until she looked into his eyes. "Are you strong enough to stand?"

"Sure as hell she's strong enough," Anthony Henson answered, and extended his hands. "Come on, Riss."

This time the male rivalry touched her heart. She smiled at the two men and sighed. "I'm sure I'll manage with a little help from both of you."

She laid her left hand on Tynan's wide, muscled shoulder and set her right hand into her father's deep, rough palm. Tynan cinched her waist with his fingers and gave her a boost at the same moment the General pulled her forward.

She leaned on her father's arm while Tynan got off the ground. The two men faced each other without the earlier glare-to-glare combat.

The General cleared his throat first. "I'll put her in the front seat with you . . ." He raised a brow. "Captain."

She would have sworn astonishment flickered across Tynan's expression. She did see his mouth twitch.

"I can't attend her while I drive," Tynan answered. "You'll have to ride up front with us." He smiled. "Sir."

She supposed she should have told both men she could take care of herself. But sensing she'd just witnessed a cease-fire, if not a full-fledged peace treaty, she held her tongue.

Tynan flicked his hand, an order for them to get moving. Sem and Dyani hurried into the back seat of the ground car, while she situated herself between Tynan and her father in the front. They followed the last service transport loaded with medical center evacuees. Behind them, the fire jumped roof-to-roof. By early afternoon, the refugee station would be smoldering ruins.

Only the sound of the ground car's undercarriage scraping rock and the whine of the engine during acceleration disturbed the silence. No one seemed eager to talk.

She rested her head on her father's shoulder, her hip against Tynan's thigh. Though cradled between the two men she loved most in her life, loss and worry weighted her thoughts. The displaced Albian refugees had given her purpose when she had none, and certainty when she doubted herself and her life's work. She fretted and fought over their future in part to keep from facing her own past and present.

Now that purpose literally had gone up in smoke. Those she protected would be scattered to Creation only knew where. She could no longer help or represent them.

She could no longer avoid the cloying emptiness inside.

Tynan's voice cut into her drowsy haze as he spoke into the portable telecom while he drove. "No, Ouray, three apartments on municipal grounds. Find one for Navarro and his wife, too . . . I know he's a common citizen, but Dyani is a Terran now, remember? And food. Make sure there's plenty waiting for us."

She glanced at his profile. Eyes steady on the road ahead, his expression grim, he commanded with only a soft voice and firm will. An officer's officer, she decided. No wonder her father had finally given him respect and deference. Without a doubt, three apartments and a meal would be waiting for them at the end of the line.

Her eyes misted with longing and love for her warrior-king, her lover-king, and she turned back into her father's shoulder before the sentiment overwhelmed her shaky self-control. Aunt Mimi always said never regret the past, cherish the present, and look to the future with hope. Somehow, she'd managed to fail at all three.

The hum of the engine soothed her to sleep. When the ground car came to stop she woke with a start. Cool, less polluted morning air rushed over her face and arms as Tynan and her father opened the doors. Revived, she righted herself and let her father pull her out of the seat.

The General held her close and stroked her hair. "Oh, Dad, I'm glad you're here. I'm sorry about so much . . ."

"Shhh," he whispered. "It's okay, Baby. I understand. Everything is okay now."

Perhaps her father did understand. She knew he cared enough to trek halfway across known space, and hundreds of kilometers in the company of bandits, to bring her home safe. Past hurt and resentment dissolved in the warm comfort of this place, and this time.

"Come on, Baby. I'll take you to your apartment."

Tynan stepped in front of them. "Sir, if you don't mind, I'll take care of Marista."

The quiet, almost humble plea cracked the thin veneer of her strained control. She trapped her bottom lip with her teeth to keep it from trembling, but her chin quivered anyway.

The General squeezed her shoulder, a gesture of possessive protectiveness she no longer found offensive.

Tynan slid his dark, pleading eyes to her face. "Will you come with me, Marista?"

Before she found the wit to nod, her father loosened his embrace, and kissed her forehead. "Go with the Captain, Riss. See you a little later."

He gave her over to Tynan's care, a gesture of trust and an unselfish consideration of her needs. She threw her arms around her father's neck. The child in her wanted to cling to him, and revel in the joy of a past forgiven. But the woman in her needed the hope for a future she found in Tynan's embrace.

The General pushed her gently toward Tynan and smiled. Then he stood ramrod straight. "You're one helluva woman, Riss." He looked at Tynan. "Don't you agree, Captain?"

Tynan drew her into his arms. His breath stirred the limp fringe of hair on her forehead. "Yes, sir, I do agree."

Twenty-five

Ouray assigned them quarters that exceeded Tynan's expectations. As Marista sat across the table from him and picked at her food, he glanced around the well-appointed apartment. "You gave up all this to live in that dilapidated hut."

She smiled around a slice of fruit. "I go where I'm needed."

That was so. But did she know how much he needed her now? She graced him with a sweet, knowing smile, as if she had read his thoughts. To hide his disquiet, he picked up a plate of bread. "Have another slice, and maybe this wedge of cheese."

She wrinkled her nose at his suggestion. He refilled her plate, anyway, though she'd already dispatched a moderate portion of the hearty fare Ouray had had waiting for them. Some color had returned to her soot-stained cheeks, but she still looked too frail and exhausted.

She leaned her cheek into her hand and nibbled at the bread crust while he chose a second piece of ripe, sweet fruit for himself. They lapsed into companionable silence, time in which he tried to untangle his chaotic thoughts and feelings.

He'd almost lost her today. When he'd jerked her crumpled body out of the smoldering debris and saw her eyes flutter open, he'd realized he could not bear to live if she were to die. Somehow, sometime, in some guileless manner, she had soothed, healed, and settled into his wounded, withered heart.

Marista Kaljin was now as vital to his existence as breathing. She had prodded him with her stubbornness, provoked him with her unshakable idealism, and forced him into awareness to all the wondrous possibilities of life after his soul's long, sad sleep.

The depth of his need for her left him dizzy and vaguely euphoric, like too much strong wine. Yet, it also left him dismayed. Their destinies crossed like two fiery meteors streaking across the sky. But their life trajectories took different paths. They had met and were united for a brief blazing moment in time, but they were bound to travel alone to their individual fates. Peace and war. Compromise and unconditional victory. Even their methods and goals worked at cross-purposes.

But the mere thought of parting with her made his insides go hollow and queasy. Why had he let this happen? As a soldier he knew better than to let personal considerations take precedence over honor and duty.

He refocused on her, and the tug of weariness around her eyes and mouth. "You look tired."

Sighing, she set down a wedge of cheese. "I'd fall right into bed if I didn't need a good scrubbing first. You and I both look and smell like we baked in hell."

"We almost did. I'm surprised you can joke about it."

"So am I. But confronting my fear wasn't as bad as living with it. Not that I'd want to go through today all over again."

He held her gaze. "You shouldn't have gone through it at all. You saved our lives at great risk to your own."

Her sea-green eyes glimmered with the same fierce determination he'd glimpsed when they'd reunited inside the burning building. "I didn't have a choice, Tynan. I . . ." She slid her gaze toward the picked-over bread platter. "I should go wash myself."

He cursed himself. He sensed she'd almost spoken from the depths of her heart, but she no doubt remembered the limitations he'd imposed upon her.

Perhaps the less said the better. For both of them.

"You'll need a hot shower to clean off just the first layer of soot," he pointed out.

"I don't think I can stand long enough to take a full shower."

"I'll help."

The idea just slipped through his mind and out his mouth. He'd meant nothing suggestive or erotic. Yet, her maidenly blush did stir a ripple of desire.

As he rose from his chair, he hoped his slow, easy grin convinced her of his honorable intentions. "I mean exactly what I say. I'll help. We'll help each other. You said I looked and smelled as bad as you do."

She skewed her mouth. "That isn't exactly what I said."

"Close enough." He held out his hand. "Are you coming? Or will I have to scrub my own back?"

She hesitated another moment, then slipped her hand into his. "All right, I'll come."

She gazed at him with such absolute trust and faith he knew he'd walk through perdition and back a thousand times over again.

With her hand entwined with his, she led him to the lavatory and turned the overhead light on low. The facility definitely outclassed her quarters in the refugee station. A long, ivory marble vanity extended two-thirds the length of one wall, and held two wash basins. Stacked on it were a half-dozen dark blue towels.

The narrow tile, chrome, and plastiglass shower stall stood next to a cavernous tub. A good long soak in sudsy water would soothe them better than a pounding, hot spray. But the mental image of the warm, wet, weightless intimacy sent a warning spasm through his belly.

He turned his rogue thoughts sharply away from the tub, but groaned when he saw his face in the mirror over one washbasin. Day-old stubble rimmed his mouth and shadowed his cheeks. Grime darkened the rest of his skin. A few streaks of lighter grayish-brown tracked old sweat. His hair was clumped in comical tufts, while some heavier strands clung to his sooty forehead. "I look three days dead."

"You look alive and whole to me."

Marista's whisper diverted his attention from the mirror. She started to say something else, but paused when he grazed her cheek with his knuckle. "And you, Little Diplomat, have never looked more beautiful."

Her eyes filled with a tender emotion he didn't want to name out loud. However, he did want to kiss her until the floor spun out from beneath them both. But he reined in the impulse because suddenly, and despite of his past intimacies with Marista, he felt awkward in her presence. "I . . . ah, suppose we should get undressed."

Quiet yearning glimmered in her gaze just before she glanced down at the zippered front of her jumpsuit. "Yes, we should."

He turned away to start the water and give her some privacy, he told himself. After adjusting the temperature to a pleasantly warm level he counted to ten and grappled with the buttons of his own shirt. "Maybe we should turn the lights lower."

He came back around, and the rest of the words stuck in his throat. The tan jumpsuit bodice hung from her waist as she stared down at the purplish blotches marring her naked shoulders, arms, and torso. One vile bruise spanned the width of her lower ribcage.

He covered the long discoloration lightly with his hands. "Marista, you were hurt! Why didn't you say something before?"

She rested her hands over his. . "It doesn't really hurt, not yet. It must have happened when the gurney hit the pile of debris and stopped. I felt the push backward. The foot bar probably caught me just right."

Anguish overcame his awkwardness. He pulled her close. "You should have let Navarro look you over. Maybe you broke a rib."

She gave his shoulder a gentle push until he backed up enough to look down. "I don't have any broken ribs. I'm fine. I'm stronger than I look."

"I think sometimes you're stronger than I'll ever be," he rasped.

"Shhh," she murmured, placing her finger against his lips. Though her eyelids sagged with weariness, her green eyes sparkled with mischief. "Are you going to shower with your clothes on?"

Her teasing drained his tension. "I should. I have nothing else to wear."

She shook her head and slipped her fingers behind the front placket of his shirt. One button popped open at her touch. "We'll send everything out to be cleaned."

His pulse struck hard in his ears. "I'll have to wrap myself in a towel, then."

Another button popped. "As my father always said, if you don't mind . . ."

"It doesn't matter," he finished, chuckling. "I suppose I can make do without my clothes for awhile."

"A sensible decision."

They finished undressing each other slowly. After they stepped into the shower, they merely stood under the warm spray, savoring the quiet intimacy and soothing rush of water. Runnels of charcoal tinged water slithered down their bodies, formed dark pools at their feet, and then swirled into the drain.

The spray rinsed Marista's face, revealing her soft, creamy skin beneath the grime. Her hair hung in saturated ropes around her neck and shoulders. Except where fire had singed the ends, the strands shimmered a vibrant auburn.

Compelled to wind his fingers into those thick tresses, he pumped a measure of liquid soap from the wall dispenser into his palm and rubbed it into a bubbling lather. "Turn around, Little Diplomat."

"As you wish, Captain." She tipped her face toward the edge of the spray.

He worked the lather over, around and through her hair. The tiny bursts of bubbles released the pleasant fragrance of the soap and mingled with the scent that was Marista's own. Her deep red curls wound tight around his knuckles and palms, defying his attempt to smooth and straighten them.

When it came time to rinse, he threaded his fingers through the thick mass and watched the spent bubbles channel down her slender body. As much as he desired to let his hands follow the same course, he refused himself the pleasure. Weariness weighted her limbs. Bruises stood out in stark contrast with her pale gold-skin. He would not press her for his own gratification.

She turned in place and smiled with drowsy contentment. "My turn. Under the spray, Captain."

With a crooked grin, he traded places. Closing his eyes to the cascade of water, he let the liquid warmth ease his strained muscles.

She first touched the back of his shoulders. After coating her palms with soap, she worked her fingers in soft slippery circles over his skin. Glad he faced the wall, he held his breath while his body reacted to her tender care. In seconds he was hot and hard and ready to pleasure her right there against the plastiglass.

Oblivious to the sensations she created, she ran her fingers over his nape, into his hair, and through the heavy, grungy strands. She paused to let him rinse away the lather, and then started down his back with the same easy motion that made his breathing erratic.

When she reached the ridge of his hips, she slid her hands around his waist and then upward. Her palms grazed the plane of his abdomen, and her left hand skimmed his scar before she tangled her fingers in the mass of springy hair on his chest. When she circled her fingers across his nipples with a sensuous, symmetrical rhythm every muscle in his body tautened.

He braced his hands against both sides of the shower stall. "Are you trying to seduce me, Little Diplomat?"

She stepped up behind him, clasped her hands around his middle, and laid her cheek against his wide back. "I'm the one who's being seduced. You have a soldier's body, Tynan. Strong. Hard. Beautiful."

The sweet compliment rocked his tenuous control. "The soldier no longer frightens or disgusts you?"

"You never frightened or disgusted me."

Snuggling closer, she pressed her soft breasts against his back. Her hips melded to his buttocks. The triangle of curls hiding her feminine depths teased his already tormented flesh. Blood throbbed inside his head. His lower body ached for release and relief.

"Tynan, let me make love to you."

Her plea cut through the building heat and haze of desire. Not only did she echo his desperate need, but she used the Terran euphemism for a sexual act of passion that spoke of the deeper sentiment he glimpsed so often in her eyes.

Let me make love to you.

A chill coursed through him despite the pleasant water temperature. Once again glad he faced the wall and not her trusting eyes, he lowered his arms and laid them over her embrace around his middle.

He would not—could not—lie to her. "Marista, I'm not sure."

"But I am sure. I love you."

He knew as much, yet the shock of hearing the words out loud stole his breath. As vapor billowed around them, he obeyed the gentle press of her hand and turned to face her. Like a man lost in a gauzy, glorious dream he gazed down at her dampened, hopeful face.

She tilted her chin upward, baring the secrets of her soul as unashamedly as she bared her flesh. "I love you, Tynan."

The words suddenly didn't terrorize him as much as they had before. With the tip of his finger he traced a bead of water from her temple to her cheek, down her throat and to the hollow of her neck where the namesake pendant lay. "Marista," he whispered past the thickness of emotion in his throat. "Little sea flower. Do you understand what you're saying?"

She nodded, so certain that he felt cowardly in comparison. "Yes, I love you. I know I can't ask the same from you. But I can't be silent any longer."

When she smiled into his mute astonishment, another bead of moisture trickled down her cheek. He couldn't tell if the drop was water or a tear.

"We've been through so much together," she went on in a quavering voice. "I know danger has forced our intimacy. But I also know what I feel is more than passing fancy. And I know you care for me, as much as you will allow yourself to care. That's why I've let you make love to me. I want you to take me again, but now take all of what I have to give. Please, let me make love to you."

For her sake, and the sake of his own honor, he knew he should deny her request. The fire and last second rescue had taken its toll on her body and, perhaps, her reason. How could he be sure he wasn't simply taking advantage of her vulnerability?

She set her palms to his shoulders, rose on tiptoes, and brushed her lips to his. The pleading innocence of the kiss aroused him more than her erotic touches had moments before.

For the first time in a long time, he let blind emotion set his course. He gripped her right hand and guided it to the swell of his full erection. "Yes, Marista, make love to me."

The clasp of her eager fingers around his flesh sent a convulsion of desire through his body, roughening his already raw voice. "And I will make love to you."

Had he actually said that out loud?

Yes. And more, he believed it. The bold promise flowed from his heart as desire flowed through his body. He trembled at the obligation that now rested on his shoulders.

She peered up at him as if his promise didn't surprise her. Her wonderful essence swirled around him on eddies of steam. Desperate and driven, he scooped her into his arms and cast himself adrift on a sea of wild, welling emotion without a charted course.

Gasping her acquiescence, she set sail with him.

***

Tynan breathed in the heady scent of spent passion and smiled with pride. The musky, salty taste of Marista's feminine depths lingered on his tongue, just as it clung to his skin and the bed linens. His erotic, deeply intimate kisses had brought her to completion almost too easily. So he brought her to completion over and over again until his own needs demanded release. Had he been capable of greater control, he would have pleased her until his heart stopped.

Indeed, she did "make love" to him with tender kisses and wild thrusts of her hips, with her hands and words and heart. She flowed in, around, and through him, encouraging him with willing, wanton whimpers. Deep, overpowering emotion poured from her, and echoed in a cry of joy during her final climax. When he let himself spill his seed into her hot, pulsing channel, he spilled some vital essence of his own heart as well.

Yes, he had made love to her. He did not recall a time when he felt so complete and whole.

Though exhausted, he felt restless. Carefully, so as not to disturb Marista, who was curled into his side, he levered his torso up and balanced his weight on his left elbow. She stirred in her sleep and rolled to her back. The movement allowed her pendant to slip from the hollow of her throat. He caught the tiny flower before it disappeared around her neck. The white metal looked fragile against his rough, tanned fingers.

She took her name from a maris stella, a little sea star flower that drew minerals to itself then glistened in sunlight. So, too, had Marista drawn him in with gentle compassion, and then struck a flame of life back into his deadened soul. Like the Terran woman, Isolde, she had healed her lover's wounds.

And like Tristan, he had to forego the love of a woman for sake of sworn duty and honor.

Duty. Honor. Even though his cause was just, the words made him shudder. Never before, not even when he "died" two years ago in order to pursue justice for Neari, had his soldier's duty and Albian pride demanded such crushing sacrifice.

A rich glow still colored Marista's skin and mouth. Beneath the rumpled sheet, the dark aureoles of her breasts peaked with the chafing of the material just as they did under his touch. Her bright, beautiful hair splayed in wild havoc over the stark white pillow. The strands were the color of the flames she no longer feared; the flames she had braved to rescue him because she could not stand to see him die.

Because she loved him.

Of course, she loved him. He had felt her love a hundred times before in her touch, in her words, and in the way she writhed beneath his body. How long had she understood the whisperings of her heart? How long had she suspected the same of him?

Her features shimmered and blurred through moisture collecting in his eyes. "What have we done, Little Diplomat?"

His choked whisper ruffled the fringe of curls on her cheek. She stirred again. "Tynan?"

He blinked away the unfamiliar tears, then bent forward and pressed his lips to her forehead. "I'm here. What is your wish?"

She tried to open her eyes, but failed and snuggled closer instead. "I wish every day could begin like this."

Innocently, she asked for something that could not be. Emotion clogged his throat, so he glanced around the room before answering. Weak sunlight streaming in the window on the far wall cast long shadows on the floor and ceiling. "It's the middle of the afternoon, not the beginning of the day."

She roused and squinted up into his face. "Is it that late? We'll have to evacuate soon."

Anxiety edged her voice. He threaded his fingers through the silky strands of hair caressing her cheek. "Not for a while. Go back to sleep."

Her gaze now wide and alert, she turned toward him and fluffed up her pillow. "I've been thinking."

He rolled his eyes in mock frustration. "If you had time to think, I didn't keep you well entertained."

She caught his hand at her cheek and brought his fingers to her mouth for a brief kiss. "I've had a few moments of lucid thought between mind-numbing pleasure."

He watched his own thumb caress her bottom lip. "And?"

"I think you should come back to Earth with me and tell your story to the Council of Seven Planets."

He stilled. He'd known this moment would come. He simply hadn't prepared himself for it.

She wound her fingers around his hand and drew it to her breast. "Tynan?"

Her quavering whisper snapped him to attention. Slowly, he untangled his fingers from hers and lay back on the pillow to face the ceiling. "I can record a statement and send it with you. Voice analysis will authenticate who I am. The Krillian military will gladly grant you access to all data files I brought with me two years ago."

"But it won't be same," she argued.

"No, but it will have to do. The Krillian government won't let me off-world for fear I'd repatriate to Albia in a double betrayal."

The sheets rustled. A second later, she covered his body with hers, stirring desire which he'd thought he'd played out hours before. "All right," she continued reasonably, "then come as far as Sarquis with me. Talk to Jace. Give him the details of your story. He can help disseminate the evidence in the media organizations. In the meantime, I can shelter you on Terran Embassy grounds."

He shook his head. "I trust you with my life, Little Diplomat. But I don't trust your kind. Or your world," he added for emphasis. "My place is with Varden's unit."

"You told me Neari's death no longer drives you," she countered, her voice too soft. "What duty is there now? You aren't even a commissioned officer in the Krillian army. Mother Creation, the war is lost anyway."

Her flesh tested his self-control. The glimmering plea in her sea-green eyes tested his suddenly fragile emotions. He gave in to his physical impulses and clasped her hips firmly with both hands. But he steeled his will. "Marista, I told you once I don't start something unless I intend to finish it. The war isn't lost until the last resistance dies."

Her chin quivered. "A soldier's answer. You're just like my father."

"I think you love me because I am like your father."

She started to protest, and then averted her eyes. "Maybe. A little."

"I know you understand," he soothed. "A soldier, any soldier, pledges himself first and foremost to his duty. I made a commitment to the Krillian cause before I met you. I have to fulfill my obligation."

Her eyes narrowed. "What about your obligation to me?"

He struggled to keep his voice low and level. "You ask again for what I can't give. I'm a Bracquar. I have no home, no nation, no family. Offering a commitment to you would debase your name and status. More than that, you're facing an inquisition of your own on Earth because of your attachment to me."

He sighed. "Your father was right. I'm nothing but a millstone around your neck. I have nothing of value to bring to a commitment."

"What about Sem and Dyani?" she argued with the first hint of desperation. "He's an infirm ex-officer, and she's a homeless expatriate. Neither has material riches or status, yet they committed themselves to each other."

"Sem is Krillian."

She stuck out her chin. "I hope you don't mean to imply that makes him less of an honorable man."

"No," he explained patiently, "it means he's a man from a different culture. In my tradition it's important for a man to provide comfort and status to a woman."

She gave him a sultry, half-smile. "In your tradition a woman doesn't pleasure a man with her touches, either."

He didn't take the bait. "This isn't a matter of how I let a woman take care of my sexual needs. This goes to the heart of who I am."

Her amusement turned to deeper, softer sentiment. "I know who you are. I want only you, not the status or wealth or family name you can offer. I love you."

He flinched and turned his face away. "Then you love a man who could destroy you."

Just as I destroyed Neari, he added silently.

"Tynan, do you love me?"

Damn, why couldn't she leave well enough alone?

"Answer me. Do you love me?"

Yes! his heart shouted, and his soul echoed the answer. But he could not tell her. She would cling to his side, just as she had literally walked through fire to save his life. He would not risk the safety of the woman he loved. Not again.

A groan of frustration left his throat. He wrapped his leg around her ankles and rolled her under him. Careful not to crush her bruised body, he nevertheless claimed her mouth with a fierce hunger.

When he had to let her up for air, he gazed down into her startled, desire-glazed eyes. "I've given you all I can, Marista. Let it be enough for now and always."

Tears welled in her eyes and spilled out the corners. "I'll find a way for us to be together. I swear."

She reached up with both arms and pulled him back down to her. As he readied her body for another frenzied climax, he concentrated only on the moment, on her smooth skin, and her passion-scented heat. For a Creation blessed wisp of time, duty and the sacrifice it demanded from both of them were part of a future he held at bay. He would show Marista with his body just how much he loved her.

And then he would break her heart.

Twenty-six

"Tynan?"

Marista sat up in bed. The strobe of an arc light pulsed through what she guessed was early evening gloom. She heard the swell of urgent voices and smelled her own fear. The depression in the mattress next to her felt cold.

"Tynan!"

Only frantic, faraway voices answered her. She threw aside the covers and switched on the bedside table light. "Tynan, answer me."

Without waiting for a reply this time, she lurched out of bed and ran to the open lavatory door. The tiled room lay in shadows. But she didn't need a light to see that his clothes were missing.

She held the doorframe to keep from sinking to the floor. Where was he?

The undercurrent of voices that woke her didn't seem so far away now.

"The noise woke me," she breathed through short, frantic gasps. "Maybe it woke him, too, and he went to investigate. Yes, yes, he'll be back soon. I'll get dressed and be waiting for him."

Comforted by her reasoning, she stumbled to the corner of the bedroom where she'd left her rucksack. Instead she found the bulging satchel propped on the dresser, and she tore into the contents. A pair of gray leggings and a long-sleeved blue knit shirt came out first. She rummaged around some more and found her undergarments.

Seated at the foot of the bed, she'd just finished slipping on a camisole and panties when someone pounded at the front door of the apartment. Her forced confidence slipped a notch. Tynan wouldn't knock.

"Who is it?" she called in a dry, screechy voice.

"Riss, it's Dad. Let me in."

He sounded calm but insistent. Maybe he had seen Tynan outside. "Just a minute."

She stuffed her arms into the sleeves of the blue shirt, and then went still. If she hadn't planted both feet on the floor she might have mistaken a steady vibration for the frantic thrumming of her pulse. The temblor gathered depth and strength until the very air hummed. Something wasn't right.

The ripple of voices swelled, but she couldn't decipher actual words. Now, boots pounded on the second story balcony just outside.

She finished dressing, hurried to the front room, and wrenched the door open to admit her father. Dissonant, urgent shouts and cries invaded her private sanctuary as the General swept into the apartment and slammed the door behind him.

"Dad, what's happening?"

Her father gripped her upper arms. "The military installations northeast of Bethel have fallen to the Albians. Time to pull up stakes and bug out. The transport to Sarquis is just outside the complex walls. I told Sem and Dyani to wait for us there."

She wiggled out of her father's grasp. "Tynan's not here. I can't leave without him."

A cool detachment, the sort of blank expression she had always dreaded, settled over Anthony Henson's craggy features. "Tynan left to rejoin his unit."

His cold delivery hit her like a body blow. "Gone?" She mouthed the word, but no sound left her airless lungs.

Her father nodded. "He came by my room about an hour ago and told me he used your personal log to record a statement for the Council of Seven Planets."

She clutched her stomach where the pitch and role mirrored the chaos of her thoughts. That's why her rucksack wasn't where she'd left it. Tynan had needed her recorder. He must have skulked about the room like a reconnaissance soldier on an escape mission from behind enemy lines.

Her father took her arm gently. "Tynan mentioned something about that old Tristan and Isolde myth. He said you'd understand."

Yes, she understood. He'd made his choice. He'd chosen for both of them. Duty and honor over love.

His betrayal was the last stone on a mountain of decades old pain. "Damn him!" she screamed with such rage her father took a step backward. "I gave him my heart, and like a good soldier he chose duty instead! !" She pinned her father with a scathing glare. "Guess that makes me collateral damage, right, Dad?"

"Riss?"

The pain in her father's voice added to her own. She'd hurt him with her verbal swipe as surely as she wanted to hurt Tynan.

She swung around and ran back to the bedchamber. For a moment, she stood in the center of the dusky room and let the terrible truth sink in. Tynan was gone—again. He'd abandoned her—again. He'd chosen duty to his personal cause over any love he might feel for her—again.

Flinging herself onto the bed, she clawed the linen and soaked it with tears, venting her fury on the place where the two of them had made glorious love just hours ago. At least, she'd made love to him. Had he plotted his escape even as he held her? How could she have been so deceived? Was she so desperate to believe he could love her in return?

His scent lifted from the bedding and filled her head. Her heart squeezed tighter with each sob, and she fisted her hands and pounded his pillow a half dozen times, each blow more savage than the one before.

"Riss, stop it!"

"No! Leave me alone!" she screamed, less at her father's voice of reason that at Tynan. He'd laid his head on this pillow, held her in his arms, and lied to her with his body . . .

"Riss! That's enough! Get hold of yourself!"

Her father grabbed her shoulders and whirled her around on the mattress. She slammed her fists twice into his chest before he shook her hard and forced her to lock her spine. Through a sea of tears, she fixed her gaze on her father's stern features. "Oh, Dad," she hiccuped, "I love him! I love Tynan, and he pushed me away, just like you did!"

She collapsed as her father yanked her to his shoulder, and she wept as she had twenty years ago on Yonar.

Her father's words finally cut through her sobs. "I know you hurt, Baby. But Tynan did what he had to do."

She raised her head and tried unsuccessfully to break free. "Of course, you'd defend him. You and he are just alike. General Henson and Captain Tynan, bound to honor and duty above all else."

He held her with firm tenderness. "And not ashamed to admit it. You listen to me, Riss. I haven't lectured you in a damn long time, maybe because I didn't feel I had a right. But I won't keep my peace now. Tynan is a fine soldier and a good man. You wouldn't have fallen in love with him if he were any less."

She squeezed her eyes shut and forced out a new flow of tears. "Do you think I don't know that?"

"Let me finish," her father commanded. "He left because he loves you."

Resentment swelled inside her. "Don't you lie to me, too. And don't make the same mistake I did. Just because he slept with me doesn't mean he loves me." She swallowed another sob. "At least he was honest. He never said he loved me."

"Don't they teach you in diplomat's school that nonadmission doesn't mean disavowal?" he asked.

She opened her mouth to argue, but hesitated. She herself had pointed out that fine but valid distinction to Tynan back at the desert outpost. "Yes, but . . ."

"But, hell," her father cut in. "He loves you. He couldn't tell you because you would have stayed here and fused yourself to his side, and he knows that's too dangerous."

As if to make the point, a muffled explosion shook the room.

The General didn't flinch. "Tynan knows you have to leave Bethel and go to Sarquis for your own safety. It was his duty to send you away because he loves you. I know. I had the same reason for sending you away from Yonar." His voice cracked. "Away from me."

Her emotions broke again. She could barely force the words past the swelling in her throat. "I didn't want to leave you."

He nodded and found a steadier voice. "I know. I wanted you to stay, Baby."

Blinking away the wash of hot tears, she gaped at her father in astonishment. "You did?"

He let her go, and his shoulders slumped. "You were all I had left in the world. I wanted you with me every second." He sighed and shifted his gaze toward the door. "But that would have been selfish of me and dangerous for you. I'd already made a bad choice and let Hannah persuade me to drag all three of you halfway across the galaxy and back."

The news rocked her. "Mother wanted to go everywhere with you?"

He struggled for breath. "She refused to stay behind. She left her career and her family to settle on every Creation-forsaken military outpost known to humankind because she wanted to be at my side. Your Aunt Mimi has never forgiven me for allowing Hannah to do it. When your Mother and Lexi were . . ." His chin quivered. "When they were killed," he went on, "Mimi hit the com-terminals with a vengeance and demanded I put you on the earliest transport back to Earth."

Her head spun with his revelations. "Mimi demanded it?"

"Yes, and I think she would have used legal coercion on me if necessary," her father answered. "But she was right. You had no business living in the middle of a hostile, free-fire zone with only one parent looking after you. Damn, Riss, as much as I didn't want to let you go, I didn't want to lose you the way I lost your mother and Lexi." He closed his eyes. "I guess I lost you anyway."

She absorbed the admission like a wilted flower absorbed rain. She wanted to reach out and comfort him as he'd comforted her moments before. One last thread of old anger held her back. "Why didn't you tell me this years ago?"

He turned and faced her squarely. "You had to live with Mimi. She was your closest relative, and a good woman. I couldn't let you resent her because she was the one who forced the issue."

"So you let me resent you instead?"

He stuck out his chin. "I've shouldered bigger burdens. I had to live without you for twenty years."

The truth made her ashamed and contrite. She crumpled into her father's arms again. "Oh, Dad, all that time! All the anger! I'm so sorry!"

"I'm the one who's sorry. I should have explained everything before. But I was afraid you wouldn't listen."

She hugged him tighter. "I probably wouldn't have."

He sighed against her hair. "Can you forgive me?"

The pleading in his voice pried open that dark, secret place in her heart where hurt and resentment had festered for nearly two decades. As the anger flowed out, the healing flowed in. "There's nothing to forgive, Dad. I now know that you did what you thought was best."

"Then try to understand Tynan, too. He's only a man. He loves you deeply and forever, the way I loved your mother. I don't know if his choice was right, but he did what he thought was best."

She leaned back. "Twenty years ago I was a child. I'll admit I didn't have the wisdom to make my own decisions. But I'm an adult, now. Tynan didn't have the right to make the choice for me. He should have trusted my judgment."

The General stroked her hair. "He did trust you. He trusted that if he had admitted his love you'd have begged him to stay, and he wouldn't have been able to refuse." He gave her a weak smile. "Then, as your nearest living kin, I'd have had to deck him and drag you kicking and screaming onto the evacuation transport."

The gentle humor didn't cajole her. "You both have the wrong impression about me. I'm not a reckless person."

"Reckless, no. A fool for love, yes."

When she started to protest, he placed a work-roughened finger against her lips. "What about that time Lexi got herself stuck on the roof chasing that damned cat? You went up after her, even though you weren't much older or bigger than she was. You managed to coax Lexi and the cat down the trellis. Then you slipped and fell two meters to the ground. There you were, your elbow shattered, Marista Kaljin-Henson protecting her kin and suffering the consequences."

He lifted her chin with his blunt thumb. "Tell me you thought twice about running into that burning building after Tynan. You nearly brought us all to our knees with that stunt."

With a swipe of her hand, she tried to dry her cheek and hide her chagrin at the same time. "Well, I know someone who spent fifteen days in the company of smugglers and thugs to get me off the front lines." She lifted a brow. "Jace is right. I am just like the old man."

Fresh tears welled in her father's eyes. "No, Riss. You're just like your mother."

The ancient grief and sweet tenderness etched in her father's face brought a new swell of affection to her heart. In likening her to Hannah Kaljin, General Anthony Henson had paid her the greatest compliment of her life. She slid her arms around his neck as her mother's memory rose between them.

And still, despite her father's arguments on Tynan's behalf, her heart ached. Like Isolde and her lover, Tristan, she and her Albian Captain would remain forever apart. Tynan said often enough he couldn't or wouldn't love her. Too much stood between them. Old pain. Cultural beliefs. Duty.

She breathed out one last, soft cry against her father's shoulder before a jarring vibration shook them apart.

Her father set her back on the mattress and stood. "We have to go."

She wiped her face dry with her sleeves and slid off the mattress. On stiff legs, she walked to the dresser, retrieved her rucksack, and slung it over her back. "I'm ready."

The General headed for the door. She followed, but paused in the archway and glanced back at the bed. Tynan's pillow lay beaten and crushed nearly flat like her heart.

"Good-bye, Tynan," she murmured and clutched at her flower namesake, as if coaxing some soothing magic from a talisman . . .

Her breath stalled as her fingers moved over a smooth, foreign surface dangling next to her pendant.

A ring.

"Riss, move it!"

She jumped at her father's command, but didn't obey. Her hands and voice trembled. "Dad, unclasp my necklace."

"What?"

"Do it. Please!"

Her father frowned, but complied. When he set the chain and its two treasures inside her palm, she let out a moan. The flower pendant lay inside the circle of gold Tynan had worn to remind himself of his higher purpose. Somehow, he'd managed to slip the ring on her necklace chain as she slept in his arms.

But she didn't want to be his higher purpose. She wanted to be his greatest love. In giving her the only remaining piece of his former life, all his worldly property as prescribed by the Albian bonding ritual, had he spoken the secrets of his heart?

She wanted to believe he had. But, as she closed her hand around the precious keepsakes, joy and hope surrendered to fear and resentment. Tynan was wrong to have abandoned her. He should have trusted her judgment. He'd never even let her say good-bye . . .

"What is it, Riss?" her father demanded.

What could she say? What did the ring mean? A promise? A farewell?

"I'm not sure," she muttered.

Her father groaned his frustration, grasped her wrist, and dragged her toward the front door. But they were barely over the threshold and into the pummeling melee when she heard her name and the order to stop.

They pressed themselves against the wall to let a crush of people pass. The cool evening air stung her flushed cheeks and gritty eyes. She wound her fingers into the front of her father's shirt and peered beyond the balcony rail to the valley below and the foothills beyond the city of Bethel.

The yellow-orange glow in the northeast confirmed that the Krillian military installation, the last line of defense against Albian incursion, lay under siege. By tomorrow morning it, and perhaps much of the city perimeter, would be nothing but rubble.

Again she heard her name. A second later Pelicia Ouray appeared from the right in the company of four Krillian home guardsmen. The Vice-Magistrate's purple tunic was stained and rumpled. Long strands of frazzled brown and silver hair escaped from a haphazard braid that lay across her shoulder. She fixed bloodshot, pale-blue eyes and a deep scowl on Marista as she drew to a halt and motioned her intention for them to move back inside the apartment.

"My father and I are on the way to the transport," Marista shouted over the tumult. "I'm leaving. Isn't that what you've wanted for the past month?"

The Vice-Magistrate looked neither amused nor relieved. "Unfortunately for both of us, Madame Kaljin, you aren't going anywhere."

Her father pulled Marista closer to his side. "Just what the hell is this about?"

Ouray ignored his bluster. "Marista Kaljin, at the request of Ambassador Radley in Sarquis, I am detaining you on the premises until a representative of the Terran Diplomatic Corps arrives in Bethel."

Marista's father shoved her behind him. "You're out of your mind, woman! Albian shock troops are going to be on these premises by daybreak tomorrow."

Ouray finally looked over at him. The resignation in the Vice-Magistrate's voice strung Marista's frayed nerves tighter. "I'm well aware of that, sir. But I have my orders to detain Madame Kaljin."

Marista stepped around her father. "On what grounds? I'm a diplomat. I have freedom to come and go as I please."

"Not any more, Madame," Ouray declared without much sympathy. "The Terran Diplomatic Corps has revoked your immunity pending the outcome of a criminal investigation."

Her heart took up a warning thunder. "Investigation of what?"

Ouray took a deep breath. "Charges of dereliction of duty, abetting espionage, gross violation of diplomatic prerogatives . . ."

Twenty-seven

The plush carpet, pastel wall hangings, and cushioned furniture of the Terran Ambassador's office did nothing to ease the knot of fear and suspicion in Tynan's gut. The last time he'd found himself on politically neutral soil, almost four months ago, he'd nearly lost his life. Here, in Sarquis, he stood to lose far more.

He flexed his right fist, hardly feeling the delicate chain inside his palm. But the metalwork flower cut deep into his flesh. Little enough pain and punishment for his dereliction of duty. By trying to keep safe the woman he loved, he'd delivered her instead into the hands of a sworn enemy and mortal danger.

A door to his right opened in near silence. He pivoted and reached for the sidearm that had been confiscated by the Terran guard escort at the city limits. The necklace almost slipped from his grasp before he drew a settling breath and anchored himself at solemn parade rest. He would not let the enemy see his fear. Loathing, however, was another matter.

The Terran ambassador entered first. White-haired and dapper in his gray uniform, the man strolled toward him with a bland smile and an outstretched hand as if greeting a guest at a social gathering. "I'm Ambassador Radley. I hope my staff has made you comfortable."

He stared at Radley's proffered palm, and then slid his eyes back to the man's face without returning the cordial gesture. "There is a desert folk wisdom, Ambassador. The friend of my enemy is my enemy."

Radley's face went as rigid as the platinum bar affixed to his breast pocket. Tynan resisted cocking a brow in triumph. Then he recognized the voice of the second man who entered the room on stealthy, rolling footsteps.

"Forgive my compatriot, Ambassador Radley. He has little respect for diplomacy, or even simple courtesy. Is that not true, Tynan?"

He snapped to alert at the sound of Sindri's mellow sarcasm and fixed the officer with a warning glare. Little about Sindri had changed except two fresh scars next to his left eye, and a new captain's chevron affixed to his uniform sleeve.

"I'm no compatriot to the likes of you," Tynan growled.

Sindri placed himself at the Ambassador's side and clasped his hands behind his back as if Tynan's threatening stance and voice were of no consequence. "You are right. I'm a loyal soldier. You are Bracquar, and always will be."

He ignored the insult, lifted his right fist, and uncurled his fingers. The maris stella lay in the crevice of his life line, pure white against bronzed skin, whole and undamaged in spite of repeated manhandling. He speared the Albian captain with an unblinking stare. "Where is she?

And listen well, Sindri. If she's harmed in any way I'll rip your heart out with my bare hands."

"Sir!" Ambassador Radley admonished.

Sindri only smirked. "Turn around, Bracquar."

"Tynan? Mother Creation, no! You can't be here!"

Though he was turning his back to the enemy, he wheeled in place at the sound of Marista's soft, frantic voice. A small, solitary figure flanked by two Terran guards, she stood in the doorway he had entered. Yet even with her hands pressed to her mouth, and her eyes wide with surprise, she exuded quiet dignity. He drank in her beauty, until he realized she wore a deep rose sari, not her uniform grays or her platinum bar. Navarro hadn't exaggerated the immediacy of her plight.

He took a step forward just as she did. Both halted when the Terran guard closed rank at her side.

Glancing over his shoulder, he skewered the Terran ambassador with a deadly glare before he returned his attention to Marista. "You're well? No one has mistreated you?"

Slowly, she lowered her hands and crossed her arms at her waist. "I'm . . . well," she stammered, and then frowned with barely concealed panic. "And for now the mistreatment has been at the hands of my own government. But why are you here?"

In her voice, he detected a brittleness so unlike her. There was another emotion lurking beneath the surprise in her eyes, too. Anger.

He should have expected such a reaction, yet he winced as he held out his hand and let the flower pendant dangle from the chain between his fingers.

She nodded. "I know. They sent Sem to lure you back here. He had little choice. But why did you come?"

The question churned up his guilt. "How can you ask that?"

She bit her lip, but shook her head. "They won't let you leave."

"How true, Madame."

Sindri stepped into his peripheral vision. "I find it odd that Navarro had no trouble finding your renegade champion, considering our Search and Seizure Squads combed the mountains for this insurrectionist the diehard Krillian patriots call 'Kae-a-tek.'"

Tynan peered into Marista eyes, hoping she understood the message of his heart. "I chose that name Sindri."

The Albian Captain snorted. "An ugly, sand-burrowing lizard."

"A tenacious desert predator," Tynan lashed back, "that pricks and bleeds larger prey to death." He nodded in deference to Marista. "The name honors me."

She granted him a tremulous smile of recognition. Yes, she remembered how he had referred in such a way to her own stubbornness.

Sindri made a low growl in his throat. "I'll wager Navarro knows more about you than he lets on. If he weren't protected by his wife's naturalized Terran citizenship, I would be pleased to interrogate him."

"Captain Sindri, please!" Ambassador Radley intervened. "We are here to conduct trilateral negotiations. I suggest we focus on the matters at hand."

Tynan's rock bottom esteem for the Terran diplomat rose a notch. "I agree."

Marista frowned. "What negotiations?"

Sindri ambled forward until he stood nearly between Tynan and Marista. "A bargain, Madame Kaljin. Your freedom in exchange for the Bracquar."

For a half-dozen solid heartbeats, she only stared at Sindri. Then she set her jaw and exhaled her answer. "Absolutely not."

Tynan had anticipated this. He stepped toward her but had to pull up short when the Terran guards closed rank again and shielded the woman he loved with their rifles.

"Marista," he explained, "if I turn myself in, Prime Minister Lares has agreed to drop all charges against you, with no chance of double jeopardy. And Earth has agreed to restore your diplomatic rank and status."

Sindri felt the need to add his opinion. "You and Tynan have always been inconveniences, Madame. Now you're both considered criminals. According to your own government, you've corrupted Terran neutrality. Tynan must answer the disgrace of making himself Bracquar."

She fisted her hands on her hips. "You lie, Sindri. Neither Earth nor the Albian government ever had substantiated proof of the charges you leveled at me. That's why I'm still here, under house arrest after more than two months. You needed me as bait to bring in the one man who can provide the truth about the true criminal conspiracy of our two governments."

She turned to Tynan. "The Albians will never openly try you as Quint of the Askanati Clan on charges of desertion and treason. They only want to drag you away and kill you before you can speak out against Lares and Osten."

Her voice took on a note of pleading. "The port authorities confiscated the voice tape you made from my father before they sent him off world. He and Jace are beating down the doors of the Council of Seven Planets, but there's nothing but circumstantial, secondhand evidence without you. Tynan, if you stay free you can rally others behind you, or at least agitate enough people from hiding to force someone to listen to your side of the story. You can't give yourself up. What of your duty?"

He wanted to yank her into his arms, tell her how his life had been empty, and his adherence to honor and duty hollow without her. But he would not speak those secrets of his heart in front of the sniveling Ambassador or the gloating Albian captain.

Instead, he took another step toward her, defying the guards and their weapons. "Resistance will continue without me. Eventually the truth will come out. But if I don't agree to this, Lares will try you in an Albian court, and that court will find you guilty. Your government won't stand behind you. If you aren't executed, you'll be sent to the military prison in Timetsuara."

He knew from the flicker of terror in her eyes that she understood what awaited a condemned soul in that place. "No," she declared in spite of that fear. "If you bargain your freedom for mine, Lares will execute you without even the formality of a trial."

He set his face in what he hoped was less of a grimace than a stern frown. "Marista . . ."

"No!" she cried out. "I won't allow it!"

He sliced the air with his arm. The delicate chain whipped against the back of his hand. "It's already done!"

She wrapped her arms around her waist and gaped at him in horror. "No! You can't . . . you can't make this decision for me . . . for both of us. Not again . . ."

"I did."

Unable to face the old pain in her eyes, he ripped his gaze from her face to Sindri's smug grin. "You have recorded us?"

Sindri nodded. "Every self-sacrificial moment. Touching, but futile. Madame Kaljin, in my capacity as representative of Prime Minister Lares, I rescind the charges against you. You're a free woman." Sindri glowered at Tynan. "You're under arrest, Bracquar."

He faced the virtual death sentence without flinching. But Marista's scream of rage and grief nearly brought him to his knees.

In a blink of time, the Terran guards moved forward and trained their weapons on his heart. He could have told them to spare their threat. Knowing he'd never see Marista again drained the fight from him.

Marista, though, rose to battle stance. Her arms went rigid at her side and scarlet slashed across her cheeks. Her ocean-green eyes shimmered fever bright as she trained them on Sindri. "The Albian government can't do this!"

Sindri shrugged. "We can do what we want, Madame. It's our world now." He sniffed and nodded with mock deference at Tynan. "Well, all but his little corner of the mountains, that is. And that territory will be under our control again soon."

Ambassador Radley tried to lay a hand on Marista's shoulder. She sidestepped his effort and advanced until she stood toe-to-toe with Sindri. But before she addressed the Albian officer, she turned to Tynan.

Her attempt to mask the pain she felt didn't completely work. Tynan knew what she was thinking. Once again he'd stripped her of control. Once again the decisions he'd made on her behalf forced them to part, this time forever. But he had no choice if one of them was to live.

Yet, as much as he cowered under her silent accusation, he feared the glint of reckless determination brewing behind her glare.

"I'll have my say now, gentlemen," she declared to all, though she kept her eyes riveted on Tynan alone. "First, I want no misunderstandings. I have been cleared of all charges and will never again be subject to prosecution for those charges."

"Yes, Madame, that's true," Sindri answered with ennui.

Mercifully, she turned her glare on Radley. "It is true, as well, that I've been fully reinstated to my position and rank within the Diplomatic Corps and have all privileges of immunity afforded by that reinstatement."

Sindri's brow flicked with uncertainty, but he held his demeanor as the Ambassador replied. "These past minutes have been duly recorded and witnessed by me and Captain Sindri, acting in the Prime Minister's stead. All statements and attendant agreements are considered legally binding in both Albian and Terran courts of law."

For the first time since Tynan glimpsed her in the doorway, her shoulders relaxed and her forehead smoothed. Even her mouth quirked a little at the corner.

She took two steps backward, pivoted gracefully to face Radley. "Very well, I accept the terms of this negotiation."

Radley sighed. "A wise choice, Madame."

Sindri rolled his eyes with impatience. "As if she could do otherwise."

Tynan breathed out hard in relief. She was safe. She would live, even if his nightmare had just begun.

Sindri flipped his hand at the Ambassador. "If you'll have your guard deliver the prisoner to my lieutenant."

Radley gave a nod. Tynan resisted the first yank at his arms. He needed only one more second to peer into Marista's beautiful face.

"Stay," she countermanded the guard. And to reinforce her order, she marched to the closest guard, grabbed the barrel of his weapon and pushed it downward. "I demand you set Tynan free."

The guards gaped at her, then each other, and finally at the Ambassador.

"Now!" she ordered, as if they were recalcitrant dolts.

Sindri stalked toward her. "What is this delay, Madame?" he shouted. "I might have granted you a few last moments with him had you asked. But not now."

"You'll grant me more than a few last moments, Captain," she retorted in a most insulting tone of voice. "You'll grant me all my rights under Albian common law."

Sindri went white, then scarlet. "What common law? What are you talking about?"

Ambassador Radley moved up from behind her. "Marista, what's going on here?"

Tynan looked on, as befuddled as the other men who formed the misshapen circle around the red-haired arc of energy. She set her scathing gaze on each man in turn before giving the guard closest to her a token shove.

When the guard refused to budge, she narrowed her eyes. "I order you to stand away from my husband."

The words echoed off the walls. No one stirred for nearly ten heartbeats.

Tynan didn't draw breath for at least that long. What had she called him? Husband?

Sindri broke the silence with a snarl. "What idiotic drama is this?"

She tilted her chin up another notch. "I'm not sure Prime Minister Lares would appreciate hearing one of his minions refer to Albian custom and tradition in such terms, Captain, especially since I stand on firm, legal ground. Under nomadic common law, which has been incorporated into Albian civil law, a woman can claim as her husband a man who shares her bed even once."

Marista's cheeks colored bright pink, but she kept her demeanor proud and sure. "Tynan shared my bed on more than one occasion during our time together." She peered at him now, her eyes soft with pleading. "Is that not so?"

Dazed, he nodded but just as quickly shook his head. "Marista, whatever you're doing, stop. You're free. Don't draw yourself back into this . . ."

"Is that not so, Tynan?" she repeated, her voice quietly demanding.

The truth, he knew, was reflected in his eyes. He had no choice but to say it out loud. "Yes, it's so."

She smiled at him, the first genuine happiness he'd seen in her expression since he'd arrived. "Then I claim you as my common law husband and extend to you the protection of my diplomatic immunity as well as my Terran citizenship."

The announcement left Tynan breathless and bemused along with everyone else in the room.

Sindri was the first to find his wits, and he lunged at the Ambassador. "I take exception. She makes her claim to strike back at my government for preferring charges against her, nothing more."

She held herself steady and proud. "My motive doesn't matter. My claim is valid."

Sindri sputtered, but Radley held up his hand. "I'll have our solicitors research the matter, Captain. But it appears that Madame Kaljin may have the law on her side. And Tynan admits to their liaison, even though he did so reluctantly."

Sindri turned his anger on the Ambassador. "Of course, Tynan would admit to bedding her. It saves his worthless neck. Their claim is grossly suspect. Furthermore, I have documentation that Madame Kaljin has a history of abusing her authority and twisting law to thwart Albian justice."

He pounded his thigh with his fist and spun toward Marista. "Madame, you have no real proof of this claim!"

"I have absolute proof," she retorted, even as she raised her left arm and fanned her hand.

A metal band circled the middle finger of that hand. Tynan recognized his ring. The one piece of himself he'd felt free to leave behind.

"This was a keepsake dear to his memory," she went on. "He left it with me as a symbol of what he couldn't say aloud, but felt in his heart." Her eyes misted. "A very wise man, a former soldier, told me as much. I believed so much in the symbolism I placed the ring on my middle finger, as would any proper Albian wife."

To Tynan, Marista had never looked so beautiful, so strong and vital. She still risked too much on his behalf. Sindri wasn't ready to stand down. He might still find cause or reason to detain her or, worse, impose new, trumped up criminal charges against her.

But at that moment, he loved her with every fiber of his being. His heart cried out that in every way important she was his wife, his soul mate, his savior. He opened his mouth to claim her in return and swear he'd cherish her to the end of their days.

Sindri didn't give him the chance to voice the sentiments. "A bit of metal means nothing," he argued. "You could have bought a dozen like it at any bazaar."

She smiled then, a secret, tender smile that seemed wholly misplaced in a room charged with the electricity of hatred and leashed violence. Slowly, she laid her left hand across her abdomen. His ring, always the reminder of his higher purpose and duty, sparkled in the sunlight pouring in through the tall reception room windows.

"Yes, I might have purchased the ring in a bazaar," she agreed, addressing Sindri. "But Tynan also gave me this."

She flexed her fingers on her abdomen, as if caressing herself. The motion sparked an old memory of Neari touching herself so when . . .

Tynan's knees went weak as water. For one, head-spinning moment he was glad for the guards' steel grip. "Marista?" he managed to rasp. "A child?"

She nodded. "Yes, I'm three months pregnant with your daughter."

Too stunned to react with any one of the dozen emotions waiting to be vented, he merely gaped. "How?"

Apprehension narrowed her eyes. Too late, he realized he had sounded less elated than simply jolted to the core of his soul.

At that moment, Sindri stepped between them. "Yes, just how did this happen? You told me yourself about the contraceptive implant Earth provided for you."

As if vaguely shell-shocked, she peeled her eyes from Tynan and lifted her gaze to Sindri. "During my abduction from the humanitarian outpost, the raid commander stunned me. My physician believes the jolt disrupted my contraceptive device." She slid her worried green eyes back to Tynan. "I was left unprotected."

Tynan knew she felt unprotected in a different way now. He opened his mouth to explain his bemused reaction.

But she returned her gaze to Sindri. "I'll undergo any genetic testing you demand to verify my claim on Tynan."

Sindri opened his mouth like a fish gasping for oxygen. He didn't look like a warrior gracious in defeat. But defeat was what Marista Kaljin had just handed him. After battles won and blood shed, the creation of love and passion won the final, greatest victory.

The end happened in a blur. Radley appeared monumentally relieved as he dismissed the Terran guard.

Tynan stood rooted and limp, staring at the woman who'd saved his life and, perhaps, his world. She'd certainly saved his soul. Now he only had to make her believe it.

Marista held her hand to her abdomen and caressed the fledging life within her while Sindri flailed his arms, let fly some ripe Albian obscenities in her direction, then stomped out after the Ambassador. When silence finally fell, Tynan was alone with her.

She was his wife. He should have rejoiced that Fate had taken his most abject failure and transformed it into success beyond his wildest imaginings.

Yet, as he peered into her wary, brooding eyes, he'd never been more afraid in his life.

Twenty-eight

Her warrior-king looked like hell in battered jackboots and mud-spattered camouflage. He'd tied his too long hair behind his neck with a piece of twine and obviously hadn't wielded a razor in a standard week. Dirt clung to the creases in his forehead and crusted deep beneath his fingernails. But he was alive and whole.

And silent as stone.

Marista told herself that Tynan was a man of action, not words. Yet he neither spoke nor moved when she wanted to declare her overflowing love and buried rage all in one breath, and then throw herself into his arms.

What are you thinking, Tynan? she begged him with her eyes. Her hand strayed to the place where their daughter nested, safe inside her body. *What can I say to you? I hadn't prepared for this. I hadn't prepared to see you again, or let you go again.*

He stepped closer to her and held out her necklace. She smiled weakly in gratitude and extended her hand. He let the chain and pendant slither off his fingers and into her palm without touching her skin.

She prayed for the strength to accept the future.

"Once again you saved my life at risk to your own, Little Diplomat."

Her heart beat in her throat. Neither his calm expression nor his even voice hinted at his emotions. "The charges against me were rescinded. I had nothing to lose."

Until now.

"Sindri will hound your ambassador."

The uncharacteristic small talk, so unlike him, intensified the terrible uncertainty in her heart. She shrugged, though she felt far from nonchalant. "Sindri can protest all he wants. The law is on my side."

He shook his head. "You never cease to amaze me. How did you know of this common law practice?"

She struggled to steady her words. "I researched Albian and Krillian civil and contractual law when I was trying to find a way for Sem and Dyani to marry. Dyani was willing to invoke the tradition, but Sem wouldn't let her. His family opposed the marriage, and he didn't want anyone believing she had entrapped him."

He peered at her with too serious bemusement. "You said you'd find a way to keep us together."

Was that an accusation? Did he feel trapped now? He seemed to have no trouble maintaining a proper distance between them. Proper for strangers. Not husband and wife.

Trembling spread throughout her body. "This pregnancy came as much of a surprise to me as it does to you," she admitted. "I was afraid at first, but never sorry. I realized I might never see you again, but at least I had a piece of you."

"Why didn't Navarro tell me about the child?" The question came from deep inside his chest, as if he had to push out the words with great effort. "Doesn't he know?"

She slid her eyes briefly to the hand resting on her abdomen. The gold band winked up from her third finger before she faced him again. "Sem knows. He's the one who finally figured out why I wasn't feeling well." She swallowed. "I didn't want you to know."

The dark eyes narrowed to obsidian slits. "What?"

"I didn't want anyone to know," she defended herself, barely controlling a bubble of emotion in her throat. "Sindri would have found a way to use the knowledge. And I didn't want the news to influence your decision to come back."

Her throat parched, she paused to swallow. "I know how you feel about doing your duty, so try to understand I had a duty as well, to myself and our child. I wanted her to know her father as a living hero, not a dead, forgotten martyr of a lost war. Besides, we both know I can take care of myself."

Genuine pain softened Tynan's dark eyes, and he finally closed the remaining distance between them. "Marista . . ."

As much as she yearned to hold him, she retreated and held up a hand to ward him off. When he frowned, she regrouped some of her poise by tapping into the anger she had nursed over the past months. "I've already named her Hannah," she declared. "Giving her a name made her even more real to me. And I . . . I wasn't sure if I would ever see you again."

He nodded slowly. "Hannah. A fitting tribute to your mother."

She tried to smile. "If you wish, we could honor your mother, too. Jamilia would be fine middle name. I'll raise her with full knowledge and respect for her Albian heritage."

His scowl halted her mid-sentence. "You'll raise her?"

She quaked as much from need and desire as in response to the challenge in his voice. Mother Creation how she wanted to feel his hands on her again, to kiss his mouth, to untie that silly piece of twine and run her fingers through his hair.

Instead, she lifted her chin. "I'm aware you still have a right to dispute my claim on you. Neither of us intended for this to happen when we entered our . . ." She stumbled to find the appropriate word. What did they share? Physical pleasure? Escape from the horror of war? Momentary happiness?

Love?

"Our liaison," she said, deciding on the neutral term. "You never expressed a wish to become my husband or the father of a child. We never made plans. You wouldn't."

The hard edge left his eyes, replaced by cold pain. Preferring her own voice to what she feared to hear in his, she went on. "I won't raise her alone. I'll have help from my father and Aunt Mimi. Even Jace. Hannah will never want for love or attention. But if you do intend to deny my claim, consider first that my status and citizenship do protect you, at least temporarily. It would be in your best interest and . . ."

Her voice clogged, and she paused to clear it. "It would be in the best interest of your duty to the Krillian cause to remain under that protection until you can find the weapons and manpower to continue your fight."

He peered at her for long, tense moments. She refused to look away from his accusatory stare. She would be strong . . .

Then his face relaxed, and he crossed his arms. "Perhaps you should ask me what I want."

The soft, almost casual comment reignited the smoldering embers of her resentments. "The way you asked me what I wanted?"

Tynan dropped his arms as if she'd slapped him. "Marista, I'm sorry . . ."

Then he reached for her, but she once again sidestepped him. This time, however, she could not keep the emotion from her voice. "I can't bear your touch if it means nothing but apology. Decide to leave again if you must, but don't lay warm, loving hands on me first. Not again. I'm not sure I can forgive you this time."

His eyes widened. "I don't think you forgave me the first time."

Now she did look away, rather than face the truth in his gaze.

"You told me once it's harder to forgive someone you love," he reminded her. "Can't you forgive me?"

The pleading in his warrior's voice tore at her heart. Yet, she pulled her arms tight to her body and spun away. "You shouldn't have left me."

She felt him draw nearer. "I thought it my duty to protect you."

"Yes," she scoffed. "You were protecting me. Just as my father did twenty years ago. But I'm no longer a child. It was your duty to respect my decisions and honor my feelings. "

She braced herself and turned. He stood so close his breath fanned the hair at her cheek, but she refused to let his nearness fluster her. "The past is past. I won't repeat it. Here, now, I demand the right to choose for us—you, me, and our daughter. And I choose to let you go back to your duty."

He retreated a step. "I see."

She shook her head fiercely. "No, you don't see. Had you allowed me a choice two months ago, I might have said the same. But you assumed I'd hold you back with my demands and keep you from what you cherish most in life."

Tynan clasped his hands about her upper arms before she could sidestep him again. "Yes, I cherish duty, Marista. And my first duty now is to be at your side."

She tried to wiggle free, but he held fast. His persistence didn't still her tongue. "You say that because of Hannah."

He gave her a gentle shake. "My duty was always to be at your side! I was just too stupid to see it. When you freed me of Neari's memory, you became my higher purpose."

"I don't want to be your higher purpose, dammit!" she shouted at him.

His fierce scowl softened. "You are what I want most in life, Marista," he whispered. "When I stared down at you while you slept in my arms that last night in Bethel, my heart told me nothing in the world mattered more than this beautiful, passionate woman. It was good that she wanted to stay at my side."

His dark eyes glazed with moisture. "But I listened to my head. I tried to protect you by pushing you away. I went back to the battlefield, but I left my heart with you. I divided myself again, and I failed you, as I failed my cause."

"The odds were always against your cause," she reminded him, though she could barely breathe with him standing so close.

He raised his arm and brushed her hair with the back of his hand. The slight breeze of his touch sent a shiver of familiar awareness through her body. "Sometimes force still is the only way."

"Force is the result of a failure to communicate," she muttered.

He chuckled. "This from a woman who shoved that Terran guard not more than five minutes ago."

She lowered her eyes in shame. "My point exactly. I failed to convince him I was right."

He expelled a slow breath of air. "You and I will always be at odds. But a good diplomat knows when to compromise." He let his finger graze her cheek and smiled when she shivered. "Likewise, a good soldier knows when to surrender. Neither my resistance on the battlefield nor my resistance to your compassion brought me victory or peace. I surrender to you, Marista."

She stiffened and backed away from his warm fingers. "I don't want capitulation. That's no victory for me. You have your freedom. You're now beyond the reach of Albian law. You can come out of hiding and come forward with your story. Perhaps it will rally the Krillians behind you again. But I won't hold you beyond that. That isn't love. It's possession."

He smiled, but the expression seemed oddly tremulous. "I will not let you send me away. What if I blunder my way back into Albian crosshairs? Who will speak for me, Little Diplomat? Who will rescue me again?"

She resisted the teasing in his voice. "How many times must I tell you I'm not a diplomat?"

He threaded his fingers through her hair and peered at her with such intensity she almost flinched. "No, you are my wife." He spoke the words with fierce pride. "Is that more than a title of status to you?"

"Of course, it is," she retorted. "But you didn't bargain for a wife, much less a child."

He drew her close and cinched her about the waist with his free hand. "I didn't bargain for most of what I got. And I will be forever grateful to the mysterious ways of Fate."

"Damn, Tynan, you have always spoken plainly before now. What are you saying?"

Instead he asked her, "Do you want me to leave?"

"I won't beg you to stay."

He smiled. "I won't make you beg for what pleases me to give."

She remembered well the first time he'd spoken those words, on their first night of shared passion.

"I won't stay with you because it's in my best interest to do so," he vowed. "Or only because force has failed me, and now I need a new strategy, or because you've become my new life's purpose. I will stay because I need you."

"I know you need me."

He pulled her closer. "I want you."

"No more than I want you."

"I gave you my ring."

"I know, but . . ."

"I love you, Marista."

She caught her breath.

"I love you, and I will not die alone and unhappy like that pitiful Tristan of your Terran folktale. I've sacrificed too much in the name of duty and honor. No more, not when I can have the comfort of your arms and the chance to see my daughter grow into a beautiful woman."

Tynan took her left hand into his, and pressed his lips to the gold band on her third finger. "I did leave this ring to say all the things I felt and had no right to say with words. Now I ask you to keep it always as a pledge of commitment. I have nothing else—no wealth nor honorable clan identity. But I give you my heart, and I consider myself bound to you as any Albian husband is bound to his wife."

She gazed at the gold band. "Oh, Tynan," she finally managed, before tears stopped her.

With his palm, he wiped away the beads of moisture. "Didn't you tell me once you never cry?"

"I never did until I met you," she said. "I love you. I can't begin to tell you how much."

"Then don't try," he whispered, bringing his mouth closer to hers with every word. "You diplomats talk too much anyway. We soldiers prefer to act."

He set his mouth to hers and kissed her with a vitality of heart that belied the bedraggled warrior-king. After a heart-trembling minute, he drew back just enough to murmur against her lips. "Do you like the way I negotiate without words, Little Diplomat?"

She slid her hand up the nape of his neck and reveled at the shiver of his body. "Yes, indeed, Captain. But words have just as much merit as actions."

He teased her lips with a brush of his mouth. "Not now, Madame."

"No, perhaps not now," she sighed and lifted on her toes, seeking another long, hungry kiss.

But before he bestowed her with his favor, he bestowed her with a promise from his heart. "I don't know what the future holds, but I want to hold you always in that future. We need each other, like the God of the Sun and the Goddess of the Desert. Some of my power. Some of your magic. Whatever battles need to be fought, we'll fight them together. I won't send you away, Marista. Not now. Not ever again."

She clung to that promise as she clung to him.

CPSIA information can be obtained at www.ICGtesting.com
Printed in the USA
BVOW011149260812

298844BV00002B/36/A